Praise for

Vulnerable

Here's what some readers have to say about the first book in the McIntyre Security Bodyguard Series...

"I can't even begin to explain how much I loved this book! The plot, your writing style, the dialogue and OMG those vivid descriptions of the characters and the setting were so AMAZING!"
– Dominique

"I just couldn't put it down. The first few pages took my breath away. I realized I had stumbled upon someone truly gifted at writing." – Amanda

"*Vulnerable* is an entertaining, readable erotic romance with a touch of thriller adding to the tension. Fans of the *Fifty Shades* series will enjoy the story of wildly rich and amazingly sexy Shane and his newfound love, the young, innocent Beth, who needs his protection." – Sheila

"I freaking love it! I NEED book 2 now!!!" – Laura

"Shane is my kind of hero. I loved this book. I am anxiously waiting for the next books in this series." – Tracy

Praise for
Fearless

Here's what some readers have to say about the second book in the McIntyre Security Bodyguard Series...

"Fearless is officially my favourite book of the year. I adore April Wilson's writing and this book is the perfect continuation to the McIntyre Security Bodyguard Series."
– Alice Laybourne, Lunalandbooks

"I highly recommend for a read that will provide nail biting suspense along with window fogging steam and sigh worthy romance."
– Catherine Bibby of Rochelle's Reviews

REGRET

McIntyre Security, Inc.
Bodyguard Series
Book 11

by

April Wilson

Copyright © 2019 April E. Barnswell/
Wilson Publishing LLC
All rights reserved.
ISBN: 9781075493423

Cover Design Copyright © 2019 April E. Barnswell
Cover Model: BT Urruela
Photographer: Reggie Deanching of RplusMphoto

Published by
April E. Barnswell
Wilson Publishing LLC
P.O. Box 292913
Dayton, OH 45429
www.aprilwilsonauthor.com

No part of this publication may be reproduced, stored in a retrieval system, copied, shared, or transmitted in any form or by any means without the prior written permission of the author. The only exception is brief quotations to be used in book reviews. Please don't steal e-books.

This novel is entirely a work of fiction. All places and locations are used fictitiously. The names of characters and places are figments of the author's imagination, and any resemblance to real people or real places is purely a coincidence and unintended.

Books by April Wilson

McIntyre Security Bodyguard Series

Vulnerable

Fearless

Shane (book 2.5)

Broken

Shattered

Imperfect

Ruined

Hostage

Redeemed

Marry Me

Snowbound

Regret

and lots more to come…

Dedication

For Lori, my sister and best friend.
I don't know where I'd be without you.

Erin O'Connor

Just as I do every weekday morning, I'm seated on a crowded public bus heading from Rogers Park, where I live with three college roommates, to my place of work, Clancy's Bookshop. I consider myself lucky to have my dream job already, and I'm not even out of college yet. I'm an assistant manager for one of the largest independent bookstores in the US, and it's located smack dab in the heart of The Magnificent Mile, a.k.a. North Michigan Avenue, in downtown Chicago. It's the perfect job for a bookaholic like me.

I'm lucky. I get to spend every day with the people I love the most... my best friend, Beth McIntyre, who owns Clancy's; her bodyguard, Sam Harrison; and Mack Donovan, who is head of security at the bookstore. Not many bookstores have their own private security force, but ours does. I guess it's to be expected when the owner's husband is the CEO of a private security company. Shane McIntyre spares no expense when it comes to his wife's protection.

Normally, I'm excited to be heading to work, but not today. Today my stomach is in knots, and I'm an anxious wreck. I'm going to ask Mack Donovan out to a New Year's Eve party tonight. The knots in my stomach morph into butterflies, and my head is spinning in nervous anticipation. It's not the first time I've asked Mack out, but I hope it's the first time he says *yes*.

As the bus rumbles along North Michigan Avenue, I lean my head against the ice-cold window and watch the new snow as it falls on the city sidewalks. Not too many pedestrians are out this early on a cold, snowy morning.

The streets are a far cry from how they looked just a week ago, when a freak blizzard brought downtown Chicago to a grinding halt. The streets are finally clear of the mountains of snow that were dumped on us with little warning, and the buses are running on schedule again. Exactly a week ago, on Christmas Eve, the streets and sidewalks became impassible because of thigh-high snow drifts and abandoned cars. I was stranded in Clancy's overnight along with Beth and her baby, Sam, Mack, and two other security guards.

The temperature this morning is still brutally cold. Even with the heat cranked on high, the bus feels like an ice box, and I sit shivering on my hard plastic seat, my arms wrapped tightly around my torso in a futile attempt to stay warm.

My bus comes to an abrupt stop just one block from my destination, and with a grateful wave to the bus driver, I hop down onto a sidewalk covered with a fresh dusting of snow. It's technically not even January yet, and I'm *so* ready for winter to be over.

Pulling my scarf tighter around my face, I make a mad dash for the bookstore, winding my way through the few intrepid pedestrians braving the cold. It's a few minutes after eight. The store doesn't open until nine, but I like to get in before the rest of the employees arrive. It's my job to power up the sales terminals, fill the cash drawers, set up new displays… generally get everything ready before the doors open.

As usual, Mack Donovan, head of security, is waiting for me at the front doors, key in hand. The moment I spot him my heart starts fluttering, and I feel the nervous-queasy excitement that hits me every single time. No guy has a right to look this good. He's the epitome of *tall, dark, and handsome*.

Mack opens the door and steps back for me to enter. "Good morning, Erin."

His deep voice sends a shiver down my spine.

I glance up at him, having to crane my neck to meet his gaze because he's so darn tall, and return his smile. I hope he'll attribute the pink in my cheeks to the cold temperature outside and not to the fact that I'm crushing on him. "Good morning, Mack."

Not only is Mack Donovan drop-dead gorgeous, but he's larger than life and literally a hero. He served his country for over a decade in the Army Rangers, completing multiple tours of duty in hot spots around the world. And after leaving the military, he worked in private security operations in the Middle East and Africa. I can't even begin to imagine the amazing things he's seen and done.

After a physical assault on his wife, Shane McIntyre hired Mack to head up the security here at the bookstore—in other words, to ensure his wife's personal safety. I nearly fainted when Mack first showed up for work. With his dark hair and trim beard, and dark eyes—not to mention muscles that just won't quit—he's a walking fantasy. The black leather jacket he habitually wears to conceal the handgun holstered to his chest in no way camouflages his muscular build. And at well over six feet tall, he towers over everyone here.

Yes, I've been crushing on Mack since I first met him. There's just one teeny, tiny little problem. He treats me like I'm his favorite little sister, when that's the last thing I want to be to him. I get it that he's thirteen years older than me, but still. I'm an adult.

"How was your bus ride this morning?" he says, following me through the store to the employee locker room in the back.

I love this time we have together in the morning before the rest of the staff arrives. I get forty-five whole minutes alone with him, and it's the highlight of my day. Our morning routine is well established. I deposit my personal items in my locker, then I get the store ready to open. He follows me around, helping me at every turn and keeping me company.

As we arrive at my locker, I tip my head up to meet his gaze. "It was cold, very cold. But otherwise, I can't complain. At least the streets are finally clear of snow."

"Good." He leans against the locker next to mine and, with his arms crossed over his distractingly broad chest, he watches me spin the combination lock on my door.

Once it's open, I hang up my purse, scarf, and my coat. Then we head upstairs to the business office to get the cash drawers. It never fails... he's always right there with me, shadowing me. He doesn't have to help me—it's certainly not part of his job description—but he does.

He carries all the cash drawers downstairs for me and sets them on the sales counter.

"Thanks," I tell him.

"My pleasure."

My God, how can one man make two words sound so sexy?

While I finish getting the sales terminals up and running, he leans on the counter and watches my every move, like a cat watching a mouse. I don't think he even realizes he's doing it. Talk about sending mixed signals! I don't understand how he can be so attentive, and yet so hands-off at the same time.

I think he likes this time we have together too. I just wish he wanted a different kind of alone time with me—the kind I want. The kind with touching and groping and kissing. And while he seems to enjoy my company, I don't think he wants the touching and the groping. Not like I do. He's very chivalrous, and apparently the age difference between us means I'm off limits to him.

"How did Haley fare during the blizzard?" I ask him, trying to redirect my thoughts away from the kissing and the groping. I know Mack had dinner last night with his seventeen-year-old daughter.

I've met Mack's tall, gangly teenaged daughter a few times when she was downtown and popped in to the store to say hello to her dad. She's gorgeous, and with her dark hair and dark eyes, she reminds me so much of her dad.

"She was sleeping over at a friend's house when the blizzard hit," he says. "They were snowed in for two days. She said it was fun—the girls made pizzas and brownies and watched movies."

Mack's a good dad, which only adds to his appeal. Even though he was never married to Haley's mother—they were high school sweethearts—he's always been active in his daughter's life. He and Haley are pretty close, and they see each other regularly.

After prepping the sales terminals, I move on to straightening store displays and endcaps. When I try to shift a heavy table laden with Harry Potter merchandise, Mack gently steers me out of the way, saying, "Here, I'll get it."

His touch burns right through my sweater and blouse to my bare skin, warming me and sending delicious tendrils of sensation through me. I bite my bottom lip in an effort not to moan. He seems oblivious to the fact that I'm about to combust.

I watch his arm and back muscles flex beneath his jacket as he effortlessly shifts the heavy table.

When he's done, he steps back, smiling at me as he makes eye contact. "How's that?"

My belly does a little flip whenever he smiles at me. For a moment, I'm caught up in his gaze, and we just stare at each other. There's always this palpable feeling of tension and anticipation between us when we're alone like this—or maybe it's just my imagination. I have to admit it could be wishful thinking on my part.

He bites back an amused grin. "Erin?"

I mentally shake myself. *What was the question? Oh, the table. Right.* "That's perfect, thank you."

We move on, and he follows me as I straighten the stacks of books on the New Release tables.

"It's New Year's Eve," I say offhandedly. The moment I broach the subject, my heart starts hammering. My roommates have invited me to a New Year's Eve party tonight at a popular hotel bar. Now's my chance to ask Mack to go with me.

He nods, and again there's that amused little smile. "Yes, it is."

I swallow hard, mentally giving myself a pep talk. *Ask him!* "I was wondering... do you have plans tonight?"

He shakes his head. "Nah. I'll stay in tonight and watch basketball, maybe order a pizza."

"That sounds like fun." To be honest, staying in tonight sounds good to me. I don't drink, so a party at a swanky hotel bar really isn't my thing. I only said I'd go because I'm trying to make an effort to be more sociable. I'm a homebody. If I had my way, I'd stay in every night and read.

"Why do you ask?" he says.

"Oh, no reason." I shrug, trying to act nonchalant. *Ask him!*

"Well, actually—"

A chime sounds at the front door, cutting off what I was about to say. An employee is out front, asking to be let in.

"Excuse me," Mack says, touching my shoulder before he walks away. "Time to unlock the doors."

As the employees begin to arrive, I continue with my straightening and rearranging. There's a cart filled with mysteries that need to be shelved, so I busy myself with that to keep my mind off Mack and the New Year's Eve party. Sadly, I realize it's pointless to even think about it. Even if I can muster the courage to ask him, he'll just say no, like he has the previous half-dozen times I've asked him to do something with me. I should have learned my lesson by now.

Once the doors are officially open, customers start streaming in, and suddenly Clancy's is bustling with activity. Beth arrives at nine-thirty with her baby, Luke, in tow, as well as with her personal bodyguard, Sam Harrison, who's with her anytime she leaves home. Beth's driver drops them off right in front of the bookstore. As usual, Mack greets them at the door, and I join them. Sam is carrying Luke, who's bundled up warmly in a darling little winter coat and hat, his big blue eyes bright as they take in the sights.

Sam holds Luke while Beth removes the baby's hat and coat. Then she takes him from Sam and hands him to me.

"Hello, sweetie," I say, kissing his cold little button nose. He's the most adorable six-month-old I've ever seen.

"Mum-mum-mum," Luke says, giving me a glimpse of the tiny

tooth peeking out of his bottom gum. He clutches my sweater as I settle him on my hip.

Beth puts her arm around me and draws me away from the doors—and away from Mack. "Did you ask him?" she says. She glances back at Mack, who's talking to Sam.

"No. Not exactly."

"What does that mean?"

Beth has been encouraging me to ask Mack to the party. "Come on, Erin," she's told me repeatedly. "Ask him! What's the worst that could happen?"

And each time I give her a *duh* look. "Hello! He could say *no*, like he always does."

"But what if he says *yes*? Isn't that worth taking a chance?"

Of course she's right. "It is." I glance back at the guys. Mack is laughing at something Sam said.

"Then you should definitely ask him."

I sigh. "I will. Later."

The guys are heading our way, and that puts an end to the discussion.

* * *

After giving her a chance to settle in upstairs, I head up to Beth's office for a little moral support. She's been encouraging me not to give up on Mack. I trust Beth's judgement, and I think she knows more than she's letting on. If she says I should ask him, then I think I should at least try.

I find her seated at her desk. Sam is lying on the sofa in front of the big picture window that overlooks North Michigan Avenue, with Luke propped up on his torso. The baby is squealing with delight as he waves his giraffe rattle and eagerly kicks his chubby little legs. "Mum-mum-mum."

"Hey, guys," I say, coming into the room.

Smiling, Beth looks up from her computer monitor. "Hey, you! Happy New Year!"

I shrug. "Happy New Year."

Sam swings his long legs off the sofa and sits up, resettling Luke on his lap. "What's wrong, Irish? You don't sound very enthusiastic."

I smile when he uses my nickname. "Hi, Red."

Sam's nickname—Red—stems from the obvious fact that he has red hair, long on top and closely trimmed on the sides. As usual, his hair is pulled into a bun on top of his head. Piercings, ripped jeans, and chunky, black boots complete the package, giving him the appearance of a bad boy, when in reality he's anything but. He's a wonderful friend to me, and a dedicated bodyguard to Beth. He once threw himself in front of a speeding car to save Beth. His act of selfless bravery almost cost him his life.

I plop down on the sofa beside him. "Is it that obvious?" I hold out my index finger to Luke, and he latches onto it and coos. And then he hands me his rattle, which is sopping wet because he's been chewing on it.

Sam laughs. "What's wrong? You look like someone stole your birthday cupcake, sprinkles and all."

Beth leans back in her office chair and crosses her arms. "She's trying to get the nerve up to ask Mack to a party tonight."

"Go for it, Irish," Sam says, nudging me with his elbow.

"There's still time," Beth says.

Sam suddenly makes a face, wrinkling his nose as he lifts Luke into the air. He definitely looks like somebody who just got a whiff of something unpleasant. "Somebody needs a diaper change." He stands, holding the baby at arm's length, and heads for the adjoining nursery. "We'll be right back. I'll leave you ladies to plot strategy."

Sam disappears through the nursery door, leaving me alone with Beth. She joins me on the sofa, squeezing my hand in commiseration. "Hang in there, Erin. I honestly think it will all work out."

I want to believe her so badly. "What makes you think so?"

"Because I see how he looks at you when you're not watching."

"And how does he look at me?"

"Like he's absolutely smitten. I really think you should ask him. He's not going to be able to hold out forever."

If only she was right.

2

Mack Donovan

Out of the corner of my eye, I observe Erin as she walks down the marble stairs, her hand skimming lightly along the handrail. At the sight of her, my heart skips a beat and heat surges through me. She reminds me of an elfin princess from a popular fantasy movie years ago... graceful, soft-spoken, beautiful. Erin O'Connor, with her bright blue eyes and shoulder-length, silky dark hair, is perfection. She takes my fucking breath away.

And I can't have her.

I'm obsessing over a girl who's way too damn young for me.

I know she's legal—she's twenty-two. But it's not just the years that separate us. She's a virgin. She's never had a boyfriend. How is that even possible? What's wrong with boys these days? She's absolutely gorgeous and sweet as hell… and the combination of those two traits wreaks havoc on me.

She hasn't yet noticed me watching her, so for the moment I can look my fill. As she skips down the last couple of steps to the ground floor, her attention is drawn to the bookstore's in-house café, where two little boys are making a ruckus over their lunch. The distraction gives me a few more seconds to drink her in. *I'm such a freaking pervert.*

Hell, my boss, Shane McIntyre, has warned me away from her so many times I've lost count. *"If you so much as touch her, Mack, you'll answer to me."* That's pretty hypocritical coming from Shane as he's almost just as many years older than Beth.

The problem is, Shane's right. I have no business getting up close and personal with Miss O'Connor. She needs a boy her own age, who's hopefully just as inexperienced and wide-eyed as she is. She doesn't need someone like me, someone who's been around the block a time or two. Someone who's done things he's not proud of. After three tours in Iraq and Afghanistan, followed by a bout as a private mercenary working in Europe, The Middle East, and Africa, I've fucked my way across three continents. I've seen it all. I've done things I shouldn't have, and frankly I'm lucky to still be alive.

My hands are sullied, and they're unfit to touch Erin.

Besides, she's only five years older than my own kid. I'm not about to rob the cradle. She deserves better. She deserves the whole Prince Charming fairy tale, not a retired mercenary with blood on his hands. No matter how I look at it, I have absolutely no fucking business putting these hands on her.

Still, I can't help watching her. I'm mesmerized by the way she moves, the way she lights up a room. The way her dark hair brushes her shoulders, one side drawn back with a gold barrette.

It doesn't help matters that Erin's got a crush on me. But that's all it is—a school-girl crush. Hell, my daughter likes a different boy each week. Erin hardly knows anything about me—she only knows the *me* she sees here at the bookstore. But when those blue eyes peer up at me with blatant hero worship, it's so fucking hard to remember she's off-limits.

God, if she knew the things I want to do to her... she'd run away screaming. If she knew how desperate I am to taste every inch of her delectable body... how I fantasize about her pert little breasts... *fuck*.

I'd give anything to have her. I'd worship every inch of her, from the crown of her head to the tips of her toes. I'd kiss every single freckle on her peaches-and-cream cheeks. I'd nibble gently on those perfect pink lips of hers... and when she gasped her pleasure, I'd be right there to drink it in.

Fuck.

I shift my stance, trying to make room in my jeans for a very inconvenient and inappropriate erection. Thank God my jacket conceals the bulge. I'll probably burn in hell for harboring these thoughts.

A raised female voice coming from the main check-out line draws my attention. Erin's now standing behind three busy cashiers as a woman in the queue starts yelling her damn fool head off. I sigh as I start moving in that direction. Customers can be such entitled asses sometimes.

I make a beeline for Erin. If things get ugly with this woman, I want to be standing between them. I know Erin—she'll step right up and do her damnedest to defuse the situation, and I admire her for that. She's got grit, and she'll gladly take the hit. But some people just won't be placated, and I won't allow Erin to get crushed in the process.

"I've been waiting in line for nearly fifteen minutes!" the middle-aged woman shouts. "I've never seen such horrible customer service! Where's the manager? I demand to speak to the manager!"

I reach Erin and plant myself at her back like a sentinel on guard, my arms crossed over my chest, my gaze locked onto the troublemaker. The other customers waiting in line either visibly cringe at the woman's outburst or roll their eyes, some of them even going as far as to try to shut her up.

"Don't shush me!" the woman yells as she gives me a nervous once-over. "I have every right to demand good service! I want to speak to the manager right now!"

Erin steps forward, squaring her shoulders like she's preparing to go into battle. "I'm the assistant manager," she says in a clear voice. "I'm sorry for your wait—"

The woman sneers at her. "You can't be the manager. You're hardly more than a child. I want to see the *manager*!"

"I said I'm the *assistant* manager."

In the meanwhile, the line continues to move steadily forward, just as it's been moving all along, and now the cranky bitch is at the front of the line, stepping up to the middle register.

"I'm sorry for your wait," Erin tells the woman as a young man rings up the lady's purchases—two paperbacks and a magazine. "We're very busy today, being that it's a holiday—"

"I don't care if it's a holiday. That's no excuse! You need to keep the lines moving faster. Open up more registers and show your customers some respect."

"I'm sorry for your wait." Erin manages to keep her voice steady, but I'm standing close enough to see that she's shaking.

The kid behind the counter finishes ringing up the woman's purchases and tells her the total due.

The old crab whips out her credit card and swipes it through the reader. "Your apology is meaningless," she says, her eyes shooting daggers at Erin. "At least you could have offered me a discount for my inconvenience."

Ah! She's angling for a discount. *Figures*.

I just happen to glance up at the second floor balcony to see Beth and Sam standing at the railing, watching the commotion down here. They must have heard the woman's strident voice from all the way upstairs. Luke's not with them, so he must be in the nursery with his nanny. I expect Beth will come down here any second to bail Erin out, like a mama bear protecting her cub, but when she takes a step toward the stairs, Sam grabs her arm and holds her back, saying something to her.

Beth doesn't look happy, but she nods and relaxes her stance. I imagine she's going to let Erin handle this situation on her own, as a confidence builder for Erin if nothing else.

Erin reaches underneath the counter and pulls out a coupon, which she hands to the woman. "I can offer you a twenty-percent-off coupon for your next visit."

The woman grabs the coupon and stuffs it into her purse. "That hardly does me any good today, does it? I'll never step foot in this store again. Do you hear me?" And with that parting shot, she stalks off toward the exit, leaving behind stunned customers and employees.

Oh, the joys of working retail. You never know when you're going to come across a gem like this one.

"I'm so sorry about that," says the next customer in line as she steps up to the register. She shakes her head in bewilderment. "Some people are so rude."

Erin smiles at the woman. "Thanks. That's very kind of you." Then she excuses herself and walks away without another word.

I follow Erin as she heads for the back of the store and disappears into the stockroom. She handled a disgruntled customer beautifully, but I'm sure the experience shook her. I want to make sure she's all right.

I step inside the cavernous room, which smells strongly of cardboard, new books, and scented candles. At first I don't see her. The room is filled with row after row of tall shelving units packed with books and assorted merchandise, so it would be easy for someone to hide in here if she wanted to. "Erin?"

"I'm in the back."

I follow the sound of that subdued voice behind a shelving unit filled with sci-fi paperbacks to find her standing in the shadows, well out of sight, her arms wrapped protectively around her torso. The sight of her shaking like a leaf kills me.

"Come here, honey." I pull her into my arms, the top of her head barely reaching my sternum, and rub her back. It's a struggle to ignore how good she feels in my arms. How *right*, like this is where she belongs. "You handled that beautifully. You should be proud of yourself."

After a moment, Erin finally relaxes into me, her arms slipping beneath my jacket and around my waist. "I hate confrontations," she says. "Why do people have to be like that?"

I try not to notice how good she feels pressed against my chest, how perfect her arms feel wrapped around me. I remind myself that we're friends. It's okay to hug a friend, right? There's nothing inappropriate about that.

As I cup the back of her head, I have to resist the urge to lean down and press my nose to her hair. "I'm sorry, honey. Some people live to cause drama."

"Erin? Are you in here?"

At the sound of Beth's voice, we break apart.

"I'm here!" Erin calls, taking a few steps back as she nervously straightens her hair.

Beth comes around the shelving unit, her gaze filled with concern. Sam's right behind her. "Are you all right?" she says. "I saw some of that from the balcony. I'm so sorry. But you handled it really well."

"That's what I told her," I say.

Erin looks flushed, but whether it's because of the recent drama or because of all the attention focused on her now, I'm not sure. "Thanks, guys," she says.

Her gaze lifts to mine, and she makes eye contact for a split second before looking away. I can't help wondering if she's thinking the same thing I'm thinking—how good it felt to hold each other.

"I should get back to work," she says, straightening her sweater unnecessarily and taking a fortifying breath. Squaring her shoulders once more, she heads back out onto the sales floor.

"You were right to hang back and let Erin handle it," I tell Beth.

"It wasn't easy," she says. "It was good practice for her, but I still felt like I was throwing her to the wolves."

I laugh. "As if I'd ever let that happen."

3

Erin

It's almost five o'clock—time for me to head home—and I still haven't asked Mack to the party tonight. With each passing hour, my anxiety has increased to the point I'm an absolute nervous wreck. After what happened in the stockroom earlier, after the way he held me to his chest and comforted me after an upsetting incident with an irate customer, it seems humanly possible that he might actually say yes this time.

I'm standing with Stacey, the evening assistant manager, at the second floor balcony as we go over the day's events and talk about anything she needs to know. There's not much to report, other than the fact we had a lot of customers in the store today. But with New Year's Eve approaching, the foot traffic has definitely died down. It should be a quiet evening.

I catch sight of Mack gazing up at me expectantly from the main floor. It's time for us to go, and he's waiting on me. He always walks me to my bus stop on his way out. If I'm going to ask him, it's now or never.

I wish Stacey a good evening and head downstairs to Mack.

"Ready?" he says.

"Yes."

Mack's locker is just inside the door, so we stop there for him to collect his things. I stand beside him, hoping I can say what I need to say without making a complete fool of myself.

"So, Mack. I was wondering...."

He glances down at me as he pulls his coat out of his locker. "Yeah?"

"I'm going to a New Year's Eve party tonight, at the Wakefield Hotel and Bar. I was wondering if you wanted to come."

He freezes in the middle of zipping up his coat, and for a heartbeat, he's perfectly still. His throat muscles work as he swallows before turning to face me. He looks... sorry.

Steeling myself for the rejection I know is coming, I gaze up at him, searching his whisky-colored eyes for a hint of what he's feeling.

"Erin—" He reaches into his locker and pulls out a pair of black leather gloves, which he shoves into his coat pockets. "Honey, I wish—"

What does he wish? That he could say yes? That I'd stop pestering him? That I'd find someone else to crush on? "You wish what?"

Mack slams his locker door shut, making me jump.

His lips flatten, and he gazes down at me with an inscrutable expression. I'd give anything to know what he's thinking. I watch his clenched jaws solidify into stone, perfectly still except for the ticking of a muscle in his cheek.

He sighs. "Erin, I'm sorry, but I can't."

My shoulders fall, along with my hopes. *I shouldn't have asked him. I should have known better!* "Right. Of course. Forget I asked."

He exhales with a grimace. "No, it's fine. It's just that... we're friends. I don't think we should blur those lines, you know?" He cups my face in his big, warm hands and leans down to kiss me chastely on the forehead. His lips cling to my skin momentarily, long enough for me to feel a warm puff of breath that makes me shiver.

My throat tightens painfully, and I'm mortified when I feel tears pricking the backs of my eyes. *Oh, God, please don't let me cry in front of him.*

"Get your things," he says as he releases me, all business now. "We'd better get going or you'll miss your bus."

Numbly, I head to my own locker and reach for the combination lock. My tears obscure the little white numbers on the black dial, and I can't see! I brush my eyes with a shaking hand. *I shouldn't have asked him. I'm such an idiot!*

"Here, let me," he says in a quiet voice, brushing my hands aside and unlocking it for me.

He opens my locker door, and I gather my things, bundling up with quick, jerking movements. When will I ever learn? Without another word, I turn and head for the door, and he follows.

"You don't have to walk me to my bus," I say, striding quickly through the store. I just want to get out of here. I don't want to see or talk to anyone.

He follows me anyway, of course. Once I'm through the door and out on the snowy sidewalk, I walk right into a gust of frigid air that practically steals my breath. I pull my scarf up to my nose and try my best to ignore the bone-chilling cold. As I trudge through the powdery snow to my bus stop, I'm painfully aware of the tall, silent form keeping pace with me.

As I stand amidst a small crowd waiting for the bus, I can feel Mack's eyes on me. He keeps a respectful distance and doesn't try to engage me in conversation. He obviously knows I'm upset.

When my bus arrives, I step inside, refusing to look back at him. I swipe my bus pass and take the first available seat. It's only as the bus is pulling away from the curb that I allow myself one glance back. And there he is, watching me leave, as he always does, so steadfast and stalwart.

My heart breaks a little, and frankly he doesn't look any happier than me. He catches me watching him and lifts a gloved hand in farewell. Sadly, I wave back, pining for so much more.

On the ride home, I relive my humiliation over and over, wishing I'd kept my mouth shut. How much rejection does a person have to take before she gets a clue?

I just don't understand him! He acts like he cares, and yet when

I ask him to do something with me outside of work, he says no. He's got me squarely in the friend zone, and while I value his friendship—I really do—I want so much more. Why can't he see me as a woman? I know I'm a lot younger than he is, but age shouldn't matter. Beth and Shane are proof of that. They're very happily married.

The bus finally pulls up to my corner stop, and I climb down the metal steps and walk a block in the frigid darkness to the two-bedroom apartment I share with three other girls. The four of us met at Chicago University, where we all major in business. We're not terribly close, but I've been rooming with the three of them since my grandma died and I had nowhere to go.

I let myself into our building and walk up one flight of steps and down the hall to our apartment. When I step inside, I don't see anyone, but I hear voices coming from the hallway bathroom. It's a small apartment, two girls to a bedroom, with one bathroom for the four of us to share. I hang up my coat in the closet and head to my room wishing I could climb into bed and hide beneath the covers.

Shelley is just coming out of our room when she sees me. "Oh, good! You're home. Get ready, girl! We're leaving in half an hour." She pauses, studying me. "Did you ask that guy you like?"

"Mack." I nod.

"What did he say?"

I swallow past the painful lump in my throat. "He said no."

Shelley frowns. "Rats. Well, it's his loss." She smiles. "At least you asked him. Good for you!" And then she squeezes past me and heads to the bathroom to flat iron her long blonde hair.

* * *

I put on a dress—a burgundy tunic that falls mid-thigh—black tights, and my black flats. Then I wait my turn for the bathroom so I can brush my hair and teeth, and at the last minute, I decide to apply a bit of lip gloss and mascara. At this point, I'd honestly rather stay home and read, but I promised the other girls I'd go, and I don't want to be a party pooper.

The four of us share a taxi to the hotel, arriving at eight o'clock, right on time. Their boyfriends are supposed to meet us here.

"Table for seven," Shelley tells the hostess.

While we're waiting for a table, their boyfriends arrive, freshly showered after their late afternoon basketball game. The seven of us hang out at the bar while we wait to be seated. The others order beers. As I'm not much of a drinker, I order a soft drink and sit on a barstool to watch the people filing into the already crowded bar.

I wonder how Mack's enjoying his evening alone at home with his basketball game and pizza. I'd rather be home myself. We've only been here a few minutes, and I'm already painfully aware that coming here was a big mistake. I'm such an introvert, and this noisy bar scene isn't my thing.

After finishing his beer, Shelley's boyfriend, Steve, orders another drink. The bartender hands him a glass of dark amber liquid. Steve points to my glass. "Is that a rum and Coke?" He has to yell to be heard over the din.

"No!" I yell back, shaking my head. "Just Coke!"

Steve reaches over and pours some of his drink into my glass. "Now it is," he says, laughing. "You're welcome."

The others laugh, too, and I force myself to smile. I don't want to be a stick in the mud. But the truth is, I don't belong here. I'm seriously thinking of grabbing a cab ride home, but then the hostess calls our group. Our table is ready.

"Come on, Erin," Shelley says, linking her arm through mine and pulling me with her to a large corner booth that's plenty roomy enough for our group.

I slide into the booth, and the others follow suit, and I end up in the middle with one couple on my right and the other two couples on my left.

Our server hands us menus and takes orders for more drinks. The guys order another round of draft beers, and the girls order shots with suggestive names like *Slippery Nipples* and *Sex on a Beach*. When I ask for a refill of my soft drink, Steve orders me a *Dirty Nipple*.

I'm already feeling the effects of the rum he poured into my soft drink. I certainly don't want to drink any more alcohol, especially since I didn't have time to grab any dinner before coming here. Alcohol on an empty stomach can't be a good idea.

We end up ordering a variety of appetizers to share—hot wings, fried pickles, nachos, onion rings. Our server returns with more drinks.

Shelley slides a shot glass my way. "This one's yours," she says, grinning at me. "Drink up!"

The alcohol is making me feel queasy, so I don't feel like eating anything. After downing my second glass of cola, and yet another shot, I excuse myself from the table, saying I need to go to the ladies' room. But the truth is, I'm hot and dizzy, and I just need an escape.

Shelley and Steve slide out of the booth to let me by.

"Do you want me to come with you?" Shelley asks, looking a bit concerned.

"No, thanks. I'll be fine."

I walk away from our table with a sigh of relief. I really don't have to pee as much as I need a few minutes alone. All that constant chatter and laughter wears on me.

There's a long line for the women's restroom, and while I'm waiting, I pull out my phone and check my messages.

I see a text from Beth.

Beth: Did you ask him?

Me: Yes

Beth: What did he say?

Me: He said no. :(

Beth: Darn

I read a little bit of a new romance novel I recently downloaded to my phone. Those of us waiting in line are hugging the wall because the hallway is packed with people coming and going from the game room in the back, where folks are playing pinball and video games.

While I've got my eyes on my phone, somebody bumps into me, sloshing some of his beer onto my arm.

"Oh, wow, sorry!" he says, using the sleeve of his hoodie to pat me dry. "I'm not normally that clumsy. Somebody bumped into me."

I look up into a pair of hazel eyes and ash blond hair. "It's all right."

He's about my age, early twenties, dressed in blue jeans and a gray hoodie. He's certainly good looking, but there's something about him that makes me uncomfortable. His gaze is way too intense.

He offers me his hand. "I'm Kurt."

I hesitate, reluctant to touch him, but when he keeps his hand hanging awkwardly in the air, I relent and shake his hand. "Erin."

"Are you here with someone?"

I nod. "Friends."

"Do you have a—"

But then the line jumps forward, and suddenly it's my turn to enter the ladies' room. "Excuse me."

"Oh, sure," he says. "Hopefully I'll see you around."

I'm so relieved when I can lock myself in a bathroom stall. I sit there with my eyes closed and try to block out all the noise. Eventually I pee, since I'm already here I might as well go, but then I remain seated for a while, wishing I was anywhere but here.

I check the time on my phone: ten-thirty already. I wonder if the others would think me rude if I begged off now and headed home.

Eventually, I give up my stall and wash my hands before heading back to our booth. Shelley and Steve are nowhere to be seen.

"They're dancing," Crystal informs me as I slide into the booth.

The dance floor is crowded, full of gyrating bodies moving in sync to a heavy beat of hip hop music. Big flatscreen TVs positioned all around the room are broadcasting the annual New Year's Eve celebration in Times Square.

Crystal and Valerie order another round of shots, and their boyfriends order fresh beers. More food comes—potato skins and more chicken wings.

When the shots arrive, Crystal pushes one across the table to me. "This one's for you, Erin. It's called a *Pink Pussy*." She laughs uproariously.

She and the other girls have been downing shots all night, and I'm pretty sure they're drunk. The guys aren't doing any better. I lost track of how many beers they've consumed, plus a few shots of their own.

"No, thank you." I push a glass containing a bright pink liquid back in her direction. "I've had enough."

"Oh, come on, Erin," Crystal's boyfriend says, intercepting the shot glass and sliding it back in my direction. "Drink it!"

"No, really, I—"

"Drink it! Drink it!" the others at our table chant, loud enough to draw a lot of unwanted stares from guests seated at nearby tables.

"Fine!" To shut them up, I swallow the contents of the shot glass in one gulp, gagging at the sickly sweet taste.

Now I definitely feel sick to my stomach. I would eat more to offset the alcohol, but the latest round of appetizers has already been scarfed up by the guys. There's nothing left.

Shelley and Steve return to our booth and slide in beside me. They're laughing loudly, their voices a bit slurred, clearly inebriated.

Steve lays a wad of cash on the table and informs us that he and Shelley are heading out, going back to his apartment. His hands are all over her, and she can't stop giggling. I'm pretty sure I can guess what they have on their minds.

Crystal and Valerie are practically making out with their boyfriends now, hands and lips everywhere.

Some random guy walks past our booth and yells, "Get a room!"

Not long after, the other two couples slide out of the booth as well, leaving money on the table to cover the bill.

"Will you be okay getting home?" Crystal asks me, giggling as her boyfriend—Rodney—slips a hand up beneath her top and pinches her nipple. She doubles over in laughter, shooing his hand away, and Rodney practically drags her to the exit.

Valerie and her boyfriend—I never did catch his name—leave right after them. And I'm left alone, which I actually don't mind. Now I can finally go home and curl up with a cup of hot tea and a book.

Just as I'm about to slide out of the booth, the guy from the bathroom hallway—Kurt—slides onto the bench beside me.

"Hey! Erin, right?" he says, giving me a blinding smile. His hot breath smells like stale beer, and I try not to make a face.

"I was just leaving," I say, hoping he'll take the hint.

"Don't go yet! The ball's just about to drop." He lifts his beer mug toward me, clearly wanting to toast. "Happy New Year!"

There's some soft drink left in my glass. I raise it to his. "Happy New Year. I'm sorry, but it's late, and I—"

"Don't run off, babe. Stay and have a drink with me."

"Thanks, but I can't, really."

"Look!" He points at one of the TV screens across the bar, and I follow the trajectory of his finger. "The ball's about to drop," he says.

The crowd is watching with bated breath as the clock counts down the last few seconds before midnight. "Three, two, one!"

I glance at the monitor just as the big colorful ball drops and the crowd cheers. In the bar, someone throws handfuls of colorful confetti into the air, and everyone's hugging and kissing.

I turn back to face my uninvited companion and grab my purse. "I really do need to go."

He pouts. "I was hoping you'd stay awhile. I'd love to get to know you better. Do you live around here?"

"Not too far. Roger's Park."

"Oh, that's not far from me at all. Maybe we could hook-up sometime. How about it?"

Rather than answer him, I slip my purse strap over my shoulder, hoping he'll get the hint.

Kurt hands me my half-empty glass of cola. "One last toast before you take off, okay?"

I sigh. "Okay." And I take a drink. Anything to get this night over with so I can be on my way.

"Bottoms up!" he says.

After setting down my empty glass, I wave for our server. She brings me the check, and I hand her the pile of cash on our table, adding a few bills of my own to pay for my portion of the total.

After the server walks away, Kurt leans close and gazes into my eyes. "You're so fucking pretty."

I pull back, feeling a bit queasy and overly warm. And suddenly, I have the beginnings of a headache. I really need to go, but Kurt sits there like an immovable object, blocking my exit. This guy doesn't know when to take a hint. He's way too … too … he's too….

"Erin?" He slides closer, his body brushing up against mine, and stares me in the face. "Erin?"

What? "Hmm?"

He smiles. "Is everything okay?"

I blink as numbness spreads through my body. "Huh?"

His smile widens as I feel myself slowly listing toward him. His arm goes around me, and he pulls me close. His lips brush against my neck, right below my ear, and his fingers graze the side of my breast.

"No," I say, my voice slurring. I try to pull away, but I don't have the strength. "Stop that," I say as he continues to caress my breast. I feel so dizzy, I just want to lie down. "Where's Mack?" My words run together. "He should be here."

He stills. "Who's Mack? Is he your boyfriend?"

"I wish." As I shake my head, the room spins, making me feel worse.

Kurt's voice lowers to a whisper as he kisses my throat. "Good. I don't want to share you with anyone."

"I think I'm going to be sick," I murmur, falling against Kurt.

He sits up and pulls me closer. "It's okay, pretty baby. Just lean on me. I've got you."

"I have to ... um ... go home."

"No, you don't."

"Yes ... I do. I should go. Home."

"Let's get you upstairs, okay? You can rest in my bed. You're going to like it there."

I shake my head. "No. I need to go...." I close my eyes. I'm so dizzy. So hot. "Something's... wrong... with me."

"No, you're fine, babe. Let's get you upstairs. You'll feel much better after you lie down."

"No...."

Suddenly the room is spinning, and the floor is moving. No, wait. *I'm* moving. And the exit is coming closer and closer. I shake my head. "No...."

"Shh," he says, his lips in my hair. His arm tightens around me. "Come upstairs with me."

"No. I can't."

"Yes, you can."

And then he laughs softly in my ear.

4

Mack

Eight-thirty Tuesday morning, and there's still no sign of Erin. She's half an hour late. That's not like her.

I stand at the shop doors and watch the heavy foot traffic, searching for a glimpse of her bright red coat among the hordes of pedestrians out shopping for post-holiday specials. She's impossible to miss. But I don't see her.

In the time I've worked here as head of security, Erin O'Connor has never been late to work. She's so damn punctual you could set your clock by her.

I suppose she might have missed her bus this morning. If she was out late last night celebrating with her friends, she might have simply overslept. That's perfectly understandable, but my gut tells me no. *This is Erin.* I once saw her drag herself in to work when she had pneumonia. I had to drive her back to her apartment myself and insist that she go to bed and stay there until she felt better.

I've already texted her twice this morning and gotten no response. I try calling her now, but my call goes directly to voicemail. Either her phone is turned off or the battery is dead.

With every passing minute, the bad feeling in my gut worsens. As the employees start trickling in, many of them looking a little worse for wear after a late night out partying, I let them know that Erin's not here yet. A couple of the employees offer to take care of getting the sales terminals ready for operation. They pick up the slack with no problem.

Nine o'clock comes and goes. Shortly after, Beth and Sam arrive, Luke in tow.

When Beth, who's laughing at something Sam said, gets a look at me, she pulls up short. "Mack? Is something wrong?"

Is something wrong? Yes, something is definitely fucking wrong! My chest tightens as the sick feeling in my gut sharpens. "Erin never showed up for work this morning."

Instantly, Beth's smile falls. She opens her mouth as if to speak, but nothing comes out. I think she's just as shocked—and concerned—as I am. "Have you tried—"

"Calling her? Yes. I've texted her. I've called her. There's been no response."

Sam pulls his phone out and taps the screen, his expression carefully guarded as he holds it to his ear. After a few seconds, he ends the call, pocketing his phone. "Straight to voicemail."

I'm already heading toward the locker room. "I'm going to her apartment," I shoot back to Beth.

She nods, looking as worried as I feel.

* * *

I practically run the two blocks to the parking garage, hopping into my pick-up truck and heading for Rogers Park. It's a half-hour drive through crowded morning traffic. I double-park, illegally, right in front of her building and run up to the main entrance, buzzing her unit.

A groggy female voice answers on my third try. "Yes?"

"This is Mack Donovan. I work with Erin at Clancy's Bookshop. Can I come up? Is she okay? She didn't show up for work this morning."

"Hold on a minute."

The intercom goes quiet, and I assume her roommate is checking on Erin.

A few minutes later, the intercom squawks as the young woman speaks. "Erin's not here."

My gut twists. "Are you sure?"

"Yes. It's not that big of an apartment. I checked everywhere. She's not here."

"Can I come up? Please?"

She hesitates for a moment, then sighs. "Sure. I'll buzz you in."

* * *

A young woman with tangled dark hair opens their apartment door. She's wearing an oversized, white fluffy robe and slippers on her bare feet. It's pretty obvious I got her out of bed.

"I'm Crystal," she says, stepping back to let me enter.

"Can I see her bedroom?"

She nods to the hallway. "First door on the left."

I pass through a tiny living room and walk down a short hallway, stopping at the first door I come to.

"That's her room," Crystal says from behind me. "She shares with Shelley."

I open the door and step inside, flipping on the light. There are two twin beds in the room, with matching nightstands between them. One of the beds is neatly made, and the other one is covered with discarded clothing. The closet door is open and there are clothes strewn all over the floor.

I can guess which bed belongs to Erin.

Neither bed looks like it was slept in last night.

"Where's Shelley?" I ask.

"She must have stayed over at her boyfriend's place last night. She hasn't been home yet."

"Tell me about last night. Erin told me she was going out with her roommates to a New Year's Eve party at a hotel bar. Did she do that?"

"Yes. The four of us went."

"Together?"

"Yes. We shared a taxi to the hotel. Our boyfriends met us there. Well, not Erin's, because she doesn't have one, but the rest of us do."

"Did you leave the hotel together, too?"

I watch the blood drain from Crystal's face, her cautious expression replaced with a guilty one. "No."

"No? You didn't leave the hotel with Erin?"

Crystal shakes her head. "Shelley left with her boyfriend, Steve, to go to his apartment. Val and I came back here with our boyfriends."

"And you didn't hear Erin come home last night? Why didn't you call someone?"

Crystal shakes her head. "We were in the other bedroom, playing music pretty loudly. We didn't hear anything. I just assumed she came home sometime in the night and went to bed."

"You never checked to make sure she got home all right?"

She pales. "No."

"So, *no one* bothered to make sure she got home safely?"

"I guess not."

I point to the bed that's neatly made. "That's Erin's bed?"

Crystal nods.

I walk over to the bed, smiling when I see a stuffed kitty wearing a pink bow lying on the pillow. On the nightstand is a reading lamp, her phone charger, and a stack of paperback books. There's no sign of her purse or phone.

The implication hits me like a blow to the gut. *She didn't come home last night.*

When I look back at Crystal, there are tears in her eyes, and she's hugging herself tightly. She shakes her head. "I'm so sorry."

I'm so fucking furious with this girl I could ring her neck. "Some friend you are," I say, and then I walk out.

* * *

Back in my truck, I grip the steering wheel with shaking hands and force myself to take several deep breaths. I need to keep a clear head. I need to find her.

I call Erin's phone again. "Come on, honey, answer!" When my call goes straight to voicemail, I slam my fists on the steering wheel. "Damn it!"

I put the truck in drive and head for the Wakefield Hotel, calling Beth on the way.

She answers quickly. "Mack! Did you find her?"

"No. It looks like she didn't come home last night. She went out with her roommates to a party at The Wakefield Hotel. I'm on my way there now to see if I can trace her movements."

"Please call me as soon as you know anything."

"I will."

I end the call, trying not to dwell on all the possible reasons why Erin might not have come home last night. None of them are good, starting with the idea that she might have simply hooked up with someone and gone home with him. The idea of her with another man makes me see red. I try not to fixate on that possibility, but if that's what happened, it still doesn't explain why she didn't come home last night, or why she didn't show up to work this morning. Or, where she is right now.

I pull up to the hotel's front entrance and skip the valet, instead opting for a short-term parking spot. Erin was here last night, presumably for several hours. There has to be some evidence of what happened to her.

I cut across the spacious hotel lobby and head straight for the bar. This early, the bar is officially closed. That's no surprise. Most of the hotel guests are in the adjacent restaurant enjoying their complimentary breakfasts. But the bar's not completely empty. There are a few guests scattered around, seated at tables where they're sipping coffee and working on their tablets or laptops.

I walk up to the counter where a young man is drying a row of tumblers.

"We're closed," he says, not bothering to look up at me as he picks up another glass.

"I'm not here for a drink."

When he finally bothers to look at me, his eyes widen as he blatantly takes me in, skimming me from head to waist. Color infuses his smooth shaven cheeks, and he sets the glass and rag down. "Hey, handsome. If you're not here for a drink, what are you looking for?" And then he winks.

"Were you working the bar last night?"

He nods. "I was."

I pull out my phone and bring up a picture of Erin, taken just last week on Christmas Eve, when we were snowed in at the store. In the picture, she's standing behind the sales counter, dressed in a red Christmas sweater and holding up a Rudolph the Red-Nosed Reindeer stuffed animal. I show him the picture. "She was here last night with a group of girls. Do you remember seeing her?"

He narrows his eyes as he stares at the image. Then he nods. "Yeah, I remember her. What about it?"

"Did you see her leave?"

He shakes his head. "Sorry. It was jam-packed in here last night, standing room only. People were coming and going all night, and I wasn't keeping track."

I nod, not the least bit surprised. "Can you tell me anything about her? What she drank? Who she talked to? Anything?"

The guy looks at me suspiciously. "Why all the questions?"

"She didn't come to work this morning. And it looks like she didn't go home to her apartment last night. I'm trying to find her. Please, I need your help."

He purses his lips. "Okay. Yes, I remember her. She stands out in a crowd, you know—she's cute as a button. Anyhoo, she and her friends were seated at that big corner booth." He points across the room. "Later in the evening, I saw her sitting alone. No, wait. There was one guy at her table. A good-looking blond kid."

"Did you recognize the guy she was sitting with?"

"No. Sorry."

"What did he look like?"

"Like I said, he was good-looking, blond." Then he shrugs. "He looked like a million other guys."

"Tall? Short? Thin? Fat?"

The guy shrugs. "Average height, maybe five-ten. Average weight. He looked pretty fit."

"Did you see her leave? Did she leave with this guy?"

"I think she was still here when the ball dropped. I remember looking at that table later, and it was empty. They were gone."

"Both of them? You never saw the guy again afterwards?"

He shakes his head. "I'm pretty sure they were both gone."

"Thanks." I pull out my wallet and lay a twenty on the counter, along with my card. "If you think of anything else, please call me."

He picks up the money and my card, pocketing them both. "Thanks."

I quickly survey the bar, counting the number of video surveillance cameras positioned throughout the room. Once back in the hotel lobby, I try calling Erin's phone again. It goes straight to voicemail. Hearing the generic, automated message just adds to my sense of foreboding. I'd give anything right now just to hear her voice. Even if it was just a recorded message.

Jesus, Erin, where the hell are you?

The longer this goes on, the more worried I get. It's not like Erin to drop off the face of the Earth, and that means something's happened to her. Just the thought makes me sick. I swear to God, if anyone's hurt her, I'll kill them.

5

Mack

My next stop is the hotel's front desk. "Can I speak to the manager?"

The young man working behind the counter nods as he gestures for me to wait. "Just a minute." He picks up a house phone and hits speed dial. A moment later, he speaks into the handset. "There's someone at the front desk asking for you."

"Thanks," I tell the kid after he hangs up. My mind is racing. The longer I can't reach her, the worse it gets.

A few minutes later, an African-American woman dressed in a burgundy suit with a white blouse comes out from the office behind the counter. She gives me a bright, polished smile. "I'm Mrs. Abney, the hotel manager. How can I help you?"

I show her my McIntyre Security ID. "Mack Donovan. I'm looking for someone. A friend." I pull out my phone and show her Erin's picture. "She was here last night with friends. I spoke to the bartender who said he remembered seeing Erin seated at a booth with a man. I need to see your surveillance camera footage from last night to see if I can spot her and see who she might have left with."

The woman's dark eyes widen. "I don't know. I'm not sure I can—"

"Please. She's *missing*, and that means she's in trouble. I've got to find her. I'm hoping your video footage will help me do that." I hold up my phone. "If you don't let me see the footage, I'll call the cops right now and report a kidnapping at this hotel. You can either deal quietly with me now, or you can deal with the police and a search warrant. It's up to you."

She looks pensive as she considers her options. "Well, I guess it won't hurt to let you look at last night's footage." She motions for me to come behind the service counter. "Let's go to the security office."

Mrs. Abney leads me down a hallway to a room marked SECURITY. She knocks briskly, then opens the door wide and ushers me inside. There's an older guy with a weathered face and a gray buzz-cut seated at a table that holds an array of monitors. The man's wearing black trousers and a white shirt with a security company logo. The name tag on his uniform shirt says MR JACK-

SON. I recognize a fellow vet when I see one.

"This is Tim Jackson. He's our security lead. Tim, this gentleman needs to see the video footage from the bar last night. He's looking for a friend—a young lady—who was here for the New Year's Eve celebration. Let's see if we can help him out."

Tim stands at attention and offers me his hand. "Tim Jackson." We shake. "Mack Donovan. Thanks for your help."

"No problem, sir. About what time?" he says to me as he takes a seat in front of the console and scrolls back to last night's footage.

"She arrived at the bar a little after eight o'clock and was last seen by the bartender at around midnight. I'm not sure of the exact time she left."

Jackson motions to the empty chair beside his. "Have a seat, Donovan. Let's take a look at what we've got."

I sit, but I'm finding it hard to be still when I feel like I should be on my feet, doing something. Jackson scrolls back through last night's footage, to the eight o'clock pm timestamp. There are three different cameras in the bar, all recording from different angles, so there's a lot of footage to skim through.

Not surprisingly, the bar was filled to capacity last night. It's a boisterous crowd. As Jackson skims through all three feeds, I watch for Erin. I spot her as she walks into the bar with her friends. Trailing behind the other three girls, Erin glances around the room with wide eyes, looking so out of place. There's no audio, but the place is crowded and bustling enough to imagine how loud it must have been last night, with multiple flatscreens broadcasting the New Year's celebration from New York.

The four girls check in with the hostess when they arrive. Erin follows her friends to the bar as they sit. The roommates order shots, and it looks like Erin has a soft drink. The boyfriends show up soon after and order drinks.

Jackson fast-forwards through the tape to the point when they leave the counter and relocate to a large corner booth. The seven slide into the booth, and a server takes their orders.

The others are clearly partnered up, but Erin sits alone, looking lost and out-of-place. God, I wish I'd been there with her. What the fuck was I thinking, letting her go to this party alone?

As I watch the video footage, my heart races, slamming into my chest. The sick knot in my stomach grows tighter and tighter with each passing second. Something must have happened to her, but I won't even let myself speculate what that could be because all of the obvious choices are unacceptable.

We speed through the footage as the night wears on. Everyone at Erin's table ends up doing shots, repeatedly. Her friends keep pushing alcohol on her, and I've lost count of how many drinks she's had. She's not a drinker. She has no idea what she's getting herself into.

She leaves the table for a while, and I'm guessing she went to the ladies' room. When she comes back, one of the couples is gone. They return for a short while, then leave again. Soon after, the remaining two couples leave, presumably to continue their party somewhere a little more private, leaving Erin alone in the huge booth.

My blood is boiling. *I can't believe they fucking left her there alone.*

Just as she starts to leave, a young man slides into her booth, blocking her exit. He says something to her, and she shakes her head adamantly, looking like she's about to bolt.

The guy looks to be near Erin's age, early twenties. I stare at the video, studying every frame for the tiniest detail that might help me identify him or find her.

According to the timestamp on the footage, it's just a couple minutes before midnight, and everyone in the bar is fixated on the flatscreen monitors, waiting for the big moment when the ball drops. Erin is reaching for her purse, looking like she's ready to leave. The guy says something to her, pointing across the room. As Erin glances up at one of the monitors, he slips something into her drink. My lungs seize up. *What the fuck! He spiked her drink!*

Erin turns back to say something to the guy. He lifts his glass and offers her a toast. She lifts her glass to his and takes a drink. Then another, finishing off her glass. My dread increases when I see her expression start to glass over. He's talking to her, and she seems to be mumbling responses, but she's clearly already impaired by whatever he gave her—most likely some form of date rape drug.

By the time they leave, he's practically dragging her out the door. And not a single person attempts to stop them.

I watch as she stumbles out of the bar with him, through the doors and out of the camera's sight.

"Where else do you have cameras posted?" I say, turning to the security guard. "I need to see where they went."

Jackson switches the monitors to a different view, and we match the time stamps. We're able to follow Erin and the suspect's progress down a hallway to the hotel lobby. But instead of leading her out the front doors of the hotel, he turns her toward the bank of elevators.

"He has a room in this hotel!" I shoot to my feet, staring down the security guard. "Can you follow them? See where they went?"

We're able to use the video surveillance footage to locate Erin and the suspect coming out of the elevator on the twelfth floor. We follow them down the hallway, Erin practically staggering as the blond holds her upright and drags her along with him. *That fucking son of a bitch!*

I'm holding my breath as I watch them stop in front of a room. I can't make out the room number, but it's the last door on the left.

"Which room is that?" I ask Mrs. Abney, who's standing behind us, looking horrified at what she's seeing.

She clears her throat as she stares at the monitor. "That's room twelve-twenty-eight."

"I need to get into that room," I tell her. "Right now!"

* * *

All three of us take an elevator up to the twelfth floor. As soon as the doors open, we race to the end of the hallway. Mrs. Abney waves a master keycard over the reader, and the lock indicator light turns green.

Not bothering to knock, I open the door and poke my head inside the room. "Erin?" I call out loudly.

The room is dark, and there's no response.

"Erin!" I switch on the entry light and step further into the room. The king-sized bed is shrouded in darkness and I can't see much of anything. But the cloying, metallic scent of blood is unmistakable, and my heart stops.

I switch on another light and approach the bed. Behind me, Mrs. Abney cries out, horrified by what she sees. The security guard immediately goes for the hotel phone.

I don't have time to think. I don't have time to feel. I race to the side of the bed where a small body lies on a blood-stained sheet. The blankets have been carelessly tossed to the floor. Erin's lying on her stomach, naked and uncovered. There are blood stains everywhere! Between her thighs, on her buttocks, streaked across her back. Her body is a patchwork of bruises and cuts. Her dark hair is matted with blood.

Working on autopilot, because I can't let myself think or process what I'm seeing, I lean over her and brush her hair away from her neck and face. Ignoring the ring of bruises encircling her slender throat, I press my fingers to her carotid artery, searching for a pulse. My heart slams into my ribs when I feel one. *She's alive!*

I drop to my knees beside the bed and stroke her sticky hair. "Erin, honey? Can you hear me?" My voice sounds like crushed gravel.

When she doesn't respond, I'm almost relieved, grateful that she's not aware of what's happening.

Jackson's on the phone with 911, giving them a run-down of the situation in a calm, professional voice.

I pull out my phone and dial a familiar number.

Shane McIntyre answers on the second ring, sounding guarded. "Mack? Did you find her?"

Beth must have told him Erin was missing. My throat closes up on me, and my free hand shakes as I lay it gently on the back of Erin's matted hair.

"Mack, talk to me."

I suck in a breath and struggle to get the words out as my throat closes up on me. "She—oh, God."

Shane is silent for a split second. "Tell me," he says. And when I don't immediately respond, his voice turns sharp. "Mack! Answer me!"

I can't bring myself to say the words. As my gaze skims over her battered and bruised body, my heart shatters. My chest is imploding, crushing my ribs and lungs. I can't catch my breath. "Shane—"

"Mack, talk to me." There's a bite to his voice I've never heard before.

"Erin—" My voice breaks. "Shane—it's Erin."

"What happened? Where are you?"

"Wakefield Hotel. She's...." But I can't bring myself to say the words.

His voice turns cold and emotionless when he says, "Is she alive?"

"Yes. Barely."

There's a muffled curse over the phone, followed by the sound of heavy footsteps. "I'm on my way," he says in an eerily measured voice.

I end the call and stow my phone. In the background, I can hear Jackson talking to the 911 operator, giving them details and answering questions. Jackson puts the call on speaker.

"Is she alive?" the female operator says.

"Yes," Jackson says.

"Is she conscious?"

"No."

"The police and an ambulance are on their way, sir. Please remain on the line."

I know there are things I should be doing right now to secure the scene. Looking for evidence. Looking for clues as to the identity of her assailant. But I can do none of those things. All I can do is kneel beside her bed and stare at her bruised and swollen face, desperate for any sign of life. Her lips are split open and caked with drying blood. Her eye sockets are bruised, her lids swollen nearly shut. Her hair—tangled and matted. And the blood... it's everywhere. She's covered in it, lying in it.

Dear God, honey. Who did this to you? I'll fucking kill him.

I probably shouldn't do this—tamper with the scene—but I grab a discarded sheet and gently cover her naked body. It's the best I can do for her at the moment. Then I press my fingers to her carotid artery to reassure myself that she's still with us. When I feel that faint, rhythmic pulse against my fingertips, I want to bawl in gratitude.

"Honey, I'm here," I whisper, my voice shredded. "Can you hear me? It's Mack, honey. I'm here. I'll take care of you, I promise." I squeeze my eyes shut against the burning sting of tears. "I'll never let anyone hurt you again."

I don't know how much time has passed before we hear a commotion in the hallway. Uniformed police officers rush into the room, followed closely by an emergency medical team with a gurney. Just as someone—a cop maybe—grabs me under the arms and hauls me back, Erin's eyelids flutter partway open, and what little I can see of her eyes is bloodshot and glassy.

"Erin!"

She stares right through me without an ounce of recognition.

"Erin, I'm here!"

"Sir, please move back," a cop says as he hauls me farther back.

Two emergency medical team members move in, blocking my view of Erin as they quickly assess her condition.

The cop releases me, and I fall onto the floor, right on my ass. I rest my arms on my knees and hang my head between them, trying not to choke on the hot bile rising in my throat. My mind is numb, and it's a struggle just to keep breathing.

Across the room, one of the police officers is interviewing Mrs. Abney and taking notes. I try to get to my feet, but I end up back on the floor. I lower my forehead to my arms and fight back tears.

Dear God, please help her.

6

Mack

Somehow, I find the strength to rise and lean against the wall as the medics check Erin's vital signs, rattling off numbers to someone on the other end of their radio. I hear words like *trauma* and *blood loss*, *contusions* and *lacerations*, but it's hard to make sense out of any of it. The blood rushing through my head is so loud it practically drowns out the chaotic voices swirling around me.

I sense motion at the hotel door and glance up just in time to see Shane stride into the room. He stops dead in his tracks and stares at Erin as the medics gingerly wrap her in a clean sheet.

The expression on his face is inscrutable, his features drawn tight. When he finally looks away, he scans the room, his gaze catching mine. We stare at each other, both of us undoubtedly in shock.

I loom closer as the EMTs transfer Erin's unconscious body to the gurney. I watch her face closely for any sign that she's aware of what's happening, but there's no response. The EMTs cover her with a blanket before they strap her down. As they wheel her out of the room, I stand there at a complete loss. I've never felt so damned helpless in my life.

Shane steps aside to let them pass, and when I reach him, he grips my arm firmly, stopping me in my tracks. "I'll drive you to the hospital," he says.

All I can do is nod as we follow the EMTs down the hallway and into the elevator.

One of the medics speaks quietly into his radio mic, undoubtedly updating the hospital on their ETA. I stand woodenly in the corner, numb, sick, my emotions tamped down as hard as humanly possible. I want to scream, to shout, to pummel something with my fists, but I manage to keep all that bottled up inside. Shane stands beside me, equally stoic. The tension in the elevator car is so thick, it's smothering.

Erin lies unresponsive beneath the covers, not a whisper of sound coming from her. She only stirred that one time, to stare a hole right through me, registering nothing of her surroundings, and then she was out again. I suppose it's a blessing she's unconscious right now.

What the hell did that asshole give her? And how much? She's pretty petite—he could have easily given her more than her body can handle. I do a quick calculation. She's been out of it for close to ten hours.

With a slight jolt, the elevator comes to a stop on the ground floor. The doors open, and the EMTs wheel Erin out and through the lobby to the main exit. There's an ambulance waiting directly in front of the doors, its emergency lights flashing.

"I'm parked over here," Shane says, nodding to his silver Jaguar.

I stare at the vintage sports car. Damn, I'll be lucky if my legs fit in that thing.

"Mack," Shane says, shaking me out of my funk.

"Don't!" I snap back, not bothering to hide my irritation with him. Where Erin is concerned, he and I have a long, unpleasant history. He's warned me away from her time and time again because of the age difference. I can't talk to him right now. I'm barely managing to hold myself in check as it is.

Shane pulls out his phone and makes a call. "Sam? I need you to get Beth to the Cook County Hospital emergency room. It's urgent."

He pauses to listen, then he says, "Yes, it's Erin. She's alive, but she's badly injured. Tell Beth to leave Luke with his nanny at the bookstore until Cooper can pick him up." After a pause, he adds, "Thank you." And then he pockets his phone.

We don't speak again on the ride to the hospital. Shane is preoccupied with his own thoughts, and I'm drowning in mine. He grips the steering wheel like he wants to choke it. I'm reeling, both physically and emotionally. I appreciate him giving me a ride—I have no business being behind a steering wheel right now—but that's as far as I'm willing to go.

The resentment I harbor for Shane with regards to Erin is monumental. But in the recesses of my mind, I know Shane's not to blame for my behavior. *I am.* I'm a grown-ass man, and I make my own damn decisions. I'm the one who decided I was too old for Erin. Blaming him is just a cowardly excuse. I had my own reasons for keeping my distance from her. I didn't need his.

Now, in hindsight, I can't escape the fact that this is all *on me.* I stare at the traffic straight ahead and say, "If I'd gone with her to that damn party last night, none of this would have happened."

Shane gives me a sympathetic look. "It's not your fault, Mack. Don't try to take the blame for this. It was a random, unfortunate incident. It's sure as hell not your fault."

I whip my head in his direction, my teeth gritted. "She fucking asked me to take her to that party, Shane, and I said no! Tell me how this isn't my fault!"

Hot bile rises in my throat, burning my esophagus and threatening to choke me. *Jesus, that poor girl!*

I'd give anything to go back in time and do things differently. If I had it to do over again, I'd gladly take her to that party. If I'd been there, protecting her as I should have been, she'd be safe at work right now, going about her business, and not lying unconscious in an ambulance.

I'm so lost in my own thoughts that I don't even realize we've arrived until Shane pulls up to the emergency room entrance.

"I'll park—"

But I'm out of the car before he can finish his sentence. Frankly, I don't give a fuck what he does.

I rush through the glass doors and head straight for the sign-in desk, where a middle-aged woman sits. "Erin O'Connor," I say, breathless, slamming both of my hands on the desk. "Where is she? She was just brought in."

The woman seated behind the desk doesn't seem to be in any hurry to answer me. She lays her folded hands on the desktop and smiles. "And you are?"

"I'm—" *Fuck! Who the hell am I? The motherfucker who let her get hurt?* "I'm her... I'm a friend. A *close* friend."

"I'm sorry. I can't give out any information on a patient without proper authorization."

My heart slams against my chest, and I have to fight the urge to pound my fist on the desk. "She's hurt, badly! She needs...a friend. She doesn't have any close family. I—"

At that moment, Beth rushes up to the counter, right beside me. And Sam is right beside her. She flashes me a brief, empathetic look and lays her hand on my back. "I'm Beth McIntyre," she says breathlessly to the woman behind the counter. I imagine she dropped everything to get here as quickly as she could.

Beth digs into her purse and withdraws a folded sheet of paper, opening it and handing it to the woman. "I have a signed medical power of attorney for Erin O'Connor. She was just brought in. Can I see her?"

The woman runs the signed form through a photocopy machine, then hands the original back to Beth. Then she picks up a desk phone and punches a couple of buttons. "Just a minute," she says, her gaze flitting up to Beth.

Finally, the woman hangs up the phone and addresses Beth. "You can go back. I'll have someone escort you."

"What about me?" I say, feeling panic rising in my chest.

The woman shakes her head. "I'm sorry, but no. Not unless the patient gives verbal approval."

Having lost my patience completely, I slam my fist on the desk. "She's fucking unconscious! She can't give approval!"

Beth lays her hand on my arm and squeezes lightly. "Mack, it's okay. I'll make sure she's taken care of."

Someone from the hospital staff arrives to escort Beth to the ER. I'm left in the waiting room, clueless, completely in the dark. I have no idea if Erin is still unconscious, or what her condition is. I pace helplessly. Shane and Sam motion for me to join them, but I can't sit. I need to be doing something, anything. Even something as useless as pacing.

Over the next hour, Shane's parents arrive, along with Beth's mother, Ingrid Jamison. Shane's two oldest brothers arrive with their girlfriends, Jake and Annie, as well as Jamie and Molly. It's shaping up to be a McIntyre family reunion. Erin would be so touched to know that these people care enough about her to drop everything and come running to her aid.

The biggest shock is when Beth's older brother, Tyler Jamison, comes striding through the doors, dressed in a black suit and white shirt. He heads straight for the sign-in desk and flashes his homicide detective badge at the woman seated there. Immediately, he's taken back to the treatment area.

I head over to Shane. "What's Tyler doing here?"

Shane shrugs. "I imagine he's here because of Erin."

"Why? He's a fucking *homicide* detective. He investigates *murders*, not—" Shit, I can't even say the words *sexual assault*.

Sam shrugs. "Maybe there's a connection."

My pulse and anxiety are through the roof as I wait for news—any bit of news—about her condition. I saw for myself the extent of her physical injuries, and I know she's lost a lot of blood, but surely to God it's not life threatening. Her mental state, though—Jesus, I can't even begin to imagine what this is going to do to Erin.

He didn't just sexually assault her. He *tortured* her. I just pray that she was so out of it from the drugs that she didn't suffer.

There's a movement at the door to the treatment area as Beth comes out. Shane is on his feet and at his wife's side in a moment flat. He takes her into his arms and holds her tightly as she sobs into his white dress shirt. As I watch Beth fall apart, my heart stutters in my chest, and I'm finding it hard to breathe.

I force myself to make my way toward her, my throat tightening as I steel myself for news. "Beth, is she—?" Jesus, I can't even say it.

Beth is so lost in grief that she's completely oblivious to my presence. She wouldn't leave me hanging like this on purpose. It's soul-wrenching sorrow that tears these sobs out of her. Shane holds her tightly, murmuring words of comfort into her hair as he rubs her back.

But I need to know. "Beth, please! How is she?"

She slowly turns her head my way, swaying in her husband's embrace. Her blue-green eyes are bloodshot and awash with tears. The sheer agony that contorts her features makes my stomach twist into a knot.

"Beth, is she alive?" I can't even believe I have to ask.

"She—" Beth nods, gasping as she tries to get the words out. "Yes, she's alive." Then she covers her face with shaking hands. "She came to very briefly, disoriented and confused, and hurting so badly. The doctor had to sedate her so he could examine her to see how extensive her injuries are. I gave consent for them to perform a rape assessment."

Beth glances up at me, her expression pained, then at her husband. "It's bad," she says, her voice little more than a whisper. "The things he did to her—it's really bad."

"Sweetheart, come sit down before you fall down," Shane says to his wife, slipping his arm around her shoulders and directing her toward the section of the waiting room that his family has essentially commandeered.

Beth's mother, Ingrid, is immediately on her feet, her arms open, just waiting to comfort her daughter.

I resume my pacing, still knowing next to nothing. I already knew she was in bad shape. *I saw her lying on that bed like a bloody, broken doll.* I should be in there with Erin. She has no family. It should be *me* comforting her.

I alternately pace and sit, pace and sit. Sam eventually steers me to a chair and hands me a paper cup of black coffee, which I gulp down, ignoring the burn. Caffeine is the only thing sustaining me right now.

Eventually, someone comes to get Beth, and she goes back into the treatment area, this time accompanied by Shane, while I'm left in the waiting room with nothing to do but pace and worry.

I lose all track of time, but I doubt it's more than half an hour before Shane returns, looking more than a little shaken.

He scrubs his hand over his mouth and trim beard. "She's still unconscious, but the good news is her vitals are stable. They gave her something to counteract whatever drug she was given last night. They're prepping her for surgery now."

"Surgery?" Shane's mother, Bridget, shoots forward in her seat. "Why?"

"To suture multiple lacerations and tears, and to check internally for damage. And there's a pretty significant cut on her right cheek that will have to be sutured."

Bridget McIntyre holds a shaky hand to her mouth as she falls back into her seat. "Dear God. That poor child."

At the news, I lean forward in my chair, dropping my head into my hands and just focus on breathing. It's all I can do right now. Just breathe. Erin is the kindest, sweetest, most gentle person I've ever known. *How in the fuck could anyone hurt her? What kind of monster—*

When I feel a hand on my shoulder, I glance up to see Shane standing beside me. He looks as pained as I feel. I shrug off his hand, not wanting him to console me. Nothing can console me right now.

Soon after, someone drops down into the empty seat beside mine, and immediately I feel a hand on my back. It's Sam.

Shane steps away from me and addresses the group. "After surgery, she'll go to recovery, and then to a room upstairs. She's been admitted, and she'll probably be here a couple of days. The main risk now is infection from her injuries. I'm going to wait with Beth while Erin's in surgery. You all should move upstairs now to the waiting room on her floor."

Sam rises from his seat, and I stare down at his scuffed black boots, noting the thick silver buckles.

He lays a hand on my shoulder. "Mack, let's go."

With a heavy sigh, I force myself to my feet and follow the others to the bank of elevators.

7

Erin

I'm floating in a sea of fire and ice.

I'm ice cold, and yet my body is burning on the inside. Every inch of me hurts. Burns. Stings.

What happened? Where am I?

I can't...think.

I can't remember.

Was I in an accident? It must have been an accident.

Someone's talking to me, a soft gentle voice. Beth? *Poor Beth.* She sounds so broken-hearted. I try to open my eyes, to look at her, but I can't. My lids won't budge. I try to call to her, but my

voice is gone.
>	*All I can do is float and burn.*
>	*Please don't cry, Beth.*

8

Mack

I've solidified into a marble statue as I stand guard outside Erin's hospital room door. After surgery and a few hours in recovery, she was transferred here to this private room. A nurse has been in and out of her room, monitoring Erin's condition. Beth's in there with her.

The only sounds I can hear from her room are the beeps of machines monitoring her vitals.

She could have died.
She lost so much blood.
And it's all my fault.

Knowing Erin as I do—probably better than anyone—I just don't see how she can come back from this.

Every so often, Beth pops out to give me an update. "She's still out, Mack. No change." And then she disappears back into the quiet, dimly lit room to stand guard like an angel over her friend's savaged body.

Savaged.

That's exactly what that monster did to her.

I feel numb. The initial seething rage that fueled me when I first found her lying battered on bloody sheets has cooled and hardened into an obsidian shell around my heart. But inside that pained organ is a spark, an ember, just waiting to flare up again.

When I find the monster who did this to her—*and I will find him*—I'll annihilate him with my fucking bare hands. This, I vow.

The worst part of this unbearable situation is that they won't let me *see* her. That means the only image I have of her in my head is the one of her lying on that hotel bed, her face so badly swollen and discolored that I barely recognized her. And her body—dear God, what that monster did to her body!

I stand upright, stiff as a board, not daring to relax my muscles for a second. I'm afraid if I do, I'll collapse.

Erin.

My sweet, gentle, perfect Erin. The young woman who always tries so hard to do good. To do the right thing. She doesn't have a mean bone in her body, and for someone to do this to her—shit. I can't even contemplate it.

Acid flows in my veins now, instead of blood, searing every

inch of my body as it eats through me.

I'm so sorry, sweetheart.

If I had it to do over again, I'd plaster myself to her side and never let go.

I snap my head to the left when I hear footsteps on the polished floor. *God damn it!*

Shane stops in front of me. "Mack, I—"

Before he can say another word, I grab him by the lapels of his expensive suit and slam him against the wall. He clutches my wrists to keep me from closing my fingers around this throat, but he doesn't fight back.

Shane's a big guy, but he's more leanly muscled, whereas I'm pure brawn. At just over six feet, he's damn strong. But he's got nothing on me. I tower over him, like I do most men.

I pull my arm back, my hand drawn into a tight fist, more than ready to smash in his face. But at the last second, I freeze. When I get a good look at his pained expression, I know I can't hit him. He's hurting just as much as I am. As we *all* are.

Disgusted—at him, at myself, at the entire fucking situation—I release him, and he staggers forward as he rights himself. I step back, my hands flexing on my hips as I fight the overwhelming urge to beat the shit out of him. I want him to suffer, just like I'm suffering. Sucking in a deep breath, I stare him down, too upset to speak.

"I'm so sorry, Mack," he says.

His tone is rough, and it's obvious he's upset. After all, Erin is one of his wife's closest friends. She's like a little sister to Beth.

But his remorse does nothing to help Erin.

I get in his face, my teeth gritted as I grind out the words. "Shut the fuck up. I don't want to hear how sorry *you* are!"

Beth pops her head out of Erin's room, her teary, blue-green eyes frantic as she looks between me and her husband. "Keep it down!" she hisses at the both of us. "She's beginning to stir."

Just as quickly as she appeared, Beth disappears back into Erin's room. A middle-aged nurse comes scurrying down the hallway toward us. "Gentlemen, please!" She's glaring directly at me. "If you don't stop, I'll be forced to call security and have you removed from the premises."

"I *am* fucking security!" I bite out. The *fuck* I'll let someone kick me out of this hospital! I'm not leaving Erin. I don't care if someone holds a gun to my head—I'm not leaving her.

Shane straightens his suit jacket, acting like I didn't just practically assault him, like I wasn't just about to crack his skull against the wall. "We're sorry for the commotion," he says to the nurse. "It won't happen again." And then he nails me with a death glare, reminding me that he's my *boss*. "Will it?"

Shaking my head, I return to my post by the door. "No."

I meant what I said. *I am security.* Even though she's in the hospital, she needs protection until the fucker who did this to her is apprehended and put behind bars. Until he's caught, she's potentially still at risk.

Shane gives me a passing glance as he enters Erin's hospital room. It grates on me that he's allowed in there and I'm not. Erin has no close family, so she put Beth and Shane down as her medical emergency contacts. That means they have access to her, and to her medical records, and I don't. At least not until she regains consciousness and gives me access.

Alone once more in the hallway, I stare straight ahead at a motivational poster hanging on the opposite wall—*A journey of a thousand miles begins with one step.*

Fuck. Erin has one hell of a journey ahead of her.

I try to switch off my mind, to still my racing thoughts. I've tried repeatedly to switch off my heart, but that hasn't worked—it's shattered into too many pieces to respond.

Finally, her doctor comes down the hallway.

"Wait!" I tell him, blocking his way into Erin's room. I grab a fistful of his white lab coat. "How is she? No one will tell me a damn thing."

"I'm sorry, I can't share that information. We have to follow regulations. You know that."

"Fuck the regulations! I want to know how she is!"

The doctor's expression softens as he gazes down at my hands. "I'm sorry. I know you're worried about your friend."

Reluctantly, I release him. "Sorry. I just need to know. Is she going to be all right?"

He lowers his voice. "All I'm going to say is that she's in stable condition. If she doesn't develop an infection, she should be able to go home in a day or two. You'll have to get the rest directly from Miss O'Connor. Now, if you'll excuse me, I need to see my patient."

I nod, grateful for the little bit he gave me. "Thanks."

9

Erin

"Erin, sweetie, can you hear me?"

Cool fingertips skim lightly across my forehead.

"It's Beth. You're going to be all right, I promise. We'll take good care of you."

I crack open my heavy eyelids, then squeeze them shut when blinding light sears my eyes.

"Shane, would you please turn down the lights?" Beth's voice again. "Erin? Can you hear me?"

"Beth?" My voice is a garbled croak, and my throat feels raw.

"Don't try to talk. Your throat hurts because they put a tube down it during surgery. Squeeze my hand instead."

Surgery? Why? Where am I? "Wha—?" But pain slices through me, stealing my breath. An agonized whimper escapes before I can tamp it down. I squeeze her hand.

"It's okay, sweetie," she says, stroking my hair. "Don't try to talk. Just rest."

Gentle fingers stroke my hair the way Gram used to do when I was little. The light touch is an odd counterpart to the sharp, stinging pains I feel all over. The worst is the throbbing pain between my legs. When I shift in bed, pain radiates throughout my body. I ache all over, as if bruised from head to toe. *What happened? Was I in a car wreck?* I try to think back, but my memories are a hazy, jumbled mess. I don't know what day it is, or where I am.

"What—" It's a struggle to open my eyes, and I realize it's because my lids are swollen nearly shut. I turn my head in the direction of Beth's voice. "What… happened? Where am I?"

"You're in the hospital, but you're going to be okay. Do you remember anything?" she says.

I try to shake my head, but it hurts too much. "No."

"Oh, sweetie." She presses her lips to my temple, so lightly I can barely feel them. "You've been hurt. Badly."

I close my lids again and try to collect my thoughts, but everything's fuzzy. It's so hard to think clearly. "I remember being at work."

"That was yesterday. Do you remember anything after that?"

"No. Just work. Did something happen?" A stabbing pain deep

in my belly makes me gasp. I try to lay my hands on my abdomen, but I can only move one of them. The other seems to be tethered. "Can't… move… my arm."

"Just lie still. You have an IV in your right arm. Try not to move it."

My brain is so sluggish I can barely think. "Was I in an accident?"

"No," Beth says. "Not an accident."

I feel a warm, gentle weight on my ankle.

"Hi, Erin," says a familiar male voice.

"Shane?"

"Yes, Shane's here," Beth says. "We've been here the entire time. We won't leave your side, I promise. Just rest."

Closing my eyes, I survey my body from head to toe. My head hurts. My lips sting, and my eyelids throb. My right cheek burns. My throat aches. My hands hurt, my wrists, and my arms. When I try to shift position, burning pain erupts between my legs, steeling my breath. I realize everything down there hurts. I can feel some kind of padding pressed up against my genitals.

A wave of panic sweeps through me, kicking my pulse into overdrive. "What happened to me?"

A hazy memory flashes through me. Heavy, oppressive darkness. A hand squeezing my throat. My lungs burning. A searing pain between my legs. Hot breath on my face.

A surge of hot bile shoots up into my throat, burning and scalding me, choking me. I turn my head and gag uncontrollably as sour liquid spills out of my mouth.

After a rustling noise and chair legs scraping the floor, I feel a pair of comforting hands on my shoulders.

"Get me a wet cloth!" Beth says. "Shh, Erin, don't cry. It's okay. You're okay. Everything's going to be fine."

As I breathe through the pain, darkness rushes over me.

10

Mack

Beth and Shane are the only ones allowed in there, besides the hospital staff. Beth says she's awake, but groggy. Apparently, she doesn't remember anything.

I need to see Erin with my own eyes. I need to tell her—*what*? What can I possibly say to make things right?

I'm sorry I wasn't there to protect you.

I'm sorry I failed you.

I won't blame you if you hate me now.

They're all empty words that can't undo the damage.

As I lean against the wall, my mind drifts back to yesterday at the bookstore. I recall with perfect clarity the moment Erin asked me to go with her to the party. I remember how nervous she was, how her voice trembled, the way her blue eyes looked everywhere but at me. She was so damn scared, but she had the courage to ask anyway.

And there's the crux of my problem. She's too sweet, too innocent for me to dare touch her. She deserves far better than me. I've lived in the trenches, slept in the mud, eaten roadkill, fought my way through hordes of insurgents, killing and maiming with my bare hands. I've fucked women I had no business fucking. I've seen and done it all, and I'm not proud of a lot of it. We did what we had to do to accomplish our missions and to survive.

And Erin? *Jesus*! She's as pure as the driven snow. And yet, for some crazy ass reason, she wants me. She acts like I'm God's gift to women, when I'm not.

I know it's just a crush. Hell, she's still in school. University, sure, but she's still a student. She hasn't lived in the real world yet. She supports herself on a scholarship, the salary she gets working at Clancy's, and the small nest egg her grandmother left her when she died.

One of these days, Erin's going to wise up and realize she's wasting her time with me. Then she'll find some nice, clean-cut boy her own age who's as pure as she is, and they'll get married and live happily ever after.

And the thought of this mythical, clean-cut kid makes me want to smash something.

Yesterday wasn't the first time she asked me out. She's asked me plenty of times to go out to lunch. If everyone else was going—meaning Beth and Sam—I'd go. I figured a group outing was safe enough. But if it was just the two of us—dinner or a movie—then the answer was always no. It had to be. I didn't want to lead her on. I figured the sooner she stopped fixating on me and moved on, the better off she'd be, and the sooner she'd meet someone more appropriate.

Shane's constant threats didn't help matters any. I'm sure as hell not afraid of Shane, but I have always been terrified of hurting Erin. She's never had a boyfriend before. What if we hooked up and it didn't work out? What if she got hurt? I'd cut my own arm off before I'd ever hurt her.

Reality hits me like a slap to the face. Someone did hurt her, though. *Badly*. In the worst way possible for a man to hurt a woman.

I can't wrap my mind around it. I can't even let myself think about it. Just the thought of what that monster did to her makes me physically ill.

If only I could turn back time and get another chance. If only I'd said yes! If I'd gone with her, no one would have *dared* mess with her.

And now, because of me, she's lying barely conscious in a hospital bed, her body torn up.

My insides burn as anger boils to the surface. I will find this motherfucker. I will find him, and I will tear him limb from limb for hurting her. I will make him bleed and cry and beg for his life. And then I'll end him as heartlessly as he shattered her.

A nurse comes scurrying down the hallway and rushes right past me into Erin's room, not saying a word. I stand in front of the partially open door and listen. I can hear Beth talking quietly to the nurse.

A few minutes later, Shane comes out. "Erin woke for a minute, then she passed out again."

"Did you call for the nurse?"

"Yeah. Erin threw up just before she blacked out. Beth was worried she might be having a reaction to the anesthesia."

"How is she?"

He sighs, scrubbing a hand over his trim beard, and shakes his head. "Not good." He looks me in the eye, and the compassion I see in his gaze sends a chill down my spine. He lets out a heavy sigh. "He—" Shane stops, his lips flattening as he wrestles for composure. I see the glint of tears forming in his eyes. "He hurt her, intentionally, methodically. It was cruel and vicious. I really can't say more than that right now. That's for Erin to decide."

I rub the back of my neck, gripping my tense muscles. "I need more than that, Shane. Come on. I've got nothing."

He runs his fingers through his hair and frowns. "She has bruising, tears, lacerations. Deep bite marks all over, some of which may leave a scar. Her face will bear a scar. And he raped her—repeatedly."

My mind races frantically, trying to make sense out of what he said. How—*why*—would someone do something like this? "When can I see her?"

"That's up to Erin, and right now she's not coherent." He

shakes his head. "But I will tell you this. I agree with Tyler's assessment that the perp never expected her to live through this. He choked her—her neck is ringed with deep tissue bruises. He must have been interrupted and wasn't able to finish what he'd started."

This news knocks the wind right out of me. *That fucker tried to strangle her?* "Why is Tyler investigating the attack on Erin? He's a *homicide* detective."

"He believes the perp who assaulted Erin is the same one who murdered two young women in the past month. The MO is the same... sexual assault, lacerations and bite marks, and ultimately strangulation."

Murder? My stomach drops and my blood turns to ice. This can't be real. Please, God, let me wake up from this nightmare.

Shane drills me with a hard look. "If Tyler's right, then Erin is in danger. If this guy thinks she can ID him...."

My mind races with the implications, and I shake my head. Not on my watch. "I'm not leaving this spot. I'll stand guard outside her door around the clock. I'll protect her."

Shane nods. "Until further notice, I'm reassigning you as Erin's personal protection. I'll have someone fill in for you at the bookstore."

I nod, swallowing hard. If he'd tried to fight me on this, there would have been words.

Shane returns to Erin's room, leaving me alone in the hallway. Alone with thoughts I can't bear to let myself think.

* * *

"Hey."

I glance down the hall to see Sam heading my way. He comes to stand directly across from me, leaning against the opposite wall and crossing his booted feet. He stands there looking perfectly casual, like he waits outside hospital rooms all the time. I don't feel like making small talk, so I don't. I just nod.

I like Sam. We see each other a lot because we're both working to make sure Beth is safe. And Sam is far more than just Beth's full-time bodyguard. He's also one of her best friends. Erin's too. I guess I could say he's my friend as well.

"She's still out?" he says.

I nod.

He watches me closely, but says nothing more for a while. A few nurses walk past us, one pushing a woman in a wheelchair, another pushing a cart of medical supplies.

Something occurs to me. "Where's Luke?"

Sam grins. "Cooper's got him back at the penthouse. I just came from there, to check on Beth and Erin. And you. When was the last time you ate anything?"

I glance at the hall clock. It's early evening now, nearly eight hours since I went looking for Erin. I shrug. "This morning. Seven-thirty probably."

Sam pushes away from the wall and steps toward me, nodding down the hallway toward the elevators. "Let's go downstairs and grab some coffee and a bite to eat. You need to eat something,

Mack. You can't fuel that big body of yours on grit and determination alone."

There's no way in hell I'm leaving my post. "No, thanks. I'm good."

He looks at me with exasperation. "Mack—"

"I'm not leaving this spot. I'm officially Erin's personal protection now."

Sam raises a brow. "Welcome to my world." He laughs. "Then how about I bring you a cup of coffee and a sandwich? You need to eat something, pal, before you collapse. You can't protect her if you can't stay upright."

He's right, of course. I've been ignoring the gnawing emptiness in my gut and the shakiness of low blood sugar all day. "All right. Fine." I fish my wallet out of my back pocket, intending to give him some cash.

"Nah, keep it," he says, waving me off as he heads for the elevators.

Sam's not been gone a full minute when Beth walks out of Erin's room. Her stance is stiff and her expression brittle as she turns to me. And just like that—like a mirror cracking under severe pressure—she breaks, her face crumpling in pain.

I automatically open my arms, and she falls against me, collapsing as her body is wracked with sobs. She presses her face into my shirt to muffle the sound. My throat tightens, and I can do nothing but hold her, my arms wrapped tightly around her. I might not be able to stop her shaking, but I'll be damned if I'll let her suffer alone.

Minutes pass, and I just let her cry it out. I'm sure she's been holding this pain inside for hours, trying to keep it bottled up tight, not wanting Erin to see it. Shane is still inside Erin's room, or else he'd be here comforting his wife himself.

I sigh, feeling as choked up as Beth. "Beth?"

She pulls back and looks up at me, craning her neck to meet my gaze. Her blue-green eyes are reddened, filled with pain and sorrow. Her cheeks are streaked with tears.

I give her time to collect herself. She'll talk when she's ready, and she'll tell me what she can. So I just stand there, holding her. Beth feels very deeply for those she loves—and Erin is definitely in that inner circle. For Erin's sake, I'm glad.

She finally lets out a heavy breath and lifts her face, glancing around as if she's not sure where she ended up. Then she steps away, self-consciously brushing back her hair and wiping her damp cheeks. "I'm sorry."

I shake my head. Hell, we're all in rough shape right now. The only difference is that Beth wears her heart on her sleeve. "There's no need to apologize."

She presses the heels of her palms to her eyes and exhales heavily, trying so hard to keep it together. I struggle not to press her for information—she'll tell me what she can, when she can.

When she meets my gaze once more, her expression shredded. "Oh, Mack." A rush of fresh tears spills over her lids and down her cheeks, and she wipes at them with the hem of her top. She sighs as if the weight of the world is on her shoulders.

"Tell me."

She shudders, clearly overwhelmed. "I hope my brother finds this monster soon. No one should suffer what Erin is suffering."

I frown. I'd like to find this perp myself, first, and dish out my own brand of justice. "Unless I manage to find him first."

She looks at me, getting my drift well enough. Her eyes tighten as she nods. "Be careful, Mack. Please don't do anything that will land you in jail. That wouldn't help Erin."

"How is she?"

Beth looks away, as if conflicted, as if she's giving away state secrets. "She's been in and out of consciousness. She doesn't remember much of anything that happened last night. She remembers being at work, and then going home to her apartment to get ready to go out. It gets fuzzy from there. She remembers nothing of meeting any guy in the bar. Her doctor told us this might happen. It's not unusual for victims of sexual assault, especially ones that were drugged, to have memory lapses."

"Does she understand what's happened to her?"

She takes in a shaky breath. "Not really, but I think it's starting to dawn on her. She's in a lot of pain all over, but especially in… her… pelvic region. I think she's figuring it out. She didn't ask, and I—" Beth stops, her expression crumpling again. "I couldn't bring myself to tell her—oh, God, Mack. I know I need to, but I don't know how to tell her."

I pull her into my arms and hold her while she cries, gently patting her back. "When can I see her?"

A nurse approaches us then, walking swiftly past us and straight into Erin's room. A moment later, Shane comes out, his gaze searching. When he sees his wife in my arms, his expression flattens. "Come here, sweetheart," he says, his voice low and calm as he holds out his arms to her.

She turns automatically into his arms, and he pulls her against his chest.

I suspect Shane must have summoned the nurse to come stay with Erin so he could go in search of his wife. He must have known she was falling apart.

"It's all right," he murmurs into her hair, leaning down to kiss the top of her head. "Everything's going to be all right." Then he glances up at me, his expression stoic, revealing nothing.

As I watch them together, I'm envious of what they have, the way he knows what she needs, the way she trusts him and leans on him.

Beth pulls back from Shane and wipes her cheeks.

He cups her face in his hands and studies her. "Are you okay?"

She nods. "As well as can be expected under the circumstances."

* * *

Sam returns from the cafeteria and hands me a cardboard tray holding a large coffee, a wrapped sandwich, a bag of potato chips, and a water bottle. I grab the coffee first.

"You take your coffee black, right?" he says.

I nod, then take a sip of the hot, strong brew. It's not the best coffee in the world, but it'll do. "Thanks."

He shrugs. "No need to thank me. Hold on. I'll be right back."

He walks down the hallway toward the waiting room and returns a moment later carrying a wooden chair with a padded seat and backrest. He sets the chair on the floor beside me. "Here. You're going to need this."

I ignore the chair and set the coffee cup and the tray of food on the floor so I can pick up the sandwich. I unwrap it and take a huge bite. "Thanks." I hadn't realized how hungry I was until the first bite hit the bottom of my hollowed-out stomach.

He raises a brow as he tips his head toward the chair. "It's a chair, Mack. You're supposed to sit on it."

When I don't take him up on his suggestion, he says, "Is standing some kind of self-imposed punishment? Penitence, maybe?"

I shrug. "Something like that."

Sam's phone buzzes, and he smiles when he checks the screen. "Cooper's on his way here with Luke. Looks like we're running low on stored breastmilk at home." Sam chuckles, and it's obvious he's pleased that his boyfriend is on his way.

They're another couple I envy for their closeness, their dedication to each other. But shit, Cooper's way older than Sam. Theirs is definitely a May-December romance. Cooper's old enough to be Sam's father. Age difference doesn't seem to matter to them.

In keeping my distance from Erin, I tried to do the right thing. And where did that get us? She's in a hospital room recovering from a horrendous assault. If we'd been together, it never would have happened.

Maybe I was wrong to keep my distance from her.

Maybe it's not too late to correct my mistake.

If she'll still have me, that is.

11

Erin

I'm pretending to be asleep so I don't have to talk to anyone. I don't want to answer any more questions. I'm scared. I'm in pain. And my heart is broken. Everything I believed about myself, about my world, about my future... it's all been shattered by a single act of violence.

I'm pretty sure I know what happened to me. The thing is, why don't I remember any of it? If I was assaulted, surely I'd remember. And how could someone do something like this to a person? How could anyone be so cruel, so heartless? I don't understand it. I *can't* understand it.

It must be evening now because it's dark outside. Beth and Shane have spent the entire day with me, with at least one of them by my side at all times, and often both of them. I'm not surprised that Beth's here for me, as she's one of the best friends I have in the world, and the closest thing I have to family. But Shane, too? That means a lot to me. He's a very busy man with a lot of responsibilities, but he's dropped everything to be here.

"Hey," Beth says quietly, her voice barely more than a whisper. "Are you awake?"

I crack open my swollen eyelids. "Yes." I glance around the room. "Shane's gone?" I heard him say earlier that he'd be back soon.

She nods. "Cooper's bringing Luke to the hospital so I can nurse him. Shane went downstairs to meet them. He'll be right back."

"You should go home, Beth. You have a baby to take care of."

"I'm staying with you," she says, reaching for my hand.

"You should go. Really. I'll be fine."

"I'm not leaving you. I can pump here at the hospital and send milk home." She lays her hand lightly on my leg. "Erin, we need to talk."

I eye her warily. I know what she's going to say, and frankly I don't want to hear it. I look away as my eyes burn. "I don't want to talk about it."

"Sweetie, we have to." She pats my leg gently. "I know this is hard, but it's important."

When I glance back at her, my eyes are swimming with tears.

"I was raped, wasn't I?"

She nods, and her own eyes fill with tears. "Yes. I'm so sorry."

"Why don't I remember anything?"

"You were drugged at the hotel bar. It's because of the drugs that you don't remember. He took you upstairs to his room and assaulted you."

"Who did?"

Beth shakes her head. "I don't know. It's being investigated."

"How did—" *How did they find out?* But I can't even say it.

"How did we find you? Actually, Mack is the one who found you. When you didn't show up for work this morning, he went searching for you. He tracked you to the hotel bar, and then through the video surveillance footage, he saw the guy who drugged your drink and took you up to his room."

I'm numb with horror as the implications of what she's just said hit me. *Mack* found me? He *saw* me? It must have been awful for him. The thought makes me sick to my stomach. How will I ever face him again?

"Oh, God." I cover my face with my left hand, flinching when I feel scratchy little threads on my right cheek. I jerk my hand away as if it's been burned. "What's on my face?"

Beth frowns. "Those are stitches. There's a cut on your right cheek. It's been sutured by a plastic surgeon."

Stitches on my face? I must look like a monster. "What else is there?" I have plenty of suspicions, but I want to hear it from her.

She looks pained, as if she doesn't want to answer.

My voice rises, in tandem with my anxiety. "What else, Beth?"

Now it's her turn to flinch. "You have a number of injuries."

"Such as?"

"Numerous bruises and cuts. And bite marks."

"*Bite marks?*" I shove the bedding down and raise my left arm, shocked to see all the small punctures marring my skin. They're deep and red, so angry looking. I feel sick. What kind of animal did this to me? And of course the worst of it is down lower, between my legs. Everything down there is swollen, painful, throbbing. There's thick padding between my legs.

Swamped with emotional pain, as well as physical, I look away, not wanting to meet Beth's gaze. "This can't be real. How could this have happened? And how could I not remember any of it?"

"Dr. Shaw told us that memory loss is not uncommon with the use of date rape drugs."

Dr. Shaw? She's my gynecologist. I pull the covers back up to my chin, feeling utterly mortified. I wish the ground would open up and swallow me. I don't want to be here. I want to forget everything and go back to my life as it was. But it's too late for that.

"There's something else," she says.

"What?"

"Your purse and undergarments were missing from the hotel room when Mack found you. Tyler thinks your assailant took those things with him when he ran off."

"He stole my *underwear?*"

Beth frowns. "Yes. Not your phone, though. The police found that in the hotel room, on the floor underneath the bed. They took it as evidence, but you'll get it back."

He has my purse? "If he has my purse, he can identify me. He has my driver's license, with my address on it." *He didn't just violate my body. He violated my privacy, my life.* "I'll never be safe again."

Beth leans in closer, her eyes teary and pained. "Don't worry, we'll keep you safe. Mack's out in the hallway right now, standing guard over your room." She hesitates for a moment, then says, "He'd like to see you."

"No!" *I can't see him. He knows everything!* I shake my head. "I don't want to see anyone."

"He keeps asking about you. He's been so worried."

I shake my head again, more adamantly this time. "No!"

"Okay, okay! Calm down. You don't have to see anyone if you don't want to."

Dear God, no! How could I possibly face him? But at the same time, I ache to see him. Just thinking about Mack makes me tear up, and that makes my eyes sting. I squeeze my lids shut and rub them hard with my free hand.

"Erin, don't. You'll hurt yourself." Beth gently pulls my hand away from my face and lays it on my belly.

I don't care.

I don't care about anything anymore.

* * *

A little while later, there's a quiet knock on the door. It swings open, and Shane walks in carrying Luke.

As soon as the baby catches sight of Beth, he reaches for her, crying "Mum-mum-mum!"

"Come here, baby," she coos, holding her hands out. Once he's in her arms, he presses his face into the crook of her neck and sobs.

"What's wrong, sweetie?" she says, cuddling him close and turning to kiss his cheek. She pats his diapered bottom as she rocks him in her arms. "Hey, it's okay. You're fine."

Shane shakes his head at me, clearly exasperated. "He was perfectly fine two seconds ago out in the hallway. He was happy as a clam when Cooper brought him up. Then he takes one look at his mama and falls apart."

"I guess he just now realized he hasn't seen his mama all day," I say. "He missed her."

Luke pulls back and grabs the neckline of Beth's top, catching her necklace in his fist and tugging.

"All right, hold on," she says, laughing as she extricates her clothing and jewelry from his grasp. "I know you're hungry."

She grabs a pillow and sits down with Luke, setting the pillow on her lap and laying the baby down. As soon as she lifts her blouse and unhooks the cup of her bra, Luke eagerly latches on, quieting as he settles down to nurse.

"I swear, he was perfectly fine a few minutes ago," Shane says, winking at me.

Shane moves behind Beth's chair so he can watch over her shoulder at his son nursing. He reaches down to cup the baby's head and give him an affectionate pat, gently ruffling the tufts of pale hair.

Seeing their closeness—the three of them—helps center me. Their dedication to each other is palpable, and right now, they're generously extending that family bond to me.

"How are you feeling, Erin?" Shane says, lifting his gaze to me.

I glance up just in time to catch the concern on his face, and reality comes crashing back. *How do I feel?* My body is a patchwork of bites and cuts and scratches. Every inch of me hurts, and I'm having trouble getting comfortable. The idea of sitting up—I can't even think about it right now, let alone walking. All I can do is shrug. "I've been better."

He nods, his gaze filled with compassion. "There are over a dozen people in the waiting room down the hall—and a few standing right outside your door—who are anxious to hear how you're doing and wishing you a speedy recovery."

My throat tightens into a painful knot. "Please tell them I said thank you."

"Do you want to tell one or two of them yourself?"

"No." I know what he's doing. He wants me to *see people*. Probably Mack. And Sam. But I can't. It's bad enough that everyone *knows* what happened to me. I can't bear to face them and see the pity in their eyes.

"I've put Mack in charge of your security for the time being," he says. He chooses his words carefully. "Until we know more, Erin, you need protection."

Realization hits me like a dash of cold water, and my stomach drops like a stone. They think I'm still in danger.

"The police are searching for the suspect," he says. "Until he's caught, it's prudent for you to have protection."

"You think he might come after me again?" The thought makes me shudder.

"You have nothing to worry about. Trust me, Mack's not going to let *anyone* through that door who doesn't belong in here. You're perfectly safe."

At the mention of Mack, guilt slams through me. He's right outside my room, and I'm sure he wants to talk to me. But I just can't face him. I feel so ashamed, so dirty, so stupid. I never should have gone to that party in the first place. "Please tell him I said thank you."

Shane sits on the edge of my bed. "He's asking to see you, Erin."

"No!" I shake my head wildly as panic overtakes me. "Absolutely not!"

He studies me for a minute. "Mack blames himself for what happened to you. He said if he'd gone with you to that party, none of this would have happened."

"But that doesn't make it his fault." My throat tightens as it clogs with tears, and I struggle to force the words out. "Tell him I said it's not his fault. Tell him, Shane! God, I don't want him thinking—" My words end in a garbled choke, and I close my eyes and cover my face. *I just want to die. I want to curl up in a ball, shrivel up into nothingness and disappear.*

Shane pats my leg. "I'll tell him, Erin. Don't worry. I'll make sure he knows."

"I can't bear for Mack to think he's responsible for what happened to me." *I'm the one who screwed up. Not Mack!* "Tell him, Shane! Make sure he believes it!"

"Telling him is one thing, Erin. But making him believe it will be easier said than done."

12

Mack

I've taken to pacing up and down the hallway, but I'm never more than ten yards from Erin's room. Her door is always directly in my line of sight so I can see who comes and goes from there. So far, the only ones allowed in are Beth and Shane, nurses, and her doctors.

I hear footsteps coming my way and glance to my left to see Tyler Jamison approaching. As he's dressed in a dark suit and tie, he must be here on official business. I expect him to knock on Erin's door, but he doesn't. Instead he joins me, standing quietly for a moment as he surveys the empty hallway.

"How's she doing?" he says.

"As well as can be expected I guess, after the hell she's been through."

He nods.

I cross my arms over my chest. "Are you here to talk to her?"

"That depends."

"On what?"

"On how she's doing."

He knocks quietly on the door, and a moment later it opens, and Shane steps out into the hallway.

"How's Erin?" Tyler asks his brother-in-law.

These two have had a rocky relationship from the start, but it appears to be getting better. Tyler seems to have accepted his sister's choice of husband.

Shane shakes his head, frowning. "She's struggling. Physically, as long as she doesn't develop an infection, she'll recover just fine. It's going to take some time, though. Emotionally, it's a very different story. She's devastated."

It kills me to hear how she's suffering. I would do anything to spare her this. *Anything*. But unfortunately, there's no magic pill that can undo what's been done.

Tyler nods, as if he was expecting as much. "Do you think I can talk to her?"

"No." Shane shakes his head. "It's too soon. She's not ready to talk about it. And besides, I don't know how much good it would do you because she doesn't remember a damn thing."

Tyler frowns as he nods. "All right. Have Beth call me when Erin's up for a brief conversation."

After agreeing, Shane goes back into Erin's room, leaving me alone with Tyler. I'm glad Tyler's here. It means he's actively investigating her assault.

He pulls a folded sheet of paper out of his inside jacket pocket and hands it to me. "I made prints of the alleged perpetrator's image. You can keep this one, as a precaution. In case he shows up here."

I stare at the photo of the asshole seated beside Erin in her booth. There are no visible identifying marks on his face and neck. No tattoos, no scars, no piercings. At least none that we can see. I memorize his face, so that *when* I see it again, I'll recognize him.

After tucking the photo into my pocket, I meet Tyler's gaze. "Do you still think Erin's assault is related to homicides you're investigating?"

He nods, looking far from pleased. "This isn't public information," he says, "but I have reason to believe this perp is a serial killer that I've been investigating. Erin bears an uncanny resemblance to the first two victims—females, early twenties, fair complexions, freckles, shoulder-length dark hair. Erin matches his type. I think he was interrupted that night and wasn't able to finish what he had intended to do."

My heart lodges in my throat. "Which is?"

"If he is indeed the same perp, his previous two victims died of asphyxiation, after they'd been sexually assaulted. The cuts and bite marks are the same. The ring of bruises around Erin's neck matches those of the two previous victims. I think he meant to kill her, but he got spooked and ran off."

"Do you think he might try to come after her?"

"Yes. It's entirely possible if he thinks she can identify him."

I shake my head. "Over my dead body."

Tyler gives me a small smile. "I was hoping you'd say that. Until we catch this guy, don't assume anything. Erin's purse and undergarments were missing from the crime scene. I think it's safe to say the perpetrator took them. That was the MO used with the other two victims as well. I think he keeps some of their belongings as trophies."

My gut tightens. The thought of this guy having Erin's belongings—her bra and underwear, for fuck's sake—makes me fume. I want to hit something. "Shit."

Tyler nods. "I don't think there's much chance that he'd risk coming here. It's much too public. But if he has her purse, which I believe he does, then it's not safe for her to go back to her apartment. He knows her address."

"What about her roommates? They're not safe there either."

"I've already warned them that Erin's assailant likely knows her home address, and that it's possible he might show up there. The police are watching their apartment for now, but the added security won't last forever. If those girls are smart, they'll move. And if Erin's smart, she'll never step foot in that apartment again."

"She won't," I say, adamant. "Not if I have anything to say about it."

He nods. "Good."

And then he's gone, leaving me to contemplate the fact that Erin's nightmare isn't over yet. As long as her assailant is alive, she's in danger. And that's not acceptable.

* * *

After Tyler leaves, Shane joins me in the hallway. I can tell he wants to talk. He nods to a spot down the hall, walking past me, and I follow him. I fall into my habitual stance leaning against the wall, my arms crossed over my chest.

Shane strikes a similar pose directly across the hall from me. "I have a message for you, from Erin."

I straighten, pulling away from the wall. "What?"

"She wants you to know that none of this is your fault."

My laugh is sharp and bitter. It doesn't matter what Erin says. I know it's my fault. "It's a fact, Shane. If I'd gone with her as she asked, it wouldn't have happened."

Shane flexes his shoulders as he rubs the back of his neck. "You couldn't have known, Mack. Hindsight is twenty-twenty. Cut yourself some slack and forget it. You can't carry the weight of this on your shoulders. Erin's going to need you to be strong, for her sake as well as for your own."

He pushes away from the wall and starts back toward Erin's room. A few paces away, he stops and turns back to face me. "By the way... Beth and I are planning for Erin to come home with us when she's released. She can't go back to her apartment. It's not safe, at least not until the perp is apprehended."

I nod, flooded with relief. Erin's apartment is out of the question. Not only is it unsecured, but her roommates aren't reliable. They *left her* at that bar. All three of them bear part of the blame, as far as I'm concerned.

And it doesn't escape me that this means Erin will be living in *my* apartment building. "What about me? If I'm supposed to be her protection, I'll need to be on-site."

"You're welcome to come to the penthouse, of course. I'd appreciate the extra security. I'm going to put extra security in the building's lobby to monitor who comes into the building. As for you, you can either be at the penthouse, or..."

"Or, I can do some investigating of my own."

Shane nods. "I figured you'd want to. The sooner we catch this monster and put him away, the sooner Erin will be safe. Until he's apprehended, we have to assume she's in danger. Tyler said she's the first one to survive—he thinks someone interrupted her assailant. Maybe there was a noise out in the hallway, I don't know, but something must have spooked him. He took off in a panic and left Erin alive. She *survived*, Mack. That makes her a target. He's got to be afraid she can ID him, and that puts her in grave danger."

"Can she ID him? Does she remember anything about him?"

Shane shakes his head. "No. She might get her memories back eventually, but right now she can't tell us anything. We've received one bit of good news. There wasn't any semen found at the scene, not in or on her body, and not on the bedding. That makes us think the perpetrator used condoms."

"Thank God for that." If the perp used a condom, that means there's little risk of pregnancy and a reduced risk that she could have contracted a sexually-transmitted disease. He probably used condoms to cover his own tracks—thinking he was hiding his DNA—and certainly not for Erin's sake.

"Mack, I want you to find this monster. Erin's like family to us, and this asshole hurt *my family.* I want to him to pay. Find him. I'm bringing in Dominic Zaretti to help you."

"Zaretti? Shit." I know this guy. He's a lone wolf, a private operator, and he's ruthless as hell. He has a well-earned reputation for getting the dirty work done, and he's good at skirting the law. He's a tattooed, pierced, six-foot-eight hellraiser. He's a fucking bruiser. Hell, he's one of the few guys who tower over *me.*

"Dominic can be very useful in certain situations," Shane says. "He can get his hands dirty when we can't. And certainly when Tyler can't."

I laugh, the sound harsh. "That's one way of putting it."

Still, none of this changes the fact that Erin is suffering. My chest hollows out as my heart contracts, leaving a painful ache. I'm not above begging at this point. "I need to see her, Shane."

He frowns. "I'm sorry, Mack. She said she doesn't—"

"I *need* to see her with my own eyes. Just for a minute."

"She said no, Mack, and I'm going to honor her wishes. Be patient. Give her time. I'm sure once she's settled in at the penthouse, she'll feel more like seeing people."

People, maybe. But that doesn't mean she'll agree to see *me*. Of course she blames me. How in the hell could she not? I wasn't there when she fucking needed me! "Tell her—" I stop and swallow hard, trying to hold it together. "Tell her I'm here for her. Tell her I'm sorry."

Shane reaches out to clasp my arm. "I will."

*　*　*

The rest of the evening passes uneventfully. People come and go from the waiting room down the hall. Shane's family, bookstore employees, even Erin's roommates stop by to check on her. Still, Erin won't see anyone other than Beth and Shane.

One of the hospital staff brings Erin a late supper, and then later a nurse comes in to check on her. After that, all's quiet in her room until around eight pm, when Shane and Beth both step out into the hallway. Luke is nestled against Beth's chest, sound asleep, his thumb tucked into his mouth, his free hand white-knuckling the sleeve of her blouse. Beth's eyes are bloodshot.

Shane pulls his wife into his arms, careful not to crush the baby, and he holds her, rubbing her back and whispering quietly to her.

He glances up over the top of Beth's head and gives me a long, pained look. "Sweetheart, please," he finally says to her, laying his hands on her shoulders and setting her back so he can gaze down into her face. "Go home tonight with Sam and Cooper. You need to rest. And Luke needs you. I'll stay with Erin. I won't leave her side, I promise." He tenderly brushes a tear from her cheek. "You can come back in the morning."

I don't blame Shane for wanting Beth to go home to rest. She looks miserable and exhausted, like she's on the edge of a breakdown herself. I wouldn't be surprised if she's experiencing a little PTSD right now, with Erin's assault hitting a little too close to home for comfort. It wasn't that long ago that Beth was physically assaulted, herself.

I look away to give them some privacy, but in my peripheral vision, I see Beth gingerly hand off the sleeping baby to Shane.

"Mack." She walks right up to me and slips her arms around my waist, hugging me tightly.

Her gesture of support means the world to me, and my arms gratefully slide around her shoulders.

"I'm so sorry," she says. "Be patient with her, Mack. She needs time to process everything that's happened. I'm sure she'll see you soon."

I give her a gentle squeeze. "I'll wait as long as it takes."

She nods, wiping her damp cheeks with the backs of her hands. "Sorry, I'm such a mess."

"You have nothing to apologize for."

Luke stirs in Shane's arms, whimpering in his sleep, and Beth immediately reaches for him and hugs him to her chest. She looks at her husband. "Okay. I'll go home tonight. I wish you could come with me, but one of us has to stay here with Erin. She shouldn't be alone right now."

Shane nods, looking more than a little relieved that she agreed to go. I was wondering if he'd force the issue if she didn't. "Don't worry, I'll take good care of Erin," he says as he pulls his phone from his pocket. "I'll let Sam and Cooper know you're ready to go."

Beth looks far from happy. "I'll go say good-bye to Erin."

13

Erin

Beth sits in the chair beside my bed, holding Luke against her shoulder and patting his back. She just finished nursing him and is trying to get him to burp. "I hate leaving you," she says.

My throat tightens, but I squelch the urge to beg her to stay. It would be selfish of me to ask. She's exhausted. The baby's upset. They both need to go home and sleep in their own beds. Besides, Shane's staying here with me tonight. He's really been here for me since… the incident.

In my mind, I've started referring to it as *the incident* because I can't bring myself to call it what it really is. I can't even bring myself to think it. "It's okay," I tell her, putting on my best fake smile. "I'll be fine. Please don't worry. You need to rest."

My heart pounds at the thought of her leaving me. She's all I have. I have no family. I was raised by a single mom—my dad left us right after I was born. When my mom died, my maternal grandmother took care of me, but she's gone now too. I think I have some distant relatives on my father's side living in California, but I don't even know their names.

I'm alone.

"Did you look?" I ask Beth as she pats the baby's back.

She lifts reddened eyes to meet my gaze. For the longest time, she hesitates, but finally she nods. She knows what I'm asking. She was here in my room when the nurse checked me over. I asked Beth to stay.

"Yes. I looked."

"And?"

She lets out a shaky breath as tears well in her eyes, letting me know without saying the words that it's bad. "Erin, it's going to take time, but your body will heal."

I haven't looked at any part of my body, other than my arms. I haven't seen my face or my torso, or my thighs. I don't want to. I saw the pity in the nurse's eyes as she examined me this afternoon. And in Beth's.

Beth reaches for my left hand, grasping my fingers and squeezing gently. "I promise you, in time, you'll be the same as you've always been."

"What about the bite marks?" *What kind of monster goes around biting people?*

She swallows hard. "I'm sure they'll fade over time." Beth scoots forward on her chair, closer to the bed. "If you need me in the night, you can call me, okay? Shane will stay with you all night, and Mack's right outside your door."

"He must be exhausted," I say, thinking of Mack standing outside my room. "He should go home, too."

Beth laughs softly, shaking her head. "No chance of that happening. He's like a guard dog out there, scrutinizing everyone who walks down the hallway." The corners of her lips turn down. "You're going to have to see him eventually, you know."

I can feel my face heating. "I can't."

"Why do you say that, Erin? He cares about you. He blames himself, and it's tearing him up."

"But it wasn't his fault. It's mine."

"It's not your fault either." She scoots over to sit on my bed. "There's only one person who bears responsibility for what happened, and that's the monster who attacked you. Not you, and not Mack."

A quiet knock puts an end to our conversation. The door opens and Shane walks in. "Ready to go?" he says to Beth. "Sam and Cooper are here."

I squeeze Beth's hand. "I'll be fine. You go get some rest and take care of that sweet baby."

Beth leans down and kisses my forehead. "I'll be back first thing in the morning."

* * *

After Beth leaves, Shane makes up the sofa bed for himself. Having him here by himself seems odd. I'm not used to seeing him without Beth around. I know he's only staying with me because of Beth—to make her happy. But now that it's just the two of us, it feels a little awkward. I mean, why would a man of his stature spend time with *me*? He's a wealthy, big-shot CEO, and he's going to babysit me tonight?

Still, having him here means the world to me. He represents safety and security, and that's what I crave.

The night-shift nurse comes in to help me walk to the bathroom and get ready for bed. Every slow step is agony, but I bite my lip to keep from crying out.

"Leave the light off, please," I tell her, as I shuffle into the bathroom.

The nurse helps me lower myself onto the toilet seat. I position my hospital gown so that I can't see anything, and I ignore the nurse as she changes the padding in my underwear.

"It looks like the bleeding has almost stopped," she says, giving me a gentle smile as she disposes of the evidence.

I shuffle to the sink to wash my hands and brush my teeth, taking great care to avoid my reflection in the mirror. I know what I must look like, with all the bruises and cuts on my face. My eyelids are fat and swollen, and so are my lips. I must look like a nightmare.

After the nurse helps me back to bed and leaves, I observe

Shane seated on the sofa. While I was in the bathroom, he changed out of his suit and into a pair of gray sweats and a plain white T-shirt—Sam and Cooper must have brought him a change of clothes. I'm not used to seeing him dressed so casually. He seems more like a normal guy now, and not so much like the imposing CEO of a multi-million dollar company.

He turns to face me. "Doing okay?" he says in a low voice.

"Yes."

"If you need anything in the night, just call for me."

I nod.

"I mean it, Erin. Don't be shy. Just holler."

"I will. I promise." I lie back and close my eyes, drawing the bedding up to my chin. I'm sure he'd rather be anywhere than here. "I'm sorry."

"Sorry? What for?"

"I'm sorry you're stuck here with me. I know you'd rather be home with your family." I turn away, staring at the sliver of door I can see beyond the privacy curtain.

There's a soft rustling sound, and a moment later the mattress dips as Shane sits on the bed. His warm hand covers mine. "Erin, I'm not *stuck* here with you. I want to be here. This is exactly where I need to be right now. You're like a sister to Beth, and she loves you dearly. You're family to her, and that makes you family to me as well. And I protect my family."

The sincerity in his voice makes my throat tighten. Tears well up, and I close my lids to keep them from spilling out. "God, I'm so sick and tired of crying! My emotions are all over the place, and the slightest thing sets them off."

He squeezes my hand. "I promise you we'll find the man who did this, and we'll make him pay."

He returns to his makeshift sofa bed and types something into his phone. He's probably texting Beth.

My last thought, as my mind starts to drift and my lids grow heavy, is that Beth is a very lucky woman to have a man like Shane in her life. I used to want the same thing, but that was *before*.

It's too late for me now. I'll never know that kind of unconditional love.

* * *

I can't breathe!

I struggle and fight as hard as I can, but my limbs are weighted down like they're full of lead.

Rough hands circle my throat, clamping down tighter and tighter, squeezing, cutting off my air and crushing my windpipe. And the laughter! That horrible laughter... it makes my blood run cold. He's enjoying this!

"Erin, wake up!"

I shoot up in bed with a strangled cry, gasping for air, my fingers clawing at my throat.

"Erin, look at me!"

A sharp male voice steals my attention, and I blink as I stare at the familiar face beside me. "Shane?" Suddenly everything comes rushing back. *Hospital.* Shane stayed with me so Beth could go home for the night with Luke.

The door to my room crashes open, slamming into the wall and letting in a stream of bright light from the hallway, blinding me. I throw my hands up to cover my face, but not before *he* sees me.

"No!" I cry, raising one hand toward the man towering in the open doorway, trying to block his view. I don't want him to see me like this.

"She's all right, Mack," Shane says in a firm, even voice. "It was just a nightmare. She's fine."

I sense Mack standing frozen to the spot, staring at me with laser intensity, but I can't look at him. I can't bear to see pity or disgust on his face.

"Mack," Shane says, the single word both reassuring and a warning.

Mack backs out of the room, closing the door behind, taking with him the only source of light other than the moonlight coming through the big window.

"Are you okay?" Shane asks me.

My lungs billow as I try to catch my breath. "Yes. I couldn't breathe!"

"It was a nightmare, not real."

He's quiet for a long moment, so quiet I turn to face him, half expecting him to have returned to the sofa. But he's still beside me. He looks… conflicted, as if he's not sure what to say. Finally, he sighs, and then he speaks. "It was just a bad dream. Don't worry, you're safe."

He says that with such conviction, I know he believes it. But the truth is, once I leave this hospital and return to my apartment, I'll be on my own again. If this monster knows who I am, then he can surely find me.

I don't think I'll ever feel safe again.

14

Mack

Hours later, I can still hear her frightened cry, the sound echoing inside my skull. Hearing her cry out like that only fuels my overactive, sick imagination. If I let down my guard even for a second, I find myself rehashing what happened to her, mentally listing the atrocities a fucking monster perpetrated on her. It makes me sick.

God, I wish she'd see me, just for a moment. Last night, when I burst into her room—after hearing her cry out like that—God, the look on her face! The way she put up her hand to block me—it gutted me.

It kills me that she won't see me, that she won't give me a chance to apologize. I want to make things right between us, but she won't even let me try.

I hear a noise to my left and turn toward the sound. One of the nurses is coming toward me, carrying a cup of coffee that looks like it came out of a vending machine.

The young woman, late twenties, pretty, her long blonde hair swept up into a topknot, stops in front of me, looking bashful, as she holds out the cup. "I thought you might like some coffee."

I give her a grateful smile. "Thank you—" I glance at her nametag. "Ashley."

She smiles, blushing as she fidgets with the ID badge clipped to her uniform top. "You've been out here so long, I figured you could use the caffeine. If you'd like to take a break...maybe grab a meal down in the cafeteria...I have a half-hour break coming up...." She trails off and smiles at me hopefully.

"Thank you, but no. I can't." I'm honestly very flattered. She's a beautiful woman, and she seems nice. But there's only one woman I'm interested in, and she's behind the door to my left.

Ashley nods, her flush deepening as she backs away. "Sure, no problem. If you need anything, just let me know. I'll be at the nurse's station."

Despite the much-appreciated injection of caffeine, exhaustion is dogging me. I've been up for nearly twenty-four hours straight. And I've had nowhere near enough to eat. But absolutely nothing could make me leave my post.

I'm going to have to get a little bit of sleep. I slide the chair

Sam brought me directly in front of Erin's door so that *no one* can come, or go, from her room without me knowing about it.

* * *

Later that morning, quiet footsteps coming down the hall alert me to the arrival of Beth and Sam. No baby this time. Beth must have left Luke at home with Cooper.

Beth looks like shit, to be honest. She's got dark shadows beneath her eyes, and her face is ghostly pale. She looks exhausted. Shane's not going to be happy about how this is affecting her. She's carrying a spare winter coat and a small overnight bag— I'm assuming the bag contains clothes for Erin to wear when she leaves the hospital, which is hopefully today.

I stand and slide my chair away from the door. "Morning, guys."

She walks right up to me and hugs me, her arms going around my waist. As I gently wrap my arms around her, I meet Sam's gaze over Beth's head. He doesn't look much happier, or better rested.

Beth steps back and looks up at me. "How did she do in the night?"

"Overall, I think she did all right. She did have a nightmare— she woke up in the middle of the night crying out. Shane took care of her, and it's been quiet after that. The nurse has been in to see her twice this morning, and someone from the hospital staff visited her earlier—I think it was a counselor. Shane's been in there with her the entire time."

I have to admit, Shane has surprised me. I know how close Beth and Erin have become over the past year, and as Erin is important to Beth, that makes Erin important to Shane. He has really stepped up and been there for Erin. I guess that shouldn't surprise me. Just because he's always been against the idea of me dating Erin, doesn't mean he doesn't care about her and isn't willing to offer her protection. Erin's essentially an orphan. Even though she's an adult, she's alone in the world. She needs family, and it looks like she's been adopted by the McIntyres. I'm glad for her sake.

Beth moves toward the door, and I open it for her. She steels herself with a deep breath, then pastes a bright smile on her face before she walks in. "Good morning, Erin!"

Sam watches the door swing shut, then turns to me. "Why don't you take a break? I'll stand guard. Go downstairs and get something to eat."

I take him up on his offer, not really having a choice. My bladder is about to rupture, and my empty stomach is gnawing a hole in my belly. "Thanks," I say, slapping him on the arm. "I won't be long."

15

Erin

"Good morning, Erin!"

At the sound of my name, I turn to watch Beth walk into the room, a bright smile on her face. She's carrying an extra winter coat and an overnight bag, which she sets down on an empty chair. After giving me a quick once-over, her gaze gravitates to her husband.

Shane's already up and moving, and he meets his wife halfway, pulling her into his arms. He holds her close, his arms wrapped tightly around her, and presses his face to the side of her head.

After kissing her temple, he pulls back to get a good look at her. "Did you get a good night's sleep?"

She murmurs a reply I can't hear, and I see her shake her head. He tips her chin up so that she's meeting his gaze, and he studies her. Then he leans down and kisses her lightly on the lips. "I'm glad you're here. How's our boy?"

"He's fine. I left him at home with Cooper and your mom."

When he gently cups the side of her face, brushing her cheek with his thumb, I look away, feeling guilty for eavesdropping on their private moment.

A moment later, Beth sits on my bed and pats my leg. "How are you feeling this morning?"

I nod. "Better."

"Mack says the nurse has been in already this morning?"

"Yes. She checked all of the sutures and changed the bandages."

"And?"

"She said everything looks fine. There's no sign of infection, and I think the bleeding has stopped. I don't have a fever." I know fear of an infection was their biggest concern.

Beth reaches for my hand. "That's wonderful! That means you can probably leave the hospital today, just as soon as your doctor gives the okay."

"I guess so." The idea of going home to my apartment terrifies me. I don't think I can take care of myself very well yet. It hurts to walk. It hurts to sit. It hurts to do anything. And I'll be completely on my own at home. Between school and their part-time jobs, my roommates are hardly ever home.

"Erin?"

I realize I'm staring out the window, lost in thought. "Hmm?"

Beth cradles my hand in both of hers. "Shane and I want you to come home with us."

My puffy eyelids widen at her suggestion, and my pulse picks up. "Really?" *I wouldn't be alone! I'd be safe.* The relief I feel is overwhelming.

She nods. "We want you to come stay with us. You're going to need some help while you're recuperating. We can give you that. You'll have everything you need."

"But I couldn't impose on you like that. You've already done so much for me."

She smiles. "You wouldn't be imposing. We want you to come. Besides, the penthouse is very secure. You wouldn't have to worry about... anything. Erin, it's not safe for you to go back to your apartment."

Shane sits at the foot of the bed, still in his sweats and T-shirt, his hair still a bit ruffled from sleep. "We want you to come home with us. We'll provide everything you need to recuperate, and we can protect you. Until this guy is apprehended, you need protection. We're not going to accept no for an answer, so please make it easy on all of us and say yes."

Beth gives me a hopeful smile. "You heard him. He's not going to take no for an answer, and neither am I. So you'll come, all right?"

How can I refuse such a generous offer? "Yes, I'll come. Thank you."

We sit and talk for a while. Beth catches me up on her night at home with Luke. I tell her about my first attempts trying to walk to the bathroom. After a while, we hear a quick rap on the door.

"I'll get it," Beth says, heading for the door. She opens it, then pops her head around the privacy curtain with a smile on her face. "It's Sam. He has something for you. Is it okay if he comes in?"

Sam's been as much a friend to me as Beth has. I'm torn. Part of me wants to say yes, but part of me is afraid.

"It's okay, Erin," she says with a cajoling smile. "It's Sam."

I nod. "All right."

A moment later, Sam walks in carrying a small cardboard box, which he hands to me. "This is for you."

I open the box to find a cream-filled chocolate éclair inside—my favorite. "Thank you, Sam."

"Can I sit?" He indicates the bed.

"Sure."

He sits down. "I can't take credit for the donut. It was actually Mack's idea. He spotted it downstairs a few minutes ago in the cafeteria and thought you'd like it."

Mack. Guilt rises up, threatening to choke me. Even after I refuse to see him, he goes out of his way to do something nice for me.

As Sam searches my face, cataloguing the multitude of injuries, his brown eyes look pained. He reaches out and touches one of the few unmarked places on my cheek. "I'm so sorry, Irish."

I press my lips together to stop the trembling. Seeing him on the verge of tears makes me want to cry. "Thanks."

"How are you doing?"

I shrug. "I'm alive."

He lifts my hand and kisses the back of it. Then he glances at Beth briefly before returning his gaze to me. "We love you, and we're going to take good care of you. You're going to be fine. And I can promise you this—he'll never hurt you again. We're going to make sure of it."

I'm not sure who the we is he's talking about, but I certainly appreciate the thought. "Thank you."

There's another knock at the door, and then Dr. Shaw walks into the room. "Hello, Erin," she says. "How are you feeling?"

I nod. "Better."

"If you'll excuse us," she says to the others in the room. "I'd like to examine Erin one last time before releasing her."

Beth hops up from the bed and holds her hand out to Shane. He takes her hand, and the two of them walk out with Sam.

Dr. Shaw sits in the chair beside my bed. "Okay, now it's just us. Tell me how you're *really* doing. Don't sugar coat it."

I drop my fake smile. "Everything hurts, especially down there."

She frowns, nodding. "Let me take a look."

I lie back and look away, my gaze fixed on the big window, and try to ignore what she's doing... pulling the bedding aside, lifting my hospital gown. She gently nudges my legs apart with gentle hands.

"You're going to feel me touching you," she says, very matter of factly. "Just a light pressure."

She's careful as she examines me, arranging my legs as necessary. Still, I flinch. No matter how careful she is, it's uncomfortable. I try to distance myself by staring at the clear blue sky outside my window, at the fat, white clouds rolling by. My throat tightens, and my heart pounds.

"There's a lot of healing to be done," she says, as she rights my gown and covers me with the bedding. "You suffered a lot of trauma to your vaginal area. The lacerations are healing well, and there's no sign of infection, but you're going to experience some tenderness and swelling for a while."

"How long will it take before everything's healed? Before I'm back to normal."

"I would give it at least four weeks, maybe a bit longer."

"Will… everything… go back to normal eventually? Will it *feel* normal again?"

She nods. "It will. There's a lot of swelling right now, and deep tissue bruising. You need to take it easy and rest. You will heal, I promise you."

I nod, too choked up to speak. I was so afraid I'd feel like this forever.

"I'm going to release you from the hospital this afternoon. Do you know where you're going to stay? You're going to need some help while you recuperate."

"I'm going home with Beth and Shane." Dr. Shaw is Beth's gynecologist too. She knows Beth and Shane well.

"Perfect," she says. "I'm very glad to hear that. The McIntyres will take good care of you. When you get home, call my office and make a follow-up appointment. I'd like to see you again next week. And if you have any concerns or problems before then, or if a fever develops, call my office right away."

* * *

The rest of the morning passes in a whirlwind. Dr. Shaw approves my release later in the day. After changing back into his suit, Shane leaves us to make some work calls and take care of all the arrangements.

"How about we get you dressed?" Beth sets the overnight bag she brought with her on the bed. She pulls out clean clothing for me to wear home—a pair of soft, pink plaid PJ bottoms, a white T-shirt, socks, and sneakers. "These are my clothes, but I'm sure they'll fit you." Then she pulls out a package of brand-new panties and a bra with tags on it, which she lays on the bed.

She holds her hand out to me. "I'll help you to the bathroom so you can change. You'll be so much more comfortable when you're out of this hospital gown."

Walking gets a little easier each time, but my pace is still slow and shuffling. When I feel a twinge of pain deep inside, I suck in a sharp breath. Right now it's difficult to imagine ever feeling normal again.

Beth opens the bathroom door and walks me inside. I catch my reflection in the mirror over the sink and stare, getting a good look at myself for the first time. My face is so bruised, battered, and swollen that I hardly recognize myself.

Beth lays her hands on my shoulders and meets my gaze in the mirror. "Erin." Her tone is a mix of sorrow and compassion.

"You're going to be okay, I promise."

I can't stop staring at my face—eyes ringed with dark purple and red bruises, lacerations on my cheeks, my complexion sickly pale. The worst is a two-inch gash on my right cheek that's been closed with tiny black stitches. "I look like a demented raccoon."

"You do not!" Beth says, stifling a laugh. She puts her arm around my shoulders and gives me a gentle sideways hug, laying her head gingerly on my shoulder. "You look beautiful. You'll always be beautiful, because I know the caring and loving person you are."

Now it's my turn to laugh. "You're just being nice. I really do look hideous."

I proceed to brush my hair and teeth and then pee. Before I can change into my temporary outfit, though, I need to take off this horrible hospital gown.

Beth steps forward. "Would you like some help?"

I nod. "I haven't undressed yet... not completely."

"Oh," she says, understanding plain on her face.

"I know the bruises will fade, and the cuts will heal. But I hate the thought of having scars for the rest of my life. Every time I see them, I'll be reminded—" I stop midsentence with a shudder. "I don't want to see them right now. I don't want to look at my own body."

"Oh, sweetie, I'm so sorry. Here, turn away from the mirror, and I'll help you take off the gown."

She closes the door half-way, so just a bit of light is shining into the bathroom, giving me a false sense of privacy. The truth is, this is my body now, and there's no escaping it.

I step away from the mirror so I can't see my reflection as Beth helps me slip off the hospital gown. She hands me each article of clothing, and I dress myself slowly and awkwardly, every movement a painful reminder of the damage that's been done. *How could someone do this? He had no right!*

Once I'm dressed, I hobble back to the bed and lie down, leaving my sneakers on the floor beside the bed. Now we wait for Dr. Shaw to finish writing up my release papers.

While we wait, I doze off, waking only when someone from the hospital staff delivers lunch to my bedside tray.

The afternoon is pretty quiet and restful. Sam brings Beth some lunch, and a nurse comes in to take my vitals. Everything checks out okay, so I'm still on track to be released.

Not long after, Shane returns to my room with my release papers and a wheelchair. "Your chariot awaits, young lady," he says, bringing the chair close to the bed. He offers me his arm and helps me transfer into the seat. "Sam's waiting at the front entrance with the Escalade."

Beth collects the few personal items I have at the hospital and hands them to me. Then, after we put on our coats, Shane rolls my chair toward the door.

"Wait!" I say, holding up my hand. "Is he still out there?" I don't have to say his name. They know who I'm talking about.

Shane stops my chair. "Mack? Yes. He's out in the hallway."

Mentally, I prepare myself to see him. Or rather, for him to see me.

Beth opens the door for us, and Shane wheels me out into the hall. I close my eyes, hoping and praying that Mack will let us walk away. But the wheelchair stops, and I feel the air shift as someone moves in front of me.

"Erin."

At the sound of his voice, so deep and achingly familiar, I squeeze my eyes shut and try to pretend this isn't happening. *I'm not ready.*

A warm hand gently covers my knee, the touch light, as if he's afraid of hurting me. "Erin, please."

I open my eyes, and there he is, his familiar face just a couple of feet from mine. He looks haggard, his brown eyes bloodshot, but he's still the handsomest man I've ever known. He swallows hard as he studies my face, a ticking muscle in his cheek the only indication of what he's feeling.

I don't know what to say to him. *I'm sorry? I'm sorry I was stupid? I'm sorry I was so gullible? I'm sorry I've been so unfair to you?*

His lips are pressed in a flat line, his jaws tightly clenched. "Honey—" His voice breaks.

He reaches out slowly as if to touch my cheek, and I turn my face away. I can't bear to see pity in his eyes.

Mack drops his hand and rises to his formidable height, towering over me. He clears his throat, and when he speaks, his voice is clear and professional. "There are some things I need to do this afternoon, but afterward, this evening… I'd like to come see you at the penthouse. Is that okay?"

I suck in a breath, wanting to say *no*, but I don't want to seem ungrateful. Everyone's done so much for me. "Okay."

He lets out a heavy sigh. "I'll see you this evening."

After Mack steps aside, Shane wheels me down the hallway, past the nurses' station to the elevators. Beth remains by my side, her comforting hand on my shoulder.

I feel nothing but turmoil after seeing Mack face to face for the first time since my world imploded. Once we're inside the elevator and the doors close, I give way to all the pain and uncertainty and burst into ugly tears.

16

Mack

With mixed emotions, I watch Shane wheel Erin down the hallway. I'm glad she's leaving the hospital. She'll be much more comfortable at the penthouse apartment. But she'll also be farther away from me. I won't be standing outside her door twenty-four-seven.

Of course I'll only be two floors below her in the same apartment building. My hope is that, when she's feeling better, I can talk her into coming down to my apartment so we can spend some time together. I want to be there for her. I want to help her deal with this in any way I can. I want to help her heal.

It's not until they disappear inside the elevator, and Erin's gone from sight, that I allow myself to process the anger and sorrow that threaten to choke me. Up to this point, I've done a decent job of keeping my emotions bottled up—I don't want her to see me lose my shit. But I'm only human. There's only so much I can take.

I collapse into my chair, my head in my hands, and let the pain out with a hoarse, muffled cry of rage. My throat is knotted so tightly I can barely breathe.

Jesus, her face! She's barely recognizable. And those are just the injuries I can *see*. What about all the ones I can't see? The ones hidden beneath her clothing? What about the emotional injuries? Those might be the worst ones of all.

Anger pulses through me, my blood on fire and I feel like I'm burning alive from the inside out. I want to hit something! I want to drive my fist through the wall. Instead, I grip my hair, fisting the strands as I try to reign in this anger.

I swear to God I'll find the fucker who hurt her. I'll rip him apart, limb from limb, with my bare hands, and I'll revel in it. I don't want him behind bars! I want him six feet underground! I want Erin to be able to live her life without fear of this monster overshadowing her.

When I feel a heavy hand on my shoulder, I open my eyes to see a pair of size eighteen black boots planted on the floor directly in front of me. I look up, having to crane my neck to see the face of the inked and pierced man towering over me. *Dominic Zaretti.*

"Dominic. Perfect timing, man." I rise to my full height, and damn if this guy isn't taller than me. I'm not accustomed to that.

But at six-eight, he's a fucking giant, all solid muscle.

He's wearing a pair of ripped jeans, a black T-shirt molded to his broad chest, and a black leather jacket. His brown hair is pulled back into a short pony, the sides shaved close, and a matching trim beard frames his square jaw. Several heavy metal rings adorn his fingers, but I have a feeling their purpose is more for offense than for looks.

Dominic's a loner with a reputation for being ruthless... a paid mercenary. Shane hires him occasionally to do the dirty work. I'm perfectly okay with that. I can live with anything that will help me catch the monster who hurt Erin.

The giant standing before me nods, his grip firm on my hand. "It's good to see you again, Mack." His voice is a deep bass, as rough around the edges as he is. He frowns. "I'm sorry to hear about the girl."

I shrug off his condolences, not wanting to talk about Erin. "I'm going to find this motherfucker and end him."

Dominic nods. "I'm pretty sure that's why I'm here."

I've heard rumors about this guy. That he was born into an organized crime family, but that he got out of the racket when he was a teenager. He's served several military tours oversees fighting in Afghanistan, Iraq, and Somalia. He's been to all the hell holes and seen it all, and that's what makes him so useful. He doesn't shy away from what needs to be done. It's part of his DNA.

I nod. "I have a meeting scheduled this afternoon with the security staff at The Wakefield Hotel, where the assault took place. We need to scour the surveillance footage to see if we can trace this guy's movements before and after the assault. We need to ID him and find him, fast, before the cops do."

Dominic motions toward the elevators. "Lead the way. My bike is parked out front."

* * *

Dominic follows me through the downtown Chicago streets on his big black Harley. Once we reach the hotel, we park in the front lot and head inside to the customer service desk.

"I'm here to see Tim Jackson," I tell the young woman working at the front desk. "I have an appointment."

Apparently, she was expecting me, because when I give her my name, she nods and invites us to come around the counter to the back where the security office is located. She knocks on the door, then opens it. Tim Jackson rises from his seat in front of a bank of video monitors.

"Tim," I say, shaking his hand.

The man's sharp gaze goes to Dominic, who's standing behind me, just inside the doorway. "Hello, Mack," Tim says to me, all the while keeping a close eye on Dominic.

I step further into the room, and Dominic files in behind me, shutting the door quietly behind him.

"This is my associate, Dominic," I tell the security guard. "He's helping me with this investigation. I was hoping you could show him the video surveillance footage of Erin from two nights ago."

Tim nods as he gazes up at Dominic, assessing him. "Of

course." He motions us to the two office chairs in front of the monitors. "Have a seat, fellas. I've already pulled up the relevant video footage showing the alleged assailant."

I sit. "That was fast."

Tim nods. "I had to locate it earlier this afternoon for a Detective Jamison. He's investigating this crime too. He said you'd likely be coming by."

Tim brings up the footage that shows our suspect approaching Erin at her booth in the hotel bar. Dominic studies the video, watching the interaction between Erin and the suspect. When the perp slips the drug into Erin's drink, Dominic's jaw tightens, and he mutters something beneath his breath.

We switch to different feeds to follow the suspect taking Erin up to his room. Seeing Erin's uncoordinated gait, and watching as the suspect practically drags her along with him, is enough to make me ill.

Watching her struggle on her feet is both infuriating and heartbreaking. I can't help returning to my original thought—if only I'd gone to that damned party with her, none of this would have happened. If I'd been by her side, this fuckwad never would have approached her in the first place.

The time stamp when they entered the hotel room is twelve-twenty am. We speed through the camera feed, watching other hotel guests come and go throughout the night and into the early morning hours. I try not to think about what must have been happening in that hotel room, but the mental images come anyway, making me sick.

Our first break appears at three o'clock am, when a drunken hotel guest staggers down the hall and tries to open the perp's door with his key card. Of course it doesn't work, but the guy's too drunk to realize he's got the wrong room. He bangs on the door and yells. A moment later, a woman opens the door to the room directly across the hall, and she motions the guy into the right room.

"That's what spooked him," Dominic says, his gaze locked on the monitor. "Somebody give that drunken fool a medal. He likely saved a woman's life and doesn't even realize it."

Sure enough, not five minutes later, our perp comes out of his room, alone, shutting the door securely behind him and hanging a *Do Not Disturb* sign on the handle. I zoom in on the guy's face, freezing the frame. It's a clear shot of him—certainly clear enough that someone might recognize him.

There are visible, bloody scratches on his face and neck. Dear God, *she fought back*. She must have been conscious at some point to try to fight him off. "Can we get prints of this image?" I ask the guard. "Two copies?"

"Sure." Tim switches on a printer.

Dominic leans back in his seat, his hand brushing his bearded jaw as he studies the image.

The security guard prints two copies and hands one to me and one to Dominic. I stare at the suspect's face, my gaze locked on the many scratches. Seeing them makes me want to kill. *She fought him, hard.*

The video footage resumes, and we watch our suspect hurry

down the hall to the elevators. He's holding something under his arm—it looks like a package wrapped up in a white cloth. In a pillowcase maybe? That must be how he carried her purse and undergarments away.

Changing camera views, we're able to follow his progress downstairs to the lobby and out the front doors. Footage from an exterior camera shows him walking briskly into the dark night, out of sight.

"Go back to the bar footage," Dominic says. "Let's see if we can spot him in the bar *before* he approaches Erin."

Tim scrolls back through the timeline. We luck out and catch the perp entering the bar around ten o'clock that night. He takes a seat at the counter and orders a beer. Sitting alone, he scans the crowd methodically, undoubtedly searching for a potential mark.

After downing his beer, he orders another. A female bartender with short dark hair pauses to chat with the guy. They seem to be on pretty friendly terms. He says something to her, and she shakes her head.

After finishing his second beer, he gets up and wanders the floor, checking out women. When he disappears down a hallway leading to the restrooms, we switch feeds.

"That's Erin!" I say, spotting her standing in line for the women's restroom.

The suspect bumps into her—probably intentionally—and initiates a conversation. She shakes her head repeatedly as she attempts to put some space between them.

As I watch the perp moving in on her, inching closer, my blood boils and anger sears my insides. *He had no fucking right to touch her!*

I realize then what an idiot I've been. I was so worried about the difference in our ages, so worried that she was too young for me, that I lost sight of the most important fact. I'm in love with her. I have been for a long time. I've been crushing on her just as hard as she's been crushing on me—I just wouldn't let myself admit it. In hindsight, after everything that's happened to her, the difference in our ages is immaterial. We're both adults. If we want to be together, we shouldn't—*I shouldn't*—let anything stand in our way.

When it's Erin's turn in the queue, she rushes inside the women's room, thinking she's free of this guy. But she wasn't. It was just an illusion.

"So that's when he made his mark," Dominic says, crossing his arms over his chest.

All the pieces are coming together now. The suspect spotted Erin in line for the restroom and made his decision then. He probably waited and watched, hoping for an opportunity to get her alone to slip her the drug.

And because her friends ditched her, he got his chance.

* * *

After watching all of the pertinent video we can find, we thank Tim and leave the security office. We head for the bar to see if the female bartender who served the perp drinks on New Year's Eve is there, but she's not.

"Her name is Terri," the manager tells us. "Her shift doesn't start until three. Come back then."

It's noon now, so there's nothing we can do here until the bartender comes on duty. In the meanwhile, there's something important I need to do.

17

Erin

"Here you go," Beth says, standing aside as Shane wheels me into my new temporary bedroom.

The focal point of my suite is a king-sized bed with pristine cream sheets and a pale peach comforter. There's a small pile of cream and gray and peach-colored pillows propped up against the tufted, gray velvet headboard.

Beth points to an open door. "That's your bathroom. There's a sunken tub in there and a walk-in shower. The closet is over there, through that door. Mack texted to tell me he's going to have someone collect your personal belongings from your apartment and bring them here."

He and Beth help me transfer from the wheelchair to the bed, and then Shane leaves us alone.

Beth sits on the bed, and I can tell from her expression that she wants to talk.

"When you're feeling up to it, I think it would be a good idea for you to talk to someone," she says. "I recommend my therapist, Dr. Carol Mosely. I've been seeing her for years. She's really good, and she makes house calls. She'll come here to see you."

"A therapist?" The thought of talking to a stranger about what happened scares me to death. I can barely face it myself, let alone talk to someone else about it. "I'll think about it."

Beth walks over to the dresser to pick up a neatly-folded, cream-colored garment. She hands it to me. "Why don't you change into something more comfortable? You can wear one of my nightgowns until your clothes arrive. And there's a robe hanging in the bathroom."

I clutch the nightgown to my chest, marveling at how soft and silky the fabric is. "Thanks." I'm desperate to get out of these clothes. Even though I'm wearing loose PJ bottoms, they feel too confining.

I shuffle into the spacious bathroom—not bothering to turn on the light—and change into the nightgown, use the toilet, and brush my teeth with the brand-new toothbrush and tube of toothpaste laid out on the counter. Beth thought of everything.

When I return to the bed, Beth already has the covers and sheet pulled back.

I sigh with relief as I slip between the cool sheets. "I can't thank you enough for giving me a place to stay."

"You don't need to thank me," she says as she helps me arrange the bed covers.

Once I'm lying in bed, I can finally relax. Just getting dressed and leaving the hospital to come here was exhausting. And painful. My private area is throbbing from all the movement. There's still so much swelling and bruising down there.

I lie back on the pillow, exhausted. Beth leaves me alone to rest. I'm tired that falling asleep isn't difficult. But my nap is short-lived, because another nightmare brings me abruptly awake. I jerk violently, shooting up in bed as I try to catch my breath.

I can't breathe!

My hands go around my throat, but there's nothing there constricting my airway.

It takes me a moment to orient myself.

It was just a dream.

I'm safe.

* * *

My new accommodations are impressive, with all the amenities anyone could wish for. There's a flatscreen TV hanging over the dresser, directly across from the bed, that gets every movie and television streaming service known to man.

I wander over to the floor-to-ceiling wall of windows and glance out at the city skyline. I feel like I've been secreted away in a castle turret, far above the bustling city below me. *I'm safe up here, right? He can't find me.*

The penthouse is a far cry from the little attic bedroom I had when I lived with my grandmother. After my mom died, when I was eight, I moved in with Gram in an old, creaky house that had been subdivided into apartments. Our apartment was a walk-up on the third floor, with access to the attic via a ladder. That's where I slept—in the attic. It was actually a charming little bedroom with lots of character and ambiance—peeling blue-and-white chintz wallpaper dating back to the 1940s, a vintage trundle bed with a little bedside table that held a small brass lamp. I did my homework seated at a child's antique desk and chair in the corner. A wooden bookcase housed my precious collection of books.

Thanks to the single-pane windows and nonexistent insulation of that old building, my attic bedroom was ice cold in the winter and boiling hot in the summer. But I didn't mind. It was my own special place. My secret oasis. I used to lie in my bed under a heavy quilt my grandmother had made me—light blue to match the fading wallpaper—and read my favorites over and over... *Jane Eyre, Pride and Prejudice, Emma, A Little Princess.*

I dreamed of the day when I'd meet my own hero. Then cold, harsh reality intervened. Grandma was diagnosed with cancer and died two years later, just a month after I graduated from high school.

The money she'd left me was just enough to supplement the scholarship I'd been awarded by University of Chicago. I'd always dreamed of going to University of Chicago and majoring in English literature, but the pragmatic side of me chose business management instead.

Still, I never stopped dreaming that I'd meet my own dashing hero one day. And when I started working at Clancy's, and Beth took over ownership of the store, her husband brought in one of his own guys, Mack Donovan, to head up store security.

And that's when I fell in love, with a dream and a man who was unattainable. I fell head-over-heels in love with the tall, dark, handsome, imposing, stoic, and yet gentle and kind, new head of security.

But it doesn't matter anymore. I'll never be able to trust a man. I'll never be able to let down my guard, or let a man see the scars on my body.

A quiet knock on my door pulls me out of my misery. "Yes?"

The door cracks open just enough for Beth to pop her head inside. "Sorry. I wasn't sure if you were awake. Someone's here to see you. Do you feel up to having a visitor?"

My heart stutters, as I'm afraid it's Mack. "Who is it?"

"It's Tyler. He'd like to ask you some questions if that's okay."

"Oh." I knew this was coming. Tyler's been kind not to rush me, but he's a police detective. He undoubtedly has questions—most of which I probably can't answer. "Does he know I don't remember anything?"

She nods. "He does. He'd still like to talk to you, though, if you don't mind. I'll stay with you if you want."

I nod, grateful for her presence.

"I'll go get him," she says. "Be right back."

She's hardly gone more than a few minutes when there's another knock on my door.

I take a deep breath. *You can do this. Just answer his questions and get it over with.* "Come in."

The door opens, and there stands Tyler Jamison, looking serious and somber in his suit and tie. I've seen Beth's brother many times before at family gatherings. He's strikingly handsome, with his short dark hair and neatly trimmed beard and mustache.

Unlike his sister, who's blonde and pale-skinned, Tyler always seems to have a sun-kissed tint to his skin that makes me think of warm, sunny beaches. Beth did tell me once that their father was biracial. Sadly, he was killed in the line of police duty when Beth was an infant. Tyler, who was eighteen at the time, helped their mother raise Beth.

I would find it hard to believe they're brother and sister if it weren't for their striking blue-green eyes, which they inherited from their Swedish mother.

Tyler stops at the foot of my bed, giving me a polite and professional nod. "Hello, Erin. Thanks for seeing me."

I pull the blanket up to my chin like it's a shield. "Hello."

He sets a small sack on the bed. "I brought your phone. It was recovered in the hotel room."

"Thank you."

"How are you feeling?"

I force a smile. "Better, thank you." *Terrible.*

He frowns, as if he doesn't believe me. "Do you feel up to answering a few questions? I promise I won't take up much of your time."

I nod, shooting a quick glance at Beth, who has claimed a seat beside me on the bed. "Yes."

Tyler pulls a chair up to the opposite side of the bed and sits.

Beth's brother makes me nervous. He always has. I don't think he does it on purpose, but he's just naturally intimidating. He's quiet, reserved, and so in *control* of himself. I can't imagine him ever letting his hair down, so to speak.

He takes a small black notepad and pen out of his suit pocket and flips the pad open. "Is it okay if I take notes?"

I nod.

"Thanks." He glances at Beth, giving her a smile that transforms his expression for a moment, softening him. He's a handsome man, but when he smiles, he's stunning.

Tyler turns to face me, his expression sobering. "Erin, I'm very sorry about what you've been through. I hope you have a speedy and full recovery."

My throat tightens, and I find it difficult to swallow. "Thank you."

He looks almost apologetic as he begins. "I'm trying to piece together your movements on New Year's Eve. I've spoken to Mack already, and he gave me a summary of your activities during the day. He said you left work about ten after five and were planning to go straight home to your apartment. I interviewed your roommates. They confirmed that you arrived home at five-forty-five, and that you changed clothes and left with them for the bar at

The Wakefield Hotel. Is that right?"

My pulse races as I nod. "Yes."

He makes a brief notation on his notepad, then looks at me once more. "Your roommates said you arrived at the hotel at approximately eight pm."

"I think so, yes."

"Now, I know you've been having trouble remembering much of what transpired toward the end of that night. I'd like to know what you do remember. Do you remember first arriving at the bar with your friends?"

I think back, my memories hazy at this point. "Yes. We sat at the bar for a while until a table opened up for us. We got one of those big, round corner booths. My roommates' boyfriends joined us."

He nods, making another notation. "So there were seven of you in all seated at that booth?"

"Yes."

"What else do you remember?"

"We talked and ate and watched the New Year's Eve celebration on the TVs. Some of them danced."

"Your friends said they left the bar shortly before midnight."

"That's seems right. This is where my memories get hazy. I remember wanting to take a cab home."

"What do you remember after your friends left?"

I pause to think, trying to remember, but my memories are so fuzzy. "I'm not really sure. I wanted to go home, I remember that much. I couldn't wait to leave that bar. It was so loud and crowded."

Tyler nods. "Do you remember meeting someone that night? A young man with blond hair?"

"No."

"In the video footage, a male about your age approaches your table after your friends left and sits down. He strikes up a conversation with you, and it seems as if you know him."

"There was a guy at my table? I don't remember anyone. I didn't know anyone there."

Tyler pulls a folded piece of paper out of his jacket pocket. "I have a photograph of the two of you seated at the booth. May I show it to you? I'd like to know if you recognize him."

My heart is racing. "Okay."

Tyler unfolds the sheet of paper and hands it to me.

I stare at the photo, surprised to see a clear, color image. I was expecting something fuzzy and black-and-white, something difficult to see. But no, it's a clear shot of me sitting with a guy about my age, just the two of us at the corner booth.

"Do you recognize him?" Tyler says.

I shake my head as I stare at the photo. He's sitting quite close to me, his arm draped across my shoulders. He's leaning into me, his lips near my ear, and there's an arrogant smile on his face. He's looking right at me, and I'm staring off into space.

My gaze flits to Tyler and then back to the photo. "Something's wrong with me. I look… stoned."

He nods, his expression perfectly neutral, giving away nothing of what he's thinking. "Yes. This image was captured after he drugged your soft drink."

"Do you know what kind of drug he used?"

"Not specifically. It'll take a while for the toxicology report to come back. But most likely he used one of the drugs commonly known as 'date rape' drugs. It doesn't really matter at this point. We know that he drugged you—the video evidence is clear—and soon after this photo was taken, he led you out of the bar and up to his hotel room. You were nearly incapacitated at that point, barely able to walk."

My stomach starts to roil, and I feel sick. I'm sweating and shaking all over, and tears scald my cheeks. "I don't remember any of this!"

"Erin, it's okay." Tyler pats my ankle. Then he stands and removes the photograph from my hand, folding it and tucking it into his pocket. He glances at his sister, then back to me. "That's enough questions for today." He gives me a sad smile. "Thank you, Erin. I'll leave you to rest now."

Beth jumps up from her seat and walks her brother out the door. I can hear their muffled voices in the hallway, but I can't make out what they're saying.

Turning away from the door, I press my hot, damp face into the pillow, squeezing my eyes shut as I fight to hold back tears.

Beth returns a moment later, quietly closing the door behind her. The mattress dips as she climbs onto the bed and lies down beside me, wrapping her arm around me and holding me close. "It's okay," she whispers.

"I just wanted to go home!" I sob, clutching my pillow tightly.

"I was going to call a cab and go home!"

"I know, sweetie." She gently strokes my hair. "I'm so sorry."

18

Mack

After arriving in Roger's Park, I luck out and find a parking spot just a block from Erin's apartment. I'm trying hard to maintain my cool, but it's not easy. I'm pissed as hell at Erin's roommates for leaving her at the bar.

When I ring the bell, a young female answers the intercom. "Yes?"

"It's Mack Donovan. Let me in." My tone is harsh, but I don't care at this point. I'm not going to bother with niceties. These girls don't deserve it.

"Oh," she says. She's quiet for a moment. "All right."

The lock disengages, and I let myself in and walk up to their apartment. I rap sharply on the closed door, and it opens promptly. A pretty blonde with green eyes greets me at the door. *Shelley.* I remember her from the hospital.

Shelley steps back to let me enter. "What can I do for you, Mr. Donovan?"

"I want to see Erin's room."

She hesitates for a moment, but as she's on the receiving end of a very dark glower, she capitulates. "Okay."

I follow Shelley to the small bedroom she shares with Erin. She pushes the door open and motions for me to enter. The room looks pretty much the same as it did yesterday. My gaze goes right to Erin's neat little bed.

I turn to face Shelley, who's standing right behind me looking wary. She should be. I'm carrying a shit ton of resentment, and I can't help glaring harshly at her. "You girls left her there."

Shelley winces and her eyes immediately tear up. She swallows hard. "I'm sorry."

"It's a little late for you to be sorry. She's been released from the hospital, but she has a hell of a long recovery ahead of her."

"She's out of the hospital? Is she coming back here?"

"No." My hands curl into fists, and I have to remind myself I don't hit women. "She's never coming back here, not if I have anything to say about it." I wander over to Erin's bed and pick up the stuffed kitty on her pillow. Then I collect her phone charger from the nightstand, as well as the small stack of paperbacks.

When I turn back to face Shelley, the girl's cheeks are wet with tears, and she looks sick with guilt.

"I'm so sorry," she says. "We all are."

"I don't give a rat's ass if you're sorry. You fucked up, and Erin paid the price. Pack up all of her personal belongings. I'll have someone stop by this afternoon to pick everything up. She's moving out, effective immediately."

For a moment, Shelley looks panicked. "But what about the lease? She signed a lease, and it's still in effect for six more months. The three of us can't afford to pay her share, too."

I grab my wallet and pull out a business card. "Here's my number. Figure out Erin's share of the expenses for the remainder of the lease and text me the amount. I'll send you a check."

Shelley looks relieved as she pockets my card. "I really am sorry about what happened, Mr. Donovan," she says as she walks me to the door. "Please tell Erin, okay?"

All I can do is stare her down. "She could have died. Do you fully comprehend that?"

Shelley looks away, ashamed, her chin quivering. She says nothing more.

I walk out the door and don't look back.

* * *

Finally, I head home to my apartment building on Lake Shore Drive, a prime piece of real estate with a front row view of Lake Michigan. Shane owns the building and occupies the entire penthouse floor with his wife and son. Sam and Cooper share the penthouse with them. Several of the top floors of the building are reserved for McIntyre Security employees, including me.

For the foreseeable future, Erin will be living in my building.

I pull into the underground garage and park my truck in my designated spot. Then I head up to my apartment, bringing with me the items I took from Erin's apartment. I'm hoping it will give her some comfort to have a few personal possessions with her. As I head up to my floor, I place a call to the McIntyre Security office to arrange for a courier to pick up Erin's belongings from her apartment and deliver them to the penthouse.

Once inside my apartment, I flip on a couple of lights. I'm tired and hungry, but my mind is focused on getting upstairs to see Erin. I down a quick protein shake to tide me over and take a shower.

By the time I make it up to the penthouse, my stomach is in knots. I have no idea how she's going to respond to my arrival. And I don't know how I'm going to tell her just how much I regret not taking her to that party.

* * *

I feel like an intruder, an interloper, as I walk into the penthouse.

The great room is impressive and serves as the center of the home. There's a fire blazing in the fireplace, which is surrounded by two sofas and two upholstered armchairs. The back wall is floor-to-ceiling windows. Besides the vintage bar along the left wall, there's a dining table to the right that seats an army, and to the right of that is a gourmet kitchen.

I've been here plenty of times for parties, but this is different. This is *personal*. The air crackles with tension.

Shane and Cooper watch me with poker faces, giving away nothing of what they're feeling. Shane leans casually against the back of a free-standing sofa, his arms crossed over his chest—I'm pretty sure his restful pose is just a ruse. Cooper stands at attention, his body rigid. The man was once a shooting instructor in the Marine Corps, in a special operations division. He was a damn fine sniper back in the day. I wouldn't put it past him to do a little target practice at my expense.

I don't know if they're happy I'm here, or unhappy, if they're judging me, blaming me... or simply wishing me luck. I honestly can't tell.

Beth joins us, having come down a hallway to my left. There's a sad smile on her face, and she looks worn out. She gives me a quick nod, motioning for me to follow her. "She said you can come back."

I let out a long-held breath, relieved. I called ahead and asked Beth if I could come up and see Erin. Beth told me to come on up, but part of me feared Erin would refuse to see me. If that happened, I doubt I'd have a snowball's chance in hell of getting past Shane and Cooper.

"I'll show you to her room," Beth says.

I follow her, half expecting Shane and Cooper to bring up the rear, but they hang back in the great room, thank God. The last thing I need right now is an audience.

Once we're out of ear shot, Beth slows her stride, falling back to my side. "Tyler was here earlier to talk to Erin, to ask her a few questions. He showed her the photo of the suspect. It really shook her up—she sort of fell apart afterward."

Beth stops in front of a closed door. "Be careful with her, Mack. Emotionally, she's very fragile right now. And physically... well, she's still in a lot of discomfort. She's scared. To be honest, we're all a bit scared for her."

I nod curtly, holding myself in check, falling back to the comfortable familiarity of a military response. It's a habit of mine when I'm on uncertain ground. "Understood."

Beth knocks lightly. Then she opens the door, slowly pushing it wide, and motions for me to enter. "Call if you need me," she says before stepping out, leaving us alone.

I take a deep breath, relieved that she's giving us some much-needed privacy. There are things I need to say to Erin... things that won't be easy for me to say or for her to hear. I gently close the door behind me and face the bed, not really sure what to expect.

Erin's in bed, beneath the covers, half sitting, half lying, her face turned away from me. Her gaze appears to be fixed on the view outside the windows. From this vantage point, she's got one hell of a view of downtown Chicago.

Steeling myself for whatever comes next, I stand quietly for several minutes, hoping she'll acknowledge my presence. I hate to intrude on her solitude. She doesn't move a muscle, though.

She just keeps staring out the window.

Finally I clear my throat. "Hello, Erin."

She flinches, but doesn't look at me.

"I brought you a few things from your apartment—things I'd thought you'd like to have."

That gets her attention. She turns to look at me, a hint of curiosity in her blue eyes.

I hold out the stash. "I brought your stuffed kitty, your phone charger, and some books from your nightstand. The rest of your stuff will arrive later today."

After setting the items on the nightstand beside her bed, I approach slowly, methodically cataloging every little detail. This is the first time I've gotten a really good look at her since the attack. Her face is mottled with a collection of bruises and lacerations. The skin that's unmarked is a pale imitation of her normal peaches-and-cream complexion. Her hair, that luxurious curtain of silky straight dark hair, hangs limply to her shoulders, flat and dull, the strands tucked behind her ears. There's a sickening ring of deep purple and red bruises around her throat, a constant reminder that a monster attempted to strangle her.

It looks like her attacker systematically hurt her, cut her, marked her. An attack like this... it's borne of hatred and rage. This perpetrator hates his victims... all young brunettes that match Erin's physical description, if Tyler's hypothesis is correct.

Erin was in the wrong place at the wrong time, and she caught the attention of a monster.

She still hasn't spoken, and I find myself craving the sound of her gentle, lilting voice.

    I take a couple steps forward. "Thanks for agreeing to see me."

    She nods, her gaze darting to the items I left on the nightstand.

    I take another few steps. "How are you?"

    She shrugs. "Okay."

    She's lying in the center of a king-sized bed, easily big enough for four of her, with room to spare. I point to the mattress. "Is it okay if I sit?"

    Again she nods, and then she looks away. Her hands clutch the comforter as she holds it protectively against her body, as tension radiates off her in waves. God, it kills me to see her like this.

    This isn't the Erin I know. My Erin is bubbly and energetic, an eternal optimist. She's a glass-half-full person who loves to chatter. This girl... she's an empty shell of herself. Alarm bells peal in my head, loud and jarring, sending my pulse racing.

    I'm careful not to jostle her as I take a seat on the mattress. I sure as hell don't want to cause her any physical discomfort.

    One hand, so pale and slight, rests on top of the bedding, lying across her abdomen. I reach out slowly, intending only to touch it lightly, but the minute my fingertips brush her skin, she jerks her hand away and slides it beneath the covers.

    I know she's been through a horrendous ordeal, but this girl lying here in front of me... I don't even recognize her. She's suffered far more than a physical assault—her spirit has been crushed.

    My chest aches so badly I can hardly breathe. My throat tightens, threatening to choke off my words. But these words have to be said. "Erin, I'm sorry." The words burst forth out of me, broken and rough, with absolutely no finesse. I'm winging this as I go. I have no real plan, other than trying not to fall apart in front of her. She sure as well doesn't need to see that.

Bruises frame her eyes, in varying shades of purple, and her lids are swollen. There are cuts and scratches on her forehead and cheeks, the worst being a vertical gash high on her right cheek that just barely missed her eye. It starts half an inch beneath her right eye and descends down her cheek. It's a deep cut, already stitched up, and it will surely leave a scar.

My gut twists. *Jesus, he used a knife on her.*

She must realize I'm looking at the gash, because her right hand comes up to cover her cheek. "You have nothing to be sorry for," she says in a quiet voice.

"Yes, I do." I blow out a shaky breath and fight the urge to reach for her. I don't dare, not after the way she reacted before. I continue, talking over the lump in my throat because I've got to get this out in the open. It has to be said. "If I'd gone with you that night as you asked, none of this would have happened. I'm so damn sorry, honey." *You have no idea how fucking sorry I am. Please forgive me.*

She nails me with glittering blue eyes swimming in tears. "It's not your fault, Mack! It's *mine!*" The words are practically ripped out of her, as pain flashes in her wild gaze. Her lips flatten, and her chin quivers violently. "It's my fault!" Her voice breaks so badly I can barely understand her. "I was so stupid!"

"Erin, no!" It breaks my heart that she would blame herself. "It wasn't your fault."

The dam breaks as tears stream down her flushed cheeks. She sinks back against the pillows and covers her face with shaking hands.

I grab a few tissues from the box on the nightstand and hold them out to her, brushing the tissues lightly against her fingers, careful not to touch her. She blindly grabs for the tissues and presses them gingerly to her bruised and swollen eyelids.

"You were a victim, Erin. That means things happened *to you*, things that were beyond your control. You are in *no way* at fault here. And it's an irrefutable fact that if I'd been there, it wouldn't have happened. So if you want to blame someone, blame *me*."

Her hands fall away, and I watch helplessly as her face screws up in pain, her eyes tightly shut, her breathing ragged. Seeing her like this tears me apart. I'm desperate to hold her. I want to wrap her up in my arms and never let her go. If she'll let me, I'll spend the rest of my life trying to make up for my failure.

"Erin, please." Her pain is my pain. Her suffering is *my* suffering. "Let me help you."

She shakes her head. "There's nothing you can do."

Resentment bubbles up inside me, and I fight to hide it from her. "You'll accept help from Beth and Sam, even from Shane. Why won't you let me help you? We're friends, too, right?"

Friends. God, that sounds so inadequate now. We're not just friends. We're way more than that. We have been for a long time; I've just been to dim-witted to realize it.

I don't know what I was expecting from her... anger perhaps.

Rage even. I wouldn't have blamed her one bit if she railed at me. Screamed at me. But I never expected this crushing sense of defeat. This hopelessness. She shakes her head as if it's too little too late.

But it's not too late because she's here, alive after a horrendous assault. I'll fix this. I'll make things right between us again. "Erin, talk to me, honey, please. Don't shut me out."

She draws the bed covers up to her chin and gingerly rolls away from me, whimpering in discomfort as she changes position. Watching her hug a spare pillow to her chest breaks my heart. She needs comfort, not self-imposed solitude as punishment.

"Erin, please." I'm at a loss here, but I refuse to give up.

"I'm tired." Her voice is quiet and emotionless. "I need to sleep now."

Her dismissal hurts. *She's kicking me out.*

"Mack, please. I need you to go."

She says those words with such finality that I have no choice but to honor her request. Now's clearly not the time to push her. She needs rest and quiet. She needs time to heal.

I stand. "All right, I'll go now so you can rest. But I'm not giving up."

I let myself out of the room, quietly closing the door behind me. Beth is waiting in the hallway, and I realize she never left us. Warily, she glances up at me.

"Did you hear any of that?" I ask her.

"No, but I'm hoping it went well."

"It didn't. She asked me to leave."

Beth's mouth falls open, but nothing comes out. She seems as dumbfounded as I feel.

I run a hand through my hair. "I begged her to let me help her, but she asked me to leave."

Fresh tears pool in Beth's eyes, and she dashes them away with a shaky hand. "I'm sorry. It seems all I do lately is cry. My hormones are a mess. I don't know what's wrong with me." She takes a deep, steadying breath. "You need to give her time, Mack."

I nod. "Don't worry. I'm not giving up."

I follow Beth back to the great room where the guys are waiting for us. Cooper is now seated on a sofa beside Sam, his hand massaging the back of Sam's neck. Neither one of them looks happy at the moment.

Shane is still on his feet, exactly where I last saw him, likely waiting for his wife to return. When he sees the bleak expression on her face, he opens his arms to her, and she walks into his embrace. His arms come around her, and he holds her tightly against him.

Shane eyes me over the top of his wife's head. "Let's talk in my office," he says quietly, tipping his head in that direction. "Go ahead. I'll join you in a few minutes."

As I turn away, I catch a glimpse of Cooper rising from the sofa to join Beth and Shane. He puts a comforting arm around Beth's shoulders and draws her away from her husband. "How about a cup of hot tea or some decaf coffee?" he says. "Come with me to the kitchen, and I'll make you something."

19

Mack

The door to Shane's home office is ajar, so I push it open and walk inside, flipping on the light switch. The focal point of the room is a dark wood desk, a black leather office chair behind it. There are two chairs positioned in front of the desk, and I take a seat in one of them.

I grip the armrests, flexing my fingers, testing the leather. My heart is still racing after getting my first good look at Erin. *God, that poor girl*. It's all I can do just to keep my composure. I want to scream. I want to hit something! What I really want to do is get my hands on her assailant. I'll show him the meaning of the word *pain*.

My first meeting with Erin didn't turn out the way I'd wanted it to, but at least I got to see her. That's definitely a win. And I'm not going to stop trying. If she'd just let me in, let me comfort her, I know I can be what she needs. *Jesus, I'd do anything for her.*

Sitting here alone is giving me way too much time to think. I don't know what's on Shane's mind, why he wants to talk to me, but I'm sure as hell not going to let him give me a hard time about seeing Erin. He might be my boss, but I'll gladly draw the line if he thinks he's going to interfere in my personal life. My relationship with Erin is my business, and no one else's. He can threaten me all he wants, but I don't give a shit.

The two framed photographs sitting on his desk catch my eye. One of them is a wedding photo of Shane and Beth, taken at their estate in Kenilworth. They make a fine couple dressed in their wedding clothes. They're facing each other, holding hands, and the love they feel for each other is palpable. The second photo is an intimate shot of Beth and Luke snuggling together in bed, Beth lying on her side as she gazes down lovingly at her infant son. Shane must have taken that one.

I hear footsteps in the hallway, and a moment later Shane walks into the room and closes the door behind him. Instead of taking the chair behind the desk, as I expected him to, he surprises me by pulling out the guest chair next to mine and turning it to face me.

He sits down and props his hands on his knees, leaning forward. Looking me right in the eye, without hesitation, he says,

"Mack, I owe you an apology."

His words take me by surprise. I was expecting a lecture or a veiled threat, not an apology. "*For what,* exactly?"

He leans back in his chair and runs his fingers through his hair, a familiar habit when he's deep in thought or upset. He sighs heavily. "You name it, I'm sorry for it. I'm sorry that Erin was assaulted. I'm sorry she's hurt. I'm sorry she's pushing you away. I know how difficult this must be for you." He brushes his hand over his jaw. "I'm sorry for all the hard times I've given you about Erin. I was wrong. As my wife has informed me—repeatedly—I should have minded my own damn business. And she's right. I know you never would have done anything intentionally to hurt Erin."

His admission comes as a complete surprise, and I acknowledge it with a nod.

He frowns. "I realize it's hardly any help to you now. Look, man, I wish you the best where Erin's concerned. I hope you two can eventually work things out. Just don't give up on her. She's hurting, and she's saying things she doesn't truly mean. Give her time."

"Thanks. I appreciate your support." That much is true. "So, what's the plan?" I say, quickly switching gears. If Shane's not going to stand in my way, then I need to leverage his assistance. "She's going to stay here for the time being?"

He nods. "Yes. She is welcome to stay with us for as long as she likes. If she eventually decides she wants her own place, I'll offer her an apartment here in the building."

In the same building where I live. "Good. What about her job?"

"She's on paid leave from the bookstore for as long as necessary. She doesn't need to worry about her job."

"And what about my job?"

He readily shakes his head, as if he's already given this some thought. "Don't worry about the bookstore. I already have someone filling in for you until this is resolved. Beth's not going to leave Erin alone, so neither of the girls will be going to Clancy's anytime soon, at least not until the suspect is apprehended. If there's even the slightest chance he's coming after Erin, I won't take any chances with her safety, or with Beth's. Sam will be here, too, for added security until the perp is caught. You're free to investigate Erin's case and to come here to see her whenever you like, as long as it's okay with her."

"Thank you."

"Don't give up on her, Mack. She needs you now, more than ever. Please don't let one tragedy become two."

I stand, anxious to get on with my investigation. If I can't help Erin here today, then I'll help her by catching the monster who hurt her. "Don't worry—I'm not giving up."

* * *

After saying goodbye to Beth and Cooper, I let myself out of the penthouse and head down to my own apartment. My mind is racing, bombarding me with mental images I don't want in my head! I keep picturing *how* Erin got those cuts and bruises. I keep seeing her lying vulnerable and helpless while some monster does unthinkable things to her.

I manage to keep it together long enough to unlock my apartment door and step inside. I slam the door behind me and lock it. I feel sick. I feel like screaming. That bastard touched her! He hurt her! He took something from her that he had no fucking right to take!

I grab the closest thing—a glass lamp sitting on the foyer table—and throw it across the room, watching the glass base shatter on impact with the wall, the pieces falling to the floor. I need to *hit* something. I need a physical outlet for the rage boiling up inside me. If I had my hands on her attacker right now, I'd gleefully rip him apart and bathe in his blood.

Blindly, I head down the hallway to the spare bedroom, which serves as my work-out room. After tugging off my boots and tossing my shirt, I pull on a pair of boxing gloves and use my teeth to secure the Velcro straps.

Beating the shit out of the heavy, weighted punching bag is the best I can hope for right now. I slam my fists into it mercilessly, wishing it was her attacker's body. Blow after blow sends the bag reeling on its chain, flying wildly as I attempt to release pent-up aggression. But it's nowhere near enough. I don't think anything can mute this raging anger festering inside me.

My knuckles are already raw and aching, but I continue to slam my fists into the bag, over and over, hoping to block out the images flashing through my mind. Some nameless bastard touching Erin. *Hurting her.* He had no fucking right!

I throw my head back and roar until my voice is raw. Then the dam breaks, ragged sobs tearing out of me, and I collapse, dropping to my knees on the hardwood floor. As tears stream down my face, I yell as loud as I can, as if she can hear me two floors away. "I'm sorry! I'm so fucking sorry!"

* * *

After my meltdown, I take another shower, scrubbing my skin raw in hopes of washing away my self-loathing. But it doesn't help. I don't think anything can help me right now.

As I'm pulling on clean clothes, my phone chimes with an incoming message. I check the screen. It's Dominic.

Dominic: I've got something. When can we meet?

Me: How about now? What's your location?

Dominic: Wakefield Hotel, main lobby. You can't miss me.

Me: On my way.

It's a short drive back to the hotel. I park out front and jog up to the front entrance, immediately spotting Dominic as soon as I walk through the revolving glass doors. He's leaning against a wall, his arms crossed over his chest. Dominic's hard to miss. He stands out in any crowd, and it's not just because of his height. Dressed in a black leather jacket and black jeans, his exposed skin covered in black ink, he's intimidating as hell.

"What do you have?" I ask him.

Dominic motions toward the entrance to the bar. "I talked to the bartender who served our suspect drinks on New Year's Eve—Terri. She knows someone who knows our suspect. Come on."

He pushes away from the wall and stalks across the lobby. I follow him into the bar, where we find the brunette wiping down the counter.

Dominic steps up to the bar and motions me closer. "This is Terri," he says. Then to the woman behind the bar, he says, "Tell my friend what you told me."

Terri scans the room, her gaze darting from one end of the bar to the other. She glances at Dominic, then at me, and shrugs. "Like I told your friend... I've seen him here before, but I don't know him. Not personally." She speaks in a quiet, husky voice. "I mean, I've served him drinks before, but we're not friendly." Then she makes eye contact with Dominic. "I told you, I don't know anything more than that. And no, I don't know his name."

I lean forward, propping my elbow on the bar, and lower the volume of my voice to match hers. I try not to take my anger out on this woman. Still, my voice is terse, tight, and my throat is raw from my earlier outburst. "This guy drugged and viciously assaulted a young woman on New Year's Eve, right here in this hotel. He met her in this bar, spiked her drink, then took her upstairs and fucking tortured her." I tap my finger to my cheek, right where Erin's worst facial laceration is located. "He cut her face," I grit out, tracing the path of the scar with my fingertip. "*Please*, help us identify him."

Her gaze widens as it bounces between me and Dominic. "But I don't know this guy."

"You told me you've seen him in here before," Dominic repeats. "You recognize him."

She nods, wiping at an invisible spot on the counter. "Yeah."

"Have you seen him talking to anyone on a friendly basis? Maybe to someone who works here? Or to a regular customer perhaps? Anyone we can follow up with?"

She shrugs. "I've seen him talking to Paul a few times. They're kind of chummy."

"Who's Paul?" I say.

She nods back toward the kitchen. "He's a busboy."

"Is he here now?"

"No. He comes in around four."

I nod. "Thanks. We'll check back then."

On our way back through the lobby, we spot Tyler Jamison standing at the check-in counter, deep in conversation with the hotel manager. Mrs. Abney frowns as Tyler speaks. Then she nods.

Dominic glances once at Jamison and keeps going.

"Do you know Tyler Jamison?" I ask him as he heads for the exit.

Dominic shrugs. "We've had our share of run-ins."

I laugh. "I take it they didn't go well."

"Nah. He's an uptight control freak, wound way too tight for my liking. We always seem to rub each other the wrong way. Why? Do you know him?"

"Yeah. He's Beth McIntyre's brother."

Dominic's brows lift. "You're shitting me. So, that makes him

Shane's brother-in-law." He chuckles.

"They've had their share of run-ins, too. But it's Tyler who introduced Shane to Beth in the first place. I think Tyler has finally resigned himself to the fact there's a man in his sister's life."

Dominic nods to the exit. "Let's go. Let's find this asshole before the cops do."

20

Mack

It won't be long before the busboy shows up for work, so we head across the street to a sub shop to grab a bite while we wait. Loaded up with sandwiches and a couple of beers, we grab a window table and kill time eating as we watch the hotel entrance.

Dominic takes a swig of his beer. "If this busboy gives us enough info that we can locate the suspect, then what? Do we go after him ourselves, or tell Tyler? It's your call."

I shrug as I set my beer on the table. "I guess we *should* inform Tyler. That would be the appropriate thing to do."

Dominic grins. "Yeah, but is that what we're really going to do? This is your show, pal. I'm just the hired help."

I take a bite of my sandwich and chew while I ponder my options. I want to get my hands on this motherfucker myself. I don't want him arrested and standing trial. But legally, that could be problematic. It won't do Erin one lick of good for me to end up in prison for homicide. "I can't do what I really want to do," I say, reaching for my beer.

"No, you can't. But that doesn't mean you can't get your hands on this guy before Jamison does. If we can get a name and an address, we can pay him a visit, hopefully before the cops do."

I nod. "I just need five minutes with this guy."

Dominic doesn't argue. He knows the score. "How's she doing?" he says. He knows I saw Erin earlier this afternoon.

"She has a hard road ahead of her. It won't be easy, but she's strong. Right now she doesn't think she is, but I know better. She'll get through this."

He checks his watch, then finishes off the last of his food. "It's four o'clock. Let's go see if we can make her journey a little easier."

At a quarter after four, we return to the hotel bar. Terri's serving drinks to a couple seated at the bar. The evening is getting under way and the place is starting to fill up with customers looking for a hot meal and alcohol.

Terri spots us standing near the entrance and waves us over. "That's him," she says, pointing at a teenager bussing a table. "Paul. I've seen him talking to the guy you're looking for on a few occasions."

The busboy is tall, gangly, with red hair and freckles, dressed in black trousers and a white T-shirt. He's busy clearing off a table, stacking plates and glasses in a gray plastic tub.

Terri busies herself putting a couple bottles of liquor on the shelves behind her. "I'd appreciate it if you fellas leave me out of it."

"Sure thing." Dominic pulls a folded bill out of his shirt pocket and leaves it on the bar. "Thanks for your help."

We approach Paul, and immediately the kid glances warily at us, his gaze going first to Dominic, then to me. I know the two of us present a pretty intimidating picture. The kid swallows hard. "What do you guys want?"

"Relax," Dominic says. "We just want to ask you a few questions."

The kid resumes clearing off the table. "Make it quick. I have work to do."

Dominic pulls the picture of the perp out of his pocket and unfolds it, showing Paul. "Do you recognize this guy?"

Paul leans across the table to look at the picture. His eyes widen for a fraction of a second before he recovers. "No."

"That's not what we were told," I say. "Look again. Are you sure?"

Once he's collected the last utensil from the table, the kid proceeds to wipe the surface down with a damp rag. He shrugs as he tosses the rag over his shoulder. "I might have talked to him a few times. We're not friends or anything."

"Do you know his name?" I say.

The kid shrugs. "Just his first name."

"Which is?"

"Kurt."

"And how do you know Kurt?"

"What do you want with him, anyway?" The kid sounds more curious than defensive.

Dominic looms closer, his expression dark and menacing. "He's a suspect in a sexual assault case."

Paul's eyes widen. "Are you shitting me, man?"

"No," Dominic says. "He almost killed a girl two nights ago, here in this hotel."

"Shit." The kid's cheeks flush. "Like I said, I barely know him. We've just talked a few times here at the bar. His name is Kurt. That's all I know. I swear."

"How do we find him?" I say.

Paul shakes his head. "I dunno—no, wait! He works at Cedric's, in the kitchen. He bitches about that place all the time. That's all I know, honest."

Dominic pulls some cash from his pocket and tosses it onto the table. "Thanks."

The busboy glances around nervously to see if anyone is watching him as he pockets the cash. Then he picks up the tub and hustles back to the kitchen.

"Do you know this place?" I ask Dominic. "Cedric's?"

He nods. "Yeah. It's a hole-in-the-wall tavern across town. Let's go see if we can dig up our rat."

Dominic leaves his bike parked at the hotel and rides with me in my truck to Cedric's. Our path takes us to a south suburb, into a sketchy part of town. I park on the street across from the tavern, and we head down a littered alley on foot to the rear of the building.

We locate the back door of the tavern, and Dominic tries the knob on the exterior steel back door. "It's unlocked," he says. "One of us should go in and see if he's in there."

"I'll go," I say. "I won't stand out quite as bad as you will."

I head for the closest dumpster and pull out an empty produce box and toss it onto my shoulder. I figure the box will give me cover for about ten seconds—just long enough to scan the kitchen for Kurt—before someone realizes I shouldn't be in there and sounds an alarm.

"Good luck," Dominic says, slapping me on the back as he opens the door for me.

As I walk into the kitchen, I'm hit immediately with a wave of hot, humid air—from the dishwashers, no doubt—and the heavy aroma of fried foods. There are close to a dozen people crammed into this small kitchen, all busy cooking, plating food, or washing dishes. But a quick scan tells me our suspect isn't one of them.

I set the produce box down on a counter and, just as I'm about to walk out, the guy loading the big commercial dishwasher calls to me. "Hey, buddy, can I help you?"

I take a chance. "Yeah. I'm looking for Kurt."

The guy shakes his head. "He's been out sick all week. Got the flu or something."

"Do you know how I can reach him?"

"Far as I know, he's at home."

"Mind giving me his address?"

The guy eyes me skeptically for a moment. Then he shrugs. "Sure. One-twenty Miller Lane. I've been there a few times to play poker."

"Thanks," I say, and then I walk out the back door.

Dominic's waiting for me in the alley. "Any luck?"

"I have an address."

"Then what are we waiting for?" Dominic says, heading for the street.

Just as I'm about to pull away from the curb, a black sedan pulls up in front of Cedric's and parks in a no-parking zone.

"That's Jamison," I say, nodding in the direction of the detective as he gets out of his vehicle and walks inside the tavern.

"Then we don't have much time." Dominic points down the street. "Drive. If he knows the identity of the suspect, then he has an arrest warrant in his pocket. I figure we have a fifteen-minute head start on him, so whatever you're going to do, you need to do it quick."

* * *

Kurt's apartment is a ten-minute drive through an increasingly rough neighborhood. We quickly find ourselves in a run-down part of town where a great deal of the buildings are boarded up and swathed in graffiti. Broken-down cars line the alleyways, and overfilled trash containers spill over into the street.

We park a block from Kurt's residence and walk the rest of the way, pausing outside to observe a decrepit, four-unit cement building with peeling white paint. According to the mail boxes nailed to the exterior of the building, our guy is upstairs in apartment C.

I try the knob on the outer door, but it's locked.

"Here, let me," Dominic says, pulling a small leather billfold out of his inside jacket pocket.

I step back as he withdraws a slender silver pick and has the door open in seconds. "That was fast," I say.

Dominic chuckles. "Just one of my many skills." He opens the door, and I head inside and up the stairs as quickly and quietly as possible.

Dominic's right behind me when I reach the suspect's door.

I knock on the door. We hear movement inside the apartment, and then a male voice calls out from behind the door. "Who's there?"

As Dominic meets my gaze, he pulls back one side of his leather jacket, revealing a Glock strapped to his chest. He rests his palm on the handle and nods. I have my own handgun holstered to my chest.

"Open the door, Kurt," I say in an even voice.

There's a moment of silence behind the door. Then he says, "Who are you?" in a shaky voice.

I'm starting to lose my patience. "I'm your worst nightmare. Now open the damned door!"

When we hear the mad scramble of running feet, Dominic

motions for me to stand back. He slams his bootheel against the door, splintering it. He kicks it a second time and sends it crashing open. I race inside, hoping to prevent Kurt from escaping out a window.

We quickly search the tiny apartment—the kitchen and living room. There's no sign of him. Then we hear the sound of a creaky window being raised coming from a back room.

"Fuck!" I take off down the hallway, throwing caution to the wind. "He's running!"

There are only two rooms back here, a bathroom, which is empty, and another room at the end of the hall. The door is closed and locked, but I kick the flimsy wood panel, busting the lock, and the door slams against the wall.

Kurt is struggling to raise the single window, which appears to be jammed. He stops what he's doing and pivots to face us, his expression frantic. He brandishes a wicked hunting knife. "Stay back or I'll cut you!"

My gaze immediately locks on the scratches on his face and neck—the scratches Erin put there. I feel nothing but disgust. "Cut us, like you cut those poor girls?"

"What girls?" he says, wildly shaking his head. "I never cut any girls."

I quickly survey the room, my eyes lighting on three purses displayed on a dresser. The last one is a rectangular, purple leather satchel with big silver buckles and a long shoulder strap. There's a tiny white kitty charm attached to the strap. It's Erin's purse. I know because I've held it for her dozens of times while she put on her coat. In front of the purses are what look to be small piles of neatly-folded women's undergarments.

I nod to his shrine. "What are those supposed to be? Trophies? Souvenirs?"

He pales as he stares at the evidence of his crimes. Then he glances back at me. "I don't know what you're talking about. I never cut any girls."

Bile rises in my throat, threatening to choke me. "What kind of monster drugs young women and assaults them? Chokes them to death?"

His face contracts into a horrible grimace, and he lunges at me with a hoarse cry, the knife raised high in the air. I rush him, meeting him halfway and blocking his arm. If he thinks I'll cower in the face of an edged weapon, he's sadly mistaken.

I grab his knife hand and twist his arm behind his back. He cries out and drops the knife and it clatters to the floor. I hear the distant sound of police sirens drawing closer. Shit! I'm running out of time.

"Make it quick," Dominic says, having come to the same conclusion I did.

I grab fistfuls of Kurt's T-shirt and slam him against the wall. My hand goes to his throat, and I cut off his air. "You choked those poor girls," I say, gritting my teeth as I grind out the words. "You fucking coward!"

Kurt struggles against my hold, clawing at my hands, his nails digging into my flesh. But I couldn't care less. I squeeze harder, fighting the urge to simply crush his windpipe and end this.

But that would be too easy. I'm not letting him off the hook that quickly.

"Who are you anyway?" he gasps, staring into my eyes. "You're not the cops!"

"No, we're not. I'm the guy who made a promise to keep someone I love safe... from you."

His eyes widen. "Erin? Holy fuck!"

Hearing him say her name unleashes a rage in me that I've been managing to control for nearly two days now. But I give in to the burning heat festering inside me, to the revulsion I've been carrying. I raise my fist and smash it into the center of his face, over and over and over, and I revel in the sound of his cartilage shattering. Blood erupts from his flattened nose, and he sinks to the floor, coughing and choking as he gasps for air.

Shouts coming from the living room signal the arrival of the cops, and presumably Jamison. I don't have much time. I crouch down and slam my fist into Kurt's abdomen, ignoring his frantic pleas for me to stop. All I can see is red. "This is for Erin O'Connor, you fucking bastard!"

Dominic lays a restraining hand on my shoulder. "They're here, Donovan."

A moment later, cops storm the bedroom, Tyler and two uniformed police officers. All three have their guns drawn.

"Freeze!" the two officers yell simultaneously.

"Mack, stand back," Tyler says in a sharp voice.

Ignoring the demand, I reach down and grab Kurt by his shirtfront and haul him to his feet. As he rises, his arm comes up in a wide arc, the discarded knife back in his hand and aimed directly at my back. Shit! I can't believe I made such a rookie mistake.

The blade cuts into my flesh, glancing off my shoulder blade and slicing through skin and tissue. The pain is searing, like someone took a blowtorch to my shoulder. I stagger back, releasing Kurt.

"Drop the knife, now!" someone yells. One of the cops.

Ignoring the order, Kurt grimaces as he raises the knife high in the air, preparing to come at me again. He lunges at me with a mad glint in his eyes. A heartbeat later, the deafening crack of twin gunfire fills the air, blasting our eardrums.

Kurt drops the knife and falls to the floor, two holes blossoming red in his chest. His eyes are wide and fixed—he's dead. Tyler sheathes his weapon and approaches Kurt's body, kicking the fallen knife aside. He crouches over the suspect to evaluate his condition, but I already know the bastard is dead. One glance was all it took.

Despite the excruciating pain I'm feeling—my shoulder's on fucking fire—I smile. The monster who hurt Erin is dead, and I didn't even have to pull the trigger.

* * *

Tyler calls a medical squad for me and the coroner for Kurt. I sit on the bed, my arms wrapped around my torso as I breathe through the pain. It's bad, but I've known worse.

Tyler searches the room, visually examining the display of

women's belongings laid out on the dresser. "Is one of these Erin's?" he asks me, indicating the purses.

"Yeah." I gasp through the pain. "The last one. Purple with silver buckles."

"You're sure."

"Yeah."

Tyler looks over the evidence, careful not to touch anything, while he waits for the crime scene team to arrive.

I grit my teeth and speak through the blinding pain. "Make sure... Erin... gets her stuff back. She loves that purse."

Tyler nods. "I will."

The ambulance arrives and, after assessing my knife wound, they pack me up for a trip to the ER.

I toss my truck keys to Dominic. "Can you see that my truck gets back to my apartment building?"

"Sure thing."

"One of you call Shane," I tell Tyler and Dominic just before the paramedics take me downstairs to the ambulance. "Let him know the perp is dead."

Tyler nods. "I will. Don't worry."

21

Erin

Luke reaches from Sam to me, extending his little arms eagerly. "Mum-mum," he says to me. That's pretty much the only thing Luke can say yet. Shane has been trying to get him to say "da-da," but it's pretty hit or miss right now.

I smile as I pull him into my arms. "Come here, you sweet little peanut."

I'm sitting on the sofa with Sam and the baby while Beth and Cooper do the supper dishes. I offered to help, but Cooper told me to sit down and rest, or else. Sam joined me to keep me company, and we're entertaining the little guy. Shane was in the kitchen helping with clean-up, but he got an urgent phone call and abruptly disappeared.

There's a fire burning in the fireplace and quiet music playing in the background, something bluesy. I try to relax and enjoy the moment and the company of my good friends, but it's hard. I can't shake the feeling that something dreadful is about to happen.

Luke grabs my hair and tries to pull it into his mouth. Sam laughs as he carefully disentangles the baby's fingers from the strands.

A moment later, Shane returns to the kitchen, his expression taut as he speaks in a low voice to Beth and Cooper. Sam notices their hushed conversation, too, and his gaze snaps to attention.

My anxiety skyrockets when Shane heads my way, coming to stand directly in front of me.

I hand Luke back to Sam and gaze up into Shane's controlled expression. "What's wrong?"

"Tyler just called. He's on his way up."

I freeze. I don't have to ask why Beth's brother is coming here. It's clearly not a social visit, not by the way Shane's acting. This has something to do with the incident. It has to.

Beth drops down beside me on the sofa and lays her hand on my leg, offering me silent support. Sam lays his arm across the back of the sofa, not touching me, but making his presence known.

The elevator chimes, and a moment later Detective Jamison walks into the great room, his piercing gaze quickly scanning the space. He heads right for us.

"Hi, Erin," he says. Then he nods to Shane and smiles at his sister, and then acknowledges Sam.

Tyler reaches out to ruffle Luke's hair. "How's my nephew?"

Beth smiles. "He's fine."

"Mum-mum," Luke says, reaching for his uncle.

Tyler picks the baby up and settles him on his hip. When his gaze returns to me, it's filled with compassion. "I have news, Erin."

My heart stutters. Good news? Bad news? Does it really matter? "What?"

"We identified your attacker. Once I got an arrest warrant this afternoon, I went to his apartment to arrest him." Tyler pauses a moment, letting that much sink in.

I can tell there's more, though. He looks a bit tense.

"When we arrived at the suspect's apartment, Mack and Dominic Zaretti were already there. They must have beat us there by minutes."

My heart jumps into my throat. "Mack was there?" The thought of Mack being anywhere near my attacker terrifies me. I grab Beth's hand and squeeze tightly. "Is he okay? Did he get hurt?" I know Mack. There's no way he wouldn't go after this guy.

Tyler frowns as he hands his restless nephew back to his mother. "He's okay, Erin."

But I can tell from the tension in Tyler's body that he's not telling me everything.

"Tell her, Tyler," Shane says, his gaze going from Tyler to me. "All of it. She has a right to know, and she'll find out soon enough."

Tyler sighs. "Mack was slightly injured."

My eyes widen. "Injured? How?"

"He sustained a knife wound to his upper back. He's being treated in the emergency room at Cook County Hospital right now. It's nothing serious, Erin, just some tissue damage."

A knife wound? I shudder at the mention of a *knife*. That monster used a knife on me too. "He was stabbed?"

Sam lowers his arm until it rests across my shoulders and gives me a side hug. "It's okay, Erin. Breathe."

But I can't breathe. I can't even think straight. *Mack's hurt because of me!*

Tyler crouches down in front of me and takes my hands in his. "He's fine, Erin. Don't worry. The last thing Mack wants is for you to worry about him."

"What about the suspect?" Cooper says.

I just now notice that Cooper's standing behind the sofa.

Tyler scrubs a hand over his short beard. Then he meets my gaze head on. "Erin, the man who assaulted you is dead."

"How?" Cooper asks.

"I shot him when he attempted to stab Mack a second time."

"He's dead?" My shaky voice is barely audible. I don't know what I should feel. Relieved? Grateful? Horrified? My throat tightens, and the air around me is suddenly hot and heavy, pressing in on me and smothering me.

"Erin?" Beth hands Luke to Shane. Then she turns to face me, her hands going to my shoulders as she peers into my face. "It's okay, sweetie. Just breathe."

But I can't. My mind is reeling. *Mack's been stabbed. My attacker is dead.* My chest caves in on itself, squeezing my ribs and lungs. My vision starts to darken as the room spins.

"She's going to pass out," Beth says, her voice urgent.

* * *

I'm back to work at Clancy's, and Mack is helping me set up a display of new children's books at the front of the store. It's as if nothing ever happened.

I see movement in the corner of my eye, and as I turn, Kurt appears right in front of me. He stares at me as if he's seeing a ghost. When his gaze latches on to the cut on my cheek, he smiles. Then suddenly, he raises his hand, clutching a wicked knife with a jagged edge.

"No!" Mack cries as he lunges between me and Kurt, blocking a knife thrust with his forearm. Mack reaches inside his jacket for his gun, but he comes up empty-handed.

He turns to face me, an apologetic look on his face. "I'm so sorry, honey."

And then Kurt drives the knife deep into Mack's back. Mack's face contracts into a horrific grimace and he falls at my feet, the knife embedded in the center of his back.

I scream bloody murder.

"Erin! Wake up!"

My eyes snap open, and I struggle to focus on the dark shape looming over my bed. Immediately, I reach out, grasping, trying to claw his face. Strong hands grasp my wrists and hold them still.

"Erin, it's okay! It's just me. Calm down!"

"Sam?" I recognize the voice immediately and stop fighting him, blinking repeatedly as I try to focus my gaze.

He blows out a relieved breath. "Yeah, it's just me, Irish. You're okay."

A light comes on in the hallway, providing some much-needed illumination in my darkened room. Now I can see the red hair, short on the sides, long on the top, and brown eyes filled with concern. His hair, which is usually pulled up into a bun on the top of his head, is hanging loosely to his shoulders. "Sam."

He drops down beside me on the bed. "What happened? We heard you screaming."

We, meaning Sam and Cooper. That's when I notice Cooper standing in the hallway outside my room. He must have been the one who turned on the light. Cooper and Sam share the suite next to mine—they heard me. "I'm sorry I woke you."

"You didn't wake us. It's still pretty early—only ten o'clock. We weren't asleep. Do you want me to get Beth? She told me to get her if you needed anything in the night."

"No, please don't bother her. It was just a bad dream. I'm fine."

Sam looks unconvinced. "Do you want me to stay with you tonight? I can sleep in here with you if you want me to."

I glance toward the door at Cooper, who's dressed in a pair of flannel PJ bottoms, his broad chest bare, his short gray hair tousled. Sam's wearing only a pair of black boxer-briefs, and there are red splotches on his bare chest—whisker burns? His barbell nipple piercing gleams in the light. My face flushes when I realize I must have interrupted something.

I shake my head, not wanting to inconvenience them any more than I already have. "No, thank you. I'll be fine, really."

Sam studies me for a moment. "You sure?"

"Yes."

"All right," he says, and then he leans forward and kisses my forehead. "Goodnight, Irish." He rises from the bed and heads for the door. "Call me if you need anything."

"Sam, wait! Has there been any news about Mack? Do you know if he's home yet?"

Sam shakes his head. "Last I heard, he was still at the hospital being treated. I'll let you know if I hear anything more."

"Thanks."

Sam quietly closes the door behind him, leaving me alone with my racing thoughts. I can't stop shaking. I've been a wreck ever since Tyler told us the news about Mack getting hurt. I fainted when I heard the news, and when I came to, everyone was watching me with such concern and worry.

I excused myself shortly afterward, claiming I was tired and needed sleep. But the truth was I just wanted to be alone.

I can't stop worrying about Mack. He was hurt because of me. He could have been killed. As I lie here in the dark, I feel his absence keenly. I miss him so much. I'd give anything to hear his voice and know for myself that he's all right.

And then there's my attacker. *He's dead.* I don't even know how I feel about that. It doesn't change anything. His death doesn't undo the damage he did to me, to my life. What am I supposed to feel? Relief? Joy? Instead, I'm more focused on Mack and wondering how badly he's injured.

I try to get comfortable, pulling a spare pillow close and wrapping my arms around it just to have something to hold. I wish I could shut off my brain for once, but I can't. I keep thinking of Mack and the pain he must be in.

My throat tightens, and my chest aches. Pressing my face into the spare pillow to muffle the noise, I give way to the pain and let it consume me.

22

Erin

When I open my eyes, sunshine floods my room. According to the clock on my nightstand, it's eight-thirty. I climb gingerly out of bed and shuffle to the bathroom to relieve my bladder and brush my hair and teeth. When I return from the bathroom, Beth and Luke are seated on my bed.

"Good morning," Beth says, smiling brightly as she helps Luke try to stand on wobbly legs.

When Luke spots me, he grins. "Mum-mum."

I take him from her and settle him on my hip. "Hello, you little cutie," I say, nuzzling his nose with my own. Luke never fails to put a smile on my face.

He grabs my hair and pulls.

"Be gentle, Luke," Beth says, jumping up to rescue my hair. Then she looks at me. "I came to see if you wanted to join us for breakfast. Cooper's making his famous homemade Belgium waffles. They're absolutely divine, trust me."

I'm surprised when I feel a pang of hunger at the mention of waffles. I'm imagining melted butter and warm maple syrup. "That sounds really good." As proof of my words, my stomach growls loudly.

Beth grins. "Come join us for breakfast. Don't bother to change. Everyone's still in their PJs." She's wearing pink-and-white flannel shorts and one of Shane's oversized T-shirts, which says I'M THE BIG SPOON.

When we reach the dining room table, Cooper and Sam are carrying in platters of food.

"Hey, kiddo," Cooper says. "I'm glad you feel up to joining us for breakfast."

Sam pulls out a chair for me, and I sit. Beth sits Luke in his highchair and straps him in, then sits beside him and fastens a bib around his neck.

Cooper comes around to my seat holding a platter of food. "How about some waffles?"

"Yes, please."

He places two thick waffles on my plate. "Butter and maple syrup?"

"Yes, thank you." It feels odd to be waited on like this.

A few moments later, he returns from the kitchen and sets a plate of scrambled eggs and bacon in front of me.

"Oh, my," I say, wondering how I'm going to eat all this food.

"What would you like to drink, Erin?" Sam calls from the kitchen. "OJ, water, milk, tea, or coffee?"

"I'd love some hot tea. Do you have peppermint?"

"Coming right up," he says.

I watch Beth as she prepares a bowl of infant cereal for Luke. He's more interested in trying to grab hold of Beth's earrings than he is in eating.

A comforting feeling comes over me, and I realize this is what it's like to have a family. It's been so long since I had my Gram, I'd forgotten. And a big family, like this one, is quite nice. I could get used to this.

When we hear a chime coming from the foyer, Beth turns to watch the door that leads into the apartment. It opens, and Mack walks in. My heart does a freefall at the sight of him. He looks… good. There's no outward sign that he was even injured.

"Hey, Mack!" Sam calls in greeting, waving at Mack to come in. "You're just in time for breakfast. My man is making waffles."

I hear a deep chuckle coming from the kitchen.

"Perfect timing," Mack says as he approaches the table. His gaze zeroes in on me. "Good morning, Erin." He comes around to my side and motions to the empty chair beside mine. "May I?"

I'm both excited and nervous about seeing him. I'm quickly reminded that I'm still in my PJs and haven't showered. I wish the floor would open up and swallow me. "Please sit," I say, watching him closely for any sign of physical discomfort. Good grief, he was recently stabbed! How can he walk around like nothing happened? "How's your shoulder?"

He carefully rotates his shoulder, flinching only slightly. "It's fine. It was just a flesh wound. Nothing serious."

He's dressed in a pair of faded blue jeans and a dark gray T-shirt that hugs his chest and arm muscles. His hair is damp, and I can smell the faint scents of soap and cologne on him.

Before taking his seat, he leans down and kisses my forehead tenderly, like he's done a thousand times before. Only this time it feels different. It feels like *more*. When he smiles at me, my heart skips a beat. "I'm glad to see you up and about again," he says in his low, rumbly voice.

My cheeks heat up, and I'm sure I'm turning all shades of pink.

"Help yourself, Mack," Cooper says as he sets a platter of waffles on the table. "There's plenty."

I feel self-conscious sitting here in my pajamas while Mack is dressed. He's seated to my right, which means he has an unobstructed view of the cut on my cheek. The tiny black stitches look like little train tracks running down my face. But he doesn't seem to notice. He's chatting away with the others as if this is just a typical morning, while I'm a hot mess.

While he and Sam and Beth talk business, I concentrate on eating. Their animated conversation gives me time to observe Mack unnoticed. I watch his long-fingered hands as he butters his waffles and pours on syrup. Since he doesn't have his jacket on and is wearing only a T-shirt, I can see a fair bit of the tattoos snaking down his left arm. My gaze is drawn to the bold, dark images emblazoned on his skin, as well as to the prominent veins running just beneath the skin.

He seems to be functioning just fine, with no outward sign of discomfort. I want to ask him how he's *really* doing, and what exactly happened last night, but not in front of an audience. For some reason, I have a feeling he's putting up a front right now. He was *stabbed*, for goodness's sake! When he catches me studying him, he smiles.

After we've both finished eating, Mack wipes his mouth on a napkin before he leans close and says, "Is there somewhere private where we can talk?"

Immediately my heart jumps into my throat. "In my room."

He rises from the table and collects both his dirty dishes and mine and carries them to the kitchen. When he returns, he says, "Ready?"

No, I'm not ready. But I rise from the table anyway. "Thank you for breakfast, Cooper. It was delicious."

"Anytime, kiddo," he says.

I'm a nervous wreck as we head to my suite. Mack follows behind me, saying nothing. I have no idea what he wants to discuss, and it makes me nervous. He beats me to my door and opens it for me, standing back to let me enter. As he follows me inside, he closes the door behind him.

I sit on my bed and try not to fidget as he paces in front of me.

"I don't know how much Tyler told you last night," he begins.

"Not much. Just that the man who attacked me is dead and that you'd been stabbed. Are you really okay?"

He shrugs. "It's just a flesh wound. He didn't hit anything vital. I figured Tyler wasn't very forthcoming with you. If there's anything you want to know, I'll tell you. You have a right to know."

"To be honest, it wasn't really his fault. I sort of fainted when he told me."

Mack's eyes widen in concern, and I realize no one told him I passed out last night. "I didn't know. Are you okay?"

"Yes. I'm fine."

He studies me for a moment, as if trying to verify if I'm telling him the truth. "I thought you might want to know more about what happened. More about the suspect."

I nod, wanting to know more, but at the same time I'm afraid to hear it.

"We recovered your purse and your undergarments," he says. "The suspect had your belongings, as well as the belongings of the two other women he attacked."

It's horrible that this monster took my stuff. My purse, yes, I can see that. But my bra and panties? That's just creepy. "Will I get my things back?"

"Yes. After they've been logged as evidence. Tyler promised me he'd make sure you get your things back."

"Thanks."

Mack begins pacing again, and I realize there's more he wants to say. "Do you have any questions?"

I nod. "How did you find him?"

He relays the information to me, about how they tracked down someone at the hotel bar who knew the suspect, and how they tracked him to his place of work. Mack and Dominic arrived at the suspect's apartment just minutes ahead of Tyler and the police.

"I wanted to kill him, Erin," Mack admits, looking conflicted as he makes his confession. "I knew I couldn't. It wouldn't do you any good if I ended up in prison. But being in the same room with this asshole made me see red. And when he picked up that knife—I realized there was a good chance it was the same knife he'd used on you—I lost it. I beat his face to a bloody pulp.

"He lunged at me with the knife. I blocked his strike, but he still managed a hit. Both Tyler and one of the uniformed officers present at the scene shot him dead." Mack steps closer. "I wanted him dead, Erin. If the cops hadn't shot him, I swear to God I would have killed him myself. He was not going to leave that room alive."

I shake my head adamantly. "I'm glad he's dead, but I couldn't bear it if something happened to you because of me. I could never live with myself."

He runs his fingers through his hair and blows out a heavy breath. "It doesn't matter now. He's dead, and it wasn't by my hand. It should have been, though."

"Are you really okay?" I ask, standing and walking behind him. I can see the impression of a bandage beneath his form-fitting T-shirt. I raise my hand, but I'm afraid to touch his back. I don't want to hurt him.

"Honestly, Erin, I'm fine."

"I don't ever want you hurt because of me, Mack. Please, promise me."

He turns to face me, gazing down intently into my eyes as a small smile teases the corners of his lips. "I'll do my best."

My nightmare of last night replays in my head, and my eyes burn with the threat of tears. "Last night I dreamed that he stabbed you—that he killed you."

"Not gonna happen," he says as he reaches out with his free hand and cups the back of my head. He steps closer, and we're almost touching. I can feel the heat of his big body sinking into my skin, warming me. I can smell him, the scent of a man, his cologne and deodorant, so different from my own. His eyes are so beautiful, the dark brown irises warm and compelling.

There was a time when being this close to him would have thrilled me. Now, it just makes me anxious. I don't want this anymore! It's not Mack's fault. I just don't want this with *any* man. I could never be with someone, never *touch* someone. Or let him touch me.

I shudder and take a step back, pulling free of his touch.

He drops his hand instantly, looking contrite. "Sorry," he says, and he takes a few steps back, giving me space. "I've been doing a lot of thinking lately."

"Oh," I say blankly, stalling for time as my mind races. I have no idea where he's going with this conversation, and I'm not sure I want to know.

"Yeah." He runs his long fingers through his hair. "I was wrong, thinking that the difference in our ages matters. After what happened to you—after coming so close to losing you—I realize it doesn't matter one bit. Age is just a number, right? How we feel about each other—that's what matters. I'm sorry, Erin. I've been an idiot."

"Mack, don't." I take another step back, and another, putting more distance between us. Immediately, I miss the heat of his body. I miss the scent of his skin. The closeness. But I have to stop him before he goes any further.

His brow furrows, tiny lines forming. "Don't what?"

I raise my hand, as if that will stop where he's going with this conversation. "I don't want that… not anymore."

"You don't want *what*?"

Part of me can't believe I'm saying this to him. There was a time not long ago when I would have jumped at an opportunity to be with him. "I don't want anyone. I don't want a relationship."

His expression softens. "Honey, I know you've been through hell and back. I—"

"Stop!" I turn and walk away. "I mean it. I'm not interested in being with anyone. It has nothing to do with you. I just don't want that anymore. I *can't*."

"Erin—"

"Mack, please! I don't want to talk about it." I can feel my heart rate shooting up, and I'm sure a panic attack is not far off. It hurts so much to say these things to him, to shut him down like this. "I think you should go."

Pain flashes across his face before he can suppress it, and I feel terrible for hurting him. He's gone out of his way for me, risked his own safety—even his life—for me, and here I repay him this way. But it can't be helped. I *know* I can't be with a man physically. I can't ever see wanting that now. Not after what's happened. Not after what's been done to my body. So there's no point in dragging this out. "I'm sorry."

He stares at me for a moment, as if he's struggling to process what I said. His jaw tightens and he looks away, his posture stiff and unyielding. In the meantime, my heart feels like it's collapsing in on itself, sharp, aching pain radiating through me.

"Erin—" He stops abruptly and clenches his jaws.

Clearly, I've hurt him, and knowing that hurts me a thousand times over. "I'm sorry, Mack."

"You have nothing to apologize for, honey." His gaze searches mine. "I care about you," he says, choosing his words carefully. "I don't want to lose you—I don't want to lose what we have. We've been friends for a long time—*good* friends. There's no reason for that to change, is there?"

"No. Our friendship means a lot to me, too. I don't want to lose that." I feel a sudden surge of hope that we haven't lost everything. If we can salvage our friendship, I'll learn to be satisfied with that.

I take a step forward, and then another, and he meets me halfway. He pulls me into his arms, like he's done so many times before, and I'm nearly overwhelmed with relief. I couldn't bear to lose him altogether.

When he kisses the top of my head, I feel a sense of peace and comfort that's been missing from my life these past couple of days. I hated being separated from him.

I wrap my arms around his waist and hug him back, telling myself nothing has changed. We can still make this work. I've lost so much since the attack, but maybe I don't have to lose my best friend too.

When we release each other, I realize I'm in my pajamas and laugh nervously. "I guess I should shower and get dressed," I say, straightening my hair as I step back.

He nods. "I have to get going. I've got some errands to run. Can I stop by again later this evening to check on you? Would that be okay?"

"Sure."

As Mack walks out of my room, I'm engulfed with a crushing sense of loss that leaves me feeling so alone. I have to fight the urge to call him back. But that would be selfish of me, and wholly unfair to him.

Seeing him hurts. It reminds me of what I've lost. I can't ever see myself being intimate with someone. There are too many obstacles in front of me now... the trust factor, my scars.

And the fact that Mack seems to be going out of his way to spend time with me just makes it all the more tragic.

23

Erin

It's not until late-afternoon that I manage to take my first shower since the incident. I leave the lights off in the bathroom so I don't see my own reflection in the mirror. After stepping into the oversized shower, I gently wash with rose-scented soap and hot water. I have to be careful not to get my stitches wet, and careful around the bite marks and the cuts and the bruises, but the rest of me I get as clean as humanly possible.

I splash warm water between my legs, where the tissue is still swollen and tender. Dr. Shaw promised that everything would eventually return to normal. I can only hope she's right.

After turning off the spray, I pat my skin dry and slip on my robe. Then I head through the connecting door that leads to the walk-in closet where all my personal belongings now reside. A courier from McIntyre Security delivered all of my worldly possessions earlier this afternoon.

My clothing now hangs on one rod, barely taking up ten percent of the available space. My precious collection of books is contained in the dozen worn cardboard boxes stacked against the back wall. I've carried these books with me ever since I had to leave the apartment I shared with Gram. I've never had any space to display my books, so they remain in boxes, tucked away for safe keeping. Maybe one day I'll have some bookshelves.

Besides my books and clothes, there wasn't much else to bring from my apartment, just some DVDs, my schoolbooks, and my prized collection of vintage tea cups that I got from Gram.

After hanging up my robe, I glance hesitantly down at my naked body, which is peppered with bruises, cuts, and bite marks. The bruises are beginning to fade, but they're still visible. The cuts are starting to heal. I glance down at my breasts and note the several prominent bite marks. There are some farther down as well, along my pelvic bones and on my inner thighs.

I can't bring myself to count all the evidence of what was done to me. It's far too nauseating to contemplate.

I dress quickly in a pair of clean panties and light-blue flannel PJ bottoms. When my gaze lands on one of my favorite T-shirts—*Waiting for Mr. Darcy*—I pull it off the hanger and slip it on. Sadly I think I've already found my Mr. Darcy, but we won't be having any happy-ever-after ending. Not now.

As I leave the closet, I don't know what to do with myself. I don't feel like reading or watching TV. I don't feel like watching a movie. I end up wandering aimlessly around the spacious suite and wind up parked in front of the huge windows overlooking downtown Chicago.

I sit in an upholstered armchair and stare at the city skyline, amazed at the view from this high up. I can see practically across town, with a perfect view of skyscrapers and apartment buildings. I glance down at the shorter buildings and spot swimming pools and grassy lawns on their roofs. The cars and buses on the streets look like tiny toys as they zip along. Everyone's going about their business, while I sit up here at the top of a gilded castle and contemplate the hopeless turn of my life.

A knock on the door pulls me out of my depressing thoughts. "Come in."

The door opens and Beth walks in with Luke in her arms and a baby book in one hand. She's still in her PJs. "Oh, good, you're dressed. How do you feel?"

Empty. "Okay."

"Would you do me a huge favor and watch Luke while I take a shower?"

"Me?" *Why is she asking me?* I'm sure Sam or Cooper would be happy to watch him.

"Of course you. Luke adores you."

And just to prove her point, Luke reaches for me, stretching his little arms in my direction. "Mum-mum-mum-duh."

It's impossible to resist that precious little face, with those bright blue eyes, just like his daddy's. I draw him into my lap.

Beth hands me a baby book. "Thank you so much! This is his favorite book." Then she heads for the door, calling back, "I'll try not to be too long!"

Luke hands me his soft giraffe rattle, which is wet with drool, and I shake it. He crows with delight at the noise it makes.

I can't resist leaning down and kissing his downy head of hair and breathing in his sweet baby smell. His warm weight is comforting. Settling him more securely on my lap, I open the book to the first page and read to him.

By the time I've read the book to Luke three times, he starts getting restless. I figure he's tired of being confined to my lap and wants to stretch out. I sit him down in the middle of my bed and hand him his rattle, which he immediately starts chewing on.

For a few moments at least, my own problems are forgotten as I entertain a six-month-old who's quite content to climb on me and be tickled.

* * *

When Beth returns, almost an hour later, Luke is asleep on my bed. He's lying between me and a row of pillows I positioned strategically to keep him from rolling off the bed.

"Sorry I took so long," she says, sitting carefully on the bed so as not to wake up her son.

"No problem. We had fun, and then the little guy got tired and dozed off."

Beth reaches out to stroke her son's cheek, and for a moment, she's lost in thought.

"Is something wrong?" I ask her.

She gives me a half-smile. "No, not wrong exactly. At least I don't think so. I'm not sure. It's too early to tell." She clearly looks preoccupied.

"Do you want to talk about it?"

She shrugs. "It might not be anything."

"Or, it might be something? What is it?"

Beth sighs. "Do you remember when I told you Shane and I had unprotected sex at Clancy's when we were stranded during the snowstorm?"

"Yes. In all the excitement, you guys forgot to use a condom."

She purses her lips. "I'm late. I should have started four days ago."

My eyes widen as the implication sinks in. "Do you think you're pregnant?"

"It's possible." She gently cups her breasts. "My breasts are tender, but that could just be because I'm nursing. It's impossible to tell."

"Have you peed on a stick?"

"No. Not yet. I thought I'd give it a little while longer. I might start my period yet."

"Does Shane know you're late?"

She laughs. "Yes, of course he does. Nothing escapes his notice."

"How does he feel about the possibility of you being pregnant again?"

She frowns as her eyes tear up. "He hasn't said much about it, but I can tell he's not happy."

That surprises me. "Why wouldn't he be happy? He adores Luke. And you both want more kids."

"I don't think he's gotten over the trauma of me going into premature labor the last time, especially under such traumatic circumstances. Plus the post-partum depression that followed was hard on all of us."

"How do *you* feel about having another baby so soon?"

She gives me a teary smile. "I'd be okay with it." She reaches for her sleeping son, lifting him carefully off the bed. "I'll put this little guy in his crib." She stands, nodding toward the door. "Do you want to come hang out with me and Sam in the great room? We could watch a movie if you like."

"Thanks, but I'm pretty tired. I think I'll take a nap."

Beth tries not to show she's disappointed. She probably thinks I'm hiding in my room—and she'd be right. "I wish you'd come visit with us."

"Maybe later, okay? I'm really tired."

"Okay." She gives me an encouraging smile. "Later. It's a date."

After they leave, I lie in bed wishing I could fall asleep, but I can't. My mind is racing after my conversation with Mack. For a moment, I indulge in wondering what things might have been like for us under different circumstances. I can't help picturing a baby boy with dark brown hair and dark eyes. But that's never going to happen now.

* * *

Finally, boredom and loneliness send me in search of companionship. I find Beth alone in the great room, curled up in an armchair with a book and a cup of hot tea.

I sit on the sofa adjacent to her chair and tuck my feet beneath me.

She looks up with a smile. "Tyler had your purse and undergarments sent over this afternoon." She points to a box on the coffee table. "It's all there."

As I stare at the plain cardboard box, my heart starts racing. I can feel Beth's gaze on me as she watches me.

"Are you okay?" she says.

I shake my head. I want my things back—that monster had no right to take my belongings. But at the same time, I'm afraid to touch them, knowing that he touched them too.

Beth lays her book down and scoots forward on her seat. "Do you want me to do it?"

I glance at her, feeling tremendous relief. She gets it. "Yes. If you don't mind."

"Of course I don't mind." She walks to the coffee table and lifts the lid off the box and studies the contents. "Everything looks fine."

I move closer and peer inside the box. My purse is there. My bra and panties are folded neatly in a sealed, clear plastic bag. But suddenly the thought of touching something that *he* touched is repulsive. "I only want my purse."

Beth nods as she pulls my purse out of the box and sets it on the coffee table. "Is it okay if I look inside?"

I nod. "Please." I know I'm staring at the thing like it's a poisonous snake that might strike at any second, but I can't help it.

Beth carefully opens my purse wide and peers inside, first just looking, and then gingerly poking around. "I'm sure it's fine," she says. "The police already inspected the contents, and Tyler wouldn't have given it back to you if there was any problem."

I move closer for a look. Everything seems to be where it should be. My wallet is there, my comb, my pen, a pack of gum, a tiny mirror. I close the purse and secure the silver buckles. "I'll look closer later," I say, setting it aside. Then I replace the lid on the box. "I don't want these other items. It's just too skeevy thinking *he* had them. He touched them." I shudder.

Beth nods readily, picking up the box and carrying it away. "I'll get rid of it. Don't worry."

After she returns, empty handed—I don't even ask her what she did with it—she resumes her seat, and I resume mine.

"Where are the guys?" I ask her a little while later.

She slips a bookmark between the pages of her book and closes it. "Shane's still at the office, and the lovebirds are downstairs working out in the fitness room. I think they have cabin fever."

Hearing her refer to Sam and Cooper as lovebirds makes me chuckle. "They've been cooped up lately because of me."

She shrugs. "They're just used to getting far more physical activity. I think they had some excess energy to burn. How about you? Do you feel like getting some exercise? We could go down to the fitness room later and walk on the track. We could start off easy."

The idea of going anywhere seems exhausting. I shake my head. "If you want to go, I'll be happy to stay here and watch Luke." I'm sure I'm hampering everyone's freedom. "Maybe I should think about going back to my apartment. Now that my attacker is dead, I don't have to worry about him coming after me again."

"No!" she says. "Don't go."

"But I can't keep imposing—"

"You're not imposing. I promise, you're not. We love having you here. Besides, you're still recuperating. You're welcome to stay here as long as you like. I love having you here."

I let out a long, slow breath, releasing the air that's been trapped in my lungs for so long. I don't want to leave, and yet I feel like I'm a fifth wheel here. Beth and Shane have each other. Sam and Cooper have each other. I'm the odd one out. And I honestly don't want to go back to my apartment—not after everything that's happened. I guess I don't fit in anywhere.

A mix of emotions wells up in me, and I look away as my eyes fill with tears. My throat tightens, and I'm trying hard not to cry. I'm sick of crying, but no matter how hard I try, the tears keep coming, often without any warning.

Beth shoots up from her chair and joins me on the sofa, putting her arms around me and holding me close.

"I'm sorry," I mutter, wiping my eyes. "I don't know why I'm crying. One minute I'm fine, and then the next I'm falling apart. It just comes out of nowhere."

"It's okay," she says, laying her head against mine. "You don't need to apologize."

The elevator chimes as the doors open. A moment later Sam and Cooper walk through the door, both dressed in shorts and muscle shirts, with towels slung over their shoulders. They're both damp with sweat and breathing hard.

"Hey, Erin!" Sam says, his face lighting up.

Cooper grips the back of Sam's neck and steers him in the direction of their suite. "Pardon us, ladies. We're going to grab a quick shower. Then how about I order in some Chinese food for dinner?"

Beth defers to me. "How does Chinese sound?"

"That sounds wonderful," I say, forcing a smile. I really don't feel like eating, but I don't want to ruin their plans.

* * *

Shane gets home from work just as the food order arrives. The first thing he does is kiss his wife and son. Then he greets me and asks me how I'm doing.

The table is covered with food cartons, sauces, and fortune cookies, bottles of beer and soft drinks and water. Shane sits at one end of the table with Luke in his arms and tries to juggle his food and his son. Beth sits beside him, then Sam, then Cooper. I sit on the other side of the table.

I do my best to appear content as I dish out a small amount of food, but inside I feel numb. The food tastes like paste to me, but

I eat it anyway.

The news that my attacker is dead is certainly reassuring, but it doesn't do anything to fix my reality. The damage to my body and my life has been done, and my attacker's death does nothing to change that.

The reason why Beth and Shane invited me to stay with them is no longer valid, and I really should go. The problem is, I have nowhere else to go. I can't afford a decent apartment downtown on my own, and I don't want to move farther out into the suburbs.

I jump when the elevator chimes, announcing the arrival of a guest.

"That must be Mack," Beth says, turning to watch the door to the foyer. "I invited him to join us for dinner."

Sure enough, when the door opens a moment later, Mack walks in. "Hey, everybody," he says with a wave. He nods to Beth. "Thanks for the invite."

"No problem," she says, and then she winks at me.

Good Lord, is she matchmaking?

"Help yourself," Cooper says, gesturing at the table. "There's plenty. Grab a plate and utensils and dig in."

Mack takes the empty chair beside me and proceeds to fill a plate. He leans close and bumps me playfully with his arm, just like old times. "How are you feeling?"

I force a smile as I reach for my glass. "Fine."

He studies me for a long moment, and I have a feeling he doesn't believe me. He frowns as he watches me pick at my food. Then he meets Beth's gaze from across the table and they share a moment of silent communication. Neither says a word, but they're speaking volumes.

My chest tightens, and my pulse kicks up. It feels like everyone's watching me, half expecting me to fall apart at any moment.

"Excuse me," I say, rising from the table. "I'm sorry, but I'm just not hungry."

24

Mack

It breaks my heart to see her hurting like this. My sweet, vibrant girl is suffering. Not just physically, but emotionally as well. The girl sitting alone across the room is nothing like herself.

Beth meets my gaze, looking just as concerned as I am. The others keep glancing at Erin, who's curled up with a blanket on a sofa staring at the fire burning in the hearth.

When she finishes eating, Beth rises and picks up her dirty dishes. She catches my gaze and nods toward the kitchen, motioning for me to join her there.

I stand and collect my dirty dishes, too, and follow her.

"She's depressed," I say to Beth once we're alone in the kitchen.

Beth nods, frowning. "I think you're right. She's been very emotional all day. She suggested that she should go back to her apartment."

"Oh, hell no!" I lower my voice to a whisper. "She's not going back there."

"I told her it wasn't a good idea, but she thinks she's imposing on us."

I shake my head. "What can we do? What can *I* do?"

"I think she needs to get out. She's been cooped up all week, first at the hospital and now here. I think a change of scenery would do her a lot of good."

"I'm on it," I say, heading out of the kitchen.

I sit next to Erin and gently pat her leg. It's too cold to take her out anywhere, but there is something we can do in this building. "How about coming down to my apartment for a while? Come hang out with me."

Her eyes widen in surprise. "Really?"

"Sure. We could watch a movie. We could do whatever you want, or do nothing at all. It's totally up to you."

"I've never been to your apartment," she says, a hint of a smile ghosting her lips.

I'm so relieved so see her smiling. I have to resist the urge to brush back her hair. Even though the bruises around her eyes have faded a bit, and the redness of the cut on her cheek has decreased, I'm afraid I'll hurt her if I touch her. "What do you say?

I've got a fresh carton of mint chocolate chip ice cream in my freezer."

That definitely gets her attention. It's her favorite flavor, which is why I bought it.

She glances down at her flannel bottoms and T-shirt. "I'm hardly dressed to go anywhere."

I stand and hold out my hand. "You're dressed just fine. It's only my apartment, not the philharmonic. Come with me, just for a little while. Please."

She glances at Beth, who's now seated on the other sofa across from her, with Luke in her lap. Beth gives her an encouraging smile. "Go ahead. It'll be good for you to get out for a little while. It's just downstairs. If you get tired, Mack can bring you back."

Erin's eyes light up with a tiny frisson of excitement. "Okay. Just let me freshen up a bit." She hops up from the sofa and heads to her room.

Beth smiles at me. "Thank you, Mack. That's the first time I've seen her smile in days."

When Erin returns, I open the foyer door and follow her to the elevator. It's a quick trip down two floors to my apartment. I unlock the door and motion for Erin to enter, and she steps hesitantly into my small living room.

"It's not much," I tell her. "Living room, kitchen, two bedrooms and a bathroom. Would you like a tour?"

She nods, so I show her the small kitchen with a dining table that seats two and a small balcony.

I show her the spare bedroom I turned into a work-out room.

It's not fancy, but I do have a treadmill, free weights, and a punching bag suspended from the ceiling by a chain.

The room next to it is a bathroom. And the last room, on the left, is my bedroom.

"That's it," I say. "It's not much, but it's plenty of space for a bachelor."

She follows me back to the living room.

"Would you like to sit down?" I say, indicating the sofa.

"Thanks." She sits down and kicks off her sneakers so she can tuck her feet beneath her.

She looks so small sitting there, and so sad. I sit, too, turning to face her. "Erin, please talk to me. Tell me what you're feeling."

As her eyes fill with tears, she covers her face with her hands. "I feel so lost."

"You're not lost, honey," I tell her, pulling her into my arms. "I'll never let that happen."

I hold her while she cries, her tears dampening the front of my shirt. As her slight body shakes, I rub her back gently, trying not to lose it myself. She's breaking my heart. I tamp down a fresh wave of anger and resentment at the fucking asshole who did this to her. The attack was over in a matter of hours, but her pain and suffering will last far longer.

When the tears end, I move back so I can see her face. "Now, talk to me." I can't resist tapping the top of her head. "Tell me what's going on in here."

She glances up at me, looking both fragile and self-conscious. "Everything's wrong. I'm scared, and I feel so alone. I can't stay with Beth indefinitely, and I don't want to go back to my apartment."

"Why can't you stay with Beth? She loves having you there."

"Because she spends so much of her time worrying about me. She has her own family to take care of. And I don't want to go back to my apartment. I was never really happy there to begin with, and after the incident, I just don't want to face those girls again."

I clench my jaws to keep myself from telling her what I think about her roommates. Instead, all I say is, "I don't want you going back to that apartment either."

"Then I have nowhere else to go. I signed a year's lease at the other place, so I'll have to keep paying my share. That means I can't afford to lease anything else."

Now is as good a time as any to tell her about the lease. "Actually, you don't have to worry about that lease payment. I paid off your portion. You're free and clear."

"What?" She looks shocked. "Mack, there were six months left on that lease. That's several thousand dollars. I can't let you do that."

"I was more than happy to do it. I didn't want you going back there anyway. Your roommates never should have left you alone at that hotel."

"Thank you. That was very generous of you. I promise to pay you back as quickly as I can."

"You don't need to repay me. I was happy to do it."

"Of course I'll repay you. I can't accept a gift like that. It's too much."

"You can stay in this building rent free. Shane has set aside an apartment for you right here, if you want it."

She looks blown away at the prospect. But then she shakes her head. "I think I'd be too afraid to live alone right now. After what happened, I just don't feel safe. And I have so many nightmares. I wake up every night in a panic, feeling terrified, and I don't know why. Sometimes I feel like I'm suffocating."

Her fingers go to her throat, gently skimming her neck, which still bears a ring of fading bruises. That sick motherfucker tried to strangle her. That's how the other two victims died. But I don't think Erin knows this. I try to keep my expression neutral, for her sake. I don't want to upset her.

"I know there are bruises around my throat. I've seen them. When I dream that I can't breathe, is it really just a nightmare, or is it something more?"

She looks right at me, clearly wanting an answer. An answer I don't want to give her.

Her eyes narrow as she watches me, way too perceptive. "Mack? Do you know something?"

I open my mouth to speak, but nothing comes out. God, I don't want to tell her. She has enough to worry about without learning that her assailant intended to kill her... and failed. I shake my head.

She frowns. "Mack, if you know something, tell me!"

"Honey—"

"You said you want to help me. Then help me by being honest

with me. I have a right to know."

Of course she's right. I just hate for her to know this. I want to protect her, not add to her nightmares.

"Mack, please."

Shit. "Honey, he choked you, just like he choked the others."

Her eyes widen and what little color she has drains from her face. "There were others?"

I nod. "Yes, two. The monster who hurt you attacked two other young women before you."

"He choked them? Are they okay?"

Shit! I really don't want to go down this path with her. Kurt's dead. It's a moot point now.

"Mack?"

I shake my head. "No, honey, they're not okay."

I can see the wheels turning as she digests that bit of information. "They're... dead?"

"Yes."

"He killed them?"

I nod, hating that she knows this. "Erin." I reach for her hand, which is ice cold. "You don't have to worry. He's gone. He'll never hurt you again."

"But he wanted to? He meant to kill me?"

"Yes."

"Why? Why would anyone want to kill someone else? Someone they don't even know? It's like a nightmare I can't wake up from."

I pull her into my lap. "It's okay," I murmur, pressing my lips against her temple. "I promise you, everything's going to be okay."

"You can't know that for sure," she says, her voice muffled against my chest.

I cup her cheeks and gaze down into her eyes. "Yes, I can. I know you're hurting now, and you're scared, but this will pass in time. You'll get your life back, and you'll feel safe again."

"I don't think I'll ever feel safe."

There's so much pain and uncertainty on her face, it kills me. So I draw her back into my arms, and she melts into me, her slight weight warm against my chest. Eventually, she relaxes with a sigh, and I'm just grateful she's finally letting me comfort her.

I settle back on the sofa cushions, adjusting her in my arms so she can rest more comfortably. "I swear I'll keep you safe."

"You can't promise that," she says, pulling away and leaning against the back of the sofa. She wipes her eyes. "You're not with me all the time."

But I sure as hell want to be. "I *will* keep you safe. Now, how about some ice cream? And would you like to watch a movie?" I'll suggest anything to keep her here longer. "Lady's choice."

She smiles. "I'd love some ice cream. And a movie sounds great."

25

Erin

I follow Mack into his small kitchen in search of ice cream.

"Here," he says, handing me two bowls he pulls out of the cupboard. Then he retrieves a brand-new carton of ice cream from the freezer. "How many scoops?"

I smile. "Two." I don't know how he does it, but when I'm with him, I'm happy.

He puts two scoops into one bowl, and four into the other. "Do you want any toppings? I've got hot fudge, whipped cream, and chocolate sprinkles."

"None for me, thanks. But I am impressed with your dessert

stash."

He grabs two spoons for us, hands me one, and we head back to the living room. He picks up the remote control for the TV. "Okay, what are we watching? You get to pick first."

"Hmm." I try to think of something we both might enjoy. "How about *Ready Player One*?" It's got action and excitement, as well as a bit of romance in it. There's something for both of us.

"Coming right up." He pulls up the movie through a streaming service, then turns down the lights in the room.

He's a good sport, putting on the movie I picked. I'm sure he would have chosen something quite different, something with fast cars or lots of explosions, but he doesn't complain. We sit side-by-side, both of us leaning back against the sofa cushions, our stockinged feet propped on the coffee table, bowls of ice cream on our laps.

"Are you cold?" he says.

A glance out the big picture window behind the sofa reminds me that it's early January. The night sky is filled with fat white snowflakes blowing hard against the glass panes. And eating ice cream doesn't help. "Maybe a little."

He grabs a soft fleece blanket off the back of the sofa and drapes it across my lap, carefully tucking it around me. "There you go."

At first, I felt self-conscious sitting with him like this. I can't believe I'm sitting here with Mack, in his apartment, eating ice cream, and watching a movie. There was a time not long ago when I would have given anything to be here with him like this...

just the two of us. *Alone.* Now, it's bittersweet. I'm here with him, sitting side-by-side, and yet in some ways we've never been so far apart.

This isn't a date, of course. We're just two friends hanging out. I have to keep reminding myself of that, in case I start to lose sight of reality.

We're about half an hour into the movie, and he's actually paying attention. He's certainly laughing in all the right places.

"What do you think?" I ask him.

"About the movie? I like it."

"Were you expecting me to pick something really mushy?"

He grins. "Well, actually, yes. I expected you to pick a romantic comedy, something like that."

"I thought this would be a good compromise."

He nods, then sticks a spoonful of ice cream in his mouth. "It's not bad."

I laugh. "The movie or the ice cream?"

"Both."

By nine o'clock, halfway through the movie, my body is starting to give out. My belly is filled with ice cream, and my lids are growing heavier and heavier with each passing minute. I just don't have much stamina lately. I try to stay alert, but I repeatedly catch myself dozing off.

* * *

"Erin? Honey?"

When I open my eyes, I find myself leaning against Mack, toasty warm beneath the soft blanket. I jerk back into an upright position. The TV has gone dark, and our empty ice cream bowls are sitting on the coffee table. "I'm sorry. I must have dozed off."

"It's okay. You need the rest."

"What time is it?"

"Almost ten."

"I get tired so easily lately. I'm sorry for passing out on you. Some company I am."

He lays his hand on my leg. "Hey, you don't have to do anything to impress me, Erin. I enjoy your company."

I'm so cozy right now I don't want to move. Even though I conked out on him, at this moment I feel a sense of peace that has eluded me for days. It's been pleasant just sitting here with him all evening, just the two of us, and I am loathe to leave him.

He lays his arm across my shoulders. "You're tired. Do you want me to walk you back upstairs?"

I shake my head. I feel safe here, hidden away from the world in his apartment. For the first time since the incident, all the noise in my head has quieted, and I don't feel like I'm on the verge of having another panic attack. I blurt out the truth. "I don't want to leave."

When he doesn't respond, I mentally kick myself, wishing I'd kept my mouth shut.

But then he surprises me. "You don't have to leave if you don't want to."

When I glance up at him, I lose myself in his beautiful dark eyes. He watches me closely, his expression giving away nothing of what he's feeling.

"But it's getting late," I say, as reality intrudes. "Beth will start to worry if I'm not back soon. And I don't want her waiting up for me."

"I'll tell her," he says.

"Tell her what?"

"That you're staying with me tonight," he says easily, as if we do this all the time. "I'm serious. You're welcome to stay here tonight. I'll make up my bed for you, and I'll sleep out here on the sofa."

"You'd let me do that?"

"Of course I would. I'd love for you to stay. I'll even make you breakfast in the morning."

My pulse quickens, but this time it's not out of fear, but rather anticipation. "Are you sure?"

He tightens his hold on me. "Very sure. It will give us more time together. I haven't seen much of you in the past few days."

"I don't have my toothbrush."

He shrugs. "I have a whole package of spares. You don't need anything else. You can sleep in one of my T-shirts."

"Okay, I'll do it."

Mack picks up his phone, types out a text message, and hits send. "There. It's done. I told Beth you're staying here tonight."

A moment later, my phone buzzes with an incoming message. I look at the screen, not surprised to see it's from Beth.

Beth: You're staying the night? Are you sure?

Me: Yes :)

Beth: Okay... sleep well

"I'll make up your bed," Mack says, rising from the sofa. "You just relax."

But I end up following him down the hallway to his bedroom. As I reach the open door of his room, he's just coming out of a large closet holding a stack of sheets, a pillow, and a gray T-shirt.

He hands me the T-shirt. "Here. You can sleep in this. It'll be a bit big on you, but at least you'll be comfortable."

I watch as he quickly strips the king-sized bed and makes it up again with clean sheets.

"There you go," he says, indicating the bed. "I'll make up the sofa for myself. The toothbrushes are in the bathroom cupboard. Help yourself. If you need anything else, let me know."

I lock myself in the bathroom and change into his T-shirt, leaving on my panties and bra. I then claim a purple toothbrush and brush my teeth.

When I come out of the bathroom, the hallway is empty, and the apartment is quiet. I return to the bedroom and come up short when I see him sitting on the bed wearing a pair of black flannel pajama bottoms and a white tank top. His thick, dark hair is slightly tousled, as if he's been running his fingers through it. I stand in the doorway, watching him. Good lord, he's so handsome it hurts.

Mack smiles as he stands and pulls the covers back. "Hop in." He points to a folded blanket at the foot of the bed. "There's an extra blanket in case you get cold in the night."

"Thank you." I climb into bed and pull the covers up to my chin.

Mack turns off the light and pauses at the door. "Do you need anything else?"

"No—wait!" Suddenly I feel overwhelmed again. My emotions are on a roller coaster, and I never know when they're going to abruptly change course. I've never felt so alone in the world as I do right now. I basically have no home, and I just want to feel like I belong somewhere, at least for a little while. I blink back tears, hoping he can't see them in the dark.

"What is it, Erin?"

When I don't answer, he comes back into the room and points at the bed. "Mind if I sit?"

"Sure." I scoot over to make room for him.

He sits down and slowly reaches out to brush my hair back from my cheek, revealing the cut beneath. "You don't have to hide this, you know," he says of the scar. "You survived, Erin. Don't ever be ashamed of any of your scars. They're symbols of your courage, of your bravery, in the face of a horrible crime."

"I'm an emotional wreck. There's nothing brave about me."

"That's not true." He sighs. "There were deep scratches all over the suspect's face and neck. That means you fought back, hard."

My eyes widen in shock. "I did? But I don't remember anything."

"You might not remember, but you did it. I saw the fresh scratches on his face when he ran from the hotel room. There was blood under your nails. You fought him, Erin. You're braver than you realize."

His gentle words bring forth a flood of anguish, and I can't hold the pain in any longer. "I hate feeling this way!" Then the ugly tears come. Ashamed of my own weakness, I press my face into the pillow to muffle the sound.

The mattress dips heavily, and then a moment later he's lying beside me, drawing me into his strong arms. The heat and masculine scent of his body envelop me, and it comforts me. "I'm so sorry, honey." His big hand cups the back of my head, and he holds me to his chest. "Everything's going to be okay, I promise you. It may not feel like it right now, but it will. You just need time."

But he can't know that. He's Superman. He's not afraid of anything, but I am. I'm terrified. I'm afraid of what I've lost. I'm afraid I'll never be able to trust anyone ever again. I'm afraid of people looking at me and seeing my scars and wondering what happened to me. "I'm afraid I'll never get past this."

"You will."

Mack rolls me to my side so that I'm facing away from him and he's lying behind me. He wraps his arm around me and pulls me close, surrounding me with his big body. His lips press against the back of my head. "I won't let anyone hurt you ever again, I swear."

"You can't make a promise like that." My voice breaks as I try to stem the tears. "You can't protect me every minute of my life."

He tightens his hold on me, and I melt into him. I know right now, right here, I'm safe. For some reason I trust him, when I don't think I could trust any other man.

My tears gradually subside, and I feel wrecked. I'm exhausted and I just want to sleep forever. He's quiet for a while, and I think he's probably wondering if I'm done.

"I'm sorry," I say.

"You have nothing to be sorry for." He kisses the back of my head, then loosens his hold on me.

"Wait!" I grab his arm. "Don't go." I know I'm not being fair to him, that I'm being selfish, but I can't stop myself. "Will you stay with me for a little while?"

"Erin."

I can tell from the tone of his voice that he thinks this is a bad idea. But I'm not above begging. "Please? Just this once? I don't want to be alone."

He sighs heavily as if he's agreeing to something against his better judgement. "All right. For a little while."

After he gets himself ready for bed, he climbs in beside me, dressed in flannel pajama bottoms and a tank top. I turn on my side, facing away from him, and scoot back against his body, reaching for his arm and pulling it across my waist. He naturally draws me into the lee of his big body, sheltering me both literally and symbolically. I don't miss the fact that his hips are nowhere near my backside, which I appreciate. I don't even want to think about that.

Once his arm is around me, and I feel his warm breath ruffling my hair and neck, my muscles finally relax. I can feel the tension seeping out of my bones.

With a sigh, I close my eyes and welcome sleep.

26

Mack

I've never felt so conflicted in my life. On the one hand, I'm lying in bed with Erin, and she's asleep in my arms, and it's pretty damn satisfying to know that, at least in this moment, I can make her feel safe. On the other hand, I'm feeling things I have no damn right to feel, thinking things I shouldn't think. She's trusting me to be what she needs me to be… her friend. Her protector.

But if I'm being honest with myself, I have to admit I want to be more than a friend to her. Not right now, obviously. She's not ready for that after what she's been through. But someday, when she's healed emotionally, I want her to see me as more than just a safe port in the storm. She used to see me as more. I'm hoping like hell she will again one day.

I check the digital clock on my nightstand—three a.m. I've been lying here with her for five hours. I've dozed off a few times, but every time she moves or makes the slightest sound in her sleep, I come full awake, on high alert and ready to slay her dragons. I probably should get my ass up and out of this bed and go sleep on the sofa, but I can't bring myself to leave her. What if she wakes up in the middle of the night, scared and disoriented? What if she has a nightmare? I want to be here for her if she does.

It shames me to think that it took a horrific attack to make me realize I was being an idiot where Erin is concerned. The difference in our ages isn't so important now when I think about how close I came to losing her. I'd give anything to go back in time and say, "Hell yes, I'll take you to that fucking party! I'll take you to the moon and back if that's what you want."

She makes a whimpering sound in her sleep, and instantly I'm on alert, ready for nightmares, for panic attacks, for anything that comes. But her breathing remains deep and even, and she's still fast asleep. It's a false alarm.

I shouldn't be thinking about how soft her skin is, or how good she feels in my arms. Or how damn good she smells. Shit! This is not what she wants from me.

When my cock hardens with a will of its own, I shift my hips back to ensure my erection never comes into contact with her body. She'll never be able to relax around me if she thinks I want sex. I shouldn't even want that in the first place, not after what she's been through. Not even subconsciously.

But sometimes a body has a mind of its own.

* * *

Sometime later, I awake with a start when she begins to stir, making small movements as her brain comes back online. She stretches with a quiet moan that sends my body into red alert. In my sleep, I had pressed myself more fully to her soft backside, and right now her bottom is nestled against my very inconvenient morning wood. Carefully, I move back so I'm not touching her.

The bright sunlight filtering through the curtains tells me it's already well past dawn. I crane my neck to see the clock. It's seven-thirty—late for me to be sleeping in. But right now I'm going by Erin's clock. I'm on her schedule for the foreseeable future.

She stretches more fully now and groans, still half-asleep, and I do my best to ignore the soft sounds she's making. I know the minute she's fully awake because I hear her swift intake of air. When she stiffens, I release my hold on her, withdrawing my arm, to give her some space. Last night we slept as close as two people can, mostly because she had a death grip on my arm the entire time. But I didn't mind. I enjoyed holding her, and I'm hoping she'll let me do a lot more of that.

She rolls to her back and glances at me.

"Good morning," I say, my voice rough from sleep.

She stifles a yawn. "Good morning."

"How did you sleep?"

"Pretty well, actually. I don't remember having a single nightmare. That's a first in days."

I chuckle. "Good. I'm glad." I prop my head on my hand as I study her. She said something that's been stuck on replay in my head all night, something that's given me an idea. "Last night you said I can't protect you every minute of your life."

Her slight smile fades. "You can't."

"What if I could?" I have no idea how she's going to react to my proposal, but I think it's a real solution in the short term, at least.

"What do you mean?" She sounds cautious, hesitant, and maybe a tiny bit curious.

I steel myself for instant rejection as I propose the craziest idea I've ever had in my life. "Move in with me, Erin."

Her blue eyes widen. "What?"

"Move in with me. That way I can protect you every minute of your life. You'll be safe living here with me, and when you're ready to go back to work, I'll be by your side all day."

She looks incredulous. "I can't do that!"

"Why not?"

"Because!"

I can't help grinning. "*Because*? That's the best you've got? I'm serious. Move in with me. It would solve the problem of where you're going to live. And you wouldn't be living alone—you'd have me for company. It's not much different than Beth having a 24/7 bodyguard. I'll be yours, as long as you need me."

She shakes her head, frowning, but I can see the wheels turning in her head as she thinks through my suggestion. "I—it wouldn't work."

"Why not? It's a damn good idea, at least until you're feeling better." No matter how many excuses she can come up with, I'm confident I can counter them all.

"Because. I—I don't want…it wouldn't be fair to you. I told you I don't want a boyfriend."

Anymore. The word goes unsaid, but we both know the trauma she experienced left her with more than physical pain. The emotional pain, the insecurity, is just as great, if not greater. The bruises will fade over time, but the damage to her sense of self and security won't disappear quite so easily.

"I know, Erin. I haven't forgotten. We'll be roommates. It'll be a purely platonic relationship, just like it's always been. Nothing will change."

"Why would you want to do that? Having me around all the time would put a big crimp in your life. You don't need to take on that kind of responsibility and commitment."

"Why would I want to do it? Because I care about you. I want to help you. And as for putting a crimp in my life… I'm a single guy and I have few commitments—my daughter and my job. Having you in my life won't impact either of those. We already work together, so that's no problem. And as for Haley, I don't think you'd mind her hanging around with us occasionally. I might be biased, but I think she's pretty darn cool."

"Your daughter?" Her eyes light up. "I'd get to meet her?"

"Sure. Why not?"

She smiles. "I'd like that."

I reach over and pat her leg. "Good. Then it's settled. I'll move your stuff down from the penthouse today."

"I'll need to tell Beth."

I sit up and stretch, then swing my legs off the bed. "How about some breakfast first? I'm starving."

"Me, too." She sits up and fusses with her hair.

I nudge her playfully in an attempt to bring back some normalcy to our relationship. "Stop that. You look fine."

The smile she gives me in return is priceless. I think this co-habitation thing might work out fine.

* * *

I open the fridge door and look inside to see what I have on hand. "I've been so busy lately I haven't had a chance to go to the grocery store, and I'm running low on provisions. How about eggs and toast?"

After taking a quick shower this morning, Erin changed back into what she was wearing last night. Her hair is damp, and she's standing in my kitchen looking a little displaced.

I study her, assessing how much her bruises have faded. Her eyes are now framed by soft purple shadows. The stitches on her cheek stand out starkly against her creamy complexion. She reminds me of a frightened rabbit ready to bolt at the first sign of danger. I just want her to relax and let me take care of her.

"That sounds good," she says, peering over my shoulder into

the fridge. "Can I help?"

I pick her up and set her on the counter top. "You can sit and watch me work my mad kitchen skills—trust me, as a bachelor, I've had to learn how to cook. I'll do all the work. You relax."

Her soft lips quiver as she suppresses a smile. The poor girl. She's afraid to let herself be happy, even for a second. My new objective in life is to make Erin smile. To make her laugh.

"I'm perfectly capable of helping, Mack. You don't need to spoil me."

I lean over and kiss her temple like I've done a thousand times. *That's platonic, right?* "Maybe I like spoiling you."

I grab the necessary ingredients from the fridge—a carton of eggs, a loaf of whole grain bread, and butter. "How do you like your eggs? Fried? Poached? Scrambled?"

"Scrambled, if that's okay."

I pull out a skillet and grab the olive oil. "Coming right up."

She watches me like a hawk, her gaze roaming over my hands as I spring into action. I really do know how to cook.

Years ago, I got tired of eating take-out all the time, and I missed my mom's cooking, so I watched a ton of videos on YouTube and taught myself how to make the basics. "Don't look so skeptical, Erin."

She gives me an honest-to-goodness grin. "I'm not skeptical."

"Yes, you are." Laughing, I hand her the bread and nod toward the toaster, which sits behind her on the counter. "You can make the toast."

I crack half-a-dozen eggs into a bowl and whisk them up. Then

I pour them into the hot pan. "Salt and pepper?"

"Yes, please."

When I catch her gaze, she's looking expectantly at me, and then at the floor.

When I stand there like an idiot, she smiles apologetically. "Can you help me down, please? So I can wash my hands." She nods toward the sink.

I could kick myself for not thinking. She's bruised and sore. Of course it would hurt her to jump down from the counter on her own. *Jesus, I can be such a dipshit sometimes.*

I grasp her around the waist and gently set her on her feet. "Sorry. I wasn't thinking."

She blushes as she pushes up her sleeves and turns on the faucet. "It's okay."

While I'm cooking the eggs—careful to make them perfect for her—I watch out of the corner of my eye as she washes her hands, then dries them on a paper towel. I hand her a plate for the toast, and she gets to work.

"How do you like your toast?" she says. "Light, medium, or dark?"

"Medium, thanks." I'm trying hard not to crack a smile. But damn, I'm loving this.

Having a woman in my kitchen is a brand-new experience for me. I've never lived with a woman. When I dated Haley's mom, we were in high school still, so we both lived at home with our folks. And then, surprise! Chrissy got pregnant thanks to a malfunctioning condom, which split on me mid-ejaculation. We both knew in our hearts that we weren't suited for the long term, so we agreed not to marry.

I helped Chrissy every step of the way during her pregnancy. I got a job after school so I could provide financially for my daughter, and so Chrissy could quit her part-time job at a local fast food joint and have more time for the baby. I was there when Haley was born—I cut the umbilical cord. And Chrissy let me bring Haley home to my folks' house two nights a week to sleep over with us. But the three of us never lived together as a family.

The closest I've ever gotten to experiencing family life was the weekends Haley spent with me when she was younger, during the rare times between deployments that I was able to come home. Now that she's a junior in high school, my daughter has her own busy life, and she rarely spends the weekend with me anymore. Still, I make a point to see her at least once a week, for either lunch or dinner, and we talk on the phone nearly every day.

The eggs are perfectly cooked, so I slide them out of the pan and onto our plates.

"What would you like to drink?" I ask her as I poke my head into the fridge. "I've got water, OJ, milk—no, forget the milk. It's gone past its date. Sorry about that. Or, you can have coffee or tea." I point to the Keurig coffee maker and the basket of assorted K-cups. "Haley likes the fancy coffees and teas."

"Actually, orange juice sounds really good right now."

We assemble our breakfast on the small two-person table in my kitchen. It's not much, but it's set right in front of a window that has a fantastic view of Lake Michigan. I serve her eggs, and she passes out freshly-buttered toast. I brew a cup of black coffee for myself using the Keurig machine and pour her a glass of OJ.

I could definitely get used to this.

I've never invited a woman to stay over in my apartment before. Erin's the first, and I'm already liking it. Before, when I hooked up with someone, I always made it a point to go to the women's places. I figured they'd feel more comfortable there.

I like having Erin here under my roof, eating a breakfast I made for her, drinking my orange juice. Well, I guess it's all *ours* now, since she'll be living here with me for the foreseeable future.

I glance at her as I take a bite of toast. She's staring at her plate, completely motionless.

"What's wrong?" I say.

She looks up, meeting my gaze with sad eyes. "This reminds me of all the times Gram and I made breakfast together on the weekends. I miss her cooking. She always said she'd teach me how to cook, but we never got around to it, and then it was too late."

Shit! I wanted to do something nice for her, and now I've brought back sad memories of her dead grandmother. I could kick myself! "I'll teach you."

She lifts her gaze to mine. "You'll teach me to cook?"

"Sure. It's not that hard."

She smiles. "I'd like that."

We eat for a few minutes in silence. Then I ask, "So, what's on the agenda this week?"

"Agenda?"

"Yeah. Do you have any appointments? Anywhere you need

to be? Any shopping you need to do?" I figure she'd at least have some doctor appointments coming up. And Beth mentioned something about therapy.

"Oh, right." She pales. "I have two doctor appointments this week and a therapy appointment. My gynecologist, my general doctor to get these stitches removed," — she points to her right cheek – "and I have an appointment with Beth's therapist."

"You don't look too thrilled about any of it."

She shakes her head. "I'm not. They're all reminders of something I'm trying really hard to forget."

I reach across the table and take her hand, squeezing it gently. "Give yourself time, Erin."

She stares at our clasped hands and I immediately release hers, not wanting to push the boundaries. "I'll take you to your appointments."

"Thanks."

I'm done eating, and she's hardly made a dent in her food. I sit back in my chair and relax, drinking my coffee and trying not to stare at her. She already feels self-conscious enough as it is.

I transfer my attention outside the window, looking out at a clear, sunny day. According to the weather app on my phone, it's going to be a pretty decent day for early January. It looks like most of the recent snow has melted. I think getting Erin out for some fresh air and a little bit of exercise might do her a lot of good.

"After breakfast, why don't we go upstairs to the penthouse? You can tell Beth that you're moving in with me, and I'll bring all your stuff down here. Then later, since it's a nice day, we could go out for lunch. How about that? We could go to your favorite sushi place."

That seems to have gotten her attention. When I mentioned the sushi place, she perked right up. But then her brow wrinkles. "You hate sushi."

"It's not my favorite food, but I don't hate it. Let's go." *Because it's her favorite food.*

She smiles as she resumes eating.

"Is that a yes?" I ask her.

She nods. "Thank you."

I wait until she's done eating before I carry my dishes to the sink. She follows suit, and we end up doing dishes together. I wash, she rinses and sets the dishes in the dish drainer to dry.

I get dressed while she brushes her teeth. If this is what it's like to have a roommate, I think I'm going to like it.

27

Erin

"Come with me," Beth hisses, grabbing my hand and dragging me into the kitchen. She peers around the corner to make sure Mack and Sam are well out of earshot. "Now tell me what's going on!"

"Mack asked me to move in with him." I feel a bit thunderstruck just saying the words.

Her eyes widen in surprise. "Really?"

"Yeah. He asked me this morning."

"And you want to?"

I shrug. "I do. I like being with him." *He makes me feel safe.*

Beth frowns, looking a bit hurt. "You don't want to stay here with us?"

"No! It's not that." I reach out and give her a quick hug. "I love being here with you, and I'm so grateful for your kind hospitality."

"But? I sense a *but* coming."

"I feel like an interloper here. You have Shane and Luke. And Sam and Cooper have each other. I feel like a fifth wheel, like I'm in the way. With Mack, it's just the two of us. It's perfect."

She sighs. "Are you sure this is a good idea? Just the two of you living together? Don't get me wrong… I trust Mack one hundred percent, but the two of you together, all the time, in close quarters? After what you've been through?"

"He knows I'm not interested in having a boyfriend. I made that very clear, and he said he understood completely. We'll just be roommates, that's all. And besides, it's not forever. It's just until I feel safe enough to get a place of my own."

"But doesn't he have just one bedroom? Didn't he turn his spare bedroom into a work-out room?"

"Yeah, there's just one bedroom."

"So, who's going to sleep where?"

I shrug. "I'll sleep on the sofa. He certainly can't. He's way too tall."

She raises a brow. "Is that where you slept last night? On the sofa?"

"Well, no. Not exactly. I slept in his bed last night."

"Then where did Mack sleep?"

My face heats up. "We both slept in his bed last night. It's a huge bed. There was plenty of room."

She looks dumbfounded. "You shared a bed with him?"

"Honestly, it wasn't a big deal. I didn't want to be alone last night, so I asked him to lie down with me for a little while. I guess he fell asleep because when I woke up this morning, he was still there. But it was perfectly innocent."

Beth shakes her head and sighs. "Are you sure you know what you're doing?"

"I know it sounds crazy, but for the first time since the attack, I slept through the night. I didn't have a single nightmare or panic attack."

"Erin!" Mack's deep, booming voice reverberates through the penthouse.

"I'm in the kitchen!"

He appears in the kitchen doorway a moment later, his arms laden with my clothes still on their hangers. "Sam and Cooper are going to help me carry your things downstairs. You'll be okay here?"

"Yes."

He smiles. "Great. I'll be right back." Then he glances at Beth. "Hey, Beth. Take good care of our girl."

"I will," she says, rolling her eyes at me. Then to Mack, she says, "Overprotective much?"

He grins. "Not at all."

* * *

While the guys are gone, Beth and I make hot tea and sit near the hearth. Seated in an armchair, I cradle my hot mug in my hands, taking comfort from the scent of peppermint rising in the steam. Beth sits curled up on the sofa directly across from me.

"Luke's asleep?" I say before taking a tentative sip to test the temperature.

"Yes." As she sips her tea, she stares pensively out the windows across the room, clearly distracted.

I join her on the sofa. "What's wrong?"

She meets my gaze warily, then looks away. "I took a pregnancy test this morning after Shane left for work."

"And? What did it say?"

She gazes down into her cup. "It was positive."

"*Oh.*"

She laughs nervously at my response. "Yeah. *Oh.*"

"Have you told him?"

She looks at me, her beautiful, yet pain-filled eyes flooding with tears. "No." She sets her cup down on the coffee table and presses her hands to her face. She makes an agonized sound, and I can tell anxiety is starting to eat away at her.

"But he loves kids," I say. "And you've both said you want more."

She shakes her head. "Yes, but not this soon. He's afraid of a repeat of what happened the last time."

I lay my hand on her arm. "It won't be the same this time." I laugh softly. "Shane will make sure of it." No one does overprotective like my friend's husband. "When are you going to tell him?"

"I don't know."

When I realize she's shaking, I slide closer and put my arm around her.

For a moment, she leans her head on my shoulder. Then she mentally shakes herself and brushes her blonde hair back from her face. "Enough about me. How are you doing?"

"I'm surviving."

"You're going to see Dr. Shaw Monday, right? For a check-up? And you're going to see Dr. Mosely on Wednesday for a counseling session?"

"Yes."

"Do you want me to go with you? I'd be happy to."

"Thanks, but Mack's taking me."

"Wow." Her eyes widen. "He's really stepping up. I'm impressed."

I smile. "He's been wonderful. Now, let's talk about something else… like going back to work. I miss the store. I want to get back to a normal routine, and that means working again. I've already missed a week."

And then I remember her condition. "You don't have to go back to work, though. If you need to, you can stay home. I'll manage the store for you just like I did when you were on maternity leave with Luke."

Beth lays her hand on her soft abdomen, where she still carries some of her pregnancy weight from the last time. "I'll work as long as I can."

* * *

Returning from their third trip down to Mack's apartment, the guys are laughing as they walk through the foyer door into the great room. When they spot us sitting together on the sofa, they join us, Sam and Cooper taking the other sofa, and Mack sitting on the sofa beside me.

"That's everything," Mack says, patting my knee. "You're all moved."

Sam sits watching Beth closely. "What's wrong, princess?"

Beth pastes a smile on her face, doing her best to hide her anxiety, but I don't think Sam is fooled one bit. He knows her better than almost anyone.

"Nothing's wrong," she says before taking a long sip of her tea. "I'm just a bit tired. Luke got me up early this morning."

Sam continues to watch her, scrutinizing her closely, but he doesn't say anything more.

"Ready for lunch?" Mack asks me.

It's already noon, and I'm getting hungry. "Sure." I look to Beth. "We're going out for sushi. Do you want to join us?"

She shakes her head. "Not this time. I think I'll take it easy today."

After thanking Sam and Cooper for their help, Mack and I head down to his apartment to get our coats.

As soon as the elevator doors close, Mack presses the button for his floor—*our floor*—and we descend. "So what was that about back there?" he says. "Why was Sam worried about Beth?"

"I'm not at liberty to say."

"I see. Well, I hope everything's okay."

"It will be." *I hope.*

We stop at the apartment so I can collect my purse. It's a nice day for this time of year, so we decide to walk to the restaurant. I need the exercise and fresh air. We bundle up warm and set out on foot, heading down North Michigan Avenue toward Clancy's. The sushi place is just a couple of blocks past the bookstore. It's only a twenty minute walk.

"Let me know if it gets to be too much," Mack says as we set off on foot.

I laugh. "Why? Are you going to carry me?"

"No. But I'll flag down a cab if you get too tired from walking."

Working in downtown Chicago as we do, we're used to walking a lot, especially in the warmer months. We walk everywhere for lunch. This will be a good test for me. If I can handle walking from Mack's apartment building to Clancy's, I'm probably ready to go back to work.

The sidewalks this time of day are crowded with pedestrians, and more than once we have to dodge people and strollers. As the lunch-hour pedestrian traffic picks up, he takes my hand and pulls me close. "I don't want you getting trampled."

Holding his hand like this is a new experience for me. With our gloves on, we're not actually touching skin-to-skin, still, his big hand has a solid grip on mine. As we walk hand-in-hand, I wonder what it might have been like for us if things hadn't happened the way they did. It's bittersweet that the attack on me brought us closer together, as I'd always hoped for, and yet it's too late for us now. I'm grateful for the friendship I still have with him, and that will have to be enough.

28

Mack

Our route to the sushi place takes us right past Clancy's. Erin stops in front of the glass doors and watches the bustling activity inside the store. I watch her closely, trying to figure out what she's feeling. She's as still as a statue as she watches people come and go.

I lay my hands on her shoulders and give her a gentle squeeze, just to remind her she's not alone. "Do you want to go inside?"

She shakes her head. "No."

I wait patiently, hoping she'll say more. She loves this place. It's her home away from home, her happy place, and these co-workers are some of her closest friends. I'd hate for her to fear coming here.

"They know, don't they?" she finally says in a voice so quiet I almost miss hearing her.

"You mean, do they know what happened to you? Yeah. It was in the news."

She pulls away and continues walking at a brisk clip, as if trying to outpace her fears.

I catch up to her in two long strides and reach for her hand. "Those people are your friends, Erin. They care about you. They'll be happy to see you return to work."

She keeps her gaze forward, not looking at me, her teeth worrying her bottom lip. "I hate that they know."

"Erin... what happened to you isn't a reflection on you. You were the *victim* of a crime—not the *perpetrator*. You have nothing to be ashamed of."

She looks away, and I figure it's to keep me from seeing the tears in her eyes. Damn it. I hate that she's suffering like this.

We walk the rest of the way to the sushi place in silence, Erin's steps quick and determined, as if she can simply outrun her insecurities. I'm afraid she's going to hurt herself at this pace. I try to slow her down, but she doesn't relent until we reach the restaurant two blocks away. I open the door for her, and she walks inside, stopping abruptly.

The restaurant is packed with a bunch of twenty-somethings—probably college kids. There's a long line at the order counter, and a lot of the tables are already full. Two guys head our way as they exit the restaurant, and as they approach, Erin backs up hastily, bumping into me. I reach out to steady her, pulling her close to allow the two guys to pass through the doorway.

She turns to me, her cheeks flushed and eyes wide. "Let's go!" she says, making for the door.

"Whoa! Slow down!" I pull her back into the restaurant and maneuver her into a quiet alcove that leads to the restrooms, where we're well out of the path of customers streaming in and out. "What's wrong?"

She shakes her head, her gaze frantic. "I can't stay here!"

This is her favorite restaurant. Normally, she'd choose to eat here every single day if she had the chance. "Talk to me, honey. What's wrong?"

I follow the trajectory of her gaze as she sweeps the restaurant. It's crowded, lots of young couples, groups of young guys, groups of girls. In other words, it's nothing out of the ordinary for this place. But anxiety and fear are written plain on her face. *Shit!* She's experiencing PTSD.

I pull her back farther into the alcove, back by the door to the women's room, and turn her to face me, my hands on her shoulders. "It's okay, Erin. You're safe here. No one's going to hurt you. I wouldn't let them."

She shakes her head, her eyes tearing. "I want to go, please. Let's go back to your apartment."

Of course I want to make her happy. I want to make her feel safe, and if she feels safe at my place, that's fantastic. But I also don't want her to fear being out in public, especially at one of her favorite places. "You've heard of post-traumatic stress syndrome, right? PTSD?"

She nods.

"You're experiencing it right now. These guys in here... they're the same age as your attacker. He could be any one of them, couldn't he?"

She stares at me like I'm speaking a foreign language and she has no idea what I'm saying. "I don't remember him," she finally says.

"But you've seen a picture of him, right?"

"Yes."

"And he would fit right in here with these guys... young, college age. Wouldn't he?"

Her blue eyes widen in realization. "Any one of these guys could be a monster in disguise. And no one would know until it was too late."

I sigh heavily as I pull her into my arms. Pressing my lips to the side of her head, I speak in a low voice, just loud enough for her to hear me over the crowd in the dining room. "You can't suspect everyone of being a monster, honey. These guys are just here to eat with their buddies, that's all. Besides, I'll be right by your side, and I guarantee you no one would even dream of bothering you."

When her arms slide around my waist, my heart contracts painfully. Her faith in me slays me. "If you still want to go back home, we'll go. But I honestly think we should stay and face your fears. If you run away from this now, you'll never stop running. At some point, you have to be comfortable out in the world again. If you ever want to return to work, you have to trust that most people are good. What happened to you was a fluke of bad luck. It's not going to happen again." I release her and gaze down into her face. "So, what's it going to be?"

She's clearly torn, her expression pensive. But Erin's very pragmatic at her core, so I'm hoping she'll trust me on this.

She sighs. "Okay."

"So, we're staying?" I say, just to confirm.

"Yes."

"Good." I give her a quick hug and pat her back. "I'll be right beside you the whole time."

As we stand in line, I'm grateful that Erin has a therapy appointment this coming week. She clearly needs some help learning how to cope with her emotions and this PTSD. I doubt it's going to magically vanish on its own.

I can tell she's an anxious wreck. The closer we come to the front of the line, the closer she sidles up next to me until she's practically glued to my side. I put my arm around her as the employee behind the counter takes our order.

"What can I get you?" the young kid behind the counter says. He looks at Erin first, but she says nothing.

"She'll have the seaweed wrap," I say. I've stood beside Erin as she's ordered her sushi rolls a thousand times. I know what she wants. "Brown rice, grilled chicken, cream cheese, carrots, cucumbers, and cranberries."

She gazes up at me in awe. "You remember?"

I tighten my arm around her shoulders. "Of course I do." And then to the guy behind the counter, I say, "I'll have the same."

She flashes me a small smile that warms my chest as I finish up the order by choosing the sauce and the crunchy topping she likes.

"Anything to drink?" the kid says.

"She'll have a lavender honey lemonade, and I'll take water."

I pay for our food, and we scout out a table for two in the corner.

"I can't believe you knew my order," she says.

I hand her a tray of sushi rolls. "I remember everything about you." It's the truth. I've always been fascinated by her, since the moment we first met. When I believed she was too young for me, I kept my interest purely academic. I never even considered making it personal. Now, I want to make it personal.

As she eats, her gaze sweeps the small restaurant methodically like she's on point, and it's her job to spot trouble before it spots us. I try not to let on that I see what she's doing. She's much braver than she realizes. I hope someday I can get her to see that.

After we finish eating, I clear our table as she slips on her coat. I pick up her scarf and slip it around her neck, tucking the ends into her collar to keep her warm. "Now aren't you glad we stayed?"

She's still wary, but she manages a smile and a nod.

"Let's go home," I say. "We can warm up with a cup of hot chocolate." *Another of her favorites.*

Once we're back on the sidewalk, she relaxes enough to start talking again. We pass Clancy's, stopping to watch through the front plate-glass windows. I could swear she's gazing longingly at the countless shelves of books and the many tables piled high with stacks of books and related merchandise.

"Do you miss it?" I ask her.

"Yes."

We step back as a mother and her three little kids walk out of the store, each child holding a book like it's a precious talisman.

Erin smiles as she watches them pass by. "I want to come back to work."

I tug her hand, gently leading her away. "Good idea, but let's wait and see what your doctor says first, okay? Rome wasn't built in a day."

As we stroll along hand-in-hand, her step lightens. She looks more relaxed, and a small smile begins to tease her lips. What she needs most of all is to take back her life, and I'll do everything in my power to help her accomplish that.

29

Erin

It's strange seeing all of my clothes hanging in Mack's closet. Neither one of us is a clothes hound, so there's plenty of room for all of our clothes and then some. His wardrobe is made up mostly of jeans, T-shirts, and sweatshirts. And then he has his collection of black slacks and white button-up shirts for work. In addition to a couple pairs of jeans, I have mostly casual knit dresses and tunics, leggings, and tights.

The closet has clothes rods on three sides. Mack hastily consolidates his clothes onto the left side, and I hang mine on the opposite rod, taking the time to organize mine by type of garment:

first tops, then jeans, then tunics and dresses. I lay my three pairs of shoes neatly in a row beneath my clothes.

On his side of the closet, Mack's clothes are hung in no particular order, and his scuffed sneakers and boots lay scattered on the floor beneath his clothes. I guess you learn a lot about a person when you move in with him.

In the center of the back wall is a built-in safe where Mack stores his guns, knives, and ammunition. My boxes of books and tea cups are stacked against the back wall on either side of the safe.

Mack leans against the door jamb, watching with a smile as I locate Gram's tea kettle and my collection of herbal teas from one of the boxes. I open one box of books and gaze longingly at its contents, wishing I had space to display them. I pick up one of my favorites—a first edition of *Pride and Prejudice*—and gently open the front cover to admire the ornate title page and the publication date.

"Would you like me to put up some bookshelves for you?" he says, nodding toward the small mountain of boxes filled with books.

"Thank you, but I don't want to cause you any trouble, or make any major modifications to your apartment."

He brushes off my concerns. "A couple of bookshelves won't hurt anything. I've got a few books of my own. We could share."

Now I'm the one smiling. I've seen a few of his books scattered randomly throughout the apartment. I find the idea of my romance novels co-mingling with his sci-fi novels and military history books rather appealing. "That would be wonderful."

Mack clears out the three drawers on the left side of his dresser for me. He crams all his socks and underwear and plain white tees into the remaining three drawers on the right side. He watches me fold my panties and tuck them into the top drawer, organized by color. I do the same thing with my bras, and then again with my socks and tights in another drawer. It feels oddly scintillating to know he's watching me organize my undergarments.

"You're such a little neatnik," he says as he observes me from his perch on the big bed.

The way he said it sounds almost affectionate. "I guess I'm a little bit OCD," I admit.

"That's okay. I don't mind. As long as you don't mind that I'm not."

"I don't mind."

He rises from the bed and stretches with a deep groan. "I think I'll change into my work-out gear and hit the treadmill for a while."

"Mack, wait! There's something I wanted to talk to you about."

He pauses at the open closet door, turning to lean against the jamb with his arms crossed over his chest. He gives me his full attention. "Sure. Shoot."

Trying not to stare at the way his muscles strain the sleeves of his T-shirt, I clear my throat and refocus my thoughts. "I wanted to talk to you about our sleeping arrangements. Since there's only one bed, and you're so tall—clearly too tall to sleep on the sofa—I think you should take the bed, and I'll sleep on the sofa."

He straightens with a scowl. "What? No way. You take the bed. I'll be fine in the living room."

I sigh. Chivalry is one thing, but now he's being impractical. "But you won't fit on the sofa."

"I'm sure as hell not letting you sleep on the sofa. All right, I'll borrow an air mattress from one of the guys in the building."

I'd forgotten there's a large number of McIntyre Security employees living in this building. "I'll take the air mattress then," I say. "I'll be perfectly comfortable sleeping on the living room floor, and you can have your room back."

"Erin." He scrubs his hand over his eyes as he exhales. "You're not sleeping on the floor. Period. You'll sleep in my bed where you'll be comfortable."

"But I don't want to kick you out of your own bed."

He moves closer and pulls me into a hug. "Honey, I've slept in the mud, in the woods, in the desert, and in the mountains. I've slept out in the open in sweltering heat with no shade, in the freezing cold, in the rain and sleet and snow. An air mattress on the living room floor might as well be the Ritz-Carlton as far as I'm concerned. Don't worry about me. I'll be perfectly fine."

Before I can say another word, Mack disappears into the closet to change into his work-out clothes.

Men! They're so stubborn.

Clearing out of the bedroom to give him some privacy, I carry Gram's tea kettle and my stash of tea bags to the kitchen to make myself a cup of tea. Before long, the kettle whistles and I fill my cup before dropping in a peppermint tea bag and letting it steep.

Once I'm settled on the sofa with my tea and a book, I hear the quiet whir of the treadmill and the solid, rhythmic thud of his shoes as he runs. There's something oddly comforting in the sound of him running and knowing that he's close by.

I don't know what it is about Mack that makes me feel so settled, so grounded, but he does, just by his very presence. This afternoon at the sushi restaurant he helped me get through a panic attack. He didn't let me run from it, but instead he made me face it.

He said I'm suffering from PTSD, and I suppose he's right. When I saw all those guys in the restaurant, it triggered all kinds of warning bells in my head and threw me right into fight-or-flight mode. I realized any one of them could be a sexual predator in disguise just waiting for a victim. I'll never be able to trust men again, at least not ones I don't know well.

I trust Mack. I trust Sam and Cooper and Shane. But other than them... my stomach sinks when I realize how difficult it's going to be to go back to work. All the men in there... not just the employees, but the customers as well, hundreds of strangers coming and going on any given day. Any one of them could be a predator in disguise, searching for a target. How in the world am I going to deal with that?

I force myself to focus on my book, reading a few chapters more as I sip my tea. Before long, the quiet hum of the treadmill stops. Mack walks out of the work-out room and into the bathroom. A moment later, I hear the shower running.

I find it difficult to concentrate on my book when I know that

Mack is naked in the shower.

* * *

For dinner, we put some potatoes in the oven to bake, and Mack prepares a marinade for chicken breasts. As he grills the chicken out on his balcony, I make a salad.

While the food is cooking, he makes a quick phone call to a friend who lives in the building and arranges to borrow an air mattress. I'm still uncomfortable with the idea of kicking him out of his own bed, but he's adamant that he's going to be the one to sleep on the floor.

After we eat dinner and wash the dishes, we crash on the sofa to watch a movie—his choice this time. He picks a sci-fi action movie with lots of space battles and explosions. It's pretty good, though. Halfway through the movie, his neighbor shows up with the air mattress.

"Here you go, man," says a tall guy with lean muscles and light brown hair. He looks to be in his late twenties. As he stands just inside the apartment, he catches sight of me seated on the sofa and smiles. "Hello there."

Mack looks from the guy to me and back again. He lets out a breath, then says, "Erin, this is Phillip. He's a bodyguard for McIntyre Security. Phil, this is Erin."

"Nice to meet you, Erin," Phillip says as he steps further into the room. "Do you live here in the building?"

My heart jumps into my throat, and I grip the fleece throw

tightly to me.

"She lives with me," Mack says as he steps in front of Phillip and blocks the guy's view of me. "Thanks for the air mattress. I don't mean to brush you off, man, but we're kind of in the middle of something."

Phillip backs toward the door. "Oh, sorry. No problem." He looks my way again. "It was nice meeting you, Erin." And then he slaps Mack on the back as he heads out the door. "See you around," he calls back to Mack. "Enjoy your evening."

Mack closes the door and locks it, then returns to the sofa. "Are you all right?"

I nod.

He sits next to me and reaches for my hand. "I've known Phillip for a while now. He's a good guy."

I glance down at our clasped hands. "How am I going to manage going back to work if I freak out every time I see a strange guy?"

He raises my hand and kisses the back of it. "Baby steps, right?" His dark eyes lock onto mine. "There's no rush, Erin. Beth will let you take as long as you need."

"But what about you? Don't you need to go back to work?"

"I've been reassigned as your bodyguard, so my timetable is your timetable. I'll go back to Clancy's when you go back, and not a minute sooner."

I feel my cheeks warming. "You're my bodyguard? Really?"

"Yes, really."

I can't help smiling. "Why? I'm a nobody."

He cradles my hand in his. "You are not a nobody. You have friends in high places who can make things happen. Shane will make sure you're taken care of. You don't need to worry about anything—not your job, not money. Not anything."

As he resumes the movie, he relaxes back against the sofa and draws me closer, his arm across my shoulders, anchoring me to him. I relax once more, relishing the heat and comfort of his big body.

* * *

After the movie ends, I hop up and stretch. It's late, and I'm tired. Outside, the night sky is inky black, the stars flickering faintly over the lake. The view is very serene.

As Mack begins setting up the air mattress on the floor, I head to the bathroom and get ready for bed. I've got my PJs on and am in bed reading when he appears in the open bedroom doorway.

"I'll just change in there, if that's okay," he says, pointing toward the closet.

"Of course."

After changing into flannel PJ bottoms and a T-shirt, he sits on the bed. "Is everything okay?"

"Yes."

He taps his index finger to my lips. "Then why the frown?"

"Are you sure you'll be okay sleeping on the floor? I feel bad for kicking you out of your own bed. I honestly wouldn't mind sleeping—"

"Erin, no. Not another word about it, okay?"

I sigh. "All right. It's just that—"

His finger returns, cutting off what I was going to say. "Nope." Then he leans forward and kisses my forehead. "I'll be right out there if you need me. Just holler. I'll hear you."

And then he's gone, leaving the door cracked open. I listen as he brushes his teeth in the bathroom. I listen to his footfalls as he heads to the living room. A moment later, the living room light switches off, and all is quiet and dark in the apartment. I hear a soft rustling as he gets comfortable on the air mattress.

He shouldn't be sleeping on the floor of his own apartment.

I tuck my bookmark into my book and set it on the nightstand, then switch off the bedside lamp. It feels odd lying in such a big bed, with so much open space beside me.

I lie awake for a long time, wondering if he's asleep yet. And if he's not, wondering what he's thinking. Does he regret inviting me to move in with him? It can't be easy on a guy who's used to living alone to suddenly have someone underfoot all the time— someone who is not his girlfriend or his wife.

I roll over and cuddle the spare pillow beside mine. It always feels good to have *something* to hold.

* * *

I shoot upright in bed, gasping for air, clawing at my throat... only there's nothing there. No hands are choking me. No fingers are squeezing my windpipe. It was just a dream.

I glance at the clock. It's two-thirty, still pitch dark outside. I'm afraid to go back to sleep. There's something niggling at the back of my mind, and I'm afraid to get too close to it. I'm afraid of what I might remember.

I climb out of bed and visit the bathroom. Afterward, I wash my hands and dry them on a hand towel. I know I'm stalling, trying to avoid going back to bed. After exiting the bathroom, I stand in the hallway, delaying the inevitable. I'm afraid of a repeat nightmare. I want Mack, but it would be selfish of me to wake him at this hour simply because I had a bad dream.

So I stand there frozen to the spot, afraid to go back, unable to go forward. I'm such a mess.

A slight sound to my left startles me, and I jump.

"It's okay, Erin. It's just me. What's wrong?"

"I had a nightmare."

He sweeps me up into his arms and carries me back to bed, laying me down on the mattress. He then climbs over me and slips beneath the covers beside me.

"What are you doing?" I say.

"What I should have done in the first place. Sleep beside you." He wraps his arm around me and tucks me against him. "Go back to sleep, honey."

And I do.

30

Mack

When I awake at seven-thirty, I'm lying on my back and Erin is still sound asleep, pressed up against me with her arm across my abdomen.

She woke up only once more in the night, shooting straight up into a sitting position, grabbing her throat and gasping as if invisible hands were cutting off her air. She was in a dead panic, scrabbling madly, her chest heaving. I had to gently restrain her to keep her from hurting herself or from clawing me. I talked to her in a low, calm voice, and she quickly settled down and fell right back to sleep. I don't think she was ever fully awake.

It took me a while to get back to sleep myself, after that. I was seething inside, so fucking angry because a selfish prick of a monster did this to her. He stole something precious from her—her peace of mind, her sense of safety—when he had no right. A lot of folks go through life feeling safe until they're not, and once that's taken from you, it's hard to get it back. I'm going to give it back to her if it kills me.

At least we've settled the question of our sleeping arrangements. I'm not going to let her go through these night terrors alone. She'll just have to get used to having me in bed with her. I don't want to invade her privacy, but I also refuse to let her suffer alone. So I guess she's stuck with me.

She sighs softly in her sleep and nestles closer, and as my gut tightens with desire my dick starts to harden. It's a natural response, and not one I can likely control. My dick has a mind of its own. If she knew I had a hard-on for her, she'd be disgusted at best, or scared of me at worst. She's off limits now more than she ever was. But God, sometimes it's hard being around her.

I give myself just one more minute to lie here with her pressed up against me, soft and warm and smelling so sweet. I lay my hand on her arm, careful to avoid touching any bruises or healing cuts. This is all I can have. Just quiet, stolen moments like this. Maybe one day she'll feel differently, but until then I'll have to make do with being her friend. I'd rather be her friend and deserve her trust than lose her completely.

Not wanting to wake her, I carefully extricate myself from her hold and slip out of bed. It's Saturday morning, and we don't have anything planned for the day, so I leave the bedroom and let her sleep. We need to establish a routine—figure out what works best for both of us. Obviously, she sleeps better when I'm with her, so I'll give up on the idea of sleeping on the air mattress, and we'll just share the damn bed. It's plenty big enough.

After making a pitstop in the bathroom, I head to the kitchen to whip up a protein shake before I hit the weights. I'm about a half-hour into lifting free weights when I see someone in my peripheral vision. I set the weights down. "Good morning."

"Good morning," Erin says, stepping into the room. "I hope I'm not interrupting you."

"No, not at all."

She eyes the treadmill, approaching it like it's a wild animal that might attack at any minute. "Would it be okay if I use the treadmill?"

"Sure." I wipe my hands on my shorts and join her next to the machine. "Have you ever used one before?"

"No."

She's still in her pajamas—flannel bottoms and a short-sleeved top. Fortunately, she's wearing sneakers. "Stand here," I say, pointing to the deck. "Start with one foot on each side of the belt. Then grip here."

She steps up onto the deck, straddling the belt, and white-knuckles the hand grips.

I clip the safety shut-off sensor to her top. "This stops the treadmill if you fall off." Then I point out buttons and features on the console. "Here's where you adjust the speed, and here's how you increase the incline. Let's have you start out on a level incline at one mile per hour. When you feel ready, you can increase the speed by pushing this. Are you ready?"

She nods.

I press the start button, and the tread starts moving. She steps on and smiles. "This isn't too bad." Then she increases the speed slowly.

When I'm sure she's got the hang of it, I return to my weights and work on my repetitions while she walks. I try not to stare, but she's directly in my line of sight, so it's hard not to. She's the prettiest thing in here, so of course I want to watch her. But then she notices me watching her, so I force myself to look out the window instead.

After a half-hour, she's climbs off the treadmill.

I set my weights down and wipe off my hands. "How about some breakfast?"

* * *

I'm cooking a skillet full of eggs for breakfast. As a general rule, I eat a protein-heavy, low-carb diet, but she probably wants more variety. I watch her peering inside the refrigerator. "What are you looking for?"

She closes the fridge door and glances around the small kitchen. "Do you have any fresh fruit or oatmeal or avocados?"

"Nope, sorry. We're running pretty low on everything. How about after breakfast we make a run to the grocery store?"

"I'll make a list," she says as she pulls out her phone and starts typing. "What do we need?"

An hour later, we're standing in the produce department at a local upscale grocery store. She asked for organic fruits and veggies, so here we are. She loads up our cart with apples, bananas, strawberries, blueberries, mixed greens, cherry tomatoes, and avocados. I grab my usual haul: bread, eggs, bacon, milk, chicken breasts, hamburger, buns, chips, a six-pack of beer. I also pick up another carton of mint chocolate chip ice cream. She grabs toothpaste, shampoo, lotion, and menstrual pads. That's definitely a first for me… there are menstrual pads in my shopping cart.

Erin seems to be enjoying herself as we shop. At first she seemed pretty self-conscious, and she stuck close to me. But eventually, she started to relax and roam farther afield in search of items she needed. I follow her, never far behind as I push the cart and scan the vicinity. I don't know what kind of trouble I'm expecting to find on a Saturday morning at the grocery store, but nevertheless, I'm keeping her within sight at all times.

I notice quite a few people staring at her. The stitches on her cheek are pretty noticeable even from a distance, as are the fading bruises on her face.

I'll be glad when she gets the stitches removed. They're the most obvious sign that she's been through something. I hate seeing strangers stare at her, wondering what happened to her. I get a few ugly looks, and I have to wonder if some of these assholes think I put those bruises there.

When it's our turn to check out, we load our items onto the

conveyor belt.

"I've got this," I tell her, stepping past her so I can swipe my credit card.

"I can pay for my own items," she whispers, sidling up beside me.

"That's okay. I'll take care of it."

The woman operating the check-out register stares at Erin's face for longer than she should, her frown deepening. I don't know if Erin has noticed, but it's sure as hell pissing me off.

"What happened to your face, honey?" the woman finally says.

Immediately my hackles rise. Erin freezes, looking up to meet the woman's gaze.

The cashier points at Erin's cheek. "That's going to leave an awful scar. What a shame! You were so pretty."

What the fuck? If that woman was a man, I'd have decked him. Instead, I'm seeing red, my pulse kicking into high gear.

Pale as a ghost, Erin shoots me a panicked look.

Damn it, I could wring that woman's neck!

As soon as I've paid for the groceries, I grab Erin's hand and pull her along with me as I push the cart out to the parking lot. I leave the cart beside my truck and walk Erin to the front passenger door, opening it and lifting her inside.

"Erin—"

She turns in her seat, facing forward, and shakes as tears stream down her cheeks. With jerky, uncoordinated movements, she attempts to strap on her seatbelt, but she's shaking too badly to manage it on her own.

I buckle her in myself, then grab her hands. "Erin, look at me."

She turns to me, her gaze stark and pained.

I bring her hands to my lips to kiss. "Don't you dare listen to her. You are the most beautiful woman I've ever known, and a scar isn't going to change that."

She sucks in a ragged breath and points to her cheek. "I hate this!" Her voice cracks as her volume rises. "I don't care if people think I'm ugly. It's this scar! It's like wearing a big neon sign on my face that says, 'Look at me! I was stupid!' It draws attention everywhere I go. It's like a part of him is still with me. I can't escape it!"

"Erin, no! What happened wasn't your fault! You weren't stupid. You were just in the wrong place at the wrong time, and you were targeted."

She pulls her hands from mine and faces forward, her expression closed off.

Shit! I'm so tempted to go back into that store and give that woman a piece of my mind. But I can't leave Erin out here alone right now. So I load our groceries into the back of the truck and climb up into the driver's seat.

Erin's silent on the drive back to the apartment. She's still not talking when we carry our bags up to the apartment and put the groceries away. When we're finished, she heads down the hallway and locks herself in the bathroom.

I stand outside the bathroom door, not sure what I should do. Talk to her? Make her talk to me? Leave her alone?

I knock on the door, but she doesn't answer.

"Erin, please. Open the door."

Still nothing.

The thought going through my head right now is... what if she hurts herself? I feel a sick knot of dread in my stomach. Surely she wouldn't do anything rash. I knock again. "Erin?"

A moment later, I hear the shower running. The doorknob is locked, but that's easy to remedy. I have it open in less than a minute. Her clothes and shoes are strewn across the floor, and I can see the shadow of her body on the other side of the shower curtain. Already the bathroom is steaming up.

I close the door quietly and stand just outside the shower curtain. "Are you okay?"

Still nothing.

I hear swift and repetitive noises, mixed with the sound of sobbing, and red flags go up. To hell with it. I pull back the shower curtain, prepared for God knows what. She's frantically scrubbing at her arms, at her chest, with her fingernails, scratching herself raw.

"Erin, stop!" I kick off my shoes and step into the shower. I grab her hands to still their frenzied movements. "Honey, stop! You're hurting yourself."

"I have to get it off of me!"

"Get what off?"

"My skin! He touched me! I can still feel it!"

Oh, my God. I wrap her in my arms and hold her tight, my chin resting on the top of her wet hair. "I'm so sorry, honey." I don't know if she's listening, but I keep repeating those words over and over because I don't know what else to do. "I'm so sorry."

She tries to pull away from me, but I hold her fast. "He's dead, Erin. He can't hurt you anymore. He can't touch you."

She needs help, I realize. More help than I know how to give her. I pray to God the counselor she's seeing Monday will know what to do.

I shut the water off, wrap Erin in a towel, and carry her to bed, tucking her in. While she lies there almost catatonic, I go out into the hallway and call Beth. "I'm sorry to bother you, but can you come down here?"

"I'm on my way," she says, without hesitation.

31

Erin

"Erin, sweetie?"

Beth sits on the side of the bed and brushes my damp hair back from my face. I look at her, at the deep concern in her gaze, but I don't know what to say. Anxiety is eating away at my insides, churning inside me like roiling acid. My muscles are locked, frozen in place, and I feel like I'm suffocating.

Mack stands at the foot of the bed, his arms crossed, his brown deeply furrowed as he watches me intently. Shane and Sam stand silently in the doorway, blocking the light.

They're worried. About me.

I swallow hard. "I'm sorry. I didn't mean to freak out and scare everybody."

"It's okay," Beth says, lightly finger-combing my damp hair. "Do you want me to comb your hair before it dries?"

I'm sure my hair is a tangled mess. I nod.

Beth looks to the guys standing in the doorway. "Can someone find Erin's purse? I need her comb."

"I'll get it," Sam says, and then he disappears from sight.

A moment later, Sam returns with my purse and sets it on the nightstand. He squeezes my foot gently before leaving the room.

As Beth retrieves my comb and begins untangling my wet hair, Shane motions for Mack to join him in the hallway. They close the bedroom door, leaving Beth and me alone.

She gently works the comb through my hair.

"Where's Luke?" I say.

"He's upstairs with Cooper."

"I miss him."

"You're always welcome to come upstairs, any time you'd like. You're one of his favorite people. He misses you too." After a moment of silence, she says, "Mack told me what happened at the grocery store. I'm sorry. That was an awful thing for someone to say to you."

I shrug. "She was just speaking the truth."

Beth shakes her head. "I disagree." She runs the tip of her index finger lightly down my cheek. "This scar doesn't detract one bit from your lovely face. If anything, it just makes you look dashing." She smiles. "You could be a female Captain Jack Sparrow."

I laugh in spite of the pain. "No one's ever called me dashing before."

"Perhaps not. But you are beautiful, and nothing could ever change that."

When I fall silent, she says, "I'm glad you're seeing Dr. Mosely on Monday. I think you need some help, sweetie, and I know she can help you. She's helped me tremendously."

I sigh. "I dread talking to someone about what happened. Especially to a stranger."

She finishes detangling my damp hair and lays the comb on the nightstand. "I know. It takes some getting used to. But trust me, in the long run you'll be glad you did."

* * *

Mack sits on the bed looking worried. "Are you mad at me for calling Beth?"

"No. I'm sorry I freaked out on you like that."

I reach for his hand, which is lying on my belly, and give it an apologetic squeeze.

"Would you like to come out to the living room and sit with me?" he says. "We could watch some TV and think about what we want for lunch."

"Okay." And then I remember I'm only wearing a damp towel. "I need to get dressed first."

"Oh, right." He hops up from the bed and heads for the door. "I'll wait for you in the living room."

After changing into shorts and a T-shirt, I leave the bedroom. I find Mack seated on the sofa, the remote control in his hand. He silences the basketball game and sets the remote down, watching me warily as I enter the room.

When I'm halfway into the room, he holds out his hand to me, inviting me to join him on the sofa. "What do you want to watch?"

"You can watch the game. I don't mind." I bring up the Kindle app on my phone. "I'll read."

"Are you sure? We can watch anything you want."

"I'm sure."

I end up sitting with my back against his shoulder, my legs stretched out in front of me on the sofa. Mack reaches for the fleece blanket and tucks it around my legs. While he watches his game, I read, and I'm surprised to find myself relaxing into him. The sound of the basketball game in the background is oddly comforting.

"This is nice, isn't it?" I say, leaning my head against his bicep.

"It is." He brushes his cheek against the back of my head. "What would you like for lunch?"

* * *

We stay in for the rest of the weekend, just hanging out together, watching TV, reading, cooking, cleaning up the kitchen. We even do two loads of laundry. There's a small closet with a washer and dryer right off the kitchen.

I can't help wondering if I'm in the way... if I'm hampering his life too much, but he seems happy. He watches me warily at times, with a hint of a frown, as if he's afraid I'm going to freak out on him again. But for the most part, we have a relaxing and enjoyable rest of the weekend.

Sunday evening, we're eating pizza in the living room while we watch the first *Guardians of the Galaxy* movie. I start getting nervous about tomorrow… my first appointment with the therapist. Beth is so sure this is going to help me. I'm not convinced.

Mack carries the leftover pizza to the kitchen, to stow in the fridge. When he returns, he's carrying two bowls of ice cream.

"I bet I've gained ten pounds this weekend," I say, spooning ice cream into my mouth.

He nudges me playfully with his shoulder. "That's okay. It just means there'll be more of you to love."

I know he meant that figuratively, in a platonic way. But still, his words fill me with contentment. I could get used to this… being with him. *Living with him.* He's the best friend I've ever had. He knows me better than anyone, and he accepts me the way I am. He's seen me at my worst and hasn't disowned me yet.

I lean my head against his shoulder, relaxing into him and feeling a moment of respite from my fears and anxieties. I'll worry about tomorrow when it comes.

32

Mack

Erin's therapy appointment on Monday goes better than expected. When she comes out of the therapist's office and into the waiting room where I'm sitting, pretending to read a health and fitness magazine and failing miserably, she looks guarded but not completely overwhelmed.

Dr. Moseley walks her out and stops to say hello to me, shake my hand, and tell me to take good care of Erin. Erin has a follow-up appointment in a week.

When we leave the therapist's office, I ask Erin, "How did it go?"

"Fine."

"Do you want to talk about it?"

"No."

"Are you sure?"

"Yes."

And that's the end of that. I'm just glad she agreed to go, so I'm not going to push her to talk about it if she doesn't want to.

On Tuesday, I take Erin to her general doctor to have the stitches removed from her cheek. I stand at her side in the examining room, holding her hand as the nurse carefully clips the tiny black threads. Erin is practically vibrating with tension, her back ramrod stiff. She squeezes my hand so hard it goes numb. Once we're back in the truck, she stares straight ahead, deeply lost in her own thoughts.

"Does your cheek hurt?"

"A little."

"Do you want to talk about it?'

"No."

"Are you sure?"

"Yes."

And that's the end of that.

She's holding so much in, and I'm not sure if that's okay or not. I don't want to put too much pressure on her to talk about things she's not ready to talk about. I just want her to know that I'm here and available if she decides she wants to talk.

Wednesday is the day she visits her gynecologist for a follow-up check to make sure everything in her lady region is healing okay. I haven't really talked to her about any injuries to her genitals, but I can tell from the occasional twinge on her face that she still has some degree of soreness from time to time.

"Do you want me to go in with you?" I ask her, when the nurse calls her name. I have no idea if she'd want company or not, but I figure I should ask. If she wants me in there with her, I'll be there. If not, that's okay, too. This is uncharted territory for both of us.

She looks at me out of the corner of her eye and shakes her head. "I'll be okay."

I nod. "I'm here if you need me."

Holding her head up high, her back ramrod straight, she follows the nurse through a door and disappears from sight. Forty-five minutes later, she comes out, and we head to the truck.

"Is everything okay?" I ask as I open her door and lift her up into the truck cab.

"Yes."

As I watch her buckle her seatbelt, I try not to feel frustrated. I know she's been through a lot, and I can understand why she'd want to keep it all private. But I want to be here for her.

I walk around the truck and climb up into the driver's seat and start the engine. When I reach for her hand, she threads our fingers together and holds our clasped hands on her thigh. At least she's not shutting me out completely.

A few minutes later, she says, "Dr. Shaw said I can return to work if I want to."

"Do you want to?"

"I should." She glances at me. "How about tomorrow?"

"So soon? There's no rush. If you need more time—"

"I need to be productive."

"Okay."

I can understand her wanting to get back to work. Erin's a hard worker, and she takes pride in her job as assistant manager at Clancy's. Beth trusts her implicitly. But I'm just not sure she's ready to go back yet. Her panic attack in the sushi restaurant is still fresh in my mind. At Clancy's, she'll be surrounded by strangers—lots of them men. I'll be there for her, but still…I'm afraid she'll be overwhelmed. But if she feels ready to go back, I'm not going to stand in her way.

* * *

That evening, we make soft tacos for dinner.

I never realized how much I would enjoy having a woman in my apartment. Something as simple as making tacos is a lot more fun with Erin. We work well in the kitchen together, divvying up the work. I brown the ground beef and prepare the beans while she dices up the tomatoes, onions, and garlic and makes fresh salsa. She makes up a salad and some fresh guacamole to go with tortilla chips. I pop the top off an ice cold Dos Equis, which goes perfectly with the tacos, but she sticks to water.

We lay our spread out on the kitchen table and assemble our tacos. I smile when I see taco sauce dribbling down her chin. Reaching across the table, I wipe it off her chin, and her blue eyes lock onto mine, widening just a tad. Her cheeks pinken and the tip of her tongue comes out to brush against her lower lip. My chest tightens as we gaze at each other for a long moment, until she abruptly looks away.

I've been trying really hard to keep my feelings to myself. I don't want to put any pressure on her. She sure as hell doesn't need to know that I'm pining for a hell of a lot more with her. I'm afraid if she knew how I felt, she'd move out, and I don't want her to leave.

That evening, we sit on the sofa together, like we do most evenings. We've settled into a comfortable groove. I watch TV, usually sports, and she reads. We often have ice cream—a weakness for both of us.

Tonight it's a basketball game, as usual. She leans against the arm rest opposite mine, her legs stretched out across the cushions, her stockinged feet in my lap. I absently massage her feet, and occasionally I'm rewarded by hearing a soft moan. When she makes sounds like that, my gut clenches in desire and my body temperature skyrockets. I pull a small sofa pillow onto my lap, pretending it's there to cushion her feet when in reality it's to conceal my erection.

As usual, she falls asleep on the sofa. When the game ends, I turn off the TV and the lights and rouse her for bed.

"Come on, sleepy head," I say, pulling her into an upright position.

She groans in protest, but heads to the bathroom to get ready for bed.

I join her in the bathroom, and we stand side-by-side at the sink as we brush our teeth. Then I leave her to change into her pajamas, giving her privacy to do all the mysterious things girls do to get ready for bed.

She's already in bed when I climb in beside her. I usually sleep in the nude, but obviously that's not an option now. I keep my boxer briefs on, but forgo a shirt.

That night she wakes up in the throes of a panic attack, shooting upright in bed and gasping for air. Her fingers claw at her throat, and I force myself to squelch the burning anger I feel at her attacker.

"Erin, it's okay," I murmur quietly to her. I've learned that she responds better when I remain calm. "It's okay, honey."

She turns to me, blinking in confusion. "I couldn't breathe."

"I know," I say, wondering if she's referring to her nightmare or a hazy memory. I brush back her hair, careful not to touch her scar. The skin on her cheek is still very sensitive.

She falls back onto the mattress, and I follow her down, tucking her close as I spoon against her. She hugs my arm to her chest and holds on tight, as if it's a lifeline.

If her attacker weren't already dead, I'd kill him myself a hundred times over, damn the consequences. He got off way too easy. He should have suffered, the way she is.

She falls quickly back to sleep, leaving me to watch over her. I press my nose to the back of her head, breathing in the tantalizing scent of her hair as I contemplate what tomorrow will bring.

Erin's first day back at work.

I'd be lying if I said I didn't have some pretty serious reservations about her going back so soon.

33

Erin

It's a pleasantly new experience to be riding in to work with Mack in his truck instead of taking the bus. We park in a garage a couple of blocks from the bookstore and walk to Clancy's. Mack unlocks the front door and holds it open for me. When I step inside, the store is dimly lit and eerily quiet. As usual, we're the first ones here.

I glance around half expecting to see the place has changed, but it hasn't. Everything looks just as I left it ten days ago. Clancy's hasn't changed one bit, but I sure have.

After heading to the employee locker room to drop off our

coats, we go about the business of getting the store ready to open. Mack helps me install the cash drawers and power up the machines. I check the new arrivals in the inventory room and read some notes that Stacey, the other assistant manager, left for me. Everything looks to be in order.

Everything *seems* to be the same, and yet it's different. One big difference is that Mack shadows me even more closely than he did before. He doesn't say much, but I get the impression he's just waiting for me to freak out on him. I don't blame him. I remember full well what happened at the sushi place and after the grocery store incident.

How will I handle a bookstore filled with hundreds of customers? Hundreds of *strangers*?

When the other employees begin to trickle in, they all come to greet me, telling me they're glad I'm back to work, that they missed me, that they're so sorry about what happened.

As I smile and accept their good wishes, I have to force myself not to cover the scar on my cheek with my hand. Trying to hide the scar will only call attention to it, so I try to pretend it doesn't exist.

At nine-thirty, Beth and Sam arrive with Luke. We meet them at the front doors, and Beth hugs me tightly.

"I'm so glad you're back," she whispers in my ear. "This place isn't the same without you."

I realize she and I need to talk soon. I've been so caught up in my own drama that I've neglected hers. I don't know if she's told Shane yet about her pregnancy. It's been a week since she peed on the stick. Surely she's told him by now.

"We need to talk," I tell her.

She nods. "Come up to my office when you get a chance." Then she hugs me again. "Take it easy, okay? You have nothing to prove. If it gets to be too much, go home, all right?"

I nod.

"Promise me," she says.

"I promise."

* * *

Everything's the same—the routine, the staff, the customers—everything except me. I feel like I have a neon sign planted on my face that says, "I WAS STUPID AND I GOT MYSELF ASSAULTED."

Of course people are staring at me, mostly my fellow employees, whose gazes invariably gravitate to the scar on my face, or to the faint remnants of purple and gray shadows beneath my eyes.

I tried putting some concealer on this morning, but it didn't quite do the trick. The bruises are still visible. Now I look like a muted raccoon.

Mack is never far from me. He follows at a distance, pretending he's not hovering when he clearly is. When I head up the staircase to the second floor, intending to visit Beth in her office, he's right behind me.

I stop halfway up the steps and turn to face him. "I need to talk to Beth."

"Okay."

"Alone."

His smile fades. "Fine."

"That means you don't have to follow me upstairs."

He doesn't seem convinced, but he nods anyway. "All right. I'll be nearby if you need me."

He hangs back as I head upstairs and down the hallway that leads to the administrative offices. As I pass through the outer business office, everyone says 'hi' and welcomes me back. Beth's office door is open, and I walk inside and close the door behind me. Sam and Lindsey, Luke's nanny here at the store, are seated on the sofa, chatting. Beth and the baby are nowhere to be seen.

The minute he sees me, Sam shoots up from the sofa and meets me halfway to give me a big hug. "She's in the nursery with Luke."

"Hi, Erin," Lindsey says as she stands. "Welcome back. We missed you."

"Hi, Lindsey. Thanks."

Sam rocks me in his arms and kisses the top of my head. Then he peers down at my cheek, studying the scar. "It looks good," he says. "The scar is very faint. The surgeon did a good job."

I try to put on a brave face, but Sam's not fooled.

"Hey, it's your warrior princess mark of courage," he says, grasping my shoulders and holding me at arm's length to study me. "Wear it proudly, girlfriend. That asshole is *dead*, and you're standing here looking fierce and gorgeous. You *won*. He *lost*."

I can't help but smile at the passionate sincerity in Sam's voice.

"Thank you."

The door to the nursery opens and Beth walks out holding Luke perched on her hip. "Hey!" she says, heading right for us.

As they near, Luke reaches for me, and I take him from her. "Hello, sweet boy," I murmur, nuzzling his soft hair. "You're a sight for sore eyes."

"Duh-duh," he says, grabbing hold of the neckline of my blouse and tugging.

"Hey, his vocabulary is expanding!" I say.

Beth reaches out to rescue my top from her son's tiny fist. "I'm so glad you're back to work. We really missed you."

I force a smile. "It's great to be back." I can tell Beth doesn't believe me, though.

"Why don't we go down to the café and have some tea?" she says. "We can talk."

Beth leaves Luke with Lindsey, and the two of us go downstairs to the bookstore café. Sam walks downstairs with us and meets up with Mack, and the two of them stand together chatting, close enough to observe us, but out of hearing range to give us some privacy.

We walk right up to the counter, where an employee named Adam is standing, ready to take our orders. He's worked here for about six months, and he's a nice guy. Tall, lanky, with his dark hair pulled up high into a messy bun. He's trying hard to not stare at my cheek.

Beth orders a decaf mocha peppermint coffee, her favorite, and a blueberry scone. While Adam makes her coffee, I watch him work, fixated on his movements. As I watch him pour a bit of this and a squirt of that into Beth's coffee, my mind is hijacked by unwanted thoughts. I barely know this guy. What's to stop him from putting something he shouldn't into a person's drink? Anyone could slip something into a person's drink without their knowledge. Just like Kurt did.

"Erin?"

I shake myself, my gaze pivoting to Beth. She's watching me expectantly. So is Adam. I realize he's done with Beth's order and is waiting for mine. I open my mouth to speak, but nothing comes out. I'm frozen. Normally I'd order peppermint tea, like I've done a thousand times before, but I can't get the words out. It's too risky. Someone could spike my drink. It happened once; it can happen again.

Beth lays her hand on my back. "Erin, is everything okay? Don't you want your tea?"

I look at her as panic builds inside me. *I can't order. I can't risk it.* "No." I shake my head as I step back from the counter. "I changed my mind. I don't want anything." And then I glance at the refrigerated case beside the counter. It's filled with a wide variety of commercially bottled beverages, all sealed by the manufacturers. "No, wait!" I grab a bottle of mint-infused green tea from the cold case. "I'll have this."

After completing our purchases, Beth and I sit at a small table by a window. I glance across the store and spot Mack and Sam watching us as they converse.

Beth picks up her coffee. "How are you doing, *really?*"

It's just the two of us, so I don't feel like I have to put up a front. "So-so. Some days are better than others." As I open my bottle of tea, I tell her about all my doctor appointments this week. "Next week I have another counseling appointment."

"Do you like Dr. Mosely?"

I nod. "She's nice. She seems to understand where I'm coming from. Still, it's hard to talk about what happened, how I feel."

"Give it some time," she says. "I think you'll find the counseling really helps. It's helped me over the years."

"What about you? Have you told Shane you're pregnant?"

She sighs heavily. "No. Not yet."

"How do *you* feel about having another baby so soon?"

She practically lights up. "I'm excited. Luke will have a playmate. Growing up, I always wished I had a sibling close in age. Tyler was eighteen when I was born. He was more of a parental figure than a sibling."

"Tell Shane you're excited about having another baby." I reach for her hand and squeeze it. "If he sees that you're happy, he won't worry so much."

Two guys in their late twenties sit at the table next to ours, sipping coffee and talking quietly. I find myself watching them out of the corner of my eye.

One of them gets up and approaches our table. "Sorry to bother you, ladies," he says as he points at the container of assorted sweetener packets on our table. "Do you mind if I steal a couple of sugars?"

He looks perfectly non-threatening, dressed in blue jeans,

a white button-up, and a brown leather jacket. His long hair is pulled back into a ponytail, and there's a pair of studious-looking, wire-rimmed glasses perched on his nose. There's absolutely nothing threatening about him, and yet, my immediate reaction is to freeze. I find myself holding my breath as my heart starts pounding.

"Help yourself," Beth says, holding out the container of sweeteners.

The guy selects two sugar packets. "Thanks."

A moment later, Mack and Sam descend on our location, both of them pulling up nearby chairs to crowd our space. I don't think it's a coincidence that they place themselves directly between us and the guys at the table text to ours.

"So," Mack says as he leans back in his chair, looking perfectly relaxed as he eyes me casually. He checks his watch. "Is anyone else ready for lunch? How about Thai?"

Beth and I exchange glances, both of us suppressing smiles.

"You are so transparent," Beth says to Mack, laughing. "Relax. She's fine."

* * *

"So, I was wondering…" Mack says to me later that afternoon as I'm pushing a cart of new romance releases out of the inventory room. He offered to push it for me, but I declined. It's time for me to get back to business as usual and pull my own weight.

It's not like him to be so hesitant. He's usually very direct.

"Wondering about what?"

"How would you feel about having dinner tonight with me and Haley?"

"Your daughter." It's not a question. I know perfectly well who Haley is. My pulse kicks up at the idea of meeting his seventeen-year-old daughter, Haley Donovan. She's a junior in high school and lives in a very ritzy section of Lincoln Park with her mom and stepfather, both of whom are attorneys.

"I usually have dinner with her once a week," he says. "But since…" His voice trails off.

"Since the incident?"

"Yeah. I haven't seen her since then. I was wondering how you'd feel about joining us for dinner."

I start shelving the new books. "Are you sure you want me there? I mean, I don't mind staying home alone… at your apartment. I don't want to intrude on your time with your daughter."

He looms beside me, tilting his head down, as he says, "I want you to come. I'd love for you and Haley to meet."

"Then yes. I'd love to."

His face lights up. "Yeah? You'll come?"

"Sure."

"Excellent. I'll let her know. I usually pick her up at her house and we go to a nearby diner."

"That sounds great."

He brushes my hair off my shoulder, his gentle touch sending unexpected shivers down my spine. When I tense, he drops his hand and grabs a book off the cart to shelve. "Sorry. I shouldn't have touched you."

"No, it's okay," I say. "It's fine. Really." Mack and I have always touched a lot, frequently kidding around, just having fun. I don't want that to change. I don't want him to feel constrained around me in any way. I want things to go back to *normal*. "No, I'm sorry. It was an automatic reflex. I don't want to be like that. I don't want to jump every time someone touches me."

He slowly moves behind me and leans close to whisper. "I'm going to put my hands on your shoulders. Just relax."

It's something he's done countless times in the past, something I shouldn't be afraid of. As if he's trying to calm a wild animal, he slowly lowers his hands to my shoulders. Even knowing that it's coming, I still tense.

"It's okay," he murmurs. "Try to relax."

I let out a long breath and will my shoulders to fall, to relax and not to respond as if I'm under attack. When I finally manage it, he gently squeezes once, twice. Then he starts a gentle massage, which feels so good, I moan.

Immediately, he lets go. "That wasn't so bad, was it?"

I shake my head, trying to make sense of the way my mind and body are reeling. "It was okay." *It was amazing!*

He gathers more books from the cart and resumes shelving. "So, dinner tonight with Haley? Six o'clock? Is that okay?"

"Yes, fine."

"Great. I'll let her know." He pulls out his phone and keys in a quick text message. "I told her we'd pick her up at six. She's been dying to meet you."

He flashes his phone at me, and I see Haley's quick reply:

Gr8t! Can't wait 2 meet her

My stomach drops. His daughter wants to meet *me? Why?* Mack and I are just friends. It's not like I'm his girlfriend or anything. We're not together—not that like. We're friends… platonic friends. I wouldn't want his daughter to get the wrong idea about us.

34

Erin

"Should I go home and change first?" I ask Mack as we walk to the parking garage to get his truck.

"Change? No. You're fine."

I trudge through the biting cold January wind, trying to keep up with Mack's long stride.

When he notices I'm lagging, he slows his pace. "Sorry. Are you doing okay?"

I nod, pulling my scarf up over my nose to keep warm. Mack offered to go get the truck by himself and pick me up at the door, but I insisted on walking with him. *Back to normal.* I want to get back to normal, even if it kills me.

It's just a few minutes after five, so we have plenty of time to get to Lincoln Park to pick up Haley. We're in the truck soon and heading to the suburb where Haley lives. My nerves are making me queasy, and I hope I can get through this dinner without making a fool of myself. "Does she know?"

Mack spares me a quick glance before returning his gaze to the road. "She knows you were injured in an accident. That's it. I had to tell her something to explain why I had to cancel our dinner plans last week."

"Thanks." I really don't want his daughter knowing what happened to me. She's so young.

We pull into the driveway of an impressive Tudor style home sitting right in the middle of a beautifully landscaped lawn. There are two shiny, black BMWs parked in the drive in front of a three-car carriage-house garage.

I peer out the window at the arched front door. "Wow."

"Yeah, Chrissy did pretty well for herself. She ended up going to law school and married a fellow classmate. They seem happy."

"That's good—for Haley's sake. Do they have any kids?"

"No. Just Haley."

Haley runs out a side door and races to the truck. It's freezing out, and she's only wearing a light jacket, and it's not even zipped up.

Mack shakes his head. "Teenagers. They have no sense whatsoever."

Haley opens the rear passenger door of the double cab and

climbs up, gasping. "Oh, my God, it's so cold!"

Mack lays his arm across the back of my seat and turns to his daughter, who is sitting behind me. "Have you ever heard of these things called coats? They come in handy when it's below freezing outside."

Haley laughs, sounding like she's truly amused by her father. I turn to face her, and she gives me a big smile. In that moment, I can clearly see the resemblance between father and daughter... hair the color of fine dark chocolate, dark eyes sparkling with humor, and a wide, generous smile. She's lovely.

"You must be Erin," she says, offering me her slender hand. "I'm Haley."

Her grip is strong and confident—just like her father's. I like her already. How could I not? "It's a pleasure to meet you, Haley."

Her expressive eyes widen as if she just now remembered what Mack had told her about me. "Dad said you were in an accident. I'm so sorry! I hope you're all right."

I paste a smile on my face. "I'm fine. Thanks for asking."

Then Haley turns her gaze to her father as she settles into her seat and buckles her seatbelt. "Mom and Dave said to tell you hello." Then she looks at me. "Dave is my stepdad."

Mack puts the truck in reverse and backs out of the driveway. "Tell them I said hello back."

Our destination isn't far—it's a quaint little diner tucked into a shopping center in an older part of town. As soon as we enter, the hostess greets Mack and Haley warmly. The woman's gaze is respectfully curious as she studies me, undoubtedly noticing the scar on my cheek and the faint remnants of bruises under my eyes.

When I casually raise my hand up to my cheek, Mack takes my hand and holds it securely in his, lacing our fingers together.

"Right this way," the hostess says, eyeing our joined hands.

When we reach our booth, Mack motions for me to take a seat. He slides in beside me. Haley has the opposite bench seat all to herself.

The hostess gives us a perfunctory smile as she passes out our menus. "Your server will be right out to get your drink orders."

Once the hostess leaves, Haley peers at us over the top of her menu. "So, are you guys dating?"

"No!" I say, my heart leaping into my throat.

Mack chuckles as he peruses his menu.

Then, in a much calmer voice, I say, "No, we're not dating. We're friends."

Haley's gaze bounces back and forth between her dad and me. "Friends with benefits?"

My face heats up. "No! We're just friends. Regular friends."

Mack eyes his daughter sternly. "You shouldn't even know what that means. Do you know what you want?"

She lays her menu down. "Yes. The same thing I get every time… crepes with blueberry topping and whipped cream."

Mack looks at me. "Haley is all about the breakfast foods."

"Actually, that sounds pretty good," I say, not bothering to open my menu. "I think I'll have the same."

"Sirloin steak and a loaded baked potato for me," Mack says, laying down his menu.

Our server comes to take our drink orders. Haley orders hot chocolate with whipped cream and chocolate sprinkles. Mack orders coffee, black."

"And for you, miss?" the young woman says as she eyes me. "What can I get you to drink?"

My throat tightens as my heart starts racing. I glance at our server, then at Mack, then down at the menu lying on the table in front of me. It's stupid, absolutely stupid, but I'm afraid to drink anything. "Nothing for me, thanks," I say hastily, not bothering to look up from the table.

"Not even a glass of water?" she says.

I shake my head. "Nothing. Thank you."

"Okay."

A heavy silence falls over our table after the woman leaves. Mack slowly lowers his arm along the back of the seat and leans close. "Are you okay?"

I glance up at Haley, who's watching me closely. "I'm fine," I whisper to Mack.

He whispers back. "There's a little grocery store next door. Why don't I run over there and get you something to drink? A bottle of juice, tea, water?"

Tears well up in my eyes. *He understands!* I nod, swallowing against the painful lump in my throat. "Just water, please. Spring water."

He squeezes my hand. "I'll be right back." Then he glances momentarily at his daughter, who says nothing as she meets his gaze head on.

When Mack is gone, I smile apologetically at Haley. "I'm sorry about that," I tell her. "I'm still... struggling a little bit."

She nods. "It's okay. My dad told me you were under a lot of stress."

I smile, grateful for her easy acceptance.

Mack is back ten minutes later. As he slides into our seat, he hands me a brand-new, unopened bottle of chilled spring water. *Perfect.*

I take it gratefully. "Thank you."

He slides his arm along the back of our seat, his fingers gently brushing my shoulders. "Any time, honey."

Haley grins as she pretends not to look at us.

* * *

"Your daughter probably thinks I'm a nutjob," I tell Mack as we're driving home that evening. I lean my head back on the headrest and close my eyes.

He laughs. "No, she doesn't. She thinks you're delightful."

I swat his arm. "No, she doesn't."

"Yes, she does. I'm totally serious."

"She hardly knows me, and I flipped out at the table over a stupid glass of water."

Mack grabs my hand and brings it to his lips, kissing the back of it. "Don't worry about it. She knows you've been going through a rough time."

He threads his fingers through mine and lays our joined hands on his thigh. It does something funny to my stomach when I feel his thigh muscles tighten and flex.

He squeezes my hand. "The next time we go out, let's remember to bring a bottle of water with us. Then you won't ever have to worry."

* * *

That evening, I walk on the treadmill while Mack lifts weights. When he finishes his reps, he pulls on his boxing gloves, tightens the Velcro straps with his teeth, and starts hitting the bag.

He's wearing a pair of black work-out shorts and a gray tank top that puts his arm and chest muscles, not to mention his tattoos, on display. I can't stop staring at his sinewy arms as they move in perfect coordination with the bag.

I never realized boxing was so sexy. His repetitive movements are graceful and powerful, absolutely mesmerizing. I try to look away—it wouldn't do for him to notice me staring at him—but my gaze inevitably wanders back. My goodness, he's magnificent. Watching him hit the punching bag heats me up on the inside, making my belly quiver. It's not a welcome sensation. I don't want to feel like this! Not for him, not for any man. I don't!

When I feel tears pricking the backs of my eyes, I abruptly step off the deck of the treadmill and shut the machine down. I walk out the door, closing it behind me, and head straight for the bathroom. There I can lock myself in and turn on the faucet to mask the sounds of my sobs.

I sit in the dark, on the side of the tub, my hands covering my face as hot tears stream from my eyes. Like a wounded animal, I rock myself, drowning in pity and self-loathing. I shouldn't feel anything for Mack. I shouldn't feel anything for any man.

I freeze at the sound of a quiet knock at the door. "Erin? Is everything okay?" When I don't answer, he knocks again.

I sit there holding my breath, hoping he'll go away. A moment later, I hear a metallic click, and then the doorknob turns and the door opens. Mack steps inside the darkened room, not bothering with the lights. There's enough light coming from the hallway to show him what he wants to see.

He lifts me into his arms, then carries me to the living room sofa, where he sits with me on his lap. He doesn't say anything. He doesn't ask. He doesn't pry. Instead, he wraps his arms around my shuddering body and rocks me.

He's hot and sweaty from his work-out, but I don't care. Right now, he's my rock, my safety net.

My hot tears flow unchecked, soaking his damp skin.

35

Mack

"She's a little better each day, but she's on such an emotional roller coaster. All it takes is one little thing to set off a panic attack."

I'm standing with Sam at the upstairs balcony railing, watching the girls down below as they eagerly restock the new release table. Apparently, some famous romance author's new book just arrived in the store that morning. Customers have been streaming in all day looking for that new release. We've heard nothing but excited squeals all day, and the books are flying off the table.

Sam frowns. "At least she's *alive*. Keep reminding yourself of that. I know she's been through hell, but she's alive. The two other victims weren't so lucky."

I run my hand through my hair trying to tamp down my anger and frustration at the whole situation. "The perp got off too easy. It was over in a flash for him, but he tortured Erin for *hours*. And she still suffers."

I watch Erin working side-by-side with Beth. They're laughing as customers snatch up the new books just as fast as they put them out. Erin's happy at the moment, smiling and relaxed. I wish she could hold onto this moment.

January has come and gone, and we're well into February. The days are short, the skies overcast, and the temperatures downright frigid. I'm looking forward to spring, when I can take Erin out more. She needs fresh air and sunshine. I can imagine us taking walks along the lake, going on bike rides, going to the zoo. Whatever she wants to do.

When Erin walks away from Beth and the display table, pushing an empty cart to the rear of the store, back toward the inventory room, I jog down the staircase and meet up with her. I have something to ask her. It's something I've been debating for a few weeks now, but I just didn't think she was ready. Maybe now she is. If nothing else, it might be a good distraction for her.

"Hey," I say, catching up to her. I walk beside her into the inventory room. "That new book is flying off the shelves."

"It is!" she says, her cheeks flushed pink with enthusiasm. "I set aside a copy for myself to take home. I've been looking forward to this book for a long time."

I help her load more copies onto the cart. "There's something I've been wanting to ask you."

She gazes up at me, curious. "What's that?"

"I usually get together with some of my old Army buddies on Friday nights at Rowdy's to shoot pool, drink beer, and just generally cut loose. The guys bring their wives. Would you like to go with me later this week?"

Her crystal clear blue eyes widen in surprise. "You want me to meet your friends?"

"Yeah. I thought it might be good for you to get out, meet some new people."

Her brow wrinkles as she mulls over the suggestion. "I would love to meet your friends, but there'll be a lot of strangers there."

And by strangers, she means *men*.

"I'll be with you the entire time."

She thinks it over a moment. "Okay," she says, pushing the heavy cart toward the door.

After holding the door for her, I follow her to the front of the store, stepping back to let her replenish the display table. There's a line of customers waiting for the new book, and Erin passes them out with a pleased smile on her face.

* * *

"Today was a great day," Erin says as she leans back in the front passenger seat.

She sighs with contentment, and that puts a smile on my face.

I wish every day could be like this for her. She's come so far. She's having fewer nightmares, fewer panic attacks. Her therapist has taught her all kinds of coping mechanisms that seem to be helping a lot. She has more good days than bad ones now.

She comes with me on my weekly dinners with Haley. Those two have become pretty fast friends and frequently side with each other to gang up on me.

That evening, she makes a salad and bakes some potatoes for dinner while I grill burgers out on the balcony. We eat at the kitchen table, then wash dishes together. As I watch her wiping down the kitchen counter, cleaning up after our meal prep, I realize how much pleasure I take in watching her do the everyday little things. Her movements are so economical, so efficient. There's just something about the way she moves that sucks me in. I just want to be in her orbit.

As usual, she dries the dishes and I put them away, because I'm taller and can reach the upper cabinets and she can't.

After dinner, we toss a load of underwear and PJs into the washer and go relax in the living room. I watch basketball and she lounges on the sofa beside me engrossed in her new book. It's pretty domestic. I figure this is a lot like being married, except without the intimacy.

This evening, she's leaning against me and stretching her legs out on the sofa, her new hardback book propped on her belly. Absently, I stroke her hair, mesmerized by its silky softness. The scent of vanilla wafts up and does things to my body, teasing my senses and heating up my body. She leans her head back against my arm and sighs, seemingly oblivious to my growing discomfort.

No matter how hard I try to focus on the game, my dick has other ideas tonight. My gaze keeps drifting from the TV to Erin, following the gentle slopes of her shoulders, the soft skin of her arms, her graceful fingers as they turn the pages of her book. I gloss right over the small scars on her arms.

My apartment is the only place she'll leave her arms uncovered. At work, she insists on wearing long sleeve blouses or a sweater. But here, with me, she's comfortable enough to let the small reminders of her traumatic experience show. Six weeks after the attack, there are still bite marks visible on her arms. They're on her legs, too. And I'm sure they exist in other places—places I'm not privy to.

I try to be subtle as I shift in my seat, trying to relieve the pressure on a steadily lengthening erection. If this keeps up, I'll have to change out of my jeans into something a bit more comfortable. The problem is, she can't know what she does to me. It would ruin everything.

She feels safe here with me, and that's my goal—to give her a safe haven. If she knew I was lusting after her, her sense of security would be shattered. And then where would she go? Move into an apartment of her own? Alone? Hell no!

"Are you enjoying your book?" I ask her, trying to shift my thoughts away from my traitorous dick.

She tilts her head back to look at me and grins. "It's fantastic! I knew it would be. How's your game?"

I have no clue. I stopped paying attention half-an-hour ago. I don't even know the score. But she doesn't need to know that. "It's good. Hey, do you want some ice cream?"

She sits up, swinging her feet to the floor. "Sure."

"I'll get it," I say, patting her leg. "You read your book."

I stand in such a way she can't see the thick ridge in the front of my jeans. "I'm just going to change my clothes first. Be right back."

* * *

That night, Erin has one of her nightmares, awakening in panic mode. She sits up in bed, gasping and disoriented. Years in the military taught me to sleep lightly and awake fully aware of my surroundings. Instantly, I'm sitting beside her, rubbing her back and talking her down from whatever ledge she's on. "Shh, it's okay. You're fine, honey. It was just a dream."

She turns to me with wide eyes, half awake, half asleep. "He's dead, right?" She's shaking, her fingers clutching her throat. Always the same nightmare. She's suffocating.

"Yes, he's dead."

"You're sure?"

"Absolutely sure. I checked the body myself."

The tension slowly leaves her body, and she slumps back down on the mattress. I follow her down, lying on my side and facing her. She covers her face and exhales heavily as she tries to get a grip.

I brush back her hair, tucking it behind her ear. "I'm proud of you, Erin."

Her hands come down, and she looks at me as if I'm nuts. "Why? For being a bundle of nerves?"

"For surviving. For getting up each morning and facing the day, taking whatever comes in stride the best you can. You're a survivor." I reach out and trace my finger down her cheek following the path of her scar without actually touching it. It's still very sensitive.

She looks up at me with her big, luminous eyes, and for a moment I lose myself in those clear blue depths. At moments like this, when it's just the two of us, together, quiet, and she stares into my eyes, I think maybe she's feeling a little bit of what I'm feeling.

Sometimes I convince myself we're on the same page—just that she needs more time. But the moment always ends for one reason or another, and I don't dare ask her. If I'm wrong, and she doesn't feel the same, it would ruin everything. I'll never take that chance. I'd rather have this with her than nothing at all.

She yawns, breaking the spell, and we both laugh softly.

"Go back to sleep, honey," I say. And then I lean over and kiss her temple.

Her lids drift shut, and she turns to her side, facing away from me. When I wrap my arm around her and pull her close, she clutches my arm with a sigh.

I'm careful to keep my hips clear of her so she doesn't feel my erections at night. Having her this close to me, her body soft and drowsy, warm from sleep, is sheer fucking torture. But that's *my* problem, not hers. I'll deal with it.

36

Erin

The minute we walk into Rowdy's Tavern my chest tightens, and I find it hard to breathe. The air is hot and stifling, and the place smells like beer and fried food—not my favorite combination of scents. The noise level is high thanks to the juke box playing loudly over the sound system and the multitude of voices competing to be heard over the din. In the background, I hear the sharp crack of someone hitting pool balls.

I've been here plenty of times before. Shane and the owner are friends, and McIntyre Security holds a lot of private social events here. I was here for Sam and Cooper's engagement party, and Jonah Locke performs here occasionally. It's a very familiar place. It's a safe place. Or at least it used to be. Now it feels... hostile. There's too much noise, too many voices, and too many strangers.

As if he can read my emotions, Mack slides his arm across my shoulders and draws me close. He points across the room at a group of people sitting around a cluster of wooden tables. "There they are. Come on. I'll introduce you."

As Mack leads me across the room, my instincts tell me to turn around and walk out. Go back home. But that would be selfish of me. These are Mack's friends. He's missed out on this weekly tradition for over a month because he's been at home entertaining me.

I force myself to smile as we approach the group. There are three women seated together at one end of the tables, and three guys are congregating at the opposite end.

"Mack!" An older man with short gray hair waves us over. He has to shout to be heard. "Hey, man, it's good to see you! We'd just about given up on you." The guy offers his hand to Mack and they shake.

Another man comes up behind Mack and slaps him on the back. "It's about time you showed your handsome face around here. Where you been?"

"I've been busy," Mack says. "This is my friend Erin," he says to the group. And then he points everyone out to me. "This is Patrick." The older man. "And his wife, Cindy." Then he introduces the other two couples. "Carl and Veronica. Marty and Michelle."

I smile at everyone, thinking I'll never remember who's who.

Mack pulls out a chair for me to sit, but one of the women, a blonde in her mid-fifties, waves me over to join the women. Cindy, I think. "Come sit with us, Erin," she says. "We're a lot more interesting than the guys."

Cindy pulls out the empty seat beside hers and I sit. "Go get some drinks, Mack," the woman says, waving him off when he moves to follow me. "We'll entertain your girlfriend."

Before Mack can correct her, I say, "Oh, no, we're not together. Not like that. We're just friends."

Mack hesitates to leave, his eyes on me.

"Go ahead," I tell him. "I'm okay."

He waits another moment, watching me for signs of pending doom, but when he doesn't see any, he heads to the bar where two of his friends are already ordering more drinks.

"So, Erin," Cindy says, a gleam in her pale blue eyes. She crosses her arms over her chest, displaying an impressive collection of thin gold bracelets on her wrists and big rings on her fingers. "Tell us all about yourself. Mack's never brought a woman here before, so we're dying of curiosity."

The other two women—one a red head, the other a brunette—eagerly await my response. They're all considerably older than I am. I feel like I've been dropped into the middle of a sorority of some sort. A military wives' group? Only I'm not Mack's wife, or even his girlfriend. So what does that make me? An honorary member?

I have to fight the urge to cover my cheek. All three women

have been trying valiantly not to stare at my scar, but it's kind of hard to miss. "There's nothing to tell, really," I say. "We're friends."

"How do you know Mack?" the redhead says. Veronica, I think.

"From work. We both work at Clancy's Bookshop downtown. I'm the assistant manager, and he's in charge of security."

"Oh, I love that place," the other woman says. The brunette, Michelle. "I'll bet you get discounts on books."

I smile. "I do. And it's a good thing, because I read a lot."

Mack returns to the table with a bottle of beer for himself and a bottle of chilled water for me. He cracks open the bottle of water and hands it to me, then lays a hand on my shoulder, squeezing gently. "Will you be okay here if I go play a game of pool with Patrick?"

I nod as I sip the cold water. "Sure."

"I ordered some food. They'll bring it out to the table when it's ready. I'll be right over there—call if you need me."

I watch him walk across the crowded bar to join his friend, who is already racking up the balls.

Michelle grins at me. "So, you and Mack, huh?"

I take another sip of water. "Oh, no. Really, we're just friends."

The other two guys join Mack and Patrick at the pool tables, grabbing cues and racking up more balls. It looks like they're settling in for a while.

"He's quite a catch, you know," the red head says. She winks at me. "Women throw themselves at him all the time."

"Oh, stop, Veronica," Cindy says. "Don't tease the girl."

"I'm not teasing. I'm stating facts."

A young male server brings several plates of appetizers to our table—hot wings, fried pickles, loaded nachos—and sidles up beside my chair. When he smiles down at me, I look away.

"Here you go, ladies." As our server leans forward to set the plates on the table, he brushes up against my shoulder, making me tense. "Courtesy of the gentlemen in your party." He straightens. "If there's anything else you need, just let me know."

When our server remains standing at my side, seemingly in no hurry to leave us, I risk a glance up.

He's looking right at me. "I haven't seen you in here before," he says. "Is this your first time?"

"Get out of here, Clint," Cindy says, shooing our server away with a laugh. "She's taken. Unless you want to deal with Mack, I suggest you move on."

The server—Clint—returns to the bar. I happen to glance across the bar and see Mack watching me. I give him a little wave. *I'm fine. Don't worry.*

He gives me a nod and returns to his game.

"So, Erin," Michelle says as she pops a fried pickle into her mouth. "What do you do besides work at Clancy's?"

"I'm a student at University of Chicago, currently taking online courses. I'm majoring in business."

"Where do you live? Downtown?"

I nod. "I live in an apartment building on Lake Shore Drive."

"Wow, fancy," Veronica says.

"Wait," Cindy says. "Mack lives over that way too. In the McIntyre Building."

I feel my face heating. I'm so not good at subterfuge. "Actually, we live in the same building." They already think there's something going on between us. If they knew we lived *together*, they'd never believe we weren't dating.

A young guy approaches our table, ash blond hair and brown eyes. He's wearing blue jeans and a college sweatshirt. "Hello, ladies!"

"Get lost, Donny," Cindy says, brushing him off. "Nobody here is interested."

This guy—Donny—turns to me. "What about you, darlin'? I don't believe I'd had the pleasure."

This guy reeks of alcohol, so badly my eyes water. He extends his hand to me, obviously wanting me to take it. I freeze.

"Donny, get lost. This one has standards, and you're not her type."

He ignores Cindy and drops down into the chair next to mine, putting his arm across my shoulders. "Hey, sweetie, don't listen to these old biddies. I promise you, I don't bite." He winks at me. "Not unless you ask nicely."

There's a rushing sound in my ears and the room starts spinning. Suddenly, Mack is behind Donny's chair. He grabs the guy by the back of his shirt and hauls him up off his chair. Mack twists one of Donny's arms behind his back and wrenches it upward until Donny cries out.

"Get the fuck away from her," Mack growls into the guy's ear. He ratchets Donny's arm higher up his back, straining the muscles and tendons.

"All right, all right!" Donny cries. "Jesus, man, lemme go!"

Mack releases the guy and steps back.

Donny gingerly tests his arm. With a grimace, he wheels on Mack. "What the fuck's wrong with you, man? I was just talkin' to her."

Mack points at me, gritting his teeth. "Stay the hell away from her. Do you understand me?"

"Yes! God, I was just bein' friendly. No call for you to go ape shit on my ass." Shaking his head in disgust, Donny saunters away, his right arm held close to his chest.

Mack turns to me, his expression clearly agitated. "Are you all right?"

I nod, too stunned to speak.

"You're sure?" he says, looking me over.

Patrick comes up behind Mack and claps him on the shoulder. "It's your turn to break, pal. Are you comin'?"

"Yeah. Just a minute."

"I'm okay," I say. Although my heart is hammering in my chest, I'm managing. "Go play your game."

When Mack returns to the pool table, Veronica grins as she says, "Does *Mack* know you're not dating?"

"Honey," Cindy says to me, laughing. "If it walks like a duck, and it quacks like a duck, it's a duck."

"Seriously, we're not dating." Then I pop a nacho chip in my mouth and chew slowly.

After the guys finish their pool games, they flock back to the table and devour the remaining appetizers. Carl and Marty order fresh drinks as Patrick pulls a chair up behind his wife and sits.

Mack parks himself in the empty chair beside mine and lays his arm across the back of my chair.

"Did you have fun?" I ask him.

He tosses back the last of his beer. "Yes. I skunked Patrick and Carl, both, and made a hundred bucks in the process." He pulls some wrinkled bills out of his back pocket and hands them to me. "Here. Book money."

The juke box changes songs, and a new one begins—*Something* by The Beatles. It was one of Gram's favorite songs, and she played it all the time. Hearing it now brings back a rush of emotions, a mix of happy and sad. I miss her so much. "I love this song."

Cindy points a finger at us. "Mack, why don't you take her dancing?"

A small section of the wood floor is marked off as a dance floor. A half dozen couples are out there now, slowly swaying to the music.

"Oh, no, that's fine," I say quickly, shaking my head.

Veronica points at her husband. "Carl loves to dance. Carl, you take her."

"Sure, I'm game," Carl says, jumping to his feet and wiping his hands on his jeans.

Mack's fingers brush the nape of my neck, sending unexpected shivers down my spine. "Do you want to dance?" he says, leaning close. "I'll take you if you want to."

The idea of dancing with Mack is very tempting. Before, I

would have jumped at the opportunity to dance with him. Now, I'm not so sure. It's a slow song, a really slow one, and that means he'd be holding me close.

"Of course she wants to dance," Veronica says. "What girl doesn't want to dance with a handsome fella? Go on, Mack! If you don't take her, Carl will."

Carl is still standing, hovering nearby, ready to do his duty. Mack stands and holds out his hand to me. "Come on. I'll take you."

I stare at his hand, and suddenly it feels like so much hangs in the balance. I want to do this. Not because I want to dance—I'm not much of a dancer—but because I want him to hold me in his arms. Does that make me a hypocrite?

I take his hand, and he pulls me to my feet and leads me across the room. When we reach the perimeter of the dance floor, clearly marked by a shiny parquet floor, Mack pulls me close, holding me at a very respectable distance. Unlike the other couples on the dance floor, we are not plastered against each other. It's for the best, I know. There's no point in confusing things between us.

Mack's hand drifts up my back, coming to rest between my shoulder blades. His other hand cradles mine, and he holds my hand to his chest. I don't know where to rest my eyes—I don't dare look him in the face—so I close my eyes and just let myself drift with the music as he leads us in the dance.

The familiar melody is mesmerizing, and soon I find myself floating. I close my eyes and simply enjoy the moment. One of my hands is on Mack's arm, and I can feel the strength in his bicep. I revel in the heat emanating from his big body, and the faint scent of his cologne makes my belly quiver.

I'm disappointed when the song quickly comes to an end. But when the last note fades, he doesn't release me. We stand there, still swaying, as the next song starts up, also a love song—*I Can't Help Falling in Love with You* by UB40. This song is just as hypnotic, and I'm convinced the fates are working to keep us together on this dance floor.

As we sway to the melody, my muscles turn to mush, and I just want to glue myself to him. When his hand slides up to cup the back of my head, he gently presses my cheek to his chest, closing the distance between us until my body is practically plastered against his.

I'm swamped with all sorts of feelings and sensations that I have no business feeling. And I don't think I'm hallucinating when I feel his lips against my temple.

Please, God, I don't want this moment to end. Right now, during this tiny sliver in time, I can pretend we have a future.

"Hey, can I cut in?" Carl says, snapping me out of my spell.

I open my eyes just as Mack's friend taps him on the shoulder.

"Sorry, man," Mack says as he squeezes my hand. "She's mine, and I don't share."

The moment he utters those words, my belly tumbles in a freefall, and I feel flushed. Something suspiciously like arousal surges through my body, unfamiliar and unwelcome. It steals my breath and leaves me dizzy. "I've had enough dancing," I say.

Mack meets my gaze, his dark eyes locking onto mine, searching for something. But the moment quickly passes, and he nods as he leads me back to our table.

I sit down, shaking, and Mack goes to the bar to get me another bottle of water. I'm not sure what just happened, but I think my body betrayed me.

37

Erin

We're both quiet on the drive back to the apartment. My thoughts are racing, and I don't know what to make of them. Something changed tonight, but I'm not sure what or how it happened. Mack is very pensive too, seemingly lost in his own thoughts.

Once in the apartment, we go our separate ways. Without a word, Mack changes and shuts himself up in the work-out room. I can hear the thud of his steps as he runs full out on the treadmill. I change into my PJ bottoms and a white cami, and grab my book from the nightstand. I head to the kitchen to put on a pot of water for some decaf tea. I need something to calm my nerves, because they're still electrified.

I sit on the sofa with my book and my tea, listening in the soothing background noise of Mack running. He runs for a good while before switching to the punching bag. The repetitive and oddly comforting beat of his shoes hitting the treadmill is replaced by the equally repetitive sound of his gloved fists slamming into the bag.

Half an hour later, Mack takes a shower, and as the water runs, I imagine him standing naked beneath the spray of hot water, soaping his muscular body.

Was that desire I felt tonight on the dance floor? Were those butterflies in my stomach for *him?* I honestly believed I would never feel anything like desire again. But right now, I can't get the image of Mack naked in the shower out of my head.

I jump when the bathroom door opens. From where I'm sitting in the living room, I can see him crossing the hall, wearing only a towel wrapped around his waist, and disappearing into the bedroom.

My heart is racing. I feel like I just ran ten miles on the treadmill myself. I'm nervous. All of a sudden, I don't know how to act around him, what to say. *Thank you for the dance? I loved the way you held me to your body, and I want you to do it again, only this time with our clothes off?*

But then reality hits me like a slap in the face. I can't get naked with him, or with any man. I couldn't bear for him to see the bite marks on my body. While most of them have faded to nothing, a number of them remain visible—three on my breasts, two on my belly, and six on my inner thighs. I can only hope they will fade one day.

Mack comes out of the bedroom wearing gray sweatpants and a black tank top, glancing at me only once as he heads into the kitchen and opens the fridge. He brings a bottle of beer into the living room and sits down, reaching for the TV remote control.

I'm relieved when he turns on the TV to a basketball game. Apparently, there's some kind of big tournament going on. The background noise of the game is comforting.

I pretend to be focused on my book, but the truth is I can't make heads or tails out of what I'm reading. I can't stop thinking about tonight. Every time I remember the feel of his hand splayed against my back, or cupping the back of my head, the butterflies return. Even now, just thinking about it makes my pulse race. I feel… breathless.

Is this desire?

Is that even possible?

I'm terrified to go down this path. What if it blows up in my face? What if I can't go through with it, and I end up hurting Mack even more?

I check the time—it's almost midnight. The game will be over soon.

I get up and head to the kitchen to put my tea cup in the sink. Then I stand in the darkened room and stare out the glass balcony doors at the night sky.

My heart's pounding, my pulse racing. I feel hot and dizzy and queasy all at the same time. When I head back to the living room, his gaze snaps up to me, and he watches me with a guarded expression. "Is everything okay?"

I stop halfway into the living room, standing uncertainly. His gaze meets mine and we both just stare at each other. Nervous, I twist my fingers in front of me.

"Erin?" He turns off the TV and sets the remote on the coffee table. "What's wrong?"

I stand there mutely, unable to say the words that could either bring us closer together or tear us irrevocably apart.

"What is it, honey? You can tell me."

I walk until I'm standing only a couple of feet in front of him. I could just tell him goodnight, say that I'm tired and heading to bed. But that would be a cowardly lie, and I'm done with being a coward. "Mack, I—"

That's as far as I get. He motions me forward, taking my hands when they're within reach, and he guides me to sit on the coffee table in front of him. He holds both of my hands in his. "Talk to me."

"I don't know how to say this."

He brings my hands to his mouth and kisses my knuckles. "Just say it. Whatever it is, just spit it out."

I don't even know what to say. *I think I want you?*

He waits, so patiently.

I take a shaky breath. "I don't even know if I can."

"Can… what? I'm sorry, I'm not following you. Can you try that again?"

I laugh nervously. "I don't know how to say this."

"Just say it, honey. Whatever it is, all you have to do is say it."

I clear my throat. "I think... that... I might still have feelings for you."

As soon as I say the words, his entire expression transforms instantly, going from mildly confused and somewhat amused to thunderstruck.

Frantically, I back peddle, trying to undo whatever damage I've done. "It's okay if you don't feel that way. I—"

"Erin, stop." He tugs me off the coffee table and onto his lap, his fingers threading through my hair as he studies me warily. He swallows hard, then brushes my left cheek with the rough pad of his thumb.

I find his intensity a bit unnerving. "I'm sorry. I shouldn't have said anything"

He presses an index finger to my lips. "Wait. Give me a minute to process this, okay?" He smiles, then presses his forehead to mine. "Honey, you've got me reeling inside."

"Do you—I mean..."

"Do I *want* you?" He laughs. "That's like asking me if I want to breathe. Of course I want you."

My heart skips a beat at his frank admission. "Tonight, when we were dancing, it was like someone flipped a switch in me. All these feelings came flooding back."

His hands frame my face. "Tell me *exactly* what you need from me, baby. I don't want to fuck this up."

I gaze into his dark eyes, searching. I can't believe we're discussing this. "I want to *try*, but I don't want to make promises I can't keep. I don't want to let you down."

He laughs again. "Honey, trust me, there is no way you could ever let me down." He shakes his head. "No way in hell." His thumb brushes across my lips, and then he looks me directly in the eye and says with utmost seriousness, "I will wait for you, for as long as it takes. I just want you to feel safe and comfortable. The rest can wait. This is your show, baby. You call all the shots. I am yours whenever and however you want me."

After hearing this vow—because that's exactly what it sounded like to me—much of my anxiety fades into the background, to be replaced by a tantalizing hint of desire.

I trust Mack with my life. He's the only person I could ever envision taking this step with. "Maybe we could start with kissing," I suggest.

The corner of his mouth quirks up. "Kissing. Yes, that sounds reasonable." Smiling, he shifts me on his lap so that I'm facing him, my thighs straddling him. His hands settle on my hips, and he clutches them lightly. "Remember, you're calling the shots here. You say when and how much."

I nod, my gaze going to his beautiful lips, which are so perfectly formed and lovingly framed by his short, dark beard. I've fantasized so many times about having these lips on mine.

His tongue darts out to wet his bottom lip, and the sight of it makes my belly clench sharply. That's arousal I'm feeling, no question about it. It's like my mind and body are coming back online after a long winter hiatus.

Insecurities and doubts bombard me, reminding me of the reason for my hiatus. They threaten to kill what little courage I have, but I forcefully shove them aside. I want this! I want a chance at a normal life with the most amazing man I've ever met.

And besides, we're just talking about kissing right now. He said I could call the shots. I think I can handle kissing. It doesn't involve taking my clothes off and exposing my body—my scars. Most importantly, it doesn't require him touching anything below my waist.

As I straddle him, I'm very much aware of the tender place between my legs. For the first time in a long time, I feel something pleasurable down there, instead of pain. My body is flushed with a growing sense of heat and wetness. My nerves are coming alive, my flesh tingling and… aching.

Mack is aroused, too. I know because I can feel him hardening beneath me, the ridge of his erection swelling until it's pressing against the thin material of my PJ bottoms. The sheer size of him takes my breath away. I tense, expecting discomfort, but it doesn't hurt. In fact, it feels… good.

Mack's warm hands slide up my back, stroking me gently through the soft material of my top. My lungs billow as I try to draw in air. The only thing stopping me from kissing him is my own fear. But I'm tired of being afraid! I want to touch his lips… with mine. I want to know what it's like to share that intimacy with him.

My hands come up to his chest, my palms flat against his T-shirt. I can feel his muscles beneath the material, hard and well defined. His chest rises and falls steadily with each breath.

Now it's my turn to lick my lips. As his gaze follows the movement of my tongue, he swallows hard. I brush back his hair, then gently trace the shape of his eyebrows with my fingertips. He closes his eyes and groans softly.

I've never touched him like this before, not so intimately, and the feeling is heady. I trace the ridge of his nose, then slide my hands down to cup his cheeks. His dark eyes open and lock on mine, his gaze hot. He holds perfectly still as if he's afraid a sudden movement will spook me.

I lean closer, staring at his lips. I kissed a boy once, when I was twelve years old. It was at a birthday party, and we were playing Spin the Bottle in the basement. That seems like such a lifetime ago. I was nervous then, but I'm far more nervous now. The stakes are so much higher.

When my lips are just inches from his, I close my eyes and press forward, gasping the instant our lips touch. He sucks in a breath and clutches my hips. But he remains as still as a statue, his only movement the rapid rise and fall of his chest.

I press my lips more fully against his, surprised by how soft his are. I expected them to be as hard as the rest of him, but they're not. They're soft. This time, his lips part just a bit, and mine follow suit. Our lips cling together, and he gently moves his, coaxing mine open as he teases me with slow, tender movements.

We kiss for a while just like this, slow, languid kisses. With each caress of his lips on mine, I feel my body coming alive as if dormant nerves are firing once more. My hands slide down the sides of his neck to his broad shoulders.

He lets out another groan, this one louder and so much more ragged than the one before. His hands are flexing on my hips now, alternately gripping and releasing. They slide to my butt cheeks, squeezing them and holding me to him.

Between my legs, I grow hotter and wetter until I'm throbbing. When I press myself down on his erection, he shudders, closing his eyes on a harsh groan.

"Do you trust me?" he says, his voice rough.

"Yes."

"Then let's take this to the bedroom."

Mack gently sets me on my feet and stands, taking me by the hand and leading me to the bedroom. I'm a nervous wreck, and I'm not sure if I can go through with this. Kissing is one thing, but any more than that? I'm not sure I can.

I realize I must be dragging my feet when he stops and turns back to face me. "I'll never ask you for anything you're not ready to give. And you can stop us at any time. You have nothing to fear."

I trust him. I know he won't ask for more than I'm capable of giving, but this is uncharted territory for us. This is going to change everything. And if it turns out badly, then what will we do?

He leads me the rest of the way to the bedroom and pulls back the covers, motioning for me to climb into bed. He follows me down, lying on his side next to me, facing me.

He lays his hand on my belly, gently smoothing the fabric of my top. "I'll do anything to make this right for you. There's no rush. We'll limit ourselves to kissing for a year if that's what you need."

When I laugh nervously, he smiles. "I mean it, Erin. We're not on any timetable. Above all, I want you to feel comfortable. I would never do anything to hurt you."

When he leans closer, sliding his hand up to cup the side of my face, a shiver courses through me. I close my eyes, praying that I don't ruin this by panicking.

When his lips gently touch mine again, I tense. He stills for a moment, then resumes, his lips teasing mine, gently coaxing them apart so he can settle his mouth more fully on mine.

As we kiss, I slide my hand along his arm, marveling at the firmness of his biceps. Even with his clothes on, he's magnificent, his body a work of art from head to toe.

As the pressure of his mouth on mine increases, his hand slides down my torso and slips underneath my top. He caresses my belly, drawing slow circles around my belly button. Mentally, I catalog the bite marks on my belly. And those aren't the only ones. The thought of Mack seeing them makes my chest contract painfully and my breathing pick up—not from desire, but from increasing anxiety.

I push against his chest. "I don't think I can do this."

I see a flash of disappointment in his eyes, but he quickly recovers. "All right." He removes his hand from beneath my top. "Can you tell me why?"

My eyes sting as the tears flow. "I have so many scars...."

He studies me for a moment before sitting up and whipping off his tank top and tossing it aside. When he turns to face me, bare chested, I gasp at the sight of scars on his chest. Horrible, deep, jagged scars. Four of them.

"Oh, my God, Mack! What happened?"

He points to one. "This one is a bullet wound." He points to another one—a long, jagged one. "This is a knife wound." He points to a third. "Shrapnel. And this last one is also a bullet wound."

He shows me his back, where the man who attacked me stabbed him in the shoulder. The wound is healed, but there's a jagged scar in its place. Besides that wound, there are several others of various sizes and shapes.

"Like you, I have scars all over my body, honey. They're proof we survived everything that life has thrown at us. And as for your scars… they're proof of your courage."

He leans close and kisses me gently. "One day, I'll kiss every one of your scars."

38

Mack

Erin stares at me with eyes that are deep, luminous pools of blue, full of wonder like I just performed some kind of miracle. She sits up, turning to me, and presses her mouth to mine. Her lips tremble against me, as shaky as her breath, and the soft sound of pleasure she makes lights my body on fucking fire.

I fall back onto the mattress, pulling her down with me. "Kiss me, Erin." Right now I want her all over me. I want everything she's willing to give, as much or as little. I've never wanted anything as badly as I want this.

She moves her lips on mine, gradually deepening our kiss. Impatient for more, I risk nudging her lips apart and slipping my tongue inside her mouth. She gasps, but she doesn't shy away from the contact. If anything, her kiss becomes a bit more heated, and our tongues mingle in a slow dance. I grip her shoulders and hold her to me, and her fingers splay over my chest, molding themselves to the shape of my muscles.

Rolling us so that she's lying on her back, I hover over her. My arms snake around her, and I hold her close, our mouths melded together. I slide one hand down from her face to cup her breast, and she flinches with a soft whimper. I freeze, gauging her reaction, but when she keeps kissing me, I think we're okay.

I mold my hand to her breast, through the thin fabric of her top. When I brush my thumb over her nipple, she cries out, her back arching beneath me. "Mack!"

"Okay?" I ask.

When she nods, I slip my hand underneath her top and cup her bare breast. She digs her nails into my biceps.

I brush her nipple once more, and it puckers tightly. "Can I kiss you here?"

Her eyes widen, but she doesn't say anything.

I reach for the hem of her top and lift it slowly, exposing a narrow swath of her soft belly. She grabs hold of my hands, gripping them tightly.

"It's okay," I say. "I'm just going to pull your top up. I want to see your breasts."

"There are scars," she says in a quiet, pained voice.

"I know. But I want to look at you, all of you, including your scars."

She reluctantly releases my hands. *Jesus, she's trusting me with this.* The knowledge floors me.

Slowly, I lift her top, exposing her belly button, then her abdomen, her ribcage, and finally her breasts. My breath hitches at the sight of her two soft mounds topped with pale pink nipples. My belly tightens with desire, and my cock begins to throb. *Fuck.* I've never wanted anyone so much in my life.

Those perfect little mounds are marred only by the presence of three sets of bite marks, one on her left breast, two on her right. Seeing them makes me seethe, anger scalding my insides. But I'm careful to hide my reaction from her. She doesn't need reminders of what she's been through.

"My God, you're beautiful," I say as I pull her top the rest of the way off. I cup one breast in my hand, shaping and molding its soft weight to my palm. I trace one scar with the tip of my finger, then the other. And then I tenderly kiss each scar.

She flinches and looks away as her body starts shaking.

My personal life philosophy when faced with a challenge is to rip off the bandage and plow through the pain and discomfort. But I'm not Erin. I can't expect her to feel the same way. She's got to find her own path through this journey.

Moving slowly, giving her plenty of time to protest, I close my mouth over one nipple, drawing the soft, supple tip into my mouth and teasing it with my tongue. She cries out, arching her back, and digs her nails into my back. But she doesn't tell me to stop.

I worship each breast, sucking and licking and stroking. I kiss each scar, over and over, tenderly marking them as mine.

Her chest rises and falls rapidly, and her soft moans are music to my ears. Every soft sound she makes, every cry, fuels my own arousal until my cock aches for release. *Sorry, pal. This is for her, not for you.*

My lips return to hers, parting them so I can slip my tongue into her mouth. She lets me in, and we leisurely explore each other's taste and texture. She laughs once when my mustache tickles her nose.

"It's softer than I expected," she says, brushing her fingers against my beard.

My hand meanders down her abdomen, to her belly. My finger circles her belly button, then slips lower, slowly making its way down to the waistband of her PJ bottoms. I run my fingertip back and forth along the seam of her pajamas.

My fingers slide between her legs, adding gentle pressure as they brush against the soft fabric. Even through the material, I can feel the heat of her, the soft mound of her springy curls. I want closer. I want inside, to taste her wetness, but this will have to do for now.

I press the tip of my index finger gently against her clit and watch her reaction. "Does that hurt?" I have to ask. I have to know.

"No," she says breathlessly, sounding genuinely surprised.

I strum my fingers gently up and down the seam of her pants. "If it's too much, tell me," I say, my voice rough.

"No, it's okay," she says, despite the fact her nails are digging into my arms.

"Can you open your legs for me? Just a bit?"

When she does, I angle the pad of my thumb so that it brushes against her clit. I begin rubbing slow circles through the material.

"Is this okay?" I say.

Her thighs are shaking. "Yes!"

So I continue stroking her clit, alternating gentle and firm pressure. God, I would love to make her come, to show her how pleasurable sex can be. I keep stroking her, gauging her arousal by her breathless pants and soft moans. When her breathing quickens, and her thighs tighten, I know she's close. *Come on, baby, please come.*

She squeezes her eyes shut as she struggles through what might be her first orgasm with a partner. She gasps as she clutches my shoulders, holding on for dear life. "Mack!"

"I know, honey." I maintain gentle pressure on her clit. "Just relax and let it happen." I continue stroking, teasing, alternating the pressure, relentlessly prolonging her pleasure. I watch her closely, noting her flushed cheeks and flaring nostrils. Her nipples are tight little points.

She presses her head back into the pillow and releases a long, wailing cry as an orgasm hits her hard. "Mack! Oh, my God, Mack!"

I cover her mouth with mine and drink in her sweet, inarticulate cries. Her lips tremble as she opens them for me, letting my tongue inside. Her body trembles as wave after wave of pleasure sweeps through her.

When her orgasm wanes, I meet her flushed gaze. "Did I hurt you?"

Breathless, she shakes her head and smiles.

Cupping her between her legs, I feel her damp heat through the fabric. Damn, I'd give anything to taste her arousal, but I don't think she's ready for that. I've already pushed my luck tonight as it is.

I lie back and pull her close, my lips in her hair. She's quiet, and I hope to God I didn't push her too far.

Her fingers play over my bare chest, and she leans close and kisses the muscle right over my pounding heart.

"What about you?" she says, glancing down at my hips.

My erection is tenting the fabric of my flannel pants, demanding attention. "Don't worry about me. Tonight was about you. Baby steps."

Trying to ignore my aching blue balls, I roll us so that I'm spooning behind her, my chest pressed against her bare back. I pull the blankets up around us both, cocooning us in.

I kiss the back of her head, then dip down to kiss the bare skin of her shoulder. "Go to sleep, honey."

* * *

When Erin's scream rips me out of a sound sleep, I shoot up in bed, my heart hammering. It takes me half a second to orient myself. She's having a nightmare, only this one is way more intense than the ones she's had before. This isn't a panic attack. She sounds like she's in pain! *Shit!* "Erin, honey, wake up."

I shake her lightly, feeling a bit rattled by the frantic sound of her cry. "Erin! Wake up, sweetheart. You're having a dream."

Her eyes snap open, and she stares blankly right at me. She jumps out of bed and backs away from me, her chest heaving as she tries to catch her breath. It's the middle of the night still, and the room is shrouded in darkness. I can barely make out her movements as she backs into the dresser, knocking it into the wall with a crash.

I swing my legs off the side of the bed and stand. "Erin? It's all right. You're safe."

She stares at me. "Mack?"

"Yeah, it's me. Everything's okay. You had a bad dream."

I approach her slowly, as I would a frightened animal, until I'm right in front of her. "Let's go back to bed." Laying my hands on her shoulders, I steer her back to bed, and she lies down without a fight.

Once I've got her covered, she curls up in a ball and cries herself back to sleep.

Shaken, I lie awake wondering if she dreamed about the attack. I know there's a possibility that her memories of the attack will surface at some point, whether a week from now or a year. It's impossible to know.

I lie on my side and watch her, listening to her breathing as it gradually slows and deepens, signaling that she's back to sleep.

The memory of her cry of pain reverberates in my skull, rattling my nerves. I don't fear pain myself, but the idea of *Erin* hurting like that makes me want to break something.

If Kurt Marshall wasn't already dead, I'd gladly kill him myself.

39

Erin

Saturday morning, I awake to find Mack lying next to me in bed, reading on his phone. As I turn to face him, memories of what we did last night return in a rush, and I blush with embarrassment. He made me *come*. He made me fly apart just by touching me.

He sets his phone down and rolls to face me. "Good morning. How did you sleep last night?"

I stretch with a moan. "Like a baby."

He cocks his head, looking a bit surprised. "You don't remember having a nightmare last night?"

I shake my head. "No."

He leans over and kisses my forehead. "Good. I'm glad you don't remember." He sits up in bed, stretching, and the covers fall to his waist.

I'm so busy staring at his rock-hard muscles that it takes me a moment to realize I'm topless.

His gaze goes to my breasts, and I feel utterly self-conscious. I pull up the sheet, but he gently tugs it back down.

"You let me see your breasts last night. You even let me kiss them. Why so shy now?"

"It was dark last night. Now it's broad daylight."

He leans in and kisses one of the scars on my breast. "That doesn't matter."

He kisses his way over to my other breast and kisses the other two scars with such tender reverence my throat tightens.

He meets my gaze. "Remember last night, when I said I was going to kiss each and every one of your scars?"

"Yes."

"I meant it. Your scars are nothing to be ashamed of. They're part of you now, and I love every part of you."

Distracted by the sight of his bare chest, my gaze meanders down his torso, past tattoos and well-defined muscles. His abdomen is ridged like a washboard. When he notices me studying his body, he lies back, letting me look my fill.

His flannel pants are riding low on his hips, and the sight of thick veins heading south beneath his waistband make my pulse race. I can't help noticing the very impressive erection tenting the front of his PJ bottoms. Last night he made sure I came, but he took no pleasure for himself.

"Ignore that," he says, glancing at the thick ridge visible through his PJs.

My face heats, but my fascination outweighs my nervousness. "You didn't come last night."

"That was for you, remember? I'll wait."

"What do you normally do about that?" I say, nodding toward his erection. "It can't be comfortable to simply ignore it. If you were alone, what would you do?"

He grins, apparently liking the direction this conversation is taking. "If I was here alone, I'd jerk off, either in bed or in the shower."

He reaches inside his flannel pants and fists his erection. "This is what you do to me. Every time I'm near you, I get hard."

I can't help staring at the sight of his hand disappearing beneath the waistband of his briefs.

"Have you ever seen a naked man?" he says, his voice deepening.

I shake my head.

"You're not comfortable with nudity, are you?" he says.

"It's not that. I'm just not used to it."

"I usually sleep in the nude," he says, watching my reaction intently.

My cheeks are burning, but I can't look away. His body is a work of art. "I don't mind if you sleep in the nude. You should do what makes you feel comfortable."

Chuckling, he lifts his hips and shoves his clothing down his long, muscular legs. His penis springs free, fully erect, defying gravity as it lifts from his body. It's surprisingly thick, the skin stretched taut, and the head flushed a deep, dark red. If I'm not mistaken, he's getting even harder as I stare at him.

"I want to watch you," I say, throwing caution to the wind. My pulse is beating so hard I can feel it in my throat. My chest grows tight, and I feel heat pooling between my legs.

He studies me for a minute, as if he's not sure this is a good idea. But I'm hungry to see his body.

"Make yourself come," I say, my voice barely above a whisper.

He wraps his long fingers around his erection, his grip confident and strong. Slowly, he begins stroking his length, from base to tip. There's fluid gathering at the tip, and he catches it in his palm and rubs it along his shaft.

My heart pounds, and I'm finding it hard to breathe.

"Are you sure?" he says, his voice deeper, rougher than I've ever heard it.

I nod.

He begins stroking himself, his fist tight on his erection, gradually moving faster and faster. His chest rises and falls with each breath, and his face darkens with arousal, his nostrils flaring. He's magnificent.

I'm mesmerized, watching him bring himself to climax, his grip tight on his shaft, his touch surprisingly rough. His gaze locks onto my breasts, and with his free hand, he reaches out to cup one of them, gently squeezing it and teasing my nipple into a tight peak with his thumb.

It's not long before he grits his teeth and bucks his hips. He arches his back with a loud, hoarse cry. "Fuck!"

He angles his penis toward his belly, and soon a stream of silky cream spurts onto his abs. Gradually, he slows his strokes, teasing out each ejaculation, until they finally stop. His belly is coated with semen.

His gaze is hot and intense when he looks at me. "How about a shower?" he says. "I need to clean up."

My heart leaps into my throat. "Me too?"

"Yes, you too." He grabs a tissue from the box on the nightstand and wipes his belly. "How about it?"

* * *

We both brush our teeth as the water heats. Mack's standing naked in front of the sink, his body a sculpted masterpiece of muscles and tendons. Sexy veins meander down his heavily inked and muscled arm. I'm pretty sure this is what they mean by the phrase *arm porn*.

I'm topless and feeling incredibly self-conscious, making a point not to look at myself in the mirror. I tried to put my cami back on before leaving the bed, but Mack pulled it from my grasp and tossed it across the room.

At least I'm still wearing my panties. But not for long I guess, as we're destined for the shower.

Mack rinses and spits, then drops his toothbrush into the cup holder. While I finish brushing, he grabs two fresh towels out of the cupboard and sets them on the counter.

He turns to show me his back and the bandage covering his stab wound. "Would you mind taking that off?"

"Are you sure it's okay to get your shoulder wet?"

He shrugs as he rotates his shoulder. "It's mostly healed by now. Take a look."

I gingerly peel off the taped edges of his bandage, revealing a six-inch long cut. The scar is pink, but it seems to be healing well. "It looks pretty good," I tell him. "It's not red or anything."

Mack grits his teeth as he flexes his arms. "It's fine." After taking the bandage from me, he folds it up and tosses it into the waste basket. He nods toward the shower. "Shall we?"

I swallow hard, my pulse racing. "Okay."

He waits patiently while I remove the last of my clothing. When I'm naked, his hot gaze sweeps the length of my body, his nostrils flaring. His jaws are clenched tightly, and a muscle twitches in his cheek.

He pulls the shower curtain back and motions for me to step in. I do, and he follows me in, letting the curtain fall back into place. We are cocooned in together in this small space, surrounded by rising steam.

My mind is reeling. Yes, I saw his naked body in bed this morning—every glorious inch of it. But he hasn't seen my naked body before now. My naked and *scarred* body. I wasn't planning on this happening so soon. I thought I'd have some time to work up to it.

Mack stands directly beneath the spray and briskly rinses the last of the semen from his abdomen. Then he trades places with me so I can wet my body. Despite the heat of the water cascading over me, I'm shivering. I feel so horribly exposed.

"Come here," he says gently, opening his arms to me.

I walk into his embrace, and he holds me for a moment, just offering comfort and support. When I finally stop shaking, he reaches for my bar of rose-scented soap, generously lathers his hands, then runs them over my shoulders and down my arms, caressing my skin, gently working my muscles.

His touch is soothing and hypnotic. My muscles soften, and my entire body relaxes. Then he moves me beneath the spray and the water rinses me clean.

He grabs his own bar of soap, something that smells very outdoorsy, and quickly soaps himself while I wash my hair. Then he rinses off before washing his own hair.

We get out of the shower at the same time, both of us toweling off. I watch, fascinated, as he applies his deodorant.

After dressing, we make breakfast together and eat at the kitchen table. We fall into a comfortable weekend routine. While a load of laundry is washing, we clean up the kitchen. Then it's off to do a little shopping.

Tomorrow is Annie and Jake's combination wedding and baby shower, so we have some gifts to buy. And this evening, we're having dinner with Haley. I always look forward to our dinners with Mack's daughter. Spending time with her gives me fresh new insight into her father.

Something momentous has changed between us since last night and this morning. The Earth has shifted on its axis, and everything's different.

Since the sidewalks are clear of snow, we decide to bundle up in our winter coats and walk to Water Tower Place to shop for Jake and Annie's gifts. The shopping mall is not that far from us, and we could both use some fresh air and exercise.

We luck out in a specialty gift shop. For their bridal shower, we choose a picture-frame made by a local artist. The frame is decorated with the hand-lettered phrase "Love Means Family." That was an easy gift to pick out for them. I've been to their new house a few times in the McIntyre family compound, and I know that Annie loves taking photographs and hanging them on the walls. The photos she's taken of her young son, Aiden, are incredible. She's even been thinking about trying her hand as a professional photographer.

For the baby shower gifts, we buy matching stuffed animals, a pair of pink, fluffy baby llamas that are ridiculously soft and adorable. And of course we need wrapping paper, bows, ribbons, and cards.

We take the gifts home and wrap them just in time to leave again to pick Haley up for dinner.

The moment we pull up to her house, Haley comes running out the front door, waving. She climbs into the back seat of the truck cab, and we're off.

"God, I'm so sick of winter!" she says.

"Get used to it, kiddo," Mack says. "We have a while to go before spring gets here."

Haley laughs. "Dad, please! I'm not five years old."

When I glance back at her, she rolls her eyes at me. Her long dark hair is pulled back into a ponytail, emphasizing her big, beautiful dark eyes. I'm struck by how much she looks like her dad. It really starts to sink in—Mack's a *father*. And then I wonder if he's ever thought about having more kids someday. I would certainly like to have kids.

Mack reaches across the truck console for my hand, squeezing it as he feigns hurt. "Did you hear what my daughter said to me?"

"I did," I reply, turning my head to share a smile with Haley.

Mack meets his daughter's gaze in the rear view mirror. "Don't be in such a hurry to grow up, young lady. I'm far too young to have a grown daughter."

When Mack asks what she wants for dinner, Haley suggests we go for pizza. We end up at a charming little mom-and-pop pizzeria in Lincoln Park, complete with red-and-white checkered tablecloths and an old-fashioned juke box that plays songs from the fifties.

We're seated at a booth, Mack and I on one side of the table, Haley on the other. Our server takes our orders—hot chocolate for Haley, a beer for Mack, and a bottle of sparking water for me. We order a giant pizza with the works to share.

Haley eyes us intently when Mack lays his arm across the back of our seat, his fingers brushing against my shoulder. He leans over without warning and kisses my cheek, his lips lingering.

Haley's dark brows rise as she looks on. "Are you trying to tell me something, Dad?"

He shrugs as he picks up his beer mug. "Maybe."

Haley's curious gaze goes to me. "Is there something you two want to share? Have you finally moved past the 'we're just regular friends' stage?"

"Oh, we're waaay past 'regular friends' now," Mack says, grinning as he pulls me close and kisses my temple.

I laugh, blushing hotly.

"Oh, my God, you two are an item!" Haley laughs as she mock glares at her father. "You told me you weren't! You lied to me!"

"I was telling you the truth at the time," he says. "But things have changed considerably since then." Mack lifts my hand to his mouth and kisses the inside of my wrist, his lips grazing my pulse point.

Haley shakes her head. "Seriously, Dad? Get a room."

We have a wonderful time talking and laughing over our pizza. Haley tells us about a boy at school she likes.

Mack pretends to be horrified as he wag his finger at his daughter. "You are too young to be interested in boys, young lady." Then he looks at me. "Right?"

Haley rolls her eyes at me. Then to her dad, she says, "Have you forgotten that you and mom were pregnant with me when you were my age? You tell him, Erin."

Haley's observation shuts Mack up pretty quickly. I love that she looks to me for support. I think Mack likes it too. She seems to genuinely like me.

Mack reaches underneath the table for my hand and brings it to his lap. He lays my hand flat on his thigh, then his hand covers mine, and he links our fingers together. I'm filled with a deep sense of satisfaction and a feeling of belonging that I've never felt before, almost as if Mack and his daughter have welcomed me into their family dynamic. It feels really good.

After indulging in ice cream sundaes for dessert, we drive Haley back to her mom's house. It's almost ten o'clock by the time we get back to our apartment, and I'm suddenly nervous. We've quickly progressed to second base. I don't know if I'm ready for more.

But the idea of *more* with Mack is quite titillating.

* * *

I'm in the bathroom, dressed in a pale blue nightgown and brushing my teeth, when Mack comes up behind me, looming over me as he meets my gaze in the mirror. He's ready for bed, dressed only in his boxer-briefs. My gaze locks onto his reflection in the bathroom mirror.

He lowers his head and kisses the side of my neck, sending tingles down my spine. "Haley really likes you."

I smile. It's hard to talk with a toothbrush in my mouth, so I rinse and spit. "Do you think so? I really like her. She reminds me so much of you, the way she smiles, her laugh, her sense of humor. And she has your eyes—it's uncanny."

"I'd love for you two to be friends." He gathers my hair in his hands and tugs playfully, sending a shiver down my spine. "Ready for bed?"

"This early?" I say, surprised. He usually watches TV before heading to bed, while I read next to him.

"Yeah." He rests his chin on top of my head and slips his arms around me, nestled beneath my breasts. The he leans down to kiss my throat. "If you're up for it, I thought we could try for third base."

Third base? I'm not entirely sure what that means. I know it's not intercourse, but it does involve doing things below the belt. "Um, is that..."

He drops his mouth to my ear and whispers in a low, gravelly voice. "It means I'm going to put my mouth on you." Then his hand slides down my torso, and he cups me between the legs. "Right here."

"Oh." My body responds with a violent shiver.

"Do you think you can handle that?"

My head spins as heat sweeps through me. "I don't know." Already my pulse is racing, but in a good way.

He kisses me behind my ear, where I'm ticklish. "Do you want to try?"

I like how he says *try*. It feels less pressureful that way. His lips skim down my throat, his beard tickling me.

"Mmhmm."

"Is that a yes?"

"Yes."

I squeal when he swings me up into his arms and carries me to the bedroom. I am SO not ready for this!

40

Erin

"Same rules apply as before," Mack says as he sets me on my feet beside the bed. "You call the shots. If anything gets to be too much, or you're uncomfortable for any reason, you just say so, and we stop. Got it?"

I nod. "Got it."

He turns the bedroom light off, but the light in the closet is still on, and the closet door is wide open letting plenty of light spill into the bedroom.

"Shouldn't we turn off the light?" I say, pointing toward the closet.

The corner of his mouth twitches as he suppresses a smile. "I wasn't planning on it. Do you need the light off?"

"Yes." He has yet to see the scars on my inner thighs. There are six horizontal scars, three on each side, looking like someone was keeping tally.

His brow furrows as he considers my request. "But then I won't be able to see what I'm doing."

I laugh as I swat his uninjured shoulder. "I don't think you need to see to do that. I'm sure you can manage just fine in the dark."

"But where's the fun in that?" he says, with a wicked gleam in his eye. "I want to see you, honey."

My face heats a million degrees. "Is that really necessary?"

"Yes, it is. How about we give it a try with the light on and see how it goes? Then, if you still want the light off, I'll turn it off."

I frown, knowing I've been outmaneuvered. He has a way of pushing me just a little bit, making it sound so perfectly reasonable, and making me laugh in the process. But he's good for me in that regard, so I really can't complain. "All right. We can *try* it."

"Good."

Without warning, he reaches for the hem of my nightgown and pulls it up and off my head, then tosses it aside. I screech in surprise, bringing my hands up to cover my breasts. "Mack! You could have warned me first."

"I could have," he says with a grin. "But it's better this way." He gently pries my hands off my breasts, holding both my hands in one of his as he pulls down the bedding. Then he sweeps me up into his arms and lays me on the bed.

I sigh nervously, wondering why I agreed to this. I'm really not ready. "Mack, I'm not sure this is a good idea."

Halfway onto the bed, he freezes. "Do you want to stop?"

I frown. "No."

He chuckles. "Okay then. Just relax and trust me." He lies down beside me and lays his warm hand on my belly. "You're so beautiful."

His words, and the sincerity with which he said them, touch me deeply.

"I mean it, Erin. You're the most beautiful woman I've ever known." He cups the side of my face and kisses me again, his lips warm and coaxing. In between words, he peppers me with gentle kisses. "You're brave." Kiss. "And courageous." Kiss. "And beautiful. And I'm the luckiest son-of-a-bitch because you chose me."

Tears form, blurring my vision, and my throat tightens.

He smiles down at me, brushing away my tears with the edge of his thumb. "It's okay." He leans down and kisses me, skimming his lips down my throat to my collar bone and then to my chest. "Technically, this is still first base," he says. "But it's good to review."

And then, even as I'm laughing, he draws one of my nipples into the wet heat of his mouth. My body jolts like it's been shocked with a live wire. As he sucks gently, I feel pleasure ripple all the way down to my core, as if the two erogenous zones are interconnected.

My sex flushes hotly, and I'm practically throbbing. I suck in air, and my hands grow restless. Crouching over me, Mack showers attention on one nipple, then crosses over to the other.

My body grows hotter until I'm practically squirming. He doesn't seem concerned about my predicament, though. He takes his sweet time trailing kisses down my torso to my belly, stopping to tease my belly button with the tip of his tongue.

I grip his shoulders and hold on for dear life. He's my port in the storm, even when he's the one making the waves in the first place. He's my rock, my safety net. He's become indispensable to me.

Shifting down the bed, he kneels between my legs and reaches for the waistband of my panties. His heated gaze locks onto mine as he slowly pulls them off.

He settles between my legs and nudges my thighs farther apart, using his broad shoulders to pin them open. My gaze is riveted to the top of his head, to his thick, dark hair. When I run my fingers through his hair, tugging lightly, he groans.

I can feel his warm breath on my clitoris, and I shiver knowing that he's going to touch me there *with his tongue*. He's going to make me come again.

I gasp when he pries the lips of my sex open with his thumbs. He stares as if mesmerized. Then, to my surprise, his gaze lifts and meets mine, holding it for a long moment as he studies my reaction. He watches, as if looking for me to fall apart, but I'm not afraid of this. I'm not scared because this is Mack, and I trust him, and he knows me. He knows *everything*, and he'll keep me safe.

Apparently, he's satisfied with what he sees, because he dips his head and gently flicks my clitoris with the tip of his tongue.

I cry out sharply, my back bowing off the bed as my hips buck against his hold. I've never felt anything so incredibly electrifying in my life. I'm fairly panting now, my hands grasping frantically at the sheet beneath me.

He proceeds to drive me out of my mind, his wicked tongue alternately tormenting my clitoris and licking my sensitized flesh. I stiffen when I feel the tip of his finger rimming my opening.

"It's just my finger," he says. He slides the tip in, barely to the first knuckle.

I tense up, expecting pain, but I'm so slick that his finger slips inside easily. There's no pain. None at all... just a rush of pleasure that intensifies when he starts stroking me.

His finger and tongue work together, teasing me mercilessly, and I have to bite my lip to keep from crying out. I try not to dwell on the high-pitched, desperate sounds coming out of me—sounds I never thought I could make.

I feel a storm gathering in my core, a swelling of heat and sensation. As the pleasure builds, my heart beats frantically and I'm gasping for breath. And then suddenly, my body implodes, sending a rush of fireworks through me. Pleasure pulses through me and my body tenses. "Mack!"

He crawls up beside me, half on top of me, and cups my hot cheeks. Gazing down, he smiles gently, clearly pleased with himself... and I think with me.

I'm panting like I've just run a marathon. "Oh, my God, that was—"

"Good?"

"Way more than good. That was mind blowing."

He grins. "So, you approve of third base?"

Pleasure reverberates throughout my body, and I just want to melt. "Oh, my goodness, yes."

When he kisses me, I taste myself on him, on his lips. It's warm and salty and earthy. I'm simultaneously shocked and intrigued.

Smiling at my reaction, he grabs the edge of the top sheet and wipes his beard. Then he rolls onto his side, facing me, and draws me close. I'm spent, and a yawn escapes me.

Mack laughs. "I didn't wear you out, did I?"

"I think you did."

"Hold on, I'll get the light." He climbs out of bed and walks to the closet to switch off the light. I stare at his backside, marveling at the sight of his muscular back and firm, sculpted butt cheeks.

When he returns to the bed, he pulls me close and I cushion my head on his chest. "I'm so proud of you," he says.

I swallow against the lump in my throat. After the attack, I was so sure this could never happen for me. I didn't think I could ever feel pleasure or desire with a man. But I was wrong.

His warm hand strokes my spine, and he kisses my forehead. "Sleep soundly tonight, honey. I'll chase your nightmares away."

41

Erin

Sunday afternoon, two o'clock. It's time to go upstairs for Annie and Jake's party, and I'm a nervous wreck. I'll be seeing a lot of these people for the first time since the incident, and I can't help feeling self-conscious.

I choose a tunic dress with a long-sleeved blouse underneath so no one will see the marks on my arms. But no matter how many different ways I try styling my hair, I can't hide the scar on my cheek.

Mack appears behind me in the bathroom doorway, looking very handsome in black slacks and a gray crewneck sweater that hugs his muscular torso. He leans against the doorjamb, crossing his arms over his chest, and watches me attempt the impossible.

Frowning, he steps into the small room. "Ready to go?"

I meet his gaze in the mirror, then look at my reflection once more. The scar on my cheek is straight, thin, and pink. And it stands out like a sore thumb against my pale complexion. I set my brush down on the counter. "No, I'm not ready. I'll never be ready."

He sighs. "What's wrong, honey?"

"This," I say, pointing at the scar. "Plus I haven't seen most of these people since *before*."

He kisses the top of my head, then tucks one side of my hair behind my ear. "Every single person who will be at this party showed up at the hospital when you were admitted to the ER. Every. Single. One. Shane's entire family, Beth's family. They all care very deeply about you and about your wellbeing. Trust me, you have nothing to worry about." He kisses my temple. "And I'll be right by your side the entire time."

I turn in his embrace and press my face against his chest. He smells good... the faint woodsy scent of his soap, a hint of cologne. He's my safety net. I pull back and clear my throat. "There's no sense in putting this off, so we might as well go."

His warm hands cradle my face, and he leans down and kisses me. "You are courageous and beautiful, and I'm so damn proud of you."

I grin as my cheeks flush at his compliment. "I don't feel very courageous."

"You are."

We collect our gifts—the wedding shower gift wrapped in silver paper, the baby shower gift wrapped in pink paper—and leave the apartment. It's a quick trip up to the penthouse. When we step out of the elevator, I hear a multitude of voices coming from the great room. But the moment we step through the foyer door, the conversations stop as everyone in the great room turns to look at us.

Mack has a tight hold on my hand, squeezing it as he leads me forward.

Beth runs up and throws her arms around me. "I'm so glad you're here."

Before I know it, there's a small crowd gathering around me—Shane's mom, Bridget. Shane's sisters Sophie and Hannah. Beth's mom, Ingrid. Beth's friend Gabrielle. Jamie's girlfriend, Molly. They all wait for a turn to hug me.

Annie Elliot, the bride-to-be, makes her way to the front of the group. "Let me in there!" she says, her arms open wide. She looks lovely in a loose, flowing maxi dress in a pretty floral print. Her abdomen is hugely distended, and the babies aren't even due for another couple weeks!

"Thank you for coming," Annie whispers to me as she hugs me. She pulls back, smiling at me with teary eyes. "A family get-together wouldn't be complete without you."

Her kind words bring tears to my eyes, and when she releases me, Sam steps in and gives me a big bear hug, lifting me off my feet. He kisses my unmarked cheek. "Hey, Irish! I've missed you."

"Careful," Mack says in a gently chiding voice as he extricates me from Sam's embrace and sets me back on my feet.

Sam laughs as he eyes Mack. "So, that's how it's going to be now? You're the big, bad protector?"

Mack doesn't even crack a smile. "I just don't want her overdoing it, that's all."

Shane steps forward and envelopes me in his strong arms. "It's good to see you again, Erin." He glances at Mack. "Has this guy been taking good care of you?"

I smile. "Yes."

"All right, that's enough," Cooper says in his gruff voice as he shoos everyone back. "Give the poor girl room to breathe."

My heart is pounding, but in a good way. It really is good to see everyone again, and their warm welcome means the world to me. I don't know what I was afraid of.

"Here, I'll take these," Bridget says, relieving Mack of our gifts. "You two make yourselves at home and relax."

Beth puts her arm around my shoulders. "Luke just woke up from his nap. Do you want to help me get him up?"

"Sure." I glance up at Mack, who's watching me like a hawk.

Shane lays his hand on Mack's shoulder. "Relax, pal, she's fine. Come with me. I'll buy you a drink."

Across the room is a full-sized bar, where the rest of the guys are congregated. Jake stands behind the bar with a dishtowel thrown over his shoulder. After having abused alcohol in the past, Jake doesn't drink anymore, so he's appointed himself the official family bartender. Two of his brothers—Jamie and Liam—

his dad, Calum; and his sister Lia's fiancé, Jonah, are all seated on barstools.

Mack looks at me, clearly hesitating to accept Shane's offer.

"Go ahead," I tell him. "I'll be fine."

"Yes, go ahead," Beth says, grinning as she links her arm with mine. "She'll be fine. Go have a drink with the guys. We need some girl time."

It's a short walk down the hallway to the nursery, which is right next to Shane and Beth's suite. Beth quietly opens the door, and we step inside, closing it behind us. The nursery walls are painted a pale, soothing blue, and there's a matching plush rug on the gleaming hardwood floor.

I follow Beth to the crib, and we both peer down at Luke, who's just starting to stir from his afternoon nap. He blinks up at us through half-opened eyes.

"Hello, sweetie," Beth says, smiling down at her son, who's drowsily stretching.

With a sleepy whimper, Luke reaches for Beth, and she lifts him out of the crib and carries him to the changing table.

"How are you feeling?" she asks me as she changes Luke's diaper.

"I'm doing better. Physically, I feel pretty good. I'm pretty much back to normal. Emotionally, well, that's been harder. I still have nightmares and panic attacks. Mack says I have PTSD."

"I'm not surprised. Speaking of Mack, how are things going with you two? How's the roommate arrangement working out?" When I bite back a grin, she notices immediately. "Oh, I think you need to tell me everything."

I laugh. "Well, for one thing, I think we're dating."

She laughs too. "You *think* you're dating?"

"We've kissed. And he's touched me."

Beth looks surprised. "Have you had sex?"

"No. We're taking it slow."

"He's not pressuring you for anything, is he? Because if he is—"

"No, not at all." I smile just thinking about how patient he's been. "He's been wonderful."

"Good. He'd better be. Otherwise, there's an entire room full of tough guys out there who would be only too happy to set him straight."

Beth picks up a freshly-diapered Luke and settles him on her hip. "Do you mind if I nurse him?"

"No. Go right ahead."

She sits with Luke in the padded rocking chair. I sit on the ottoman facing them.

"How are *you* doing?" I ask her. I've been trying not to pry. "Have you told Shane?"

"About the pregnancy? Yes, I told him."

"How did he take it?"

She unclips her bra cup and latches the baby onto her breast. "About how I expected." She starts rocking gently, patting the baby's bottom as he nurses. "He was upset initially, but he wasn't surprised. He figured I'd already tested, and when I didn't immediately tell him the results, he assumed it was positive. I tried to reassure him that it would be different this time. I know what to expect, and I'm not afraid. And as for the closeness in their ages, that's a good thing. Bridget and Calum had their first four children very close together. It's not uncommon." She pats her belly. "It'll be fine."

I reach out to stroke Luke's hair. "I'm sure this little guy will be a fantastic big brother."

"We haven't told anyone yet," she says. "We're going to wait until after Jake and Annie's wedding, and until after their twins are born."

"I won't tell anyone."

"Thanks. Sam and Cooper know. And it's okay if you tell Mack. But we'll wait awhile before we make any announcements. We don't want to take away from Jake and Annie's special day, you know?"

She holds Luke to her shoulder to burp him.

"I wonder if he's going to have a little sister or a brother," I say, as Beth lays him down to resume nursing.

She smiles. "We're going to wait to find out. We want to be surprised."

"There have been so many recent additions to your family... Aiden, Luke, and before long Jake and Annie's twins, and then your new baby."

"It's bound to happen with seven adult children in the McIntyre family. Personally, I love it. I grew up in a very small family. I love being part of a big one."

After she's done nursing, we head back out to the great room. Beth's friend Gina Capelli is busy at the dining room table putting the finishing touches on an amazing spread of hot finger foods. The guys, including Mack, are congregated around the bar, talking and laughing. The women are congregated in the seating area around the fireplace.

"Erin, come sit with me, sweetie," Bridget McIntyre says as she pats an open spot beside her on the sofa. Shane's mom reminds me so much of my Gram, and I'm grateful that she seems to have adopted me.

As we approach, Bridget holds her hands out for her grandson, and Beth hands him over.

"I'll be in the kitchen helping Gina with the food," Beth says, heading for the table.

A moment later, I feel a pair of hands descend on my shoulders. I look up at Mack, who is standing behind the sofa.

"Doing okay?" he says.

His sudden presence makes my pulse quicken and my belly do a little flip. "Yes."

He nods toward the impressive display of food on the table. "Do you want anything to eat? I'll get you something."

"Thank you, but not quite yet."

Jake brings a plate of food to Annie, along with a napkin and a glass of water. He sets the items on the coffee table and leans down to give her a long, lingering kiss. Then he pats her burgeoning belly. "How are my girls doing?"

Annie smiles up at her soon-to-be husband, her eyes alight with affection. "They just woke up," she says, laying her hand on his. "Right now, they're doing cartwheels."

With his hand pressed firmly to her abdomen, he grins. "Somebody just kicked me."

Lia sits on the arm of one of the sofas, beside her sister Sophie. "Hey, Erin. I'm glad you could make it." Then to Annie and Jake, she says, "The guys are betting on what comes first… the wedding or the birth."

Annie laughs. "Oh, dear God, please let it be the wedding. I can only handle one major event at a time. Getting married with two newborns on my hands would be a challenge."

"Don't worry, Elliot," Jake says, as he steals a strawberry off her plate and pops it into his mouth. "I promise you… whatever happens, we'll make it work."

Tyler approaches quietly out of nowhere. "Hi, Erin. How are you doing?"

I nod. "I'm okay."

Tyler was there when Mack was stabbed, and he was the one who shot my attacker. Seeing him suddenly brings it all back. My chest tightens painfully, trapping the air in my lungs. I hear a loud rush in my ears, shutting off all other sounds.

Looking concerned, Tyler crouches in front of me, taking hold of my hands, which are shaking. His lips are moving, but I can't hear a thing. Everything is muffled as if I'm submerged underwater.

Suddenly Bridget vacates her seat and Mack is there in her place, turning me to face him. He's talking, but I can't make out the words.

Mack cups my cheeks and peers down at me, his lips moving

with precision. Finally, the words sink in. "Look at me, honey. You're okay. Just breathe."

As if waking from a bad dream, I snap out of it, surprised to meet with a sea of concerned faces, starting with Tyler's. He's still crouching in front of me, his hand on my knee.

"I'm so sorry," I say, feeling horribly self-conscious. "I'm okay."

Mack settles back on the sofa, holding one of my hands in his.

I glance around, mortified that everyone's watching me.

"All right, gang," Bridget says, drawing everyone's attention away from me. She tucks a strand of her wavy, strawberry-blonde hair behind her ear. "Go grab yourselves a plate of this delicious food. After we eat, we'll play some games, and then Annie and Jake can open their gifts."

42

Mack

Erin seems to have fully recovered from her sudden panic attack. Still, I'm sticking close to her side, just in case.

My guess is that seeing Tyler again brought everything crashing back on her. I was seated clear across the room, over at the bar with the guys, all the while keeping one eye on Erin. As soon as I saw the concern on Tyler's face, I knew there was a problem, and I headed right for her.

I know full well what those panic attacks feel like, and they're not pleasant. I dealt with them frequently right after leaving the military. I still occasionally wake up in a cold sweat after reliving some horrendous experiences in my dreams. I hate knowing she's experiencing something similar.

Once the excitement's over, I get a few curious glances from some of the others. I'm not surprised—no one really knows that my relationship with Erin has turned a corner. I think it's time they knew.

I stand and offer her my hand. "Let's grab something to eat."

"Okay." She smiles as she slips her hand in mine and lets me pull her to her feet.

We head over to the dining table, which is loaded with food and beverages. At the far end of the table is an impressive three-tiered white cake, decorated with pale pink flowers and tiny silver beads. Perched on top of the cake are two pairs of pink baby shoes.

I chuckle. Annie and Jake sure didn't waste any time reconnecting after a decade apart. I'm happy for them.

Five-year-old Aiden, Annie's son from a previous marriage, races up to the table and slips between me and Erin. I reach down to steady him before he crashes into the table.

"Sorry, dude!" Aiden says, grabbing a mini quiche off a platter and taking off. "My mom wants another qweesh!"

"It's called a 'quiche,' pal! Not a qweesh!" Jake hollers after him, shaking his head with a grin as he joins us at the table. "Sorry about that. Aiden can be a little exuberant at times."

"I think he's adorable," Erin says, grinning.

When Annie and Jake reunited recently, Jake became an instant step-father to Annie's young son. The guy seems to have taken to his new role well, which is a good thing as they're expecting twin girls in a few weeks. Their little family of three will soon become a family of five. Jake seems more than ready for the challenge.

As I hand Erin a plate, I gaze down into her face, and I lose myself in her blue eyes and the light dusting of freckles on her cheeks. The bruises are all gone now, and her peaches-and-cream complexion has returned. The only difference now is the thin scar on her right cheek. It doesn't detract from her beauty—nothing could do that.

God, she looks so young. But then again, she *is* young. It's something I'll just have to come to grips with. I can imagine having a party like this for us one day... our friends gathering to celebrate *our* marriage. Maybe *our* pending bundle of joy. I'm pretty sure Haley would be happy to have a little brother or sister.

Before long, Erin has her hands full juggling her plate, a fork, and a napkin, so I take her plate and hold it for her. Right now, she looks like she doesn't have a care in the world.

Beth is filling up her own plate as Shane hovers close to her. He reaches out and brushes his wife's hair back, tucking the strands behind her ear. With his hand on her lower back, Shane leans close and whispers something to Beth, making her blush hotly. Then he kisses her on the mouth, his lips lingering on hers.

I carry Erin's food to the seating area and set it on the coffee table as she takes a seat on the sofa. I head over to the bar to grab a bottle of water for her out of the mini fridge. She smiles gratefully when I screw off the cap and hand her the bottle. Giving her sealed drinks is a small thing, but it gives her so much peace of mind.

I grab a plate of food for myself and join her, sitting on the arm of the sofa next to her as all the seats are taken.

As I watch these people, I'm glad that Beth's family has welcomed Erin into their fold. She needs people. She needs family. She soaks up their attention and affection like a sponge.

I run my hand down her back, and she shivers. Then she leans into me.

"Finish up eating, everyone," Bridget says. "We're about to start the baby shower games."

I hear more than a few male groans coming from the audience, but I don't mind. I'm content to be here with Erin. When she's finished with her food, I collect her empty plate and fork, along with my own and carry them to the kitchen.

I walk in on a quiet moment between Shane and Beth. He's holding her to his chest and talking quietly to her. I get the feeling something's up with these two. They're always lovey-dovey, but this is a little unusual. I'll have to remember to ask Erin if she knows anything.

The baby shower games commence, accompanied by lots of good-natured laughter and ribbing. The ladies make the guys join in when they'd probably rather return to the bar and talk sports.

Of course Jake is right there at Annie's side. He's not going anywhere. Aiden climbs onto Jake's lap and watches his mom open gifts. There are lots of pink baby girl things, cute little matching outfits, pink blankets, pink sleepers. And, of course, the pink stuffed llamas we bought for them. There's definitely a theme here.

"Good luck, Jake," Cooper says, laughing. "You and Aiden are about to be outnumbered."

Jake laughs as he leans over and kisses Annie's cheek. "Our next baby will have to be a boy then, to even out the numbers."

Annie groans loudly, trying not to laugh as she frames her huge belly with two hands. "It's a little premature to be talking about more babies. We haven't even had these yet."

Jake sweeps his gaze around the room. "You're marrying a McIntyre, Elliot," he says, putting his arm across her shoulders. "Big families come with the territory."

43

Erin

Late that evening, after changing into his PJs, Mack crashes on the sofa to watch a recorded basketball game. Normally, I'd be sitting beside him, reading on my Kindle, but tonight I'm hiding out in the bedroom, trying to get up the nerve to tell him *I'm ready*. At least I think I am.

I realized something at the party today. Mack and I aren't *sort of* dating. We *are* dating. We're just as much a couple as those other couples. We think about each other's needs. We care about each other. Mack was there for me when I needed him, during my panic attack.

My hands are shaking as I put on a pale blue, sheer nightgown that falls to the tops of my thighs. The nightgown is see-through, and I'm not wearing anything underneath. It's sexy.

I stare at myself in the mirror over the dresser, trying to psych myself up for this. Mack calls me courageous. I guess it's time for me to live up to the compliment.

Wearing the nightgown and nothing else, I head to the living room, pausing just inside the room.

Mack has his feet propped up on the coffee table as he watches his game. When he realizes I'm standing here, he glances up at me, freezing when he sees what I'm wearing. Immediately, he grabs the remote and turns off the television.

"That was a nice party today," I say, nervous and not knowing what to say. *Let's have sex* doesn't strike me as a good idea.

His gaze is hot on me. "Yes, it was."

He waits patiently for me to say something, but when I don't, when I just stand there awkwardly, he motions me forward. "Come here, honey."

Slowly, I approach him, noticing how he tracks my every movement. Because the nightgown is so sheer, I'm sure he's getting an eye full.

I come to a stop directly in front of him. He slips his hands around to the backs of my thighs, sliding them up beneath the hem of my nightgown to stroke my bare bottom cheeks. His warm hands feel good on my skin.

His nostrils flare as a muscle in his cheek flexes. He opens his mouth as if to speak, then closes it.

My heart is in my throat as I try to summon the courage to say what I want to say. But the words don't come easily.

He waits patiently, watching, giving me time.

Finally, I just blurt it out. "I want to be with you."

He smiles as he takes hold of my hands, which are shaking. His expression is almost wary, as if he's not sure of my meaning. "We *are* together," he says carefully.

"No, I mean… entirely together. Completely."

He cocks his head as he considers my words. "Can you be a little more specific?"

"I want to have sex with you." Well, that came out a little more bluntly than I meant it to, but he definitely got the message.

He straightens, his eyes widening. "That was pretty specific. Are you sure? I don't want you to feel pressured. *I'm* certainly not pressuring you. Whether we wait a month or a year—"

I squeeze his hands. "I'm not feeling pressured. It's just that I want everything with you. I want to *try*."

He pulls me onto his lap so that I'm straddling his thighs and brushes my hair back. Then he cups my face in his hands. "You're sure?"

"Yes."

He gazes at me for the longest time. "God knows how badly I want to make love to you, but I'm trying really hard not to be a selfish bastard. I'm trying to give you your space."

The building heat in his gaze sets butterflies loose in my belly. This is it. *There's no turning back now.* "Maybe I don't want space."

He pulls me close and kisses me, and as he deepens the kiss, one of his hands sweeps up to cup the back of my head.

Then he pulls back and meets my gaze. "I want you more than I want my next breath. Okay, we'll *try*. But if you change your mind at any point, tell me."

I lay my hand over his heart, and I swear I can feel that organ thudding beneath his ribs. "I will."

He stands abruptly, lifting me in his arms. I squeal as I wrap my legs around his waist. His jeans press against my bare flesh, and it feels shockingly intimate. I wrap my arms around his neck and hold on tightly as he carries me to the bedroom.

44

Mack

Fuck, this is really happening.

Well, maybe it is. I'm still not convinced she's ready. And I'm sure as hell not going to push her. Our first time together has to be perfect. A lot is riding on this... not just her physical and emotional comfort, but her trust in *me*.

I set her down beside the bed and turn down the light. She looks uneasy, like she could bolt at any second.

I reach back and grab the neckline of my T-shirt and whip it off. Her gaze locks on my chest first, then travels down my inked arm. Her fingers twisting together nervously. I can't begin to imagine what she's feeling right now. Uncertainty, I'm sure. Fear of the unknown coupled with the trauma she experienced.

"Come here," I say, pulling her into my arms, holding her close and secure. I want this badly, but it's more important to me that she feels safe and comfortable.

As I stroke her back, she melds into me, her face against my bare chest, her body soft and warm against mine. I lower my head to kiss her temple and breathe in the scent of her skin, of her hair... delicate, sweet, feminine. My cock hardens.

I've had a lot of sex in my life, but it's never been anything like this. It usually consisted of me picking up a woman in a bar, both of us a bit drunk. We'd find a dark hallway or a broom closet, and we couldn't rip our clothes off fast enough. It was usually a frantic coupling, and then we'd go our separate ways without a look back. But this... this is couldn't be more different. This is about building trust. It's about making promises. And I do promise to make this right for her.

I stare down at her in awe. She's a vision in a skimpy nightgown that's so sheer I can see the dark shadow of curls between her legs and the pink tips of her nipples pressing against the fabric. She looks so beautiful, I almost hate to take the nightgown off her, but naked is even better.

I grab the hem of her nightgown and lift up. She raises her arms and the garment slips right off, leaving her bare. I stare down at her breasts, perfect little mounds tipped with lush pink nipples that make my mouth water. When those nipples pucker into tight little peaks right before my eyes, my belly clenches with desire. I can feel my blood racing south, making my cock throb with need. My balls tighten, and already I'm aching for release.

I pull her back into my arms, her soft breasts pressing against my chest, and run my hands down her bare back.

She shudders, but doesn't baulk. Her arms slide around my waist, and her hands explore my back. Damn! Just that innocent touch sets my body on fire.

Hungering for a taste, I bend down and capture her mouth with mine. She tastes like peppermint and pure innocence as she exhales a shaky breath. The soft noises she makes goes right to my cock, which is painfully constrained in my jeans.

Sweeping her up, I lay her on the bed. My hands automatically go to the waistband of my jeans, but I hesitate, thinking better of it. I should wait until she's fully aroused and distracted by her own needs and desires before I give her an eye full. I doubt she's ever seen a naked man before, let alone one who is fully aroused.

I crawl onto the bed and stretch out beside her, careful not to crowd her too quickly. She watches me a bit warily, and her hesitation is a painful reminder of how I failed her once. It haunts me that I wasn't there to protect her when she needed me most, but I'm here now. And I sure as hell won't fail her again.

She looks up at me with concern etched on her pretty face. "What's wrong?"

I blink and only then realize there are tears in my eyes. Damn it.

"Don't!" She clutches my hand. "It's not your fault!"

I force a smile I don't feel, and I think she sees right through me. So I shake myself mentally. She needs me to keep it together right now, not wallow in self-recrimination.

I lower my head to kiss her, and we share slow, gentle kisses, the easy kind. No pressure. No rush. I try not to think about what she's been through. Her body was traumatized, victimized, and I have to fight to keep those sickening images out of my head.

Pretty soon her breathing picks up, in a good way. Her hands flutter restlessly, skimming up and down my arms and across my shoulders.

I cup the soft mound of her breast and brush my thumb lightly across her nipple, watching it tighten into a pale pink bud that I'm desperate to taste. When I draw her nipple into my mouth, she arches her back with a shocked cry that cuts right through me. I freeze, waiting to see if that was a good response or a bad one. But her hands continue their exploration of my body, moving around to the back of my head, her fingers threading through my hair. It's all good.

Every new sound she makes, every whimper and cry, every harried breath just fuels my own arousal to the point that my dick is aching for relief, and we've only just started. I don't know how I'm going to survive this.

When I draw her other nipple into my mouth, her hands slide off my shoulders onto my biceps and she digs her nails in hard. I smile, reveling in the feel of her exerting her power. She can claw me all she wants.

I release her nipple and trail kisses down her abdomen. My fingers follow the path of my mouth, but her thighs are closed tight as a drum. They're also shaking, which breaks my heart. So I sift my fingers through her dark curls, gently petting her and giving her a moment to get used to my touch before pushing forward.

As my index finger teases the seam of her labia, I trail kisses up her throat to the sensitive spot behind her ear. When she moans softly, I smile.

"Open your legs, honey." I suck on her earlobe before I whisper, "Let me in."

She makes a sound, part pleasured moan and part plaintive whimper.

Slowly, I slip my fingers between her thighs and gently nudge them apart. I'm walking a fine line here between coaxing her and pressuring her. "You can say stop me any time. Just say the word."

When she makes a quiet humming sound deep in her throat, I laugh softly.

Gradually, she relaxes her legs, letting them fall apart enough that I can slip my hand between her thighs. I'm relieved to find her wet. My finger glides easily through her arousal and over her clit. She cries out as she digs her nails deep into my arms, but I don't mind. She's welcome to claw me all she wants if it will help her through this. I want her to feel that she has control over what we do together.

She's silky soft and so wet, I'm desperate to put my mouth on her, to taste her sweetness. But I have to remind myself to slow down. I don't want to push her too fast and ruin this.

I slip a finger into her opening and tease her clit with the pad of my thumb. With a whimper, she rocks her body against my hand, which is surely a good sign. I'm not even sure she's aware she's doing it.

I draw my finger out, then slide it back in, pausing to rim her opening. She's breathing harder, making plaintive sounds as she clutches me in a death grip. But she hasn't put on the brakes.

My cock is aching like a bitch now, so fucking swollen. I can feel my veins throbbing in demand, and I know I'm leaking pre-come already—I can feel the damp fabric of my boxer-briefs against the head of my cock. My balls tighten, drawing up in anticipation.

When I begin stroking her g-spot, her cries intensify. "That's it, honey," I murmur against her trembling lips. I can tell she's already close. Her leg muscles are taut, her hips rocking harder against my hand. "Relax and let it happen."

She's breathing hard, her nostrils flaring, her eyes closed tightly. She's right on the edge, so close, almost frantic. I lean down and suck one of her nipples into my mouth. When I tongue the tip, she arches her back with a long, whimpering cry as her legs stiffen. "Mack!"

I kiss her through her orgasm, using my finger and thumb to gently prolong her pleasure. When her chest deflates with a heavy exhale, I smile to myself.

After shucking off my jeans and briefs, I reach over to the nightstand to grab a condom. I sheath my cock quickly, then kneel between her thighs.

"We'll go slowly," I say, my voice rough with arousal. She's soaked and softened from her orgasm, so I hope she can take my cock without too much difficulty.

She gazes up at me with an expression that's part sated and part wonder. Her cheeks are flushed a pretty pink, and her pupils are huge.

"Doing okay?" I say.

She nods.

I begin to feed my cock into her opening, slowly, carefully pressing the broad head inside. She gasps, her body tensing. Her expression is part pain, part fear. Her hands grip my arms. "Mack."

I hold my position when her nails dig into me.

"Don't stop," she pants.

Damn, she's tight. Even after coming, she's still as tight as a fist. Her body clenches down on the head of my cock. It's mind-blowing pleasure for me, but I'm not so sure it is for her. Her lips flatten, and her nostrils flare.

Part of me wants to stop. I can't bear the thought of causing her pain, but she hasn't put on the brakes, so I'm not going to either. I resume pressing into her, pushing through her soft, wet tissues. Her face screws up, and I know it's uncomfortable for her. I'm a lot for most women to take, and despite what she's been through, Erin is still very much a virgin.

When she bites her bottom lip hard, my heart cracks wide open for her. She's so damn brave. And she fucking *trusts* me enough to let me inside her body.

I let gravity do its job and use my weight to sink slowly inside, feeding myself into her an inch at a time. My erection slides through any last resistance and I'm finally buried fully inside her.

When she tenses, this time surely in pain, I lock my lips to hers and absorb her cries. "Just breathe, honey. Relax and breathe."

As I start to move, so carefully at first, just letting her adjust to my size, I'm swamped with a sense of rightness. For the first time in my life, I feel like I'm where I belong. My calling is to protect this young woman, stand by her side, love her, make her laugh, give her joy, tease her, challenge her, and most importantly, love her unconditionally.

The pleasure of being inside her is mind-blowing. Her silky, wet heat grips my cock like a velvet fist, and the friction is enough to steal my breath. I groan loudly, helplessly as I fight not to completely lose myself in her.

My cock is throbbing, my ballsac tightening, and I'm so fucking close. My chest heaves as I try to catch my breath.

I move inside her, slowly and steadily, monitoring her panting breaths and soft cries. Her nails are digging into my arms, but she hasn't told me to stop.

I've wanted this for so long, and I'm so close already, it doesn't take much to put me over the edge. When my climax rips through me, my body tenses and pleasure fries my brain. I throw back my head and shout to the fucking rafters, so loud I'm sure my neighbors can hear me. But I don't give a fuck. This feels too damn good.

After the last of pulse of my throbbing cock, I hold myself perfectly still inside her, mindful of the condom. It takes me a moment to realize she's shaking. When I gaze down at her, my heart lurches at the sight of tears spilling down her temples. Her eyelids are screwed shut.

Shit! "Did I hurt you?" I must have.

Wordlessly, she shakes her head.

"Are you sure?"

"Yes," she breathes.

I don't linger, but instead pull out carefully and remove the condom, quickly tying if off before tossing it into the waste basket beside the nightstand.

I pull her into my arms. "Then why are you crying?"

She wipes her cheeks with shaky fingers, brushing away the tears. "I—"

That's as far as she gets before sobs overtake her, wracking her entire body. I lie back and draw her to me, holding her close and stroking her back. I let her cry. I don't know what else to do. I figure she's got a whole mess of emotions and anxiety coursing through her right now, and it's just too much to hold in. So I hold her, comforting her as best I can, all the while murmuring to her about how brave she is, how courageous. How beautiful.

After she cries herself out, she stills, and I realize she must have fallen asleep. My heart aches for her. I want to talk to her. I want to know how she feels, find out exactly what she thought of what we just did, but I don't want to wake her. After tonight, she needs the rest.

I suppose it's for the best. If we'd got to talking, I probably would have told her how much I love her, and that would be a big mistake. In the emotional state she's in right now, it would be wrong for me to declare my feelings. It wouldn't be fair to her. I'm her first, and she has her whole life ahead of her to decide what she wants. Just because I've found what I've been searching for my whole life doesn't mean she has.

I lie awake for a long time, just watching her sleep. With every passing minute, her grip on my heart tightens.

When she whimpers in her sleep, the soft, quiet sound draws me close, and I roll her to her side so I can spoon with her.

I am caught, hook, line, and sinker. And I couldn't be happier.

45

Erin

The first thing I notice when I awaken is the tenderness between my legs. When I shift position, I feel a twinge deep inside. I'm not surprised. Mack was a lot to take last night.

It's still dark outside. A glance at the digital clock on the nightstand tells me it's only three-thirty.

I'm lying on my side, and Mack is plastered to my back. Sleeping with him is like sleeping next to an oven, which for me is a good thing. I'm always cold, especially this time of year. He keeps me toasty warm. His arm is snug across my waist. Even in his sleep, he protects me.

Last night was one of the most momentous nights of my life. *I did it.* I had sex. And I didn't run away screaming. I didn't even raise a red flag and make him to stop. There were a couple times last night when I feared *he* would stop, but I didn't want him to. I wanted to get through it, once and for all, and put the anxiety of having sex behind me. It's got to be easier the next time.

Physically, it was painful at first, but I think that's true for every girl's first time. Mack is well endowed and, well, it hurt. A lot. But I tried not to let him see how much. But once he was all the way inside me, my body adjusted pretty quickly. I could feel myself softening and opening for him, and then suddenly the pain faded away to be replaced by an electrifying thrill.

Emotionally, it was transcending. I was terrified at first, afraid it would hurt. Afraid it wouldn't feel good, at all. *Ever.* But once my body got used to him inside me, the pain was quickly replaced with pleasure. I loved feeling him stroking inside me, slowly at first then gradually faster. I loved feeling his power and his strength as he controlled his body. I loved how careful he was.

We did it! My sense of relief is overwhelming.

As far as I'm concerned, last night really was my first time. What happened before—that horrible incident—doesn't count. The only memory I have of being with someone is being with Mack, and I want it to stay that way.

"Erin?" His voice is quiet in my ear, rough from sleep. He stretches with a groan. "Is everything okay?"

"Yes," I whisper. I roll to face him, feeling a bit self-conscious as I'm naked. But so is he. My nipples brush against his chest, and the intimate contact feels good.

He brushes my hair back from my face. "How do you feel?"

"Pretty good actually." I lay my hand on his warm chest. "Relieved."

His hand comes up to cover mine. "Yeah, me too," he says. "I admit I was a bit apprehensive." He brings my hand to his mouth and kisses my palm. "But you were amazing." He hugs me tight. "I'm so proud of you."

I cup his face, brushing my thumb across his cheekbone along the top edge of his beard. "Thank you for last night. I just want to be normal, and you made that possible."

I slip my hand to the back of his head and coax him down for a kiss. He complies eagerly, his lips parting mine. When his hand cups my breast, and his fingers gently tease my nipple, I feel a corresponding flare of liquid heat between my legs. When his erection prods my belly, my entire body tightens in anticipation. If he's hard, then he's aroused. And if he's aroused, then maybe he wants to do it again. "Mack?"

"Yeah?"

"I know it's late, and we have work tomorrow, but I was wondering..."

"Wondering what?"

"If you want to—I mean, I want you. Again."

He kisses me again. "Honey, there's no such thing as too late or too early for sex." His hand slips down my abdomen to the junction between my thighs. When his finger slides easily between my labia, he makes a sound of pure male appreciation. "God, you're so wet. Are you sure?" he says. "You're not too sore."

I am a bit sore, but that's a small price to pay for feeling normal, for knowing that I can have a healthy relationship with a man. "I'm sure."

He raises my leg and drapes it over his hip, opening me up to the eager press of his erection against my clit. I groan and rock against him, eager to increase the pressure. As his cock slides through my wetness, my belly tightens.

"Condom," he groans, rolling to his back and reaching for the top drawer of the nightstand. A moment later, he's got a condom packet in his hand and soon he's sheathed.

He touches me, his fingers gentle as they explore the wet, sensitized flesh between my legs. I tense automatically, expecting pain. Already my heart is pounding, and I can hardly catch my breath. I'm excited—I want this again. But I'm also nervous. What if the first time was a fluke?

He teases my clitoris with the pad of his thumb, rubbing slow circles, and it feels amazing. My nerves are electrified as pleasure and heat radiates throughout my body. My hips start rocking on their own, and I press harder against his touch.

I gasp, clutching his arm, when he slips a finger inside me and proceeds to slowly work it in, pressing through my sensitized opening an inch at a time. Soon after he starts rubbing inside me, my body starts throbbing. I press my face against him and smother a groan.

He nuzzles the tender spot behind my ear and whispers, "It's okay, honey. Just relax."

I nod, not trusting myself to speak. The combination of his thumb on my clitoris and his finger stroking deep inside me is too much. My entire body is already wracked with pleasure, and we've hardly just begun.

I see stars when pleasure detonates deep inside me. He strokes me relentlessly, all through my orgasm, driving my arousal higher and higher as my body quakes. His hot, eager mouth locks onto mine, muffling my cries.

When I finally settle back down, he angles himself at my opening and guides himself into me, slowly sinking inside. Despite some tenderness, it's much better than it was the last time. It's like my body knows what to do now, and he sinks more easily inside. It's still a stretch, and there's a bit of a burn, but soon any discomfort is pushed out by sheer pleasure.

As he begins to move inside me, my body is still reeling from my climax. The moonlight coming through the curtains is just enough that I can make out Mack's expression. As he rocks carefully into me, his jaw tightens, and his gaze locks onto mine.

When his own climax nears, he throws back his head and grimaces with pleasure, his own rough cry filling the room as he empties himself, thrust after thrust.

When he comes down from the high, he relaxes against me for a moment as he catches his breath. A moment later, exhaling roughly, he slides out of me and rolls to his back.

I watch him dispense with the condom.

"Be right back," he says, climbing out of bed and heading toward the hall bathroom. I hear the water running, and a few moments later he's back in bed with a warm wet washcloth in his hand.

He smiles. "I would have done this the first time, but you passed out on me." Then he proceeds to wash me clean before he tucks me back into bed. Both of us are a little out of breath, and I don't know about him, but my pulse is still racing.

"I think I could get used to this," I say with a sigh.

He laughs and he spoons behind me once more. "I'm very glad to hear that." His hand claims one of my breasts, and his lips tickle as he kisses the back of my neck. When I shiver, he tightens his hold.

I fall back to sleep thinking about how lucky I am.

* * *

When I awake later that morning, I'm alone in the bed. I check the time—seven o'clock. Time to get up and get ready for work. I shower and dress quickly, then head for the kitchen where I can hear Mack rattling cookware.

"I'm making your favorite breakfast," he says as he dishes scrambled eggs onto a plate. "Scrambled eggs and half an avocado. There's toast, too."

He's dressed, and his hair is damp. He must have showered already.

"You're up early," I say.

He sets two plates on the small kitchen table. "I wanted to let you sleep in as long as you could. You had a busy night last night. I figured you needed the extra sleep."

As we're sitting down together to eat, he reaches across the table for my hand. "How are you feeling?"

I feel myself blushing as I answer. "Good."

"You didn't have any nightmares last night."

I smile. "I think I was too worn out to dream."

After breakfast, we head for Clancy's. As usual, we're the only ones in the bookstore for a good half-hour. We settle easily into our routine, but it feels different now. We're not just co-workers anymore. We're together. And more than that, we're *lovers* now. I have something with him that I feared I could never have.

He watches me as we load up a cart of new releases. "Hey."

I pause and meet his gaze. "Yes?"

Leaning over the cart, he kisses me. "You look beautiful."

Heat suffuses my cheeks, and I resist the urge to cover my scarred cheek. "Oh, stop."

He follows me out onto the sales floor. "I'm serious!"

The employees begin to arrive, and while he lets them in, I start shelving the new books. Our day begins, and I can't stop smiling. Even these simple, routine activities have taken on a new significance, and I can't help smiling.

Before long, the store is buzzing with activity as shoppers file in. Mack comes up behind me and slips his arms around my waist and draws me close. "What can I do to help?"

I turn in his arms, gazing up at him with a stupid grin on my face. I know people are watching us. The employees try not to stare, but I catch them doing it anyway, smiles on their faces.

"Not a thing," I tell him. "Just be with me."

"Wild horses couldn't drag me away," he says as he kisses my forehead. "I'd like to see them try."

Epilogue

Erin

When we arrive back at our apartment building after work, Mack surprises me when he pushes the button for a floor two levels below ours.

"Where are we going?" I ask him.

His grin lights up his handsome face. "You'll see."

When the elevator doors open, he takes my hand and leads me down the hallway, stopping at a closed door. He pulls a key out of his pocket and unlocks the door, pushing it wide and motioning for me to proceed him.

When I step inside, he follows behind me and switches on the lights. I'm speechless! Our furniture is here! At least it looks like our furniture and our living room. It looks like our sofa and coffee table, but there are two matching recliners that we don't have. It looks like our flatscreen TV mounted on the wall, our surround sound speakers. But the living room as a whole is much bigger than ours.

As I glance around, I realize that this entire apartment is bigger than ours. The living room is almost twice the size, and I can see that the kitchen is bigger, too.

Dumbfounded, I turn and gaze up at him. "What's going on?"

He smiles and motions me toward the kitchen. "Take a look around."

I walk into the kitchen, which is larger than ours. It has a spacious walk-in pantry and a separate laundry room with washer and dryer. Even the balcony off the kitchen is larger. Instead of our small kitchen table which seats only two people, there's a larger table in here, with enough chairs to seat six.

I spot our Keurig coffee maker on the counter, and my little teapot sits on the stove.

I continue exploring, my heart racing. He follows me through the apartment, saying nothing, just observing me with an amused grin on his face.

After viewing the kitchen, I stop next at the spare bedroom. Sure enough, all of Mack's work-out equipment is here. The room is bigger though, so it feels much more spacious.

Next is the hall bathroom, also bigger.

The master bedroom is filled with our furniture, only the room itself is much bigger and has a private bathroom with a fancy tub and a separate walk-in shower. I step into the large walk-in closet, and there are our clothes, his and mine, arranged just as they are in our apartment.

I turn to face him. "I don't understand."

"Keep going," he says, steering me back out into the hallway. He turns me to the left and gives me a gentle nudge. There's a door at the end of the hallway—a door that doesn't exist in our apartment. I open it and step inside. "Oh, my God."

Shocked, I scan the room. There are built-in bookshelves lining two of the walls. In the corner of the room, in front of a large picture window, is an upholstered, light gray armchair and a matching ottoman. Beside the chair, a mahogany end table holds a reading lamp and a vase of fresh flowers.

I gravitate to the bookshelves and examine the neatly shelved collection of books. *Jane Eyre, Pride and Prejudice, The Little Princess.* My throat tightens painfully as I run my fingertips along the dozens of familiar and beloved spines.

"These are my books," I say, my voice barely audible. I turn to face him. "I don't understand. What is this?"

"It's ours, if you like it."

"*If* I like it? Are you kidding me? It's perfect!"

I lunge at him, and he catches me. "How did you manage this? How did you—" But I can't speak for the lump in my throat.

When he sets me down, I turn to survey the room. It's difficult to take everything in at once. There's a rug on the hardwood floor that features a floral pattern with pale yellow and white flowers, and a light gray border. The walls are painted light gray, the trim white. The lampshade is pale yellow. There's even a little antique writing desk and chair against another wall.

Tears prick my eyes. "I don't know what to say."

He pulls me back into his arms. "I wanted you to have your own space, somewhere you could display your books. I checked with the building manager and found this apartment had recently been vacated, so I jumped on it. Sophie arranged everything. She hired the contractors to build the bookshelves. She found the furniture and accessories. It was her idea to match the colors in your grandmother's teacups. She thought you'd like that."

When I glance at the bookcases, I notice something I'd missed before. My Gram's collection of vintage teacups is displayed on one of the shelves.

"Do you like it?" he says.

My cheeks are wet with tears as I throw my arms around his waist. I can't even speak. *It's everything I've ever wanted, right here in front of me. Mack. This place. My books. Everything.* The only thing missing is Gram. I wish she could have met Mack. I know she would have loved him as much as I do. My chin trembles. "It's perfect."

He leans down and kisses the top of my head, his arms securely around me. "Don't cry, honey. This is supposed to make you happy, not sad."

"I *am* happy," I say, wiping my tears with shaky fingers.

"Good." He gazes down at me, his dark eyes glittering with intent. "This might be too soon, but I'm going to say it anyway. I love you, Erin. And if you'll let me, I'll dedicate the rest of my life to making you happy."

I go up on my tiptoes to wrap my arms around his neck and pull his face down to mine for a kiss. "I love you, too. I've loved you for so long."

"I know." He sighs as he drops gentle kisses on my right cheek, right over my scar. *My badge of courage.*

His big hands cradle my face as he gazes down at me, his dark eyes glittering with emotion. "I'm sorry it took me so long to give myself permission to love you back. I promise to make it up to you."

Without warning, he swings me up into his arms and carries me to the master suite, setting me down beside the big bed. "I think we should christen our new home. What do you say?"

I smile. "I think that's a fine idea."

The end... for now.

Coming Next!

Stay tuned for more books featuring your favorite McIntyre Security characters! Watch for upcoming books for Tyler Jamison, Sophie McIntyre and Dominic Zaretti, Hannah McIntyre and Killian Deveraux, Charlie Mercer, Cameron and Chloe, Liam McIntyre, Ingrid Jamison and Joe Rucker, and many more!

For updates of future release, follow me on Facebook or subscribe to my newsletter. I'm active daily on Facebook, and I love to interact with my readers. Come talk to me on Facebook by leaving me a message or a comment. Please share my book posts with your friends. I also have a very active reader group on Facebook where I post weekly teasers for new books and run lots of giveaway contests. Come join us!

You can also follow me on Amazon, BookBub, Goodreads, and Instagram!

Please Leave a Review on Amazon

I hope you'll take a moment to leave a review for me on Amazon. Please, please, please? It doesn't have to be long… just a brief comment saying whether you liked the book or not. Reviews are vitally important to authors! I'd be incredibly grateful to you if you'd leave one for me. Goodreads and BookBub are also great places to leave reviews.

Acknowledgements

Ever since they first appeared in *Fearless*, I've been dying to write Erin and Mack's story. Their story is a tale about healing and acceptance, forgiveness and hope. Their relationship moved at their own pace, and the end result was just perfect for them.

As always, I owe a huge debt of gratitude to my sister, Lori, for being there with me every step of the way. Her tireless support and encouragement are priceless.

Thank you to Sue Vaughn Boudreaux for her unwavering support. With her many excellent skills, Sue is an invaluable help and instrumental at keeping me on track.

Also thank you to my dear friend Julie Collier, who has helped me immensely in getting the word out about my McIntyre Security Bodyguard series.

Thank you to Becky Morean, my soul sister and author buddy. Thank you to my dear friend across the pond, Laura Williams, for being there with me every day; thank you for your generous and unwavering encouragement.

Finally, I want to thank all of my readers around the world and especially the amazingly kind and wonderful members of my reader group on Facebook. I am so incredibly blessed to have you in my life. Your love and support and enthusiasm mean the world to me. You've become dear friends to me, and I am grateful for you all. Thank you from the very bottom of my heart for every review, like, share, and comment. I wouldn't be able to do the thing that I love to do most—share my characters and their stories—without your amazing support. Every day, I wake up and thank my lucky stars!

With much love to you all... April

Printed in Great Britain
by Amazon